PENGUIN BOOKS

THE BRETTS

Rosemary Anne Sisson was born in London, the second daughter of the famous Shakespearian scholar Professor C. J. Sisson. Her first ambition to be an actress was frustrated by the outbreak of the Second World War. She served in the Royal Observer Corps and, after the war, took a B.A. Honours degree in English at University College, London, and was studying for her Doctorate at Cambridge when she was unexpectedly invited to America to become a lecturer in English at the University of Wisconsin. She promptly settled for an M.Litt. and went. On her return, she lectured in the universities of London and Birmingham before, on the production of her first play, *The Queen and the Welshman*, she made writing her full-time career. She has since had seven more plays produced in the theatre, including *A Ghost on Tiptoe*, which she co-authored with Robert Morley, and *The Dark Horse*, which was produced at the Comedy Theatre, London. An extremely successful television playwright, Miss Sisson wrote plays for the BBC television series *The Six Wives of Henry VIII* and *Elizabeth R* and was one of the principal writers for the internationally acclaimed series *Upstairs, Downstairs*. She has also written a number of films, notably *Ride a Wild Pony*, *Escape from the Dark* and *Candleshoe* for Walt Disney, and also has the unusual distinction of working on one of their recent animation films, *The Black Cauldron*. Her first published works were children's books, but she recently turned to novels, among them *The Exciseman*, *The Queen and the Welshman*, *Escape from the Dark*, *The Stratford Story*, *The Manions of America* (Penguin), *Bury Love Deep* and *Beneath the Visiting Moon*.

With *The Manions of America* she became the first English writer to create an original mini-series for prime-time American television, and subsequent television series seen on both sides of the Atlantic include *Seal Morning*, *The Irish R.M.* and *The Bretts*.

Rosemary Anne Sisson

The Bretts

Based on the Central television series

PENGUIN BOOKS

Penguin Books Ltd, 27 Wrights Lane, London w8 5tz (Publishing and Editorial
and Harmondsworth, Middlesex, England (Distribution and Warehouse)
Viking Penguin Inc., 40 West 23rd Street, New York, New York 10010, USA
Penguin Books Australia Ltd, Ringwood, Victoria, Australia
Penguin Books Canada Ltd, 2801 John Street, Markham, Ontario, Canada L3R
Penguin Books (NZ) Ltd, 182–190 Wairau Road, Auckland 10, New Zealand

First published in paperback by Penguin Books 1987
Published simultaneously in hardback by Viking

This book is based on the Central Independent Television series *The Bretts*

Copyright © Rosemary Anne Sisson and Central Independent Television plc, 1
All rights reserved

Filmset in Monophoto Times
Made and printed in Great Britain by
Richard Clay Ltd, Bungay, Suffolk

With my best love to Robert Morley, who first taught me that the theatre was not only a highly professional business but also splendid fun.

R.A.S.

Chapter One

The milkman's horse came to a halt outside Nightingale Grove. Naturally, he didn't know that the
square redbrick house with the large gate posts and the
short drive was called Nightingale Grove. He was just a
thick-set, work-a-day horse, rather hairy about the heel,
and of limited intelligence, which, however, sufficed to
teach him, like any of his more elegant and showy circus
relatives, to respond to training and memory. He paused
outside the houses where his milkman delivered milk,
and trudged stolidly past those who patronized another
dairy. If you had told him that he had a great deal in
common with the inhabitants of Nightingale Grove, he
would not have understood, his brain not being condi-
tioned to receive such information. Certainly, the young
lady who descended from the taxi which drew up behind
the milk cart looked more like a racehorse than a poor
old drudge of an Irish vanner, although her grandfather,
still barnstorming his way doggedly round Ireland, might

have recognized, however reluctantly, some kinship with the old horse.

The milkman came to the back of the cart and collected a crate of milk bottles. Most houses in that quiet Hampstead road were what you might call reliable. Same order every day, except when the Mistress had an At Home or a Bridge Party. But with Nightingale Grove, you never could tell. Sometimes six pints of milk, sometimes eight, sometimes twelve. While he was putting a couple of extra pints into the crate, just in case, he became aware of the young lady paying the taxi-driver, who, having descended to hold the door open for her, was gazing at her with a mixture of respect and astonishment, both of which were clearly reinforced by the size of her tip. The milkman picked up his crate. Some people might have been surprised to see a young lady arriving home in a taxi at seven o'clock in the morning, wearing a very skimpy pink dress, a velvet evening coat and a jewelled turban, but not the milkman. He had seen it all before.

'Morning,' said the young lady, heading for the front door.

'Good morning, Miss,' replied the milkman, advancing up the side path which led to the back door.

Inside the house, the little maid, Emily, was doing the stairs. At least, she hoped that was what she was doing. It was her first day in the job – or, indeed, in any job – and she was far from sure what was expected of her. Emily's mother had been in service, or rather, she had been maid-of-all-work in the house of a bank clerk in Wood Green, until she met Emily's father, and got in the family way, and had to get married in a hurry. When Emily came home to Edmonton to say that she'd got the

8

job, Mrs Watkins sipped her tea, and her eyes rested on the tin bath which hung on the hook by the outside privy.

'The Bretts!' she said. 'Well, I never! That's a really posh place, that is.'

'They got a butler and a cook,' said Emily.

'So they would 'ave,' responded Mrs Watkins, with immense satisfaction.

'And Mrs Brett was in a bit of a hurry, on account of she'd got to go to the theayter, but she said she hoped I'd be very happy.'

'She's a real lady,' said Mrs Watkins. 'Not like that common bitch, Mrs Tupman, what I worked for. No, once you worked there, you can get a job anywhere.'

'Yes, Mum,' said Emily, happily.

The youngest of ten, and always treated as though the supply of brains had run out just before she arrived, she was delighted to think that at last she had done something clever, even if it was only getting a job as housemaid.

Now she was not so sure.

'Do the stairs,' Miss Evans had said, 'before the family gets up. Don't want them falling over you when they come downstairs – especially the master.'

And there was an ominous note in her voice when she spoke of 'the master' as though he was an ogre who ate little housemaids alive. So Emily, though she had never been taught what 'doing the stairs' meant, had found a dustpan and brush and swept her way carefully down the pale-blue stair carpet and white paint, and had even polished the brass stair rods, hoping to goodness she could get it all finished before the terrible master came out and caught her at it. What she didn't expect was the sound of a key in the front door, and a young lady walking briskly past her up the stairs, wearing a very short pink dress, a short velvet coat, silver shoes and a jewelled turban.

'Good morning,' said the young lady, without pausing. 'Would you tell Flora that I've had breakfast?'

'Yes, miss – madam,' replied Emily, dazedly, wondering who Flora was.

The young lady paused.

'You're new, aren't you?' she asked.

'Yes, miss – madam,' said Emily, still on her knees, but with a vague feeling that she ought to be making a curtsey.

The young lady, however, was already on her way again.

'You'll soon get used to us,' she said, and vanished round the bend.

Emily was not so sure.

Outside Nightingale Grove, the milkman, returning down the path towards the gate, encountered a stout man in a tight blue suit and brown boots.

'Is this Mr Brett's house?' the man inquired, in an unexpectedly belligerent manner.

'That's right,' answered the milkman.

'Mr Charles Brett, the actor?'

'That's right.'

'Huh!' said the man in the tight blue suit, and set off up the drive.

The milkman looked after him, mildly surprised, but his horse was already plodding on towards the next house, so the milkman followed him.

Emily had finished doing the stairs and was wondering what to do next.

'You be glad it's a warm spring,' Miss Evans had said, in that Welsh accent which made her so difficult for a cockney like Emily to understand. 'In the winter, you'll have to do all the grates before breakfast. If you stay that long.'

Emily had caught the look which Miss Evans exchanged with Mr Sutton, the butler, who was drinking a cup of tea at the kitchen table in his shirt-sleeves, and she wondered what Miss Evans meant. Why shouldn't she stay? she thought, and then, with a nervous glance towards the kitchen, it occurred to her that perhaps if she didn't look busy enough, she'd get the sack. Emily decided to dust the hall. She had just selected a cleanish duster from her wooden housemaid's box and risen to her feet, when she gave a little scream. She had seen at the window a face – a round, red, angry face. Emily looked desperately towards the door which led to the kitchen, wondering if she should tell someone. Then she looked back towards the window. The face had vanished.

In the kitchen, Alfred Sutton was struggling to attach the collar to his shirt with a recalcitrant collar stud. He always left this till last, probably because of his days in the theatre, when you made up first, so as not to get make-up on your collar. Thank goodness, he thought, looking at himself in the wooden-framed mirror by the sink, that he didn't have to make up now. He had never been very good at it.

'Goddammit, Sutton!' the guv'nor used to say. 'What are you doing with all that eye-black? You look like a bloody geisha girl!'

Sutton finally managed to attach the collar to the shirt at the back of his neck, and turned it up. Just the black tie and the coat, and then he was on. Funny, he thought, that even now he never quite thought of it as 'going on duty', but always as 'going on'. It was all those years of playing butlers. Probably no one remembered that now, except for Miss Lydia, bless her! The rest of the family just thought of him as Sutton, the butler. He turned away from the mirror.

Flora Evans was putting a big white apron over her nanny's navy-blue dress, with its white collar and cuffs. Like Sutton, she had changed her avocation. Once nanny to the children, when the children grew up and no longer needed her, she had become instead cook and housekeeper. She was not, truth to tell, a very good cook, but, like Sutton, she was loved and trusted by the family, and theatrical people, like royalty, need, above all, love and loyalty.

'Guv'nor was late home last night,' remarked Sutton. '*And* he'd spilt wine all over his new dress shirt.'

'Better than lipstick,' responded Flora.

Sutton looked at her, startled. One never knew with Flora. Born in a Welsh mining village near Port Talbot, brought up all teetotal and Nonconformist Chapel, and then, when you least expected it, she came out with something that showed she knew quite well what it was all about. That was why the older Brett children, Edwin, Martha and Thomas, grown up as they were, still came to her in the kitchen when they were in trouble, just to hear her say, 'Well, I never! You ought to be ashamed of yourself!' or, 'I dare say it's not as bad as you think,' or, 'Now, you just sit down and have a nice cup of tea.' To them, Flora was still nanny, whereas to everyone in the household, Sutton was just the butler – well, to everyone except Miss Lydia, bless her!

Emily, surveying the hall, duster in hand, could not see a great deal to dust. There was a telephone, however, which stood on a table in the alcove beside the front door. Emily had never actually seen a telephone, except on the pictures, but she knew that if you took that little handle off the hook and put it to your ear, you heard voices. She advanced to the table and diligently dusted it, and then, succumbing to temptation, she took the little handle off and put it to her ear. There was a sort of buzz. While she was waiting to hear the voice, she was frightened nearly out of her wits by a tremendous hammering, which she thought at first came from the telephone, but then realized came from the front door. She dropped the earpiece, juggled with it in her lap, caught it, and guiltily put it back on its hook, just as there was another thunderous knock at the door.

'Miss Martha,' remarked Flora, 'forgotten her key again.'

'Doesn't sound like her,' Sutton answered, 'unless she's a bit the worse for wear.'

He finished tying his black tie and took his black coat from its peg, just as there was another even louder knock at the door.

'That's never Miss Martha,' said Sutton, 'drunk or sober.'

He set off for the hall, struggling into his coat, but he was too late. Emily, following her instincts as she usually did, had trotted to the front door and opened it. She saw a big man in a bowler hat silhouetted against the early morning light.

'Mr Brett?' he demanded.

''E's in bed!' answered Emily, instinctively truthful.

'Is he?' replied the large man. 'He'll have to get up, then, won't he?'

He pushed past Emily into the hall, just as Sutton emerged from the door which led to the kitchen.

''Ere, just a minute –!' protested Emily.

Even she knew that wasn't right.

Sutton advanced, the perfect butler.

'Excuse me, sir,' he said. 'Can I help you?'

'I doubt it,' replied the man. 'I want to see Mr Brett,' and, taking a couple of steps towards the staircase, he bawled, 'Mr Charles Brett!'

'Keep your voice down!' exclaimed Sutton, really shocked. 'You'll wake the mistress!'

Flora pushed the door open and came out into the hall.

'Mr Sutton,' she said, 'whatever is going on? I could hear you right out in the kitchen. Who is this man?'

'Yes, sir,' said Sutton, throwing her a distracted glance, 'if I might have your name?'

'Burroughs,' said the big man. He raised his voice again. 'My name is Burroughs, and I want my money!'

'Money, is it?' said Flora. 'You'll get what for if you wake the master!'

Burroughs was beginning to regret his incursion into the house. It was not going quite as he had meant. But he was there now, and must make the best of it.

'I hope I do wake him up,' he responded, belligerently. 'Then perhaps he'll pay my bill.'

A voice came unexpectedly from the staircase.

'Who is Bill?' it said.

Burroughs saw a young lady with dark hair and immensely long legs, who was wearing a very short pink silk dress with a very low V-neck. She began to descend the stairs.

'What's happening, Sutton?' she inquired. 'I was just

going to bed, but I thought this sounded more interesting.'

'Going to bed?' exclaimed Burroughs, distracted from his purpose, and thinking of Mrs Burroughs's nocturnal long-sleeved flannelette. 'Is that her nightdress?'

'That's none of your business!' said the butler, in a tone of outrage.

But Burroughs became aware that the young lady, after a long and thoughtful look, had lost interest in him.

'Any chance of a cup of tea, Flora?' she asked.

'I'll bring it up to you, Miss Martha,' replied the middle-aged Welsh lady. 'Now, do put something on or you'll catch your death of cold.'

But the young lady sauntered on downstairs, yawning, and addressed the butler in confidential tones.

'Actually, Alfred,' she remarked, 'I think I'd rather have one of your pick-me-ups. I've been drinking gin all night in the Silver Slipper, and I really do think they make it in the bathtub.'

'Yes, Miss Martha,' said Sutton, with just a hint of agitation in his voice. 'If you will let me deal with this gentleman first –'

He turned to Burroughs, putting the palms of his hands together, and spoke in a plummy voice, just like a blooming butler on the stage, thought Burroughs, disgustedly.

'If you wish to see Mr Brett,' he said, 'you must write a letter and request an appointment. Now, sir, I really must ask you to –'

He was clearly hoping to shift Burroughs towards the door, but Burroughs stood firm.

'I've *written* a letter!' he said, raising his voice again.

'I've written ten bloody letters! He don't bloody well answer letters!'

'We'll have none of that language in *this* house, thank you very much!' said the Welsh lady.

(Cook? thought Burroughs. Nanny?)

'Quite right, Flora,' said the young lady, with a primness that didn't quite seem to go with her skimpy dress and plunging neckline. 'I should hope not, indeed! Whatever next?'

Next was another voice from the staircase.

'What's all the row about?'

Burroughs, with a sinking sense of unreality, looked up and saw a handsome young man in riding breeches and a white shirt, who, like the young lady, paused as he first appeared, and then slowly began to descend. Just as Burroughs, determined to assert himself, prepared to tell him that he had come to demand payment of his account, and wouldn't leave until he had it, the young man unexpectedly spoke again.

'Flora,' he said, 'what's happened to my morning tea?'

'I'm so sorry, Master Edwin,' said Flora. 'We've had a bit of trouble. Emily, go and make Mr Edwin's tea.'

'Yes, Miss Evans.'

The little, round-faced maid, with the tousled fair hair under a crooked cap, set off with evident reluctance to leave the scene of action, but she had only taken half a dozen steps before she was halted by Burroughs' infuriated bellow.

'Never mind his tea!' roared Burroughs. 'I want to see Mr Brett!'

'I *am* Mr Brett,' said the young man. 'Who the devil are you?'

But, before Burroughs could tell him, another young

man appeared on the bend of the stairs, wearing striped flannel pyjamas and an old camel-hair dressing-gown.

'Hullo?' he said. 'What's going on?'

'There, now!' exclaimed Flora reproachfully. 'Master Thomas heard you right up in the nursery!'

Burroughs was once more distracted from his purpose. This second young man had untidy brown hair, and, though not handsome, had a bright, intelligent look, like a clever child. Still, he was twenty if he was a day.

'Nursery?' Burroughs repeated. 'He's a bit old for the nursery, isn't he?'

'Never mind that,' said the first young man. 'Sutton, who is this man?'

'He seems to be a tradesman, sir,' replied the butler, 'who has forced his way in to demand payment of his bill.'

'What infernal cheek!'

'Oh, I don't know,' said the young man in the dressing-gown. 'If I had a bill, I think I'd want someone to pay it.'

The other young man glared at him.

'You keep out of this, Thomas,' he said, and descended the stairs. 'Sutton, do you want me to throw him out?'

'Master Edwin –'

'I'd like to see you try!' said Burroughs, clenching his fists.

'If you ask me,' said the young lady, sitting down and crossing her long, silk-stockinged legs, 'this man is becoming a bore.'

'Oh, all right,' said the young man in the dressing-gown. 'Let Eddie do his Douglas Fairbanks bit and throw him out.'

Sutton stepped forward, and Burroughs could see that, like him, the butler thought the whole thing was getting out of hand, and was endeavouring to assert himself.

'Now, if you would all leave this to me,' he was beginning to say, when another voice spoke from the direction of the staircase. It sounded rather like a church organ, with just a dash of brass band thrown in.

'May I ask,' it said, 'what is the meaning of this?'

'Oh no!' said the butler, with a note of exasperation. 'Not the guv'nor!'

Burroughs saw a handsome man of medium height with grey hair and clear blue eyes, who was dressed in silk pyjamas and an expensive silk dressing-gown.

'Do you realize,' he said, 'that it is seven o'clock in the morning?' As he descended the stairs, Burroughs noticed that both the young men, as though instinctively, stood out of his way. 'Sutton,' he demanded, 'what the devil is going on?'

'I am very sorry, sir,' said the butler, in a very butlerish voice. 'If you will leave it to me, I will take care of it.'

The older man hesitated, and for a moment it seemed that he had decided that, whatever it was, he didn't want to be bothered with it.

'Right, Sutton,' he said, and turned to go back upstairs.

But Burroughs had now grasped that this was the man he had come to see, and he wasn't going to be cheated.

'Are you Mr Charles Brett?' he demanded.

The gentleman turned back instantly, with a look of astonished indignation.

'Of course I'm Charles Brett!' he roared. 'Who the devil are you?'

'My name's Burroughs,' said Burroughs, doggedly, 'and I want my money.'

He was unprepared for the look of amusement in the gentleman's face, and for the Irish chuckle in his voice.

'Good God, Sutton, don't tell me we have the bum-bailiffs in the house!'

The butler advanced and endeavoured to speak confidentially.

'I'm very sorry, sir. The new girl opened the door by mistake, and –'

'What new girl?'

His eyes turned towards the little, round-faced maid.

'Emily, sir,' she said.

He smiled at her kindly. Why, thought Emily, he wasn't an ogre at all, and she beamed back at him.

The gentleman's eyes rested on her rosy young face for a moment longer before he turned to the butler.

'I'm sure it wasn't her fault,' he said. 'Sutton, you'd better deal with it. Tell the fellow to leave, and if he won't, send for the police.'

It was that word, 'fellow', that did it. Burroughs' partner, Fred Carter, had said that Mr Brett was a famous actor, and that you had to expect gentlemen like that to be late payers. But Fred had flat feet. Unlike Burroughs, he had not fought in the Great War. He hadn't been told that he must unthinkingly obey an officer and a gentleman, only to discover that there were some officers and gentlemen who were better and braver than he was, and who went over the top first, and were probably killed, while other officers and gentlemen were confirmed cowards and self-seeking bastards, who hung back, and got jobs as staff officers in a château and drank Burgundy and sent better men to their deaths. The Great War had taught Arthur Burroughs to take men as he found them, and to judge them accordingly. Perhaps Mr Charles Brett was a great actor, but he was a late payer, and late payers drove little firms into bankruptcy. Fred Carter had kept their firm going for four years while Arthur Burroughs was serving King and Country in the trenches, and they weren't going to lose it now just because so-called gentlemen wouldn't pay their bills. 'Fellow', indeed! So, as the butler stepped towards him, Burroughs took a step back, and addressed the actor gentleman over Sutton's head.

'Don't bother,' he said. 'I'm leaving. And the next time you see me, it'll be in the County Court.'

He had the satisfaction of seeing Mr Charles Brett stop short, and all the others exchange startled glances. He turned towards the front door, but paused and turned for a parting shot.

'Should get in all the newspapers, that should. "Famous actor refuses to pay his debts!"'

There was a stunned silence, in which they all stared at Burroughs, and he looked triumphantly back at them.

And then it happened. Round the bend of the staircase came the most beautiful woman in the world. She was wearing what Mr Burroughs supposed would be called a négligé, all soft white net and lace, and there was a rose pinned to her bosom. Quite by chance, she had paused in the spot where the morning sunlight from the tall window illuminated her golden hair. Her beautiful blue eyes seemed to survey the scene, and then focused on Mr Burroughs, and she smiled that dazzling smile which he knew so well.

'Good morning,' she said. 'I'm afraid I don't know you, but *I'm –*'

Burroughs suddenly realized that he was still wearing his bowler hat. He clutched it off his head and took a step forward, eagerly interrupting her.

'Oh *yes!*' he exclaimed. 'You're Miss Lydia Wheatley!'

Lydia Wheatley came gracefully down the stairs, as Burroughs had so often seen her descend before. As she passed Charles Brett, she smiled at him sweetly, and, for some strange reason, he scowled at her in return. She advanced towards Burroughs, addressing him as though he was the one person in the whole world whom she wanted to meet.

'Now, do tell me your name,' she said.

Burroughs, clasping his bowler hat in both hands on his chest, stammered as he replied.

'It's Burroughs, Miss Wheatley. Er – Carter and Burroughs, Builders and Decorators.'

'Of *course*,' she said. 'I met your charming partner, Mr Carter.'

'Er – yes.'

Fred had simply spoken of her as Mrs Brett. He never said that she was Lydia Wheatley.

'I was working on another job at the time,' he said, apologetically.

'Of *course*,' she said, understandingly. 'Still, it was *your* men who did such a beautiful job painting my garden room. But –'

Her beautiful blue eyes were clouded with grief.

'Did I hear – your bill hasn't been paid?'

Burroughs was embarrassed.

'Well – er –' he said.

'No, *please*!' said Lydia Wheatley. 'Do let me see it. How much is it for?'

Burroughs reached inside his pocket and produced the account, written out in Fred's best Board School writing, with the firm's name printed at the top. Miss Wheatley took it, looked at it, and held it out at arm's length.

'Twenty-seven pounds, four shillings and eleven pence, madam,' said Burroughs, apologetically.

'Of course,' said Miss Wheatley, and turned to him. 'Now, Mr Burroughs,' she said, and gazed into his eyes, 'I want you to do me a great favour.'

'Certainly, Miss Wheatley,' said Burroughs.

Fancy Lydia Wheatley asking a favour of *him*!

'I want you to leave this bill in my hands,' she said, 'and I will *personally* make sure that it is paid.'

'Oh – I don't want to put you to any trouble.'

'Nonsense,' she replied, with a wonderfully caressing note in her voice. 'It's the *least* I can do.'

She gave him that wonderful, dazzling smile, and, dazed, he turned away. Sutton moved briskly towards the front door. Burroughs turned back.

'Er – Miss Wheatley,' he said.

He saw a startled look in her eyes as he reached inside his pocket. Did she think he was going to produce another bill? He hastily took out his wallet and drew from it a slightly dog-eared picture postcard. The picture was in fact a photograph of Lydia Wheatley, wearing a frilly dress much like her present négligé, and reclining in a swing which had roses entwined round its ropes. Her little slippers with rosettes on them were together, and her little hands held the ropes as she leaned back and smiled adorably.

'Mrs Burroughs and I went to see you in *Singing Sunshine* when I was on leave and – well, she wasn't Mrs Burroughs then, but – she sent me this postcard to the trenches afterwards, and – that was when I wrote back and asked her to marry me, and – I just wondered – would you be so kind as to sign this for me?'

Miss Wheatley took the postcard and a tender look came into her face. Burroughs knew that she understood all that it meant to him and to his wife, all the grace and romance and elegance which was not normally a part of their lives, but which had brought to their apparently mundane marriage something secret and beautiful.

'Of course,' she said. 'I would be delighted.' She looked vaguely round. 'Has anyone –?'

The young man in the dressing-gown came down the stairs and produced a fountain pen from his pocket. Rather odd, thought Burroughs, to have a fountain pen in his dressing-gown pocket, but then everything in this house was rather odd. Thomas took the cap off the pen and offered it to Lydia Wheatley, who put the postcard photograph down on a side table. He pointed helpfully.

'Here, Mother,' he said, as though she couldn't see where to sign it.

Lydia Wheatley's smile did not have quite its usual radiance. It was almost icy.

'Thank you, Thomas dear,' she said.

She signed the photograph, and gave it back to Burroughs.

'There,' she said with that intoxicating note of intimacy. 'Please give my kindest regards to Mrs Burroughs. And thank you *so* much for coming to see us.'

Burroughs took the photograph, that photograph which meant so much to him and to Edith, and which now had additional magic because of the charmingly feminine signature wandering off the edge. He received a last impression of those delicate features and that sweet smile, and was vaguely aware of the butler moving to the doorway, and of going through it into the spring sunshine. The door of Nightingale Grove closed behind him, like a curtain falling at the end of a performance.

As Sutton closed the front door behind Burroughs, Lydia turned towards Charles, abandoning her pure vowels and gracious tones for the splendid stridency of her native Clapham.

'Why can't you pay the bloody bills,' she demanded, 'before the bloody duns are in the 'ouse?'

Chapter Two

It was with a sense of relief that Charles Brett entered the Garrick Club later that morning. Whatever the Suffragettes had achieved elsewhere, at least women weren't yet admitted to the Garrick Club. He collected his letters from the porter, and opened the first one in the hall, in the faint hope, almost concealed even from himself, that it might be from a successful author begging him to appear in a new play. Instead, it was from a charity, requesting a donation. The cause was a good one, but the request could only be an embarrassment. If he sent a guinea, they would think he was a mean bastard, but how could he send more when he couldn't even pay his bills? He stuffed the envelope into his pocket, and acknowledged the greeting of a couple of old fogies who were sitting by the fire in the hall. It was a warm day, but presumably, because they were old, they felt the cold. With an involuntary shiver, Charles began to mount the wide staircase.

He tore open the other two envelopes and realized with a sinking heart that they were both disguised begging letters from actors, asking for jobs. The first, from a contemporary began, 'Dear Charles', and went on to say that the writer had so much enjoyed playing with Charles in his last play, and understood that he was just opening in another, and hoped to be with him again. The second, 'Dear Mr Brett', was the all-too-familiar desperation ploy by the young unknown, saying how much he admired the great man's talent, and what a privilege it would be to play with him.

Charles paused halfway up the stairs, pretending to read the letters again, but really thinking with rising panic that he had no play to offer them, because no one had offered a play to him. It was all very well for Lydia, thought Charles, bitterly. She could go to her hairdresser every week and have her hair dyed gold. But he flatly refused to dye his hair, or to wear a wig outside the theatre. He thought of poor old Guy, with his ginger wig which everyone laughed at behind his back. But, when you had been a 'matinée idol', like Gerald du Maurier or Charles Brett, what happened when the hair turned grey and the waist thickened – and you had a son thirty years old?

'Oh, what the devil!' thought Charles.

He stuffed all three letters into his pocket (where they would stay until Sutton found them, read them, and either threw them away or put them on his desk with all the rest of the unanswered letters and unpaid bills). Something would turn up, Charles thought. It always did. After all, he was just going to see Willie Sutherland about this new play he'd written. Perhaps it would be better than the last one. Ever the optimist, Charles walked forward into the bar.

The big room was full of that interesting assortment of Garrick Club members whom Gerald du Maurier, in one of his more saturnine moments, had described as 'actors, lawyers and gentlemen'. Annoyingly enough, the first man Charles saw was Bertie Sanders. God knew how *he'd* become a member! He wasn't even a good actor.

'Hullo, Bertie,' said Charles, with a pleasant smile. 'I hear that little play of yours is doing well.'

He called it a little play because it *was* a little play, but it was also rather a jolly little play which could well have done as a stopgap for himself.

'Can't complain,' replied Bertie, complacently. 'Had the "House Full" boards up twice this week.'

'Well done!' said Charles, heartily.

Bertie leaned close and spoke confidentially, with a whiff of whisky and cheap cigar.

'You know,' he said, 'I thought Toby Stevens might have sent it to you. I suppose he thought it was too lightweight.'

'Never can tell with authors,' replied Charles, vaguely.

Probably decided I was too old, he thought, bitterly. Everyone thinks I'm too old nowadays.

'I hear Willie Sutherland's writing a new play for you,' remarked Bertie.

'Yes,' Charles replied. He added with what even he knew was forced geniality, 'Well, we shall have to see. I've got a lot of other irons in the fire.'

As he moved on, he saw a look of unbelief on Bertie's face, and he didn't blame him. Every actor knows when he has given a poor performance. He also knows when the lines which he has been given to speak are not very convincing. Out of the corner of his eye, Charles saw the fashionable barrister, Sir Mortimer Cranmer, bearing down on him, and hoped to avoid him, but Sir Mortimer hailed him genially, newspaper in hand.

'Hullo, Brett,' he called. 'I see this American chap, Lindbergh, has flown the Atlantic.'

'Yes,' Charles answered, blandly. 'Prefer travelling by Cunard myself.'

There was a general laugh from the other men at the bar, and Charles felt a satisfying glow and prepared to move on. (Always exit on a laugh or a round of applause!) Unfortunately, Sir Mortimer prevented him.

'When are we going to see you on the stage again?' he inquired. 'My wife was asking only yesterday. She's a great admirer of yours.'

'Oh, really?' Charles replied, and felt his smile stiffening on his face. 'Very kind of her.'

Wish I knew myself, he thought, as he continued on his way, exchanging smiles and waves with his fellow members.

It was, however, with increasing gloom that Charles made his way towards the table in the corner where Willie Sutherland was awaiting him. Willie, soon after leaving Cambridge some thirty years before, had written a slightly sub-Oscar Wilde drawing-room comedy called, rather daringly, *She Could If She Would*. In that play, Charles and Lydia had first become recognized as a good romantic husband-and-wife team, as if her career as musical-comedy beauty and his as a promising and handsome dramatic actor had suddenly come together. One might say that, instead of just being fellow actors who happened to be married, they became 'The Bretts'.

Willie Sutherland was such a pleasant young fellow, so delighted with the success of his first play, so happily ready to sit, beaming, in the stalls throughout rehearsals, and to bring large parties of acquaintances to almost every performance throughout the run, so eager to buy champagne for all the cast at the merest hint of a birthday or anniversary, that he had somehow become a friend, not only of Charles and Lydia, but of the whole family.

Over the years, Willie had managed to come up with moderately successful pieces for Gerald du Maurier, Gladys Cooper, Owen Nares, and even a few decent short-run plays for Charles and Lydia, but the awful truth was that he had only ever written one good play, and that a sort of fluke. Upon the success of *She Could If She Would*, his reputation had depended ever since, and upon its royalties he had principally lived, with the assistance of a not inconsiderable private income. His membership of the Garrick Club and his friendships with all the leading actors and actresses of the day ensured him a happy niche in the world of the theatre, and yet, to an old professional campaigner like Charles, there was always something irritating about this amiable gentle-man-playwright, cushioned as he was against the financial triumph and disaster which, since the time of Shakespeare, had been the condition of those who made their living in the theatre.

'Good news, Charles,' said Willie, smiling up at him with that impenetrable amiability of his. 'I've finished the play.'

He fished up from beside his chair a sturdy envelope and drew out of it a dismayingly stout typescript and plonked it on the table.

'I'll get you a drink,' he said, 'while you glance through it.'

Charles sat down, eyeing the large script uneasily. Willie's plays were always beautifully typed and expensively bound, with the title and the author's name in gold. It made them look like the Bible, and gave the impression that, like the Bible, every word had been handed down from a high literary mountain, and that anyone given the privilege of interpreting it should count themselves blessed. Charles picked it up and weighed it in his hand. It was an old actor's trick which always annoyed authors, but it was surprisingly reliable. Charles knew, even without opening it, that the damned thing was about three hours long. He put it down again.

'I'd rather take it home', he said, 'and read it at a sitting.' He added gloomily, 'If I can.'

Willie beamed happily. He was not alert to nuances, which was why the dialogue in his plays was always so leaden.

'Splendid!' he replied. 'I know you'll love it. Great big part for you – lots of duelling – nice love story – just what you've been looking for.'

'Hm,' said Charles. 'Long time since I've done any duelling.'

'That's what I thought,' Willie agreed, enthusiastically. 'Not since *The Laughing Cavalier*. After all, that was your first really big success. This is even better.'

He was right about one thing. *The Laughing Cavalier* had been Charles's greatest success, and his name had been associated with it ever since. It was a very effective fast-moving melodrama, something between *The Only Way*, *The Prisoner of Zenda* and *The Scarlet Pimpernel*, but with plenty of humour and a strong love story. It ran, astonishingly, for more than a thousand performances in London, and when they took the whole company to New York, it was hugely successful there. In fact, the dear old *Laughing Cavalier* had given them affluence for the first time in their lives, and it was upon its proceeds that Charles had been able to buy the big house,

Nightingale Grove, in Hampstead, where they had lived ever since.

But, Charles thought, that had all been a long while ago, before the war, and times and tastes had changed since then. Now and then, when he woke in the night with indigestion, hearing Lydia's peacefully regular breathing in the big bed beside him, he would have a nightmare vision of himself, an aging matinée idol, hacking round the provinces with *The Laughing Cavalier*, like dear old Martin Harvey doggedly playing Sydney Carton in *The Only Way* to audiences who remembered him not as he was but as he used to be. In his blacker moments, Charles even remembered the great Sir Henry Irving, worn out and ill, appearing on the bill like an old music-hall performer, giving them *The Bells* or *Becket*, and finally dying in the wings, still in his make-up, with Tennyson's last lines on his lips: 'Into thy hands, O Lord, into thy hands – '

Charles's sense of humour, never very far below the surface, rose to his assistance. Irving had not, in fact, died in the wings, but back in his hotel in Bradford. It was true that he was only fifty-eight years old and penniless, but he was also, to the end, a tremendous draw, and was planning a tour of America which, no doubt, would have been a tremendous success, and when he died he was buried in Westminster Abbey. Dammit, thought Charles, that was the way to go, and if he had to do it with the dear old *Laughing Cavalier*, why not? On the other hand, if, by some lucky chance, Willie had come up with another winner – Charles seized the envelope and stuffed the script into it.

'Thanks very much, Willie,' he said. 'I'll take it home and read it, and then we'll see what Freddie Carson thinks of it.'

The drinks had arrived, and Willie was busy signing for them. He turned back to Charles.

'I'm not sure about Carson,' he said. 'I did hear that he has a piece that he wants Lydia to do.'

'Oh, really?' answered Charles. 'He hasn't mentioned it to her, or she'd've told me.'

But as he took a sip of whisky, a nasty little voice at the back of his mind inquired, 'Or *would* she?'

Charles didn't think about Freddie Carson again until he was in the taxi on the way home. He and Willie had an enjoyable luncheon at the long table, where the conversation was witty and scandalous, and the company included the Attorney-General, who was splendidly indiscreet about the police raid on the offices of the Soviet Trade Delegation and the extraordinary bundle of documents which they had carried away, varying from a hilariously earnest account of the importance of trams to the London transport system to some quite horrifying secrets relating to the armed forces. This was what the Garrick Club was all about – inside knowledge indiscreetly revealed to fellow members who could be trusted not to pass it on.

But, during the drive from Garrick Street to Hampstead, Charles had time to think.

'You ought to buy yourself an automobile,' Willie had said, climbing into his Lagonda, as Charles was waiting for the porter to get him a taxi.

'Yes, keep meaning to,' Charles had replied, but added inwardly, 'if only I could afford one.'

Now he sat, glaring at the thick envelope containing Willie's play, and pondering Willie's words about Freddie Carson. Carson was one of the few remaining old-fashioned producers who owned a theatre and actually put plays on in it. It had long been accepted that if Charles and Lydia had a play they wanted to do, they took it first to Freddie, and if he liked it, the whole thing was settled over a cup of tea at Nightingale Grove or a nice little dinner at the Savoy. On the other hand, if he came upon a play which he felt would be right for them, the same thing applied. All very simple and gentlemanly, with the terms settled on the spot, and the written contract merely a formality. Now and then, since they did not always appear together, there would be a play which was suitable for Lydia but not for Charles, or vice versa, and then they would discuss it in the same amicable manner, the three of them together. But if Freddie Carson had really approached Lydia about a production without telling Charles, and if she had kept quiet about it –!

As the taxi rattled along Oxford Street, Charles felt a slowly rising tide of anger. His marriage with Lydia might best be described as a highly enjoyable but frequently destructive form of guerrilla warfare, and, exasperatingly, after thirty years she could still surprise him. When he married her, she was a ravishing, blue-eyed blonde of seventeen, and he was a handsome and, as he thought, worldly wise young actor of twenty-four. What he had yet to discover was that Lydia's parents were music-hall performers, and that she and her sister, Elsie, had trod the boards since they could toddle, and, as the Winsome Wheatleys, had topped the bill and dealt with recalcitrant managers since they were twelve years old. Lydia's sister, Elsie, became a chorus girl, and married an extremely wealthy 'Stage Door Johnny', Sir Harry Carstairs, at which point Elsie firmly dispatched her parents to discreet and strictly non-theatrical retirement in a nice house by the sea in Rustington. Lydia, more beautiful and more talented than Elsie, began to achieve success as a light-comedy actress as well as a musical-comedy performer, and when she and Charles fell in love and got married, it was quite definitely a case of lighting the blue touch-paper and swiftly retiring, as their careers soared off into the theatrical heavens, scattering sparks as they went.

Somehow that love, which had struck in Manchester and led to an exchange of vows on Crewe station, had survived all vicissitudes. Somehow, that sexual passion which was first consummated in a wrought-iron bedstead in Southend still worked its magic in the big bedroom overlooking the valley where nightingales once sang for Keats. Somehow Charles's inveterate philandering, which was as much a part of him as his power to work an audience, had always stopped short of the total destruction of their marriage, and Lydia's need to prove that she was still desirable had, as far as Charles knew, gone no further than candlelit dinners and flattering bouquets of flowers. But if Lydia had really been conniving with Freddie Carson behind his back, that was *quite* another matter!

Slowly Charles's anger gave way to a subtle satisfaction. Lydia didn't know that he knew, and he certainly wasn't going to tell her. As the taxi turned into Finchley Road, a gratifying scene unfolded itself in his mind.

In the kitchen of Nightingale Grove, Sutton sat in his shirt-sleeves reading a copy of the *Stage*, as he did every week, but he was well aware of what was going on. Flora was stamping out scones on a pastry board with a glass which she periodically moistened in a bowl of water, and Emily watched her, eager to help, but not sure of her role.

'I want these scones served piping hot,' said Flora. 'They're Miss Nell's favourites, as well as the master's.'

'Is Miss Nell the only one that's married?' inquired Emily.

Flora eyed her coldly.

'Mrs Caldwell to you,' she said, 'thank you very much! Miss Martha *was* married, but her husband was killed in the war.'

Sutton, glancing up from his paper, saw the expression on Flora's face, and smiled to himself. Flora always had a soft spot for Miss Martha, which was funny really, considering the rackety life that Miss Martha lived, but there! Flora always saw her as the little girl whose nanny she had been long ago.

'Mr Basil was such a nice gentleman,' said Flora, 'and they only had three days together before he went back to the front. Two weeks later, she heard that he was dead.'

'Ooh!' said Emily, deeply impressed.

It's all *Peg's Paper* to her, thought Sutton. She doesn't know what the war was all about. She doesn't know what it was to be not quite sure whether or not you loved a man, but to know that a subaltern's life on the Western Front was three weeks at the most. She doesn't know anything about the mixture of love and blackmail which drove young girls like Miss Martha into a short-lived marriage, followed by long, confused years of sorrow, guilt and confusion.

'So what's Miss Martha's married name?' inquired Emily.

'If you must know, it's Mrs Holroyd,' Flora replied, stamping out the last scone, and scrumping up the remains of the dough. 'But, being an actress, she's gone back to her maiden name. So you call her "Miss", and the mistress and Mrs Caldwell, you call "Madam".'

'Oh,' said Emily, struggling with the intricacies of a culture alien to her own.

Sutton closed the paper and put it down and rose.

'And when you help me take in the tea,' he said, 'don't goggle at the master like one of them idiots at the stage door. *He* may like it, but it's not correct.'

'I wouldn't think it's "correct" to 'ave the duns in the 'ouse, either,' said Emily, mutinously.

Flora, rising from putting the scones in the oven, glared at Emily indignantly, but Sutton, as the door swung to behind him, grinned to himself. That girl might find her place in the Brett household yet.

Chapter Three

'Good heavens!' exclaimed John Caldwell. 'There are unpaid bills here going back for three or four months.'

'Oh, Dad!' said Nell, looking reproachfully at Charles.

Ellen Brett Caldwell, who was named after Ellen Terry but always known as Nell, was in some ways the most extraordinary of the Brett family. It took an extraordinary degree of ordinariness to live her entire childhood, either with her Auntie Elsie or at boarding school, knowing that her parents were notable theatrical personalities, and to emerge to play Cordelia to her father's King Lear on the London stage, and then, as obstinate in reverse as any stage-struck daughter, to say that she wanted nothing to do with the theatre, never wanted to be an actress, and that she insisted on marrying John Caldwell, a stockbroker, whose sole connection with the stage was that he had given Charles some good advice on investments and had, in recompense, been invited to one of the Nightingale Grove Sunday lunches. The fact that John's business acumen proved to be useful, and that, in spite of all that Nell could do, he had become drawn more and more deeply into the affairs of the Brett family was, of course, inevitable, but still, to Nell, exasperating.

'What do all these bills relate to?' inquired Edwin, helping himself to a hot scone and going to sit beside Martha on the sofa.

Tea was the Brett family's favourite meal. Breakfast was too early, and they frequently had luncheon engagements, while dinner interfered with the evening performance of anyone who happened to be in work. But, except for matinées, teatime marked that magic span of time when ordinary people prepared to go home and theatre people prepared to go to work, and the Brett family, jostling round the garden room, helping themselves to scones and cakes, and accepting the cups of tea poured by Lydia, were like racehorses in the paddock, lively and eager, enjoying each other's company and ready for off.

'Most of them,' said Charles, gloomily, 'are for the redecoration of this room. Blame your mother. She would insist on getting Syrie Maugham to do it up – though I didn't notice Syrie paying for any of it.'

Lydia's face, as she poured a cup of tea for Thomas, had a beautiful Pre-Raphaelite detachment. Nell took a plate of Flora's rather soggy Dundee cake to John, and he helped himself to a slice and thanked her with a smile before turning back to the pile of bills and letters.

'Most of them,' he said, 'haven't even been opened. "Tennis Racket, sixty-three shillings." "Wireless Cabinet, thirteen pounds." "Lady's gold brocade purse, twenty-one and sixpence."'

Lydia, her attention caught, put the teapot down with a bang.

'*What?*' she said.

Charles buried his face in his cup of tea.

'Wine,' John concluded, oblivious of this little piece of by-play, 'a hundred and thirty-eight pounds.'

'What about the letters?' inquired Thomas, sitting, as usual, slightly apart, on the higher level of the garden room, and leafing through Willie Sutherland's play.

'Father only reads letters from admirers,' answered Martha.

'And he doesn't answer those,' Edwin added, 'unless they're from ladies, preferably titled, and young. Agèd governesses don't stand a chance.'

'Really, Charles,' remarked Lydia, 'you are too heartless.'

'Nonsense,' Charles replied, relieved that she seemed to have decided to let the brocade purse pass for the time being. 'They enjoy writing them. They don't really expect me to write back.'

Nell knew as well as John did that it was necessary to be firm if the family were not to skate away from tiresome business matters into more amusing discussions.

'Yes, Father,' she said, looking over John's shoulder at the unwieldy mass of papers, 'but the trouble is that the letters are all mixed up with the bills.'

She gave John the kind of look which from husband to wife is more like a command, and turned away.

'The truth is, sir,' said John, clearing his throat, 'you need a secretary.'

'How can I afford a secretary?' demanded Charles. 'I'm nearly in Carey Street now, according to you!'

'Why don't you have Miss Jones?' Lydia suggested. 'She's not expensive.'

'Miss Jones?' inquired Charles.

'The nice little woman who types Willie's plays,' said Lydia.

Thomas languidly helped himself to a hot scone.

'Got ginger hair,' he remarked, 'and talks all the time in a high-pitched voice, like a chicken laying eggs.'

'I'm certainly not having *her*!' said Charles.

Lydia glared up at Thomas, as he took his first bite of buttery scone.

'Thomas!' she said. 'Really!'

He swallowed, and then grinned.

'Sorry, Ma,' he said.

'And don't call me "Ma",' said Lydia, with unexpected sharpness. 'You know I hate it.'

Edwin and Martha exchanged a glance, and Martha intervened, but, as always with Martha, with an ulterior motive.

'Father,' she said, warmly, 'I know exactly the right person – the most charming young man – he's a great admirer of yours, and he wants to get into the theatre. He's written a play which I've promised to read, and –'

'And he's absolutely beautiful,' Thomas finished.

They all looked at Martha, who endeavoured to look unconcerned.

'Really, Martha!' exclaimed Nell. 'Father doesn't want one of your young men imposed on him in the guise of secretary – however beautiful he may be!'

'I must say, Nell,' Martha drawled, 'that since you married John, you have become the most crashing bore.'

Nell took an outraged breath, but John intervened.

'Let's keep to the point,' he suggested.

He looked round at this talented but exasperating family into which he had married.

'I think we should advertise,' he said.

Instantly, they were all composing interesting advertisements: 'Wanted, charming young lady, able to type.' 'Wanted, elderly lady, able to add two and two but not too susceptible.' 'Secretary wanted, honest and industrious and willing to double as soubrette.' Charles, who had been very quiet for several minutes, suddenly spoke.

'There's no need for any of that,' he said, brightly. 'I've just had a brilliant idea.' He smiled at Lydia, but with a hint of nervousness which he was doing his best to conceal. 'I know just the person,' he said. 'She's a war widow. I met her at one of Emerald Cunard's charity shows.'

Lydia frowned. Clearly she was trying to remember the event.

'Poor as a church mouse,' said Charles, with a note of deep and sincere sympathy, 'and she has a little boy, too.'

'He can't be *very* little, Father,' Edwin remarked, 'if she's a war widow. Her son must be eleven or twelve at least.'

'Unless he's a little bastard,' Thomas contributed.

'Yes, well, anyway,' Charles went on with a hint of haste, 'she's just the – the woman for the job. She told me she was hoping to do a little secretarial work, so as to earn some money. It'd be doing her a favour. I'll send a note round to her and she can start tomorrow.'

'It's very odd,' remarked Lydia, thoughtfully. 'We went to that charity show together, and I seem to remember everyone glittering with diamonds, and Emerald Cunard looking like a rather large fairy off the top of a Christmas tree. I certainly don't recall an impoverished widow, with or without a little boy.'

'Oh, really, Mother!' Nell exclaimed, with unusual

irritability. 'What does it matter, as long as Father has someone to help him with his letters and make sure that the bills get paid?'

Charles suddenly saw the opening he had been waiting for. Rise. Move stage centre in front of fireplace. Speak with winning sincerity.

'That's all very well, my dear Nell,' he said, 'but getting a secretary is only the first step. If I am going to pay the bills, I need to have some money coming in.' He turned towards Lydia. 'Time we got back to work, Liddy.'

He saw Lydia's face stiffen and her eyes glaze, like an actress who has forgotten her lines but hopes no one will notice, and he was well satisfied. He beamed round at his assembled family.

'One success for your mother and me like *Marriage for Two*, and I'll have plenty to pay those bills, and enough left over to buy a yacht.'

John Caldwell looked, aghast, at Nell.

'Don't even think about it,' she said.

'Well, Liddy,' said Charles, 'what do you suggest?'

Lydia gazed vaguely round her, and then spoke in the manner of an actress who has finally recalled a line that might cover the hiatus.

'Thomas,' she said, 'would you ring the bell for Sutton? Tea is such an untidy meal.'

'I suppose,' Charles remarked, casually, 'that if there's nothing else, we might offer Freddie Carson this new play of Willie's.'

Thomas, having rung the bell, turned sharply towards him.

'Pa!' he exclaimed. 'You can't do that play! It's appalling.'

'Rubbish,' said Charles.

'It certainly is,' replied Thomas.

Charles decided to rise above this undoubted score by Thomas.

'Edwin?' he said, with what he hoped was a flattering note of confidence. 'I thought perhaps you and I and your mother might take it on. Willie says it has a very nice part in it for you.'

'No, thank you, Father,' Edwin replied, decidedly. 'I've just agreed to do *She Stoops to Conquer* at Richmond. Besides, from what Thomas says –'

Charles stormed across the room and picked up the script which had already lost much of its pristine freshness. Obviously, most members of the family had found time to leaf through it.

'We all know Thomas's taste in plays!' he said. 'If it isn't written by some damned Russian and performed in the Euston Road –'

Leafing through the script himself, he came upon a line which struck gloom to his heart. 'Sire, it is my duty to save you from yourself.' He'd never get his tongue round that. He hoped to God the rest of it was better.

'Pa,' said Thomas, earnestly, 'you don't have to appear in a piece of old-fashioned rubbish, just because you've been out of work for three months.'

The rest of the family twitched slightly, and Martha moaned, 'Oh, Tom!'

'I am *not* out of work!' Charles roared, just as Sutton came in. 'I am simply looking round for the appropriate piece for your mother and me.'

In that moment, Charles saw Sutton and Lydia exchange a quick glance. I was right, he thought. Dammit, I was right. Lydia smiled graciously at Sutton.

'Oh, thank you, Sutton,' she said, as he stood there, attentively waiting. 'Would you clear away the tea?'

'Certainly, madam.'

His eyes met hers as he came to stack the tea things. Lydia looked across at Charles with a pleasant smile.

'You could always ask Freddie Lonsdale to write you something,' she said. 'Or even Noël Coward.'

'You'd be lucky to get anything from *him*,' said Thomas.

'Huh!' said Charles. 'Don't want him, anyway. Five successes in a row, his next play is sure to be a flop!'

He kept his eyes on Lydia's face.

'What do you say, Liddy?' he demanded. 'Shall we send Willie's play to Carson and see if he feels like putting it on for us?'

There was a brief pause before Lydia raised her beautiful blue eyes to Charles's face.

'I may as well tell you, Charles,' she said. 'There really wouldn't be any point. Freddie Carson never puts on more than one production at a time, and he already has something he wants *me* to do.'

Charles gazed at her, stunned astonishment in every line of his face.

'You don't mean – on your own?'

'Well, it's hardly suitable for you,' Lydia replied, with an acerbity which Charles was happy to think was born of guilt. 'It's a musical comedy called *Twinkle-Toes*.'

Charles sank into the nearest chair like a wounded stag subsiding heroically on the hillside.

'And might I make so bold as to ask – have you agreed to do it?'

'More or less,' Lydia replied. 'I'm seeing Freddie tomorrow morning, to meet the author and hear the music.'

'I suppose,' said Charles, tragically, 'that I am the last to know?'

Fortunately, the chair into which he had sunk was in a commanding position from which he could gaze round

43

at each member of his family in turn and, stricken, see each of them avoid his eye. Gratified by the success of the little trap which he had sprung on Lydia, he looked back towards her, and, to his annoyance, was in time to surprise a glance between her and Sutton which was a silent but unmistakable criticism of his performance. He rose to his feet, but Lydia was too quick for him. Her rise was faster than his.

'Charles, dear,' she said, with that sweet reasonableness which, as she well knew, always drove him mad, 'I'm very sorry if you're upset, but Freddie Carson's piece is just right for me. If I don't do it, he'll only offer it to Boo Laye or Jessie Matthews – and we really do need the money.'

'I dare say,' said Charles, 'but –'

'Besides,' Lydia continued, expertly cutting in, 'we've been in the business long enough to accept the fact that sometimes a part comes up for you, and sometimes for me.'

Yes, bugger it! thought Charles, but lately all the parts seem to come up for you and none of them for me! Long years of experience kept the thought out of his face.

'I am not in the least upset,' he said, loftily. 'It doesn't matter to me. Do whatever you like. *I* shall do Willie's play.'

They all spoke at once.

'Now, Charlie, really –!' cried Lydia.

'Oh, Pa!' said Martha.

'I shouldn't rush into anything,' said John Caldwell.

'Father –' began Nell.

'Pa, that play is simply appalling!' said Thomas.

Edwin's voice came in later than the others and crystal clear.

'Quite honestly, Father,' he said, 'I don't think you'll get anyone to put it on.'

That did it. Charles's Irish temper rose up within him.

'Oh, *don't* you?' he said.

He walked to the door and delivered his exit line.

'I shall do Willie's play,' he said, 'if I have to lease a theatre and put the blasted thing on myself!'

Chapter Four

By next morning, Charles had recovered his temper. He had also had time to read Willie's play. Lydia had her breakfast in bed as usual, and then went off to meet Freddie Carson. Perhaps, thought Charles, he had better let her do *Twinkle-Toes* (especially since he couldn't stop her, and they really did need the money!). Meanwhile – Charles went happily off to his study to prepare for the arrival of the new secretary.

In the kitchen, as the morning wore on, Flora and Emily were preparing luncheon and Sutton, drinking a cup of tea, was keeping an ear open for the front door bell. The secretary still had not arrived, and Flora was out of temper.

'You're sure the secretary's having luncheon with the family?' she demanded.

'That's what Miss Lydia said. Only the first day, though. After that, she'll have a tray in the study.'

'Huh!' said Flora, and pummelled her pastry on the board in a way that boded ill for the steak and kidney pie she was planning. 'If you ask me,' she said, 'a secretary is as bad as a governess. Can't eat with the family, and too proud to eat in the kitchen. You mark my words, it'll be trays, trays, trays, all day long. I just hope this one knows her place.'

Her eye fell on Emily, polishing an entrée dish.

'You'd better clean the other entrée dish as well,' she said. 'If there's any fish left, I'll do it up with a bit of curry powder for supper.'

''Ow many will there be for lunch?' inquired Emily.

'Luncheon,' Sutton corrected her. '"Lunch" is a bit of bread and cheese in the middle of the morning.'

Emily ignored this. Young and foolish as she was, she had already grasped the fact that this was not the kind of household in which one learned the finer points of etiquette of life in service.

'There'll be the master and the mistress, and the secretary –'

'If she ever arrives,' Sutton intervened, glancing at the apple-and-pears kitchen clock on the mantelpiece.

'And Master Thomas,' Emily pursued.

'Unless he's working on one of his plays. Then he prefers a tray up in the nursery.'

''Ow about supper?' inquired Emily, with a note of resentment.

'Never can tell,' Flora replied, rolling out a by now rather leathery piece of pastry. 'The master and mistress, Mr Thomas, Miss Martha, I dare say, unless she's got something better to do –'

'You said she'd got her own flat,' Emily interrupted. 'Why don't she stay there?'

Flora looked at her, astonished.

'That flat of hers isn't big enough to boil an egg – if Miss Martha could boil an egg, which she can't. And Mr Edwin has his service chambers in Jermyn Street, but it's not the same. He likes to come back home for a chat and a bit of comfort. They both do. So we just like to make sure that it's all here for them if they want it, and if they don't, no harm done.'

Emily went to fetch the other entrée dish, but sent a resentful glance back at Flora.

'It wasn't like this at my Mum's place,' she said.

Sutton drained his cup of tea and put it down.

'I dare say your Mum's place wasn't with a Theatre Family,' he said.

'No,' Emily answered, 'but –'

Sutton, amused, saw her young brain struggling with the problem. Her Mum had said that Mrs Tupman was a bitch, but, on the other hand, she was paid good wages and all you had to do was open a tin of herrings in tomato sauce for supper, and butter a bit of bread. Was it worthwhile being in a Theatre Family and never knowing what to expect or how much work you were expected to do, just for the privilege of working for them? Sutton, ever alert, heard the key in the front door, and instantly forgot everything else.

'There's Miss Lydia!' he said.

'Oh, Alfred,' said Lydia, 'could you lend me a half-crown for the taxi?'

Sutton resignedly felt in his waistcoat pocket and went out to pay the taxi-driver. It had always been like that, right back from the old days when he was a walk-on, and the great Miss Wheatley sent him out to buy a bottle of stout between the houses. 'Oh dear,' she would say, fumbling in that little kid purse of hers, 'I don't seem to have –' 'Never mind, Miss Wheatley,' he would say, great gawky lad that he was. 'I've got it here.' And off would go the best part of his week's wages, but he'd never grudged it then, and he never grudged it now. If he hadn't turned up at the Prince's Theatre, Manchester, just for a dare, to volunteer as a super in the touring company of *The Scarlet Pimpernel*, and been bewitched by the beauty of Miss Lydia, what would he be doing now? Serving out fruit and vegetables from his father's greengrocer's shop? He would have money in the bank, no doubt, but what value could one put on magic? And, as long as he lived, Miss Lydia would represent magic to him.

'Is the secretary here?' inquired Lydia, as Sutton followed her into the garden room.

'Not yet,' Sutton replied. 'She's late.'

He never used his butler's voice when he was alone with Lydia, and she never called him 'Sutton'. It was always 'Alfred' and 'Miss Lydia'.

'Mm,' she said. 'I wish I knew who this woman was. He's up to something, I know it.'

There was a screech of brakes from the direction of the drive, and they both rushed to the window. The departing taxi had very nearly collided with a smart little open two-seater, which, with a slight crash of gears, was now speeding towards the front door.

Sutton, opening the door, felt his mouth come open. Even the sight of the two-seater and the imperious ring of the doorbell had not prepared him for the lady who confronted him. Exquisitely dressed in the latest fashion which yet was hallowed by money and breeding, she was about thirty years old. She raised enormous eyes from beneath her silk cloche hat, but while they rested on his face, she did not really see him. Ladies of her unmistakable quality never actually *saw* butlers.

'Mr Charles Brett,' she murmured, in a voice that seemed to have accidentally combined husky seductiveness with the exaggerated vowels of the upper classes.

'Yes, madam,' replied Sutton.

Obviously not the secretary, but who the devil was she?

'Lady Agatha Danvers,' she said, advancing. 'He is expecting me.'

'Yes, ma– m'lady,' responded Sutton, falling back.

Was it possible that –? He became aware of Charles emerging from his study and coming towards the lady with arms outstretched.

'My dear Lady Agatha!' he cried. 'So good of you to come!'

As Charles escorted her towards his study, Sutton looked down at the white fox fur, which, without even looking at him, she had deposited over his arm, and then, looking up, saw Lydia in the doorway of the garden room.

'Secretary, eh?' he remarked. 'Bit overdressed for the part, I'd say.'

Lydia's face, always superbly, if subtly, expressive, indicated that all was now revealed to her, and that she didn't like it one bit.

If Lydia had been able to accompany Lady Agatha into Charles's study, she would have been able to discover that, twenty minutes later, he was far from happy himself. This beautiful young woman was just as delightful as he had remembered, just as flattering in her admiration of himself, and declared herself now too, too thrilled at the notion of being able to help him in his wonderful work.

He poured her a second glass of sherry, and she crossed those long, silk-stockinged legs of hers, and looked up at him with that gaze of seductive purity, like Diana Manners as an unbelievably pure Virgin in *The Miracle*, but as he turned away, his eye fell on those appalling piles of unsorted letters and bills. If he didn't do something about it, the duns really would be at the door again.

'Well,' he said, regretfully, 'I suppose we should get to work. Did you – er – did you leave your typewriter in the car?'

'Oh,' said Agatha, seeming slightly taken aback, 'well – no. You see, I'm borrowing Selena Davenport's – she bought it because she thought she might write a novel, you know, but she says writing is dreadfully difficult, much more trouble than she expected – so she said I could borrow the typewriter.'

'Ah,' said Charles, feeling slightly dazed.

'But the only bother is,' Agatha continued, 'Selena says it needs a new ribbon, and she doesn't know how to put it in.' A puzzled frown briefly furrowed her pure brow. 'Apparently,' she confided, 'typewriting ribbons get holes in them if you use them long enough – too absurd! Why not put in ribbons that last?'

'Quite,' Charles responded, as best he might, and poured himself another glass of sherry. Lady Agatha, delighted, came up with an idea.

'But I'll buy a new ribbon,' she declared, in a sudden

burst of enthusiasm. 'I dare say one can get them at Harrod's – and I'll bring it along, with the typewriter, and I expect your butler will know how to put it in.'

'Er – yes, I'm sure he will,' said Charles.

Agatha drew the satisfied breath of one who has just settled the main problem of the day and now has time to enjoy herself.

'Now,' she said, 'what do you want me to do? Could I type a play for you? I'd simply love to type a play!'

'Ah – well – I don't actually write plays myself. I only act in them. And when people send them to me, I'm afraid they're already typed.'

'Oh, what a shame!' said Agatha. 'I've been telling all my friends that I was going to type your plays. I rang absolutely *everyone* up last night, and said that we could all go to the theatre, and when we saw you on the stage saying all those marvellous things, I could say, "*I* typed those!"'

'Never mind, my dear,' said Charles. (Really, she was like a charmingly innocent child!) 'If you want to help me, you know what would mean more to me than anything?'

'Oh, *what*?' she cried, eagerly. 'Do tell me!'

'Well,' replied Charles, 'it's all these dreadful letters and bills. They are making my life a misery. What I thought was that, if we could have a spot of lunch together here, and then make a start on them this afternoon –'

Lady Agatha's face was suddenly clouded with sorrow.

'Oh, I'm *terribly* sorry,' she said, 'but I *can't*. I arranged to meet Barny Harrington at the Ritz Grill. You know Barny? He was such a friend of my darling

Raymond – not a penny to his name, poor sweet, but then none of us have any money since the war, have we?'

Charles experienced that sensation familiar to him in nightmares, and even occasionally in real life, of endeavouring to deliver a scene from one play and realizing that his fellow actor was performing quite a different piece. The clock on the mantelpiece struck the half-hour, and Lady Agatha started up.

'Goodness!' she exclaimed. 'Is that the time? I must dash. Oh, I'm so looking forward to being your secretary. Too thrilling!'

Charles rang the bell for Sutton. The great thing, he thought, in situations like this, was to regain control.

'You're going to be absolutely invaluable,' he said, and then proceeded before she could speak again. 'When do you think you could start?'

'How about tomorrow?' suggested Lady Agatha.

Charles drew a breath of relief. After all, Lady Cynthia Asquith had acted as Barrie's secretary, and, from all accounts, had not been a total disaster. Perhaps he was in luck after all.

'Splendid!' he said. 'What time shall we say? We don't start work too early in the theatre, you know. Shall we say – ten o'clock?'

He saw again that sorrowful look which made any man feel a brute for having caused it.

'Oh – well –' said Lady Agatha, 'that is a teeny bit – I mean, I usually have breakfast in bed –' (again that unconsciously seductive note!) '– and then I have to get dressed –'

'Of course,' said Charles, and their eyes met.

'And Hampstead is such a long way out. How about eleven o'clock?' Lady Agatha added, with an air of inspiration. 'Then we can work for at least an hour and a half before lunch.'

An hour and a half! thought Charles. How long did she think secretaries usually worked? Eight thirty until five thirty? Clearly not. He decided to make the best of a bad job.

'Splendid,' he said, heartily. 'Splendid! And – I suppose we really should talk about – about a salary. You're not going to do all this work for nothing,' he added, playfully, putting his arm round her shoulders.

It was unfortunate that Sutton should appear at the door in that moment. Charles had forgotten that he had rung for him. He couldn't very well take his arm hastily away from round Lady Agatha's shoulders, so instead he smiled down at her in a fatherly manner. She gazed adoringly up at him.

'Oh, I'd *love* to,' she said, 'if only I could afford it. I'm such a great admirer of yours.'

'Ah, Sutton,' said Charles, as though he had only just become aware of him. 'Lady Agatha is leaving.'

Sutton stood aside, and Charles took the opportunity to remove his hand from around Lady Agatha's shoulders and instead to put it on her elbow. He would have preferred not to discuss her salary in front of Sutton, but it couldn't be helped, so as they proceeded across the hall, Charles remarked, casually, 'I believe secretaries earn something like – twenty-five shillings a week – or – perhaps – two pounds?'

Agatha paused and turned to him, as Sutton went past her to open the front door.

'Money's such a bore, isn't it?' she said. 'And I'm so hopelessly unbusinesslike.'

Charles smiled down at her sympathetically.

'So am I,' he murmured, 'but – one has to –'

'I tell you what!' exclaimed Agatha. 'Why don't you just give me a fiver a week, and that will include expenses – petrol and all that sort of thing?'

Charles had trouble keeping the smile on his face. Five pounds! Sutton only got three pounds a week. Mind, that included his keep, not to mention a bottle of Whitbread every day, and the odd bottle of wine which he thought Charles didn't know about. And, of course, a secretary should get more than a butler, although one expected to pay a woman less than a man – though perhaps not a lady – Charles was all too conscious of Sutton, stone-faced, standing holding the door open, but, on the other hand, the most important thing was to settle the matter and get Lady Agatha out of the house before Lydia returned from seeing Freddie Carson, thus postponing the inevitable row. Besides, Lady Agatha was such a deliciously charming young woman –

'Is that fair, do you think?' inquired Lady Agatha, anxiously.

'Of course!' said Charles, gratefully accepting the cue, no matter what the consequences. 'Five pounds. Yes. Very fair.'

Charles escorted Lady Agatha out to her two-seater, and helped her into the driving seat, well aware of the fine display of silk-stockinged leg which this manoeuvre entailed. He leaned down to take her hand and kiss it.

'See you tomorrow,' he said. 'Eleven o'clock.'

'Oh *yes*!' she replied with enthusiasm, and added, 'I'll try not to be late.'

The tyres tore up the gravel as she zoomed away down the drive. Charles returned into the house, and Sutton closed the front door behind him. Heading for the study with a considerable sense of relief, Charles heard behind him the words: 'War widow, indeed!'

It was Lydia at her most acid. God damn and blast! thought Charles. So she was home already. Trust her to get back early. He almost continued his move into the study and closed the door behind him, but decided that this would look like guilt, whereas he was as innocent as the driven snow. He turned and walked past Sutton into the Garden Room.

'So she is,' he said, defiantly. 'Her husband was killed on the Somme. Poor girl, she's inconsolable!'

Lydia was taking a script and sheet music out of the tapestry bag which, as long as he could remember, had been her version of a Gladstone bag and holdall.

'From all I've heard,' said Lydia, 'she has been doing her best to console herself ever since his death – and she didn't do too badly, according to Edwin, while Raymond was at the front.'

Charles, seeming to remember now something of the same himself, thrust the thought aside and, as usual in their quarrels, decided that attack was the best means of defence at his disposal.

'Such a mistake, dear,' he said, 'to be acid and cynical. So ageing. If you're not careful, you'll find yourself playing dowagers in Oscar Wilde plays.'

'*You*,' Lydia responded instantly, 'will end up playing Charley's Aunt. Very vulgar and not at all funny. Always supposing,' she added, 'that you are not such a nincompoop as to take on that play of Willie's, which would finish your career once and for all!'

Charles, having almost decided against Willie's play, found himself driven back towards it, like a man whose wife forces him into the arms of a mistress he never wishes to see again.

'I have every intention of doing Willie's play,' he said, loftily, 'but thank you for your vote of confidence. I

56

know I can always count on *you*.'

'Yes,' Lydia responded, her accent beginning to slip, as it always did when she was angry, 'and I can always count on *you* to behave in a cheap and stupid way with any bit of skirt that's around!'

She was heading for the door, and if only Charles had let her go, everything would have been different, but unfortunately the perfect riposte came into his mind, and he delivered it.

'What a vulgar expression, my dear,' he remarked, 'and quite inappropriate, too. Unlike you, she is a lady.'

He knew as he said it that he had gone too far, and so, certainly, did Lydia. She stopped short and turned very slowly to look at him.

'Charles,' said Lydia, in quite a different voice, 'I am warning you. I won't have it. I won't have that woman in the house. Either she goes, or I do.'

Sutton, listening in the doorway of the dining room across the hall, just as he always used to stand watching from the wings, heard these words with alarm. She was backing the guv'nor into a corner, and that was never a good idea. He had his pride, and all the more because, just as all actors were insecure, he was more insecure than most, having started his career with his mother and father, touring Ireland and the provinces with a broken-down fit-up company, and, deep down, was always afraid that he might end up the same way.

'Oh, don't be childish!' said Charles. 'I've offered Lady Agatha the job of my secretary, and I couldn't possibly go back on my word.'

'Well,' said Lydia, 'I'm certainly not going back on mine!'

Sutton heard the note of panic in her voice, and knew that she had realized that she had inadvertently gone past the point of no return. He was aware that she was now covering the moment of panic with another burst of temper.

'Have you forgotten', she demanded, 'dear little Maithie Parshonth, with her dear little listhp and her shock of red hair?'

It is a feature of matrimonial quarrels that ancient wrongs are unexpectedly dug up, like evil-smelling bones.

'For God's sake!' Charles exclaimed. 'You're not bringing *that* up again?'

'Why not?' inquired Lydia. 'I told you then that that was your last chance. Perhaps you'd forgotten – or perhaps you thought I didn't mean it?'

Come on, Miss Liddy, thought Sutton, you didn't, did you? But he was uneasily aware that the quarrel was now acquiring a momentum of its own.

'All I can say,' Lydia continued, 'is that if you want to spend the rest of your life kissing Lady Agatha's – *hand* – pray do. I certainly shall not be here to see it!'

She thrust her script and music sheets into her tapestry bag and walked out into the hall, shouting, 'Sutton!'

Sutton, hastily stepping back into the dining room, stepped sedately out again, every inch the butler.

'Yes, madam?'

'Would you ask Flora to come upstairs and help me pack?' she said. 'And then I'll need a taxi.'

Charles followed her out into the hall.

'What on earth do you mean?' he demanded. 'Where are you going?'

'I am going to stay with Elsie,' Lydia responded. Halfway up the stairs, she turned to look at him. 'Once and for all, Charles, will you get it through your head? I am leaving you!'

Chapter Five

The ensuing week was a miserable one in the Brett household. They were all accustomed to what Charles called 'alarums and excursions'. In a way, they all flourished upon these quarrels, just as the internal combustion engine proceeds by little bursts of energy. But at the end of a day of tantrums and tears and wounded feelings (sometimes quite deeply wounded feelings), they all knew that Charles and Lydia would kiss everyone goodnight and retire upstairs to that elegant yet comfortable bedroom, where, as in their connecting dressing rooms at the theatre, they would undress, Lydia would take off her make-up, and they would give a few notes to each other and comment on the performances of the rest of the family, and then they would climb into the big bed with its opulent blue satin bedspread and come to terms together with the day's events, knowing that in life, as in the theatre, nothing is ever quite perfect.

But now, for the first time, there was no Lydia. Even

when she had been away in America, or on tour, they had all been conscious of her presence, reinforced by letters, telephone calls and telegrams, but this deliberate absenting herself, cutting the threads of trust and affection between herself and Charles, was like a gratuitous and unaccepted death. Sutton and Flora knew, if no one else did, that Lydia was spoilt, wilful and ingeniously manipulative, and that she got her own way much more often than Charles, for all his bluster. But it was Lydia who, in the midst of everything else that was going on, was most aware of other people's feelings, first to see when, in the rough and tumble of the Brett family life, real injury had been done, and she would pause to salve the wound and mend the damage as best she could. If Charles was the chief source of energy in the household, Lydia was its heart, and a family, like a play, or a human being, cannot exist for long without a heart.

Lady Agatha arrived at half-past eleven next morning, and Sutton, much to his indignation, was obliged to fetch the typewriter out of the car and carry it through to the study. He was even more indignant when he was asked to take out the old ribbon and replace it with a new one, a task which he did not accomplish without a great deal of suppressed profanity and a vast amount of indelible ink on his fingers. Lady Agatha and Charles meanwhile indulged in cheerful badinage on the hearthrug. Clearly Lady Agatha had no intention of watching what Sutton was doing, so that next time she could do it herself.

'Thank you *so* much,' she said, when he had finished. 'Do you think now you could show me how to work it?'

'I am very sorry, m'lady,' replied Sutton. 'I am not familiar with the machine.'

And upon that he withdrew and firmly closed the door.

A very short time spent in watching Agatha strike the wrong key with one immaculately manicured forefinger convinced Charles that Selena's typewriter, with or without a new ribbon, was not going to be a success.

'How would it be,' he suggested, 'if you answered some of these letters for me in your own hand?'

'Oh, *yes*!' she cried. 'I *love* writing letters. If you just tell me what to say –'

'Of course,' answered Charles, relieved. 'You see, I've sorted out these letters which are from people I don't know from Adam, and I've written at the top, "Refuse", "Agree" or "Many thanks for writing". If you could take care of those while I write some cheques to clear off some of these bills – and then perhaps you could address the envelopes –?'

'Goodness!' exclaimed Agatha.

It occurred to Charles that never in her whole life, except for brief spells in the schoolroom with her governess, had Agatha ever done any work of any description, and, judging from the haphazard nature of her spelling, she had not applied herself to any great extent even then. However, she cast her hat aside and sat down very readily to dash off the first of the letters in her large, illegible handwriting. Unfortunately, it emerged that Lady Agatha enjoyed reading letters almost as much as she enjoyed writing them, and it was just when Charles had written the last painful cheque, and realized that he would also have to address the envelopes, and was wondering whether there was enough money in the bank to cover them all, that Sutton entered to say that he was wanted on the telephone by Mr Sutherland.

'Hullo, Charles,' came Willie Sutherland's cheery

voice. 'Just wondered if you'd had time to read the play.'

'Ah – yes,' Charles answered.

It might have been different if Sutton had not been standing waiting firmly, if deferentially, by the kitchen door. Charles was damned if he was going to back down in front of Sutton. That would be just like backing down in front of Lydia. He knew damned well that Lydia would ring Sutton from her sister's house when he was out, just to see how things were going along, and whether there was any news.

'Guv'nor had to cave in over Mr Sutherland's play,' Sutton would say. 'You were right, Miss Liddy. He had to admit that it would never go in the West End.'

'Of course I've read it, Willie,' said Charles. 'Wants a bit of work on it, but –' he inadvertently caught Sutton's eye and finished on a note of defiance. 'You're quite right. It's just what the public wants, after all this modern rubbish. As a matter of fact, if you can find anyone who wants to lease a theatre, I'm quite willing to put it on myself.'

Charles put the receiver back on the hook and turned towards the study.

'Excuse me, sir,' said Sutton. 'Flora was asking – how many will there be for luncheon?'

'Myself and Lady Agatha, naturally,' said Charles, 'and – is Mr Thomas –?'

'Mr Thomas has intimated,' responded Sutton, exasperatingly overacting his butler role, 'that he would prefer a tray in the nursery.'

'I don't give a damn what he prefers!' Charles exploded. 'You can tell Mr Thomas that I expect him to come downstairs and eat luncheon with my guest!'

'Guest, is it?' said Flora. 'I thought she was supposed to be his secretary.'

'Ah, but she's a lady,' replied Sutton. 'That's why she gets five pounds a week.'

'Five pounds a week!' exclaimed Emily. 'Getting that much, I should think she ought to wait on us!'

'That's quite enough from you, Emily,' said Flora. 'What the master chooses to do is no business of yours.'

She looked at Sutton.

'Did the master say what he wanted for luncheon?'

'Didn't say,' responded Sutton, expressionless. 'Left it up to you.'

Emily, glancing up, was surprised to see Flora and Sutton exchanging a slow, subterranean smile.

Thomas was furious to be told by Sutton that he had to come downstairs to take luncheon with the war widow. It made him feel disloyal to his mother, but, even more, it interrupted his writing. Like all the Bretts, Thomas was single-minded, and he was single-mindedly certain that he was destined to be a writer. At school, his essays were always marked ten out of ten, and his sketches for the Cambridge Footlights were enormously admired. He had come down from the university with a third-class degree, which had enraged his father, but with one play completed and two more in his head. The play which was finished he confidently sent to the Royal Court Theatre, and it was a nasty shock to get it instantly returned with a curt rejection slip. It was the Royal Court which had put on many of the plays of George Bernard Shaw, to the plaudits of a small, unfashionable but faithful audience, and Thomas privately considered that his play was a great deal better than any of them. The rejection knocked him out for a couple of days, especially since his justification for the third-class degree was to be an instant triumphant production of a brilliant play. If he was not to be a famous writer, what *would* he be? A third-rate teacher of English in a fourth-rate prep school? He thrust the humiliatingly unsuccessful play beneath a pile of papers and prepared for a life of failure. The third day, however, he awoke with a peculiar surge of energy and optimism. He had suddenly remembered an idea he had had for a light comedy. Perhaps it had been a mistake to try first for a serious play. Comedies were much easier. 'If The Truth Be Told', he wrote at the top of the page, and then, 'Act One'. In a fine new access of self-confidence he wrote the first three scenes, and then ground to a halt. It was a funny first act, but what happened next? Oh, damn! It had all seemed so clear, so simple. But was it possible that his comedy was really just a one-acter? Were funny lines not enough?

It was at that moment that Sutton broke the bad news that his father demanded that he should go downstairs and eat luncheon.

As a social occasion, it was doomed from the start, although Lady Agatha did her best. Somehow, the subject of the war came up, and she remarked that it was so fortunate that Thomas had been too young to be involved in it.

'None of us', she said, movingly, 'who lived through the war will ever *quite* recover from it.'

'"Never glad confident morning again,"' quoted Charles.

'Oh – absolutely,' replied Agatha, floundering. 'And, I mean, everyone so hard up. Like poor Barney Harrington – both his father and his older brother killed, and he's crippled by death duties. And, of course, he limps as well.'

'Twice crippled,' remarked Thomas, blandly.

Charles glared at him, but Agatha warmly concurred.

'Oh, absolutely!' she exclaimed. 'So horrid for him. And it's ruined his dancing.'

'Beastly for him,' said Thomas.

'You said your son, Edwin, was in the war?' said Agatha, turning towards Charles.

'Yes,' he replied, cheerfully. 'Came through without a scratch. Well, that's not quite true. He was slightly wounded –'

'Oh yes, but only slightly,' Thomas said. 'A shell exploded and killed Martha's husband, who was Edwin's best friend, and was standing right beside him, and Edwin was hit by a piece of shrapnel.'

'Goodness, how dreadful!' exclaimed Agatha.

'Yes,' Charles agreed. 'He was hit in the face, too. It could have scarred him for life, but luckily it didn't.'

Sutton served the pudding – pêche Melba, which Flora knew Charles detested. So did Sutton, deferentially presenting the silver dish with an inky forefinger well in evidence. Charles very well knew that he was being punished by the staff on behalf of Lydia, and also that he couldn't possibly make a row in front of Lady Agatha. His eyes met Sutton's.

'Not for me, thank you,' he said, coldly.

Some part of Thomas was aware of this amusing little by-play, but at one remove, as though he looked in on the scene from outside. Somehow he had moved away into that author's world which, while taking part in a scene, also acts out another one in some mysterious region of the mind, like people who, while apparently lying unconscious, travel into mysterious worlds beyond the grave. He was brought sharply back into the present by Lady Agatha.

'Mr Brett tells me you're writing a play,' she said. 'Too thrilling!'

Thomas looked at Charles reproachfully. Surely his father knew that a play in its early stages was like a performance in rehearsal, too fragile to be displayed to outsiders? Wounded, he took his revenge.

'Oh, I'm afraid you wouldn't like it, Lady Agatha,' he said. 'It's only a light comedy. I imagine you would prefer something more intellectual.'

'Oh – well – yes,' replied Agatha. 'That is – of course, I like anything if – I mean, if it's good, and, of course, amusing.'

'Of course,' said Thomas. 'I did hear, Father, that the Royal Court Theatre was considering reviving *The Lower Depths* by Gorky. You really ought to take Lady Agatha to that.'

'If they do decide to do it, I certainly will,' replied Charles, smiling at Agatha, who had no more conception of *The Lower Depths* than of how to clean a kitchen grate.

Charles turned back to Thomas.

'Thank you, Thomas,' he said. 'We won't delay you if you want to get back to work. Naturally, you're anxious to complete your play. After all, now you've left the university, you have your living to make.'

'Thank you, Father, for reminding me!' said Thomas. He rose and stormed out of the room and slammed the door behind him.

Charles smiled apologetically at Agatha.

'So sorry,' he said. 'I'm afraid all my family are somewhat temperamental.'

He felt guilty all the same. It had been unpardonable to have said what he did to Thomas in front of a stranger. But, dammit, Thomas had provoked it! He had the power to irritate Charles more than any of his other children – and, of course, for a very good reason.

Thomas raced up the stairs two at a time, banged into the nursery, and slammed the door with such force that he hoped his father would be able to hear it in the dining room three floors below. How dare he! How dare he remind me that I'm a failure, and dependent on him for everything! And to do it in front of that woman!

In a blazing temper, Thomas walked up and down the big, bare room, with its schoolroom furniture and sloping window looking out over the garden. How could he possibly work now? How could he ever work in this house, where no one ever treated him as an artist, but belittled him and invaded his privacy? It would be days now before he could get back to writing his play.

And yet, all the time, his rage had a kind of life-giving energy in it, like a rising tide of sexual passion. He stopped and looked at the pile of paper on the schoolroom table. There were words beating in his mind, like a melody waiting to be written down. 'It could have scarred him for life, but luckily it didn't.' He sat down at the table, and found himself thinking of Edwin. Came through the war without a scratch, did he, that older brother of his? The war had been over for nearly ten years, and yet Edwin still had that curious air of detachment, of being an observer, of never quite having returned from the front, or rather, of still only being home on leave. And then, there was his lack of involvement with girls. It wasn't that he didn't like them, and certainly not that they didn't like *him*. Edwin was like a younger and even handsomer version of their father, with his pencil moustache like Douglas Fairbanks' and that slightly enigmatic smile of his. But it was as though, having seen Martha, his twin, widowed by the war, and so many of his friends killed before they could find love and marriage, he felt that he himself, in finding happiness, would be robbing the dead.

Thomas remembered that day in 1917 when Edwin, home on leave, had come up to the nursery, where Thomas, an awkward schoolboy of thirteen, was struggling with a holiday task before returning to Marlborough. As though the scene now acted itself out before him in that very room where he was sitting, Thomas saw Edwin, in his romantic uniform with the new M.C. ribbon on his breast, sitting on the windowsill and gazing out at the garden and the valley beyond.

'War's a rotten business, Thomas,' he said. 'People at home say it's glorious, but it's not. It's bloody and frightening, and when we're in the trenches we're covered in mud and lice. If any of us get out of it alive, we'll be lucky. Or will we?'

He had turned to look at Thomas as he sat there, an inky schoolboy, confused and overawed, and smiled.

'Sorry, old chap,' he said. 'I can't tell Mother or Father – and certainly not Martha – and I had to tell someone.'

He got up and walked out, ruffling Thomas's hair as he passed in a gesture of affection and apology.

Thomas drew a clean sheet of paper towards him and wrote at the top, 'If The Truth Be Told', and then 'Act One'. But he pushed the light comedy aside. The play which was coming into burgeoning life in his mind was quite a different play.

Chapter Six

Somewhat to Charles's dismay, Willie Sutherland, always very active where his own interests were concerned, wrote almost immediately to say that he had heard of a suitable theatre, and, in no time at all, they were sitting in the Garrick Club, waiting for the owner to arrive.

'Glad you liked the play, Charles,' said Willie, beaming. 'Good title, isn't it?'

'Very good,' Charles replied, glad to be able to praise something. *The King Shall Not Die* certainly had a ring to it. He took a cautious sip of sherry. 'Er – Edwin seemed to think that the play might be – rather old-fashioned.'

'Nonsense!' said Willie, unperturbed. 'It's just what people want after all this modern rubbish. Getting dressed up and going out to the theatre just to watch Gerald du Maurier light a cigarette!'

'You can't say he's not a big draw,' remarked Charles.

'Ah,' responded Willie, with the author's usual

desperate eagerness to turn a criticism into a selling point, 'well, you can smoke a cigarette in this play – a Russian one, anyway. Come to think of it,' he added, triumphantly, 'I've actually called the country "Sobrani".'

'Ye–es,' said Charles, gloomily. 'We'll have to change that.'

He glanced round, his impatience and irritation increasing. What the devil was he doing here, preparing to discuss the production of a play whose only virtue was that it had a great big leading part for himself? Was he really reduced to that – and, if he was, did he have the power to carry such a play to success? Conscious of rising terror, he saw a way of escape.

'This fellow Brewster is late, isn't he?' he said. 'Is he a member?'

'Good Lord, no!' replied Willie. 'He's a mill owner from Bradford. A war profiteer. Made his pile selling blankets to the army, and then bought some theatres as an investment. Not really in the "business" at all.'

'Oh,' said Charles. 'Don't like the sound of that. I don't mind dealing with a gentleman like Freddie Carson, but I'm damned if I'm going to wait around here for –'

About to rise and depart, he was forestalled by Willie.

'There he is!' cried Willie. 'Mr Brewster!'

Charles saw approaching a four-square man, dressed in a worsted suit made, no doubt, in his own mills, and with a face that looked like Cromwell's, warts and all. No Laughing Cavalier about *him*! He advanced on Willie and shook him firmly by the hand. His Yorkshire accent sounded like something out of *Hobson's Choice*.

'Good day, Mr Sutherland,' he said, and turned to Charles. 'Mr Brett?'

'How do you do?' said Charles, reluctantly accepting a hand like a rough-edged vice.

'Sit down, Mr Brewster,' said Willie, with an ingratiating note in his voice. 'What will you have to drink?'

'I never drink, thanks,' said Mr Brewster, sitting down and putting his hands on his tight-trousered knees. 'Just a whisky before I go to bed, but I never drink in working hours.'

'Ah,' said Charles. He and Willie exchanged an alarmed glance. How did one deal with a man except over a congenial glass of something? 'Well, now,' Charles pursued, deciding that, for better or worse, it was up to him, 'about Mr Sutherland's play, *The King Shall Not Die* – Good title, isn't it?'

'I'm not too keen on the word "die" in the title,' replied Brewster. 'Might put people off.'

Since the title was about the only thing Charles liked about the play, this was a bit of a facer. However, he pressed on.

'You've – um – you've read the play?' he inquired. 'What did you think of it?'

'I got one of my advisers to read it,' Brewster replied, crushingly. 'He seemed to think it was a bit old-fashioned.'

Charles eyed him coldly. He never accorded to persons outside the 'business' the right to criticize plays or performers.

'Not old-fashioned, Mr Brewster,' he said, loftily. 'I would say rather that it is in the classic tradition of *The Scarlet Pimpernel* or – or *The Laughing Cavalier*. I have every faith in the play. That is why I am considering putting it on myself.'

'Yes,' said Brewster. 'Mr Sutherland tells me that you want to lease the Princess Theatre.'

'Er – well –' said Charles.

He saw Willie nodding and smiling, and knew that he had been committed much further than he had intended. Brewster produced a sheet of paper from his pocket.

'I've worked out a few figures here,' he said, 'and what I suggest is that you should pay a fixed rent of £400 per week.'

Charles drew his breath in sharply.

'Four hundred?' he repeated. 'That's a bit steep. The usual arrangement is to have a lower rent, and you take a share of the profits.'

Brewster's pale eyes met his.

'That's true,' he said, 'but in this case, I don't have quite the same confidence in the play that you do. Best to be honest.'

'Quite,' said Charles, hoist with his own petard.

He saw a way of escape, and took the paper and affected to study it.

'But I still think that rent is too high. We'd have to play to full houses every night to cover that, and –'

'I can't come down much more,' said Brewster. 'Don't forget, I've got the ground rent to pay.'

'Well, in that case,' said Charles, returning the paper with a feeling of profound relief, 'I'm afraid I don't feel that I can –'

Before he could finish, Brewster had taken the paper from him and was studying it.

'I tell you what I'll do,' he said, and took a pencil from his pocket. 'We'll make the rent three hundred and fifty and I'll take the bar receipts. That'll cover me in case of loss.'

'The bar receipts?' exclaimed Charles, aghast. 'But I need those to fall back on, in case – I mean, it's an expensive production to mount, and –' Endeavouring to return the paper to Brewster, he was prevented by Willie.

'Charles,' said Willie, 'you don't need the bar receipts. You'll get your money back from the box office.'

'Yes,' Charles said, 'but –'

'The audience won't be coming to the theatre to drink in the bar,' said Willie, firmly. 'They'll be coming to see you. They'll be coming to see you – and my play.'

He beamed, happy and confident.

'That's a deal, then,' said Brewster.

And, somehow, before Charles knew quite what was happening, it was.

Thomas, up in the nursery at Nightingale Grove, lived and ate and wrote and slept the play. It had taken over his whole life. He was simply an amanuensis, proud but dazed to be chosen to write the words and feelings that flowed so inevitably from his pen on to the paper. It was a shock when the door was banged open, and Martha barged in, followed by Edwin.

'Clear your junk off the table, Tom,' said Martha. 'Sutton's bringing tea up here. The garden room's like a morgue.'

Edwin languidly crossed the room and sat on the windowsill.

'How did it go at Richmond?' asked Thomas, and, with a belated access of guilt, 'Sorry I didn't get to see it.'

'All right,' Edwin replied. 'Mother came, and so did Father, though not at the same time.'

'Oh.'

'By the way,' Edwin added, 'I dropped in on Father's rehearsals at the Princess Theatre this morning.'

'Bad?' inquired Martha.

Edwin shrugged.

'I made the mistake of trying to tell him what he was doing wrong.'

Thomas and Martha both laughed at that.

'Ma's the only one who can do that,' said Thomas, 'and he doesn't always listen to *her*.'

Sutton came in with the big wooden tray of nursery tea, and Martha threw the darned white linen cloth over the wooden table.

'Martha,' Edwin asked, 'have you seen Mother?'

'No. She's gone down to the country with Auntie Elsie "to work on her songs". If you ask me, she's avoiding us.'

'We've got to do something,' said Edwin. 'It's all very well Tom saying, "She'll be back, she'll be back!"'

'Of course she will,' Thomas said. 'She's just flounced out in a temper, and when she's got over it, she'll be back.'

Sutton had put tea, bread and butter and a fruit cake on the table, and they all came to sit down.

'What do you say, Alfred?' asked Martha.

'I'd say,' replied Sutton, 'that it has gone too far. You know what they are – he'd rather die than admit he's wrong, and she'd rather die than spoil a good exit.'

He went out and closed the door neatly behind him. Martha, Thomas and Edwin glanced at each other, and then towards the door.

'So would Sutton,' Edwin remarked.

Charles was sitting in his study, gazing at a lot of official-looking documents, of which he could understand only one paragraph in three, when he heard the door open behind him, and, looking round, saw Martha.

'I'm off, Pa,' she said. 'Eddie and Thomas and I have just had tea up in the nursery. We should have asked you to join us. Do you remember what fun we had in the old days, when it was Flora's day out, and you and Ma used to come up and play pirates with us?'

'Yes,' said Charles. 'I remember.'

Martha, about to withdraw, saw him sitting motionless at his desk, and paused.

'Dada,' she said, using the old familiar Irish term, 'are you all right?'

He didn't answer at once, and she came back into the room.

'Dammit, Mart,' he said, 'I never realized that going into management would mean dealing with all this stuff. I always had the sense to keep out of it before – take my salary and run.'

Martha frowned. She didn't want her father to be worried and weak. She wanted him to be strong and powerful.

'I don't know why you took it on,' she said, with a note of irritation.

'Didn't have much choice,' Charles replied. 'Must do something – and no one sends me any plays these days. I suppose they think I'm too old.'

'Oh, Pa, of course they don't!' cried Martha.

She meant, I don't want you to be old, or even thought of as old. I want you to be strong and powerful and wonderfully talented. I want you to be my father.

'It's just that there's been nothing suitable,' she said.

'Nobody writes anything suitable for me now,' replied Charles, gloomily. 'That's the trouble. So I fetch up with a play of Willie Sutherland's that no one wants to put on, and all this rubbish to deal with.'

He poked distastefully at all the papers with his forefinger, thus succeeding in making the muddle even worse.

'Where's Lady Agatha?' inquired Martha, zooming in on the relevant immediate problem.

'Oh,' replied Charles, uneasily, 'she – she's spending a week at Chatsworth. She said she needed a holiday. She's a charming girl. Just not used to working regular hours.'

'At least,' said Martha, 'if you got rid of *her*, Ma might come back.'

Charles rallied in an instant.

'Certainly not,' he replied. 'If I gave in on this, your mother would have me on toast for the rest of our lives.'

'Pa,' said Martha, 'marriage is supposed to be a partnership, not a battle to the death!'

'That's what you think!' responded Charles.

The same thought came to them both in the same instant, the same unseen but always vividly imagined vision of Martha's husband, Basil, blown to pieces as he stood beside Edwin, nothing left of him but his boots. That was what Martha's marriage had been – a brief, shattering marriage to the death. Martha turned towards the door.

'Martha,' said Charles.

She paused, and turned back.

'You and I,' said Charles, 'never talk seriously about things.'

'What sort of things?'

There was a long silence.

'Well –' said Charles at last, 'Basil?'

'I can't talk about Basil,' said Martha.

'Right,' said Charles.

It almost was the end of it, but Martha, lingering in the doorway, said. 'I did love him.'

'Yes,' said Charles. 'I know.'

'So I married him,' said Martha, 'and then he was killed.'

Charles was almost afraid to speak, but at last he said, 'And he was a hard act for anyone else to follow.'

There was a long silence, and then he looked up at her, and saw her smiling at him, fondly and gratefully. Thank God, he had got it right!

'Yes,' she said. 'He was a hard act to follow.'

She turned towards the door again.

'I must go,' she said, 'or I'll be late.'

She was appearing in a revue at the Fortune Theatre called *Hey-Ho!*

'It can't take you long,' said Charles, 'to get into that Venus costume of yours. I can't think how you get away with it.'

'Considering the fact that Venus came out of the sea naked –'

'I dare say, but the Lord Chamberlain wasn't there to see her. You'll be arrested one of these days.'

'If I am, Dada,' said Martha, 'I'm sure you'll come and bail me out.'

She was about to go out, but, looking back, saw him sitting quite motionless, staring at the script of *The King Shall Not Die*. She returned, and put her arms round his neck.

'You're not really worried, are you?' she inquired. 'I mean, about the play?'

Charles responded with the instinctive swiftness of a boxer countering a right hook.

'Good heavens, no!' he responded. 'I haven't been in the business all these years without knowing a good thing when I see it!'

Martha smiled, her cheek against the top of his head. That was something else they had in common. Neither of them was good at talking about their own private emotions, and they were both incapable of admitting that they had made a mistake.

'Darling Pa!' she said, and kissed him.

The production of *The King Shall Not Die* ground inexorably ahead. Charles never had any trouble casting. He was known for splendid first-night parties, and, if it was a good run, for highly enjoyable summer outings to Maidenhead or Box Hill. In the other principal leading role, that of the villain, Sir Hugo, he cast Vincent Kendall, whom he had known for years. They had shared digs together first in Bolton about thirty-five years earlier, and, although Vincent had never risen above 'supporting cast' status, he was what is known as 'reliable'. He was, in fact, a few years younger than Charles but, fortunately, with make-up, he could look rather older – which was just as well, since he was supposed to be the father of the girl with whom Charles fell in love. The part of Celestine was more tricky. One didn't want to look as though one was cradle-snatching. On the other hand, Charles knew that his faithful following, gazing at his famous profile, still thought of him as thirty years old – thirty-five at most. In the end, he auditioned the part, and chose a twenty-eight-year-old actress who could look twenty. For the part of Maria, he decided to play safe and engage Anne Vere. She was a charming actress, who had been a friend of his and Lydia's for years. Never quite possessing Lydia's star quality, she had usually played second female lead, but now and then, if Lydia had a better offer, Anne had gone with Charles to take productions on tour, playing Lydia's role with grace and charm, even if without that indefinable sparkle and brilliance which made all Lydia's performances so memorable.

'Anne Vere, as Maria?' Edwin had remarked. 'She's a bit old, isn't she?'

'Not at all,' replied Charles. 'She's the same age as your mother – and *she* would have been playing the part if she hadn't got involved in this *Twinkle-Toes* rubbish.'

'Mother gets away with it better,' said Edwin. 'I suppose you'll have to have Guy Vere, too?'

'I've offered him two parts,' said Charles, gloomily. 'He can take his pick.'

'That means neither of them is very good,' observed Edwin.'But then Guy isn't very good, either.'

'If you can't say something constructive,' exclaimed Charles, irritated, 'you'd be better saying nothing!'

Of course, Edwin was right. Anne's husband had the kind of wooden good looks that carry a young man into the theatre and then leave him stranded, too old now to play those undemanding juvenile roles which at first came to him so easily, but incapable of acting himself into anything better. Unable to recognize his own shortcomings, he carried about with him a sense of injustice and ill-usage which hampered him still further from advancement, since he was not particularly pleasant to work with. He also carried about with him a hip flask of whisky from which he would frequently take a nip in the wings before going on. This did nothing to improve the quality of his acting, and it didn't improve his temper, either.

'Damn Guy!' thought Charles. 'Damn him for a rotten actor, and a rotten husband, too!'

But the truth was that it was worth putting up with Guy for the sake of Anne. He felt safe with Anne. No tricks and no temperament, and if he forgot his lines or got in a muddle with a bit of business, she'd always be ready to help him out. If he couldn't work with Lydia,

Anne was the next best thing – and, what's more, she wouldn't upstage him, either.

Sitting in the stalls on the morning of the dress rehearsal, Charles realized that he was falling into the habit of most older actors – and especially actor-managers – in surrounding himself with old friends, or at least with familiar fellow players. He'd even got old Sophie Parker playing the Grand Duchess. She never knew her words, rarely remembered her moves, and half the time forgot what play she was in, but whenever he and Lydia had a part for a fierce old dowager or wise old grandmother or dotty old lady in one of their productions, they had always offered it to Sophie. She might drive him mad, thought Charles, but at least he knew her little ways and could watch out for them. All old actresses had their little ways, and he didn't in the least want to break in a new one. Besides – Sophie needed the work. She had once been a famous beauty and still lived in the style of a West End actress, though parts were now few and far between. There were times, thought Charles, when Sophie had just a fleeting look of Lydia – Lydia as she would be in old age. Charles threw off the unwelcome thought, and sat up.

'Come on, everyone!' he roared. 'You're playing like a lot of sleepwalkers! This is the opening scene. I don't want to make my entrance and find that you've put the whole bloody audience to sleep!'

The actors on the stage gave an uneasy glance and giggle, then peered out at Charles and Willie Sutherland in the stalls.

'How would it be, Charles –' Willie began, with the author's usual desperate desire to help the floundering scene, 'if I rewrote –'

'No, thank you, Willie,' Charles replied, succinctly. 'If

the play isn't any good now, it never will be.' He raised his voice. 'Just a little more pace!' he called. 'More energy!'

He sank back in his seat. Gazing at the anxious little group on the stage, now acting their socks off, it occurred to him that there was not a single member of the cast except for himself who was worth a penny at the box office. Thanks to the ludicrous arrangement he had made with Brewster, he would have to play to at least 80 per cent just to break even, and the whole production depended on him. He felt the energy seeping out of him at the very thought.

'Splendid!' he called. 'Much better! Well done, every-one!'

Chapter Seven

Sutton always dressed for a first night as carefully as if he were going on stage himself. Like most theatricals, both onstage and backstage, he hated the dress rehearsal, that long-drawn-out struggle for perfection, with, all the time, the knowledge that if perfection was achieved, then it would not be there when it was needed, for the audience. The worst thing about a dress rehearsal was its unpredictability. The lighting went wrong, or the door stuck, or the actors had trouble with the props. The dress rehearsal was full of meaningless panic, with none of that unique and subtle excitement which said, 'Here are we, and there are the audience, and, like lovers, we will come together when the moment comes.'

Unless the dress rehearsal had been so disastrous that there was nothing for it but to struggle on, come what may, to get the damned thing right, the guv'nor always came home to Nightingale Grove before the performance. It was his way of saying to himself, 'I'm not just an actor. I have a wife and family who will never abandon

me, and if the audience don't love me, *they* always will.'
But this afternoon, thought Sutton, there would have
been no Miss Lydia there to say, 'Oh, nonsense, darling,
you know Vincent's always slow on his cues in rehearsal,'
or, 'Oh, darling, doors always stick at rehearsals; Bert
will have it right by tonight.' So Charles had said,
casually, 'Think I'll stroll round to *Il Piccolo*, Sutton,
and have a quiet bite,' and Sutton had replied, 'Very
good, sir, if you don't mind, I'll take a cab back to the
house; I seem to have left your silk handkerchief behind.'
He always took care to leave something behind, so that
he could be sure to get away and put his feet up before
the evening's exertions.

'Well, I'm off again,' he said to Flora, when he had had
his sandwich and cup of tea and changed into his best
black suit. 'With this play, it takes an hour to set up the
guv'nor's make-up, let alone anything else.'

'I wish *I* could see a play,' said Emily, returning from
upstairs with Thomas's luncheon tray. 'What's it like?'

'Why don't you go and find out?' answered Sutton.
'Go to the matinée on your next afternoon off. Only
costs sixpence in the gallery. I dare say the guv'nor would
give you a seat, if you asked him.'

'Ooh, I couldn't!' Emily exclaimed. 'But I might try
the gallery. I've been to the music-hall.'

'Same thing,' replied Sutton, cheerfully, 'only a bit
posher.'

'Now, Mr Sutton,' said Flora, reprovingly, 'don't
encourage the girl. The music-hall's not respectable.
Nor's the theatre, come to that. My father always used
to call it the Devil's playground.'

'Ooer!' said Emily. 'And the master works there.'

Flora realized that her Nonconformist zeal had rather carried her away.

'Well, he acts in a nice class of play,' she said, 'for the most part. But it's a pity he's not in the Moving Pictures instead. They're quite different. Really educational, they are. Really artistic.'

Sutton, combing his hair in front of the mirror in the dark corner by the back door, grinned to himself. Many years before, Flora, greatly daring, had gone with her friend, Mrs Jones, from the Welsh dairy round the corner, to one of the early Biograph shows. That one *was* educational, and, by good fortune, the next movie they saw was a highly devotional work called *From the Manger to the Cross*. Thus the Moving Pictures were established as both educational and religious, and Flora was free to enjoy them to her heart's delight – which is what they undoubtedly were. She had never had a lover, and probably, thought Sutton, never even held hands with a boy. She had left the Welsh valleys as a raw young girl, barely speaking English, and had become maid of all work to Charles and Lydia when they were first married and, as Charles cheerfully told her, 'hadn't two pennies to rub together'. When the children came along, Flora found herself acting as their nanny, and when they grew up and no longer needed a nanny, it happened that the cook had just left, so Flora did a bit of cooking, to oblige, and somehow stayed on.

It might have seemed a dull life – even a wasted life, giving all her devoted service to a family who, for all their affectionate ways, were so entirely self-engrossed – but Flora had her own entirely satisfying secret existence. That passion which had never found expression in human terms was directed in total innocence and sublime joy towards the lovers of the silver screen. She, who would have been utterly aghast if a man had even put his hand on her knee, sat glowing with excitement and ecstasy as Rudolph Valentino sent his burning glance of lust towards the shrinking heroine who, without her knowing it, was always Flora herself. She loved Rudolph Valentino dearly, and mourned his death, but fortunately she was fickle or, rather, promiscuous in her devotion. On Sundays, of course, she went to Chapel, but every Wednesday afternoon there was a different rapturous experience, a different lover. And all very artistic, very educational.

'Why don't the master go in for the movies, then?' inquired Emily, clattering the dishes in the sink.

'Because he's an actor,' Sutton replied, turning away from the mirror. 'And his father's an actor, and so's his mother. That's all he knows. You won't find *him* playing a part where he hasn't any lines.'

'There's some beautiful words in the movies,' said Flora.

A dreamy look came over her face. '"Beloved, do you think I could ever leave you?" "Forgive me. I am not worthy of you."'

'I dare say,' replied Sutton, briskly. 'Written on the screen, and him not there! That would never do for the guv'nor. He likes to hear the sound of his own voice. No, the theatre's where he belongs, and he knows it.'

He fetched his raincoat and his bowler hat from the pegs in the corner, and turned towards the door.

'Mr Sutton,' said Flora.

He paused.

'Will Miss Lydia be there tonight?'

'She'll be out front,' replied Sutton. 'They all will. But – it's not the same, is it?'

Outside the Princess Theatre, big, shiny, chauffeur-driven cars drew up outside, and, as though performing in a Hollywood film, ladies and gentlemen in full evening dress descended with practised grace, and, apparently quite unconscious of the gawping masses, moved with smiles and cries of 'Oh, too thrilling!' towards the foyer. The shabbily dressed crowds outside, mostly female, were eagerly gazing at each car, hoping to see their own heroes and heroines from the Society pages of the new popular press, some theatrical like Jack Buchanan and Jessie Matthews, and some combining that heady mixture of power and aristocracy, like Mr Winston Churchill and his wife.

Charles sat at his dressing table, finishing his make-up. He wore a rather becoming frilly shirt and dark trousers, with his slightly shabby but familiar dressing-gown over them. The dressing room had that hushed and sacred seclusion of a chapel, with the smell of dust and make-up instead of incense. Sutton, busying himself with the costumes on the rail at the back, was like a well-trained and silent verger.

'Fifteen minutes, please, Mr Brett,' shrilled the call boy. 'Fifteen minutes!'

'Thank you!' called Charles.

He eyed himself in the mirror with a certain satisfaction. In a highly becoming dark wig and judicious make-up, he was beginning to resemble the matinée idol his public so eagerly awaited. Behind him, Sutton was examining the rich-looking velvet frogged jacket in which Charles was to make his first appearance.

'I'll take this to the wardrobe, sir,' he said, 'and get a stitch put in it.'

'Right,' said Charles. He felt a sudden qualm. 'That

costume,' he said, 'it is all right, is it? I mean, Mrs Brett usually gives my things the once-over.'

'Quite all right, sir,' replied Sutton. 'Very becoming.'

Charles turned back to the mirror.

'Not – er – not too close-fitting, is it?' he inquired, casually. 'You said it needed a stitch.'

'Oh, nothing like that,' replied Sutton, hastily. 'It's just that Mr Kendall caught the pocket with his rapier at the dress rehearsal.'

'Ah,' said Charles. 'Hm. Damned awkward duel, that. Just hope we get it right tonight.'

'Don't worry, sir,' replied Sutton, cheerfully. 'You will.'

With a slight recurrence of satisfaction, Charles put an additional touch of shadow on his cleft chin, which, he knew, was always a source of pleasure to his female admirers. Leaning back again, his eye fell on the open script beside him. How did that line go? 'Nay, Sire, it is your duty to save me from myself.' No, that wasn't it. 'Nay, Sire it is my duty to save me –' Oh, blast! He put his glasses on the end of his nose and peered at the heavily underlined page. 'Sire, it is my duty to save you from yourself!' Stupid line, he never would get it right! In a fit of temper, he picked up a stick of make-up and scored it greasily across the page, and slammed the script shut. Got it. 'Sire, it's my job – your duty –' Damnation! He tried to open the script, which was now stuck together with the make-up.

'Blast!' he said, aloud.

He was suddenly flooded by despair. He took off his glasses and sat quite still. Supposing the play was as bad as he thought it was? Supposing he couldn't carry it? Supposing he was actually booed at the end? God! it was a long time since that had happened to him! People thought that you became more confident as you became more famous, but it wasn't so. Everyone expected so much more of you, and failure was no longer anonymous. Besides, you didn't have the resilience of a twenty-year-old. A failure at twenty could mean that you hadn't yet succeeded. A failure at fifty could mean that you were finished.

'I know what I need!' thought Charles.

He reached down into the Gladstone bag beneath the dressing table. He remembered his father saying, 'Never take a nip before going on, Charlie. One nip leads to another, and before you know where you are, it's the whole bloody bottle! But it's that first nip that leads to the downward path.'

'That's right, George,' his mother had agreed in her soft Irish voice. 'It's the downward path. Mind, there's no harm in half a glass of Guinness at the end of the second act, just to give you strength.'

'Yes, yes, Maeve!' George had said, irritably. 'But I'm not talking about that. It's the little nip that's the downward path.'

'Damn the downward path!' thought Charles, as his fingers closed round the flask at the bottom of the Gladstone bag.

He was just about to unscrew the top when he heard a tap at the door, and, looking round, saw Lydia. She was stunningly dressed, in all her customary first-night finery. Charles had seen her reclining in bed in a satin nightdress and her most seductive attitude. He had seen her looking as though she had been scalped, with her hair scragged back ready for the wig, and no make-up. He had even seen her after the twins were born and she had very nearly died, lying there drained of blood, lifeless except

for a tiny glint of love and courage in her blue eyes. He
had always thought she was the most beautiful woman
in the world, but he wasn't thinking about that now. He
just knew that he had never been so glad to see anyone in
his life. He hastily shoved the flask under the script and
rose and turned.

'May we come in?' asked Lydia.

Those were the words which made Charles remember
that things were not what they used to be.

'Yes,' he said, awkwardly. 'Of course.'

He saw Edwin behind Lydia.

'Hullo, Father.'

'Edwin. Glad to see you.'

'Well, we thought we'd – just come and – and –' said
Lydia. Then, 'How's it going?'

'Fine!' replied Charles, much too heartily. 'Fine!'

'Good,' said Lydia.

It was dismaying to find themselves talking like
strangers. Charles saw Lydia forcing another smile to
her face.

'Elsie and Harry are in front,' she said, 'and Martha
sends her love, and says she'll be round as soon as her
curtain comes down.'

'I hope she remembers to change,' remarked Charles.
'If she goes out in the street in that last costume, she'll be
arrested.'

They both smiled, but Charles was aware that Lydia
was watching him attentively.

'Is – Thomas here?' he inquired.

'He stopped to have a word with Willie,' Edwin
answered. '*He* seems happy.'

'I dare say he is,' said Charles, bitterly, eyeing the
script. 'He doesn't have to say this rubbish! Bloody
authors!'

He saw Edwin and Lydia exchange a swift glance.

'I'll just slip along and have a word with Sophie,' said Edwin.

'Ask her to remember to enter upstage in the first scene,' Charles begged him, and was rewarded by an encouraging and sympathetic smile.

'What does she usually do?' asked Edwin.

'Tries to get through the fireplace,' responded Charles.

Edwin grinned at him, and then glanced at Lydia.

'Be back in a minute,' he said.

Lydia sat down in the chintz-covered armchair, and Charles sat down again at the dressing table. His eyes met hers in the mirror.

'Liddy,' he said, 'I've got a nasty feeling that this is a bloody awful play.'

'Oh, Charlie,' said Lydia, 'of course it isn't! Willie's plays are always effective.' She paused. 'Showy,' she said, 'but –'

'Stagey,' said Charles.

'Stagey,' Lydia agreed, 'but effective.'

'Yes,' said Charles.

Suddenly he could tell the truth to the only person in the whole world to whom he could tell the truth.

'I just hope I can remember the thing!' he said. 'What with Willie popping up and down all through rehearsals like a jack-in-the-box, changing the lines and then changing them back again – and old Sophie's worse than I am. She keeps throwing me the wrong cue, and then just stands there with her mouth open while I wonder what the devil I should say next – and with all that tricky business in the first scene – and you know how hopeless I am with business, especially if I'm not too sure of my words –!'

'I know, darling,' said Lydia.

She did know. That was the point. No one else knew his weaknesses, but she did, every one of them.

'I suppose,' said Charles, bitterly, 'that if I were Gerald du Maurier, I would just stand there and light a cigarette!'

Lydia stood up.

'Would you like me', she said, gently, 'just to go very quietly through the first scene with you?'

'Oh, *would* you?' cried Charles.

Lydia took her lorgnettes out of her silver evening bag and came and picked up the script, thus revealing the flask. A lesser woman would have put the flask back in the Gladstone bag, but Lydia merely pretended not to have seen it at all. She picked up the script, and flicked it open, unsticking the stuck-up pages, and turning back to Charles's first scene. Charles drew a deep breath of relief. He'd be all right now.

It was at that precise moment that the door opened, and a high-pitched voice, surrounded by other high-pitched voices yelped, 'May we come in?' It was Lady Agatha.

With a sickening lurch of the heart, Charles remembered that moment when Lady Agatha, having told him all about her week at Chatsworth and scrawled one quite unsuitable letter to a Shakespeare scholar seeking information on his views about the character of Macbeth (name of ill omen!) had said, 'May I come and see you on the first night and wish you luck?'

'Of *course*!' Charles had cried, and, O God! there she was, with a set of what Charles supposed would be described as 'Bright Young Things'.

'Eeow, my dear!' he heard. 'Is this really "Backstage"? It's more like a public lavatory. Not that one has ever actually been in a public lavatory!'

Suddenly they were all in the dressing room, whooping and giggling.

'Oh, Mrs Brett!' cried Agatha. 'Isn't it all too thrilling?'

Lydia closed her lorgnettes with a snap, closed the script and put it down, and turned.

'Too, too thrilling for words,' she said. Her eyes met Charles's for a second, before she turned towards the door.

'Ah, there's Thomas,' she said.

She was overacting slightly, and Charles saw that Thomas had taken in the whole situation as Lydia swept towards him and turned, with a lavish gesture, towards Charles.

'Good luck, Charles, darling,' she said.

'Good luck, Pa,' said Thomas.

'Yes,' said Charles. 'Thank you.'

And then they were gone.

The small room was full of Lady Agatha and her entourage of fellow aristocrats.

'My *dear*, did you see Bootsie Prendergast arriving in that dreadfully vulgar Daimler of his?'

'Yes, with darling Felicity. It's the first time they've been out together in public since the divorce fell through.'

'She kept trying to vamp the judge.'

'That was a waste of time.'

'If you knew the judge as I do, it certainly was!'

There were whoops of laughter, in the midst of which Sutton entered, astonished. His eyes met Charles's.

'Sutton –?' said Charles, desperately.

'Yes, sir,' replied Sutton. 'My lady? Sir? Mr Brett allows nobody in his dressing room immediately before the performance.'

'Of course!' cried Agatha. 'My dears, didn't I tell you? We can only stay for a teeny moment!'

The teeny moment, however, turned into several minutes before, with the others finally jostling out into the passage, Agatha turned in the doorway to cry, 'Oh, I just know it's going to be the most tremendous success!' And, as Charles was managing a heroic smile in reply, Agatha's friend Selena suddenly reappeared beside her.

'And, just think, Atha, darling,' she trilled, 'you typed *the whole play* on my typewriter! Simply spiffing! Honestly, Mr Brett, I can't think how you manage to remember all those words!'

After all that, it was, perhaps, not entirely surprising that Charles's performance lacked some degree of finely honed perfection, or that, as he ran up the stairs at the end of the second act and paused to deliver his exit line, the words which sprang to his mind were not, 'Sire, it is my duty to save you from yourself!' but, 'Sire, if I don't save you from yourself, what will you do?' The unfortunate actor who was playing the King opened and shut his mouth, a look of horror on his face. He had not expected to be called upon to speak again in that scene, and had no idea what to say. Charles smiled and raised his hand in a noble gesture.

'Don't answer, sir,' he declaimed. 'All I ask is that you should trust my loyalty!'

As he raced, rather breathlessly, up the staircase and off, to the swish of the curtain and a gratifying round of applause, he was aware of a parting glance of justifiable exasperation on the face of his fellow player, but he couldn't help that. In such situations, it was every actor for himself!

Charles could afterwards remember very little of the first-night party, which took place, as usual, on the stage, with a buffet and champagne. It was not that he was drunk, but that, even at the time, he had endeavoured to detach his mind from the whole ghastly event. Edwin, Martha and Thomas came, looking solemn, and Edwin brought a message from Lydia saying that she was terribly sorry but she had suddenly developed the most awful headache, and so had gone home with Elsie and Harry. So the Carstairs were also absent, although Lady Agatha and her entourage were there in full force, saying that it was too thrilling actually to be on the stage. The only really happy man was Willie Sutherland, as he 'istened to his friends telling him that he had written a simply marvellous play which would run for ever.

Charles escaped as soon as he could, and drove back to Nightingale Grove in the hired car, with Thomas totally silent beside him, and Sutton in the front seat, his rigid head beneath its bowler hat registering strong disapproval. As Charles climbed into bed, he thought that he had never been so tired in his life – and he didn't need the next morning's papers to tell him what the critics would think of the play. He could just imagine Sutton carefully scanning them in the kitchen before bringing them upstairs, and remarking to Flora, 'I think we've laid an egg this time.'

But next day, it was not just the morning papers that Sutton laid before Charles. There was also a letter in Lydia's handwriting, delivered by hand from the Carstairs' house in Regent's Park.

'Dear Charles,' it read, 'I really think it is time to call it a day, don't you? I would like a divorce as soon as it can be arranged. Lydia.'

Chapter Eight

Charles glared indignantly at Edwin across the small table in the Ivy.

'We have the advance bookings,' he said, 'and that's about all.'

'What are you playing to?'

'Fifty per cent,' Charles replied, 'and that's just about enough to pay the rent and the actors' salaries. As for running costs – the next thing we know, we'll be playing in the dark!'

'The weather's been against you,' said Edwin.

This was a safe remark. Weather is always against the theatre. Either it's too foggy, or raining, or snowing, or too hot.

'I might just have got by with the bar receipts,' said Charles, gloomily, 'but that crook Brewster insisted on having them. I'll tell you something, Eddie, this blasted play is going to bankrupt me. And it's all your mother's fault!'

The waiter brought their onion soup and endeavoured to offer cheese.

'No, no!' said Charles, irritably. 'Never mind any of that!'

'Er – I'll have some,' said Edwin, asserting himself.

Charles glared at him impatiently, and, the moment the waiter had departed, he added, 'And now there's all this rubbish about a divorce! I mean – why *now*, after thirty-one years?'

Edwin eyed him thoughtfully. How could he possibly explain what his mother had said to him at their last meeting? How could it be that a man of fifty-five, a distinguished actor and apparently a man of the world, could be so innocent? Even his lifelong philandering had something innocent about it. One could not call it womanizing, because it was not essentially sexual. The sex, where it existed, was incidental. What Charles needed, above all, was to know that he was still desirable, still attractive, still loved. Edwin's own exploits in that field had been of a very different nature. From the bored older actress who had first initiated him into the practice of sex, just to keep her hand in (if that was the right expression!) to the cheerful little barmaid cum tart whom he had taken back to his chambers the night before, his relationship with them had always derived from a need to prove himself sexually. He needed to prove that his slightly baby-faced good looks were not effeminate, and that those tentative approaches which had been made to him by various young actors and older touring managers had been purely experimental, and not provoked by any unconscious signal from himself. Thinking of his relationship with women, in bed and out, Edwin found himself remembering his friendship with Basil, who later had married his twin (was that significant?). He and Basil had never had anything resembling a homosexual relationship, and yet he had never enjoyed such a close and satisfying friendship with any woman. Perhaps, he thought, he never would.

'You don't think your mother really wants a divorce, do you?' Charles demanded.

'I'm not sure,' Edwin replied. 'I think perhaps she does.'

He had invited his mother to tea at his chambers, dashing out to Fortnum and Mason's to buy some cream cakes. Lydia gazed at them, smiling.

'Darling Eddie,' she said, 'they look delicious, but you do remember that I'm rehearsing for a show called *Twinkle-Toes*, and that it opens next week? If I'm going to dance as well as sing, I can't afford even an extra ounce.' She raised her eyes to his. 'And, actually, Eddie darling,' she added, 'I don't really think you invited me here to eat cream cakes.'

Edwin put the plate down, and laughed.

'No, I didn't,' he agreed. 'Mother, dear, you don't really want to divorce Father, do you?'

Lydia sipped her tea and didn't answer.

'I know you said you did,' said Edwin, 'but it was only because you were in a temper.'

'Was it?' replied Lydia. 'I'm not sure. Sometimes in a temper, you say things you really mean.'

'Oh, come on, darling!' Edwin exclaimed. 'You know we all need you, and so does Father. That's why he always comes back to you.'

'He always comes back to me,' replied Lydia, her voice sharpening, 'because I give him hell until he does!'

'Of course you do,' said Edwin, with a sense of relief, 'because you love him, and you know he loves you.'

Lydia put her cup down and looked at him.

'That's just the trouble, Eddie,' she said. 'I'm not sure any more.'

'Not sure that Father loves you?' demanded Edwin, astonished.

'Oh, no,' Lydia replied, calmly. 'I'm sure he does, in his own infuriating way. But *I* –'

'You –?'

Lydia stood up and walked to the window, and stood looking down into the street.

'You have to love someone an awful lot,' she said, 'to go on fighting for them, and the truth is that I really don't think I love him enough any more.'

Edwin felt a sudden chill. They were all accustomed to the rows and squabbles, the neat exchange of insults and the precarious reconciliations that had made up the fabric of their parents' marriage. But somehow there had always been something a little theatrical about it, a sense that when the curtain fell, they would be standing there hand in hand to take their bow together. Now, suddenly, Lydia wasn't acting, and it alarmed him.

'I always thought you were made for each other,' he said.

'Oh, nonsense!' cried Lydia, with that down-to-earth common sense which had always been such an invaluable counterbalance to Charles's romantic self-deceptions. 'It happened the way most marriages happen – by chance.'

She returned to sit down.

'There we both were,' she said, 'hacking round the provinces with a series of tatty touring companies. And he was rather good-looking, and I was pretty. And one day we met on the platform at Crewe, travelling in completely different directions. I had an hour to wait for my train, and he had two hours for his. We could only afford a cup of tea each at the station buffet, and a Bath bun between us, and we sat and talked, and looked into each other's eyes, and then my train came in, and he carried my case and saw me into the carriage, and as the whistle blew and the train began to move, he ran alongside, and I hung out of the window, and he ran faster, and he said, "Liddy! please marry me! Liddy, I can't live without you!"'

She glanced up and saw Edwin's expression, and smiled bitterly.

'Oh, yes,' she said, 'very romantic! But of course it wasn't true. As a matter of fact, that was the first of his lies and, as far as I'm concerned, the war widow was his last.'

'She can't get a divorce, anyway,' said Charles, peevishly, 'because I haven't done anything, not with Lady Agatha. Does she expect me to go off to Brighton with some damned professional co-respondent?'

'She might think,' Edwin replied, 'that after all your past peccadilloes, you owe her that, at least.'

'Dammit, whose side are you on?' Charles demanded, indignantly.

Edwin knew better than to answer that. He decided to change the subject.

'Hullo, there's Willie,' he said. 'He seems to be looking for someone. He's not joining us, is he?'

'I hope not,' replied Charles. 'If he does, he can damn well pay for the lunch. *He's* all right! Even if the play comes off, *he* won't be bankrupted. God, how I hate authors! They never have to go on stage. Just sit back and take their royalties!'

Scowling, he began to dissect his Dover sole, as Willie Sutherland came beaming up to them.

'Charles!' he cried. 'I've been looking for you everywhere!'

He waited for a chair to be brought, sat down and waved the menu away.

'No, no, I lunched at the Garrick, and I had the most extraordinary conversation with Bernard Whitgift.'

'Who?'

'One of the King's private secretaries. We were at school together. He said he knew I was a friend of yours, and he wanted to know how approachable you were.'

'If he wants to lend me some money,' Charles remarked, 'he'll find me extremely approachable.'

Willie did not recognize this as a joke. His simple-mindedness was the secret of his success, if not with the critics, with a large portion of his audience.

'No, no,' he said, earnestly. 'He said this inquiry came directly from the King.'

'The King?' Edwin repeated, startled.

'*He* won't lend us any money,' said Charles, carefully extracting a fish bone.

Willie leaned forward with a conspiratorial air.

'My dear Charles, he spoke of a particular honour that the King had in mind. That can only mean one thing.'

'Oh,' said Charles, 'and what's that?'

Willie leaned back in his chair.

'My dear Charles,' he repeated, 'it can only mean a knighthood!'

Charles swallowed, took a sip of wine, gazed at Willie Sutherland, and a smile slowly crept over his face. Show the world an actor who says he does not desire a knighthood, and the world will behold a liar.

'Oh,' he said. 'Ah.'

Edwin spoke quietly.

'Not if you're divorced, it won't,' he said.

It was hard to say who actually organized the council of war. Perhaps it was Flora, who said, 'Why not have a nice tea party, talk the whole thing over?' Or perhaps it was Sutton who said, 'Miss Lydia's coming in on Wednesday to pick up some things; that's the guv'nor's matinée.' Or perhaps it was Nell, oldest and, after all, toughest of them all, who said, 'Let's just tell Mother we are all involved, and we want to meet and talk about it.' In any event, there they all were in the garden room, drinking tea.

'Mother,' said Nell, 'you must know by now that Father doesn't give a damn for the war widow.'

'Anyway,' added Thomas, 'you must be used to Father's little bits of fluff by now.'

Trust Thomas to say the wrong thing!

'I may be used to them,' responded Lydia, tartly, 'but that doesn't mean I like them!'

'Still,' Nell pursued, 'after all this time, suddenly to –'

'There's nothing sudden about it,' said Lydia. 'I told your father long ago that I would leave as soon as Thomas was old enough to – to fend for himself.'

'Why Thomas?' asked Edwin, and then found Martha and Nell and Lydia looking at him, and concluded, 'Oh. Yes.'

Thomas looked round at them all, and back at Edwin, and inquired, 'What do you mean – "Why Thomas – oh yes"?'

Martha languidly interposed.

'Presumably, Thomas, dear, because you were then the youngest.'

'Oh, yes, of course,' said Thomas.

There was a quick exchange of glances between Nell, Edwin and Martha which Thomas didn't see.

'Then,' Lydia continued, 'Perdita arrived – rather unexpectedly – but she will be leaving school soon, and, anyway, she can live with me.'

'What about the rest of us?' inquired Edwin. 'Don't you think we care if you and Father are together?'

'You have your chambers,' said Lydia, 'and Martha has her flat, and you can still come home whenever you like. Your father will still keep the house on, presumably.'

'If he can afford to,' said Edwin.

'Supposing he doesn't,' said Thomas, with the sublime self-engrossment of the young. 'What about me?'

'You will just have to get a job and find some lodgings,' replied Lydia, with a sharpness she tended to display to Thomas more than to any of her other children. 'That won't hurt you.'

'Thanks, Ma,' said Thomas.

'And don't call me "Ma"!' said Lydia.

Nell came to put an affectionate arm round Lydia's shoulders.

'Mother, dear,' she said, very reasonably, 'have you thought about the scandal? Apart from anything else, it would be dreadfully bad for John's reputation –'

Edwin's eyes met Martha's in a moment of instinctive communication. Wrong again!

'My dear Nell,' said Lydia, 'if you think I am prepared to arrange my private life for the benefit of John's stockbroking firm –'

Nell straightened up sharply.

'You never liked him,' she said. 'You none of you liked him.'

Martha and Edwin exchanged another cautious glance. Nell, apparently so calm and placid, was extremely touchy about John. The slightest hint that he might be dull or boring, and that hidden temper of hers would flare up with all its old, childhood fierceness and unexpectedness. Edwin put his hand to his forehead, where a very small scar derived not from any war wound but from the Hornby train engine Nell had flung at him in the nursery during some small squabble, and Martha grinned. Lydia, however, remained undisturbed, possibly because she really did like John Caldwell, and had always got on very well with him, so she didn't feel the pang of guilt which always assailed the others.

'Nonsense, Nell,' she said, 'I like John very much. He's not one of us, but he happened to suit you, and he knew quite well what sort of family he was marrying into.'

'He didn't know he was marrying into a divorce!' said Nell, very sharply for her.

'That's his bad luck,' replied Lydia.

She looked round for her gloves and handbag, preparing to make a move.

'Come on, Mother,' said Martha, 'you don't really want to do Father out of his knighthood, do you?'

'I most certainly do!' responded Lydia.

They all gasped, and their mouths came open. She looked calmly round at them.

'He's quite sufficiently pleased with himself as it is,' she added. 'As Sir Charles Brett, he'd be insufferable.'

'Ma's quite right, of course,' remarked Thomas, with his usual infuriating air of detachment. 'He would.'

'Oh, you're a great help!' said Edwin, exasperated.

He and Martha and Nell looked at each other in despair, and at that moment, as though on cue, which it certainly was, Sutton made his entrance. Sutton listened at doors in the same spirit in which he waited in the wings, to keep abreast of the plot and put a hand where necessary.

'Excuse me, madam,' he said, addressing Lydia with great formality, every inch the butler, as he always was on these occasions, 'but will you be staying for dinner?'

'No, thank you, Sutton,' replied Lydia, with equal stateliness. 'I only called in to pick up some things.'

She knew that he had been listening at the door, and he knew that she knew. With silent dignity, he began to clear the tea things.

'How is Lady Carstairs, madam?' he inquired.

Was there just a tiny emphasis on the title 'Lady'?

'Very well, thank you,' answered Lydia, surprised.

'Her ladyship is looking forward to Ascot, I dare say,' Sutton remarked, casually.

'We're all looking forward to Ascot,' answered Lydia.

'Yes, but it's not up to much, madam, is it, unless you're in the Royal Enclosure?'

'Well, of course we shall be in the Royal –!' Lydia stopped short.

'Not if you're divorced, you won't,' said Martha.

Lydia took an angry breath, but Sutton was too quick for her, stooping down to put some plates on the bottom tray of the trolley.

'By the way, madam,' he slid in, neatly, 'Flora was asking, when Miss Perdita comes home from school, will she be going to stay with her ladyship?'

'Well, either with me, if I have got my own flat by then, or with – with me at Lady Carstairs' house.'

She began to put her gloves on, as a sign that she really was going. Sutton, totally expressionless, continued to fetch teacups with a priest-like calm, casually remarking, 'I suppose Miss Perdita will be coming out next year?'

Thomas laughed.

'"Coming out"?' he repeated. 'I can't quite see Perdita as a débutante!'

'Why not?' Lydia demanded, a note of defiance in her voice which indicated that she knew quite well why not.

Martha, Edwin and Nell glared at Thomas, but Sutton was equal to the occasion, delicately interposing before the argument could get under way.

'Still, madam,' he continued, as though there had been no interruption, 'if you do decide to have Miss Perdita presented at Court, *her ladyship* can do it.'

This time, there was no doubt where the emphasis lay, and Lydia reacted to it. Much as she loved her sister, and happy as she had been when Elsie married her dim if amiable baronet, she had always found it extremely irritating that, at social functions, the famous actress Lydia Wheatley (Mrs Charles Brett) had been forced to yield precedence to Lady Carstairs, especially since Elsie, well versed in stagecraft, had never failed to take full advantage of the opportunity.

'If I *do* decide to have Perdita presented at Court, I'll do it myself,' she said, 'thank you very much! And, before you think of something clever to say, it is perfectly possible for me to arrange to be presented first.'

'Not if you're divorced,' said Edwin. 'Or even separated.'

Lydia finally lost her temper.

'Shut up, all of you!' she yelled. 'Alfred, get out!'

'Certainly, madam,' replied Sutton, and he picked up the tea tray and retired in the silent and stately manner of a priest removing the Host.

After he had gone, there was a brief silence, which Martha cautiously broke.

'Mother,' she said, 'you know Sutton's right, as usual. It's always annoyed you that Auntie Elsie has a title and you haven't.'

'Huh!' said Lydia. 'Well, I certainly wouldn't have married Harry Carstairs to get one.'

'Now you don't have to,' remarked Edwin, very softly.

There was a much longer silence. Lydia looked at her watch and finished putting her gloves on. Charles's matinée would just be drawing to a close, and fortunately Elsie's car and chauffeur had brought her to Nightingale Grove and were awaiting her pleasure. If she was really going to be Lady Brett, thought Lydia, she would make damned sure that she had a car and chauffeur of her own. She rose and walked to the door and paused, and turned, surveying each of her offspring in turn. They all looked guilty, and even Thomas knew better than to say anything.

Emerging into the hall, she shouted in her most raucous tones, 'Sutton!'

Sutton emerged from the door which led to the kitchen. He didn't exactly recoil when he saw her expression, but he did suddenly go very still.

'I am leaving,' said Lydia. 'I may be back, or I may not.'

'Yes, madam,' said Sutton, and sedately crossed to open the front door for her.

'One day, Alfred,' said Lydia, 'you will go too far.'

It was supposed to be her exit line, but Sutton topped it.

'So will you,' he said, 'if you're not careful.'

Lydia had time to think while she was being driven to

the Princess Theatre, and she also instructed the chauffeur to drive her twice round the Park. Bonesy, the stage-door keeper, was delighted to see her. They all respected 'the guv'nor' but Lydia, since the age of four, had learned to use her feminine charms to earn a quite different, and slightly subversive loyalty.

'Lovely to see you, Miss Wheatley!' cried old Bonesy, stubbing out his cigarette. 'We've missed you.'

'Is Mr Brett here?'

'Just arrived, Miss Wheatley.'

As Lydia had hoped, Charles, having left his meeting, had come early to the theatre to have a little nap before the evening performance, and when she tapped on the door of his dressing room and entered, he was taken entirely by surprise.

'Charles,' she said, immediately, 'I am prepared to delay the divorce until you have your knighthood, but on certain conditions.'

'I'm far from sure I want a knighthood!' said Charles.

As a master duellist herself, Lydia appreciated the speed of his reaction, but the words that followed this instinctive parry sent a glow to her – perhaps 'heart' would not be quite the right word – to her confidence in her own expertise.

'What conditions?' inquired Charles. He saw her look of triumph, and, metaphorically, took a step backwards. 'I agree with my father. Actors are travelling players, and they should all be equal.'

'Quite,' said Lydia, and waited.

'What conditions?' asked Charles.

This time, Lydia kept the triumph out of her face, but they both knew she had him on toast all the same. She walked across the room to sit down in the chintz-covered chair.

'First,' she said, 'the war widow goes, lock, stock and b – beastly little two-seater.'

She looked at Charles. He had his countenance under excellent control. It showed neither pleasure nor pain.

'Secondly,' Lydia continued, 'I'll come back to live at Nightingale Grove –'

'Good!' said Charles, heartily.

'But I'm not coming back into our bedroom,' said Lydia.

Charles looked outraged.

'If you feel like *that*,' he said, 'I'll sleep in the dressing room.'

'It wouldn't be the first time,' said Lydia, coldly, 'but, no thank you. With a communicating door? That really would put paid to the divorce. Besides, I know our family. If I move back into our bedroom, they'll say, "Ah, we knew she didn't mean it!" I shall camp out in Martha's room.'

'What about Martha?'

'She can either stay in her flat or use the little room.'

'She won't like that,' remarked Charles. 'All those hot-water pipes, and no room to swing a – a bottle of champagne.'

Lydia was supposed to smile at that, but she didn't.

'I can't help that,' she said. 'I want it clearly understood that I am not cancelling the divorce. I'm simply postponing it until you get your knighthood.'

'Lydia,' Charles exclaimed, 'this is ridiculous!'

'Not at all,' she said. 'I refuse to spend the rest of my life trying to look the other way, while you engage in a series of ridiculous flirtations, interspersed with passionate, if short-lived, love affairs.'

Charles saw a piece of safe ground and stepped firmly on it.

'My relationship with Lady Agatha,' he said, with dignity, 'has been perfectly innocent.'

'Just a bit of pat and purr,' said Lydia. 'I dare say. But she goes, just the same.'

She rose and went to the door.

'You'd better have a nap,' she said, 'before the evening performance. I'm sure you need it.'

Charles ignored this. He obviously had other things on his mind.

'But – Lady Agatha –' he said. 'What on earth am I to tell the poor girl?'

Lydia could hardly believe her good fortune. He really *must* be out of practice! She turned at the door.

'I'm sure you'll think of something,' she said. 'You always do.'

Charles had thought of an intimate little supper after the theatre at *Il Piccolo*, but he decided that he couldn't risk it. A nice luncheon at the Ivy, with all his friends there to attest to the total innocence of the occasion, that was the answer. Lady Agatha really was a lovely girl, and Charles was pleasantly aware of envious glances, and of the waiters being even more attentive than usual. He waited until they brought the coffee before he leaned forward.

'My dear girl,' he said, 'I had a very special reason for asking you to come and have luncheon with me today. I'm afraid we have to part.'

'Oh,' said Agatha, puzzled, and then her great big eyes opened wide. 'You don't mean – that I'm not to be your secretary any more?'

Charles took her hand.

'I'm going to miss you dreadfully,' he said. 'You're so young and beautiful. You've been like a beautiful shaft of sunlight in my tired old life.'

'You're not old!' cried Agatha.

What a natural performer she was! Charles smiled sadly.

'Perhaps not,' he said. 'But I'm too old for you. My dear – I dare say you didn't realize it, but I was beginning to fall in love with you, and that wouldn't be fair to you, or to my poor Lydia.'

Agatha's face showed that she was deeply moved.

'No,' she said. 'Of course not. But – Charles – May I call you Charles?'

He pressed her hand, smiling tenderly.

'Charles,' said Agatha, 'now that I know, I don't think I *can* leave.'

'Know?' Charles repeated. 'Know what?'

'How you feel,' said Agatha. 'You see – I feel the same.'

Alarmed, Charles realized that Agatha had seen even better dramatic possibilities than those he was offering her. Keeping the tender look on his face, he withdrew his hand, while doing a quick mental rewrite of the scene.

'Dearest Agatha,' he said, 'you shouldn't have told me. That wasn't fair.'

'No,' she said. 'I'm sorry. It's just that it's meant so much to me to help you with your work.'

With relief, Charles realized that all was once more set for the grand renunciation.

'I know,' he said. 'It's meant so much to me, too. I can't bear to think that it's all over. But what you've just said makes me all the more determined. I must be strong for both of us.'

This moving line was almost too much for Agatha. Overcome, she took a tiny, lace-edged handkerchief out and pressed it to her face.

'I suppose – I had better go,' she said.

Charles was on his feet in a moment.

'You are right,' he said. 'One should never prolong a parting. It hurts too much.' Putting her coat round her, he allowed himself a brief, delicate pressure on her shoulders. 'Goodbye, my dear, brave, loving girl,' he said.

The first night of *Twinkle-Toes* came and went, and still there had been no word from the Palace.

'I suppose Willie didn't imagine it,' said Lydia.

'Perhaps Father made it up,' said Martha, resentful at her banishment to the horrid little room with its thunderous hot-water pipes and hard little bed.

Meanwhile, except for the separate bedrooms, life at Nightingale Grove almost resumed its old course. Lydia's frivolous little musical comedy was extremely well received by the critics, and did excellent business, unlike *The King Shall Not Die*, which was staggering perilously along, just about kept above disaster line by Charles's admirers and those playgoers who cherished a fond regard for *The Prisoner of Zenda*, especially if they had seen the movie version with Ramon Novarro, and who hoped that *The King Shall Not Die* might resemble it – which, God knows, it did! But still that elusive collection of indispensable ignoramuses known as 'the fashionable' flocked in to *Twinkle-Toes* and stayed away from *The King Shall Not Die*.

'I'll have to close,' thought Charles, looking at the returns, sinking every week lower and lower. 'Oh, damn! I'll have to close!'

It was that very night when Charles and Lydia returned together to Nightingale Grove (playing in neighbouring theatres, it was absurd not to travel together) that Sutton presented Charles with a crested envelope marked 'Private and Confidential'. Sir Bernard Whitgift had something of a particularly private and confidential nature to discuss with Charles, and begged to propose himself for tea on a day convenient to Mr Brett and Miss Wheatley.

'I wonder if the King has ever knighted a bankrupt,' remarked Charles.

'Funny thing, though,' Sutton remarked to Flora. 'I always thought they wrote to people if they were going to give them a knighthood. I never knew they came and saw them.'

'It's a great honour, I'm sure,' Flora replied, nervously beating butter and sugar for a sponge cake.

'Mm,' said Sutton. 'I know the King's a stickler for inspections, and everything being done properly, him having been in the navy. Likes it all shipshape and Bristol fashion, as they say. P'raps he wants to make sure the guv'nor doesn't bite his nails.'

'Mr Sutton!' cried Flora. 'As if he would! Mr Thomas, now, he always bit his nails. I just hope the mistress remembers to watch her tongue. She can come out with some funny things at times – not always quite right for a lady.'

'Don't worry, Miss Lydia knows how to play her part,' said Sutton.

And so, when the moment came, did everyone. It's true that Martha, having forgotten her latchkey, rang the front doorbell and was greeted by Emily crying, 'Blimey, Miss! we thought you was Buckingham Palace!' But Sutton soon quelled this incipient hysteria, Martha hastily retired upstairs, and Sir Bernard Whitgift was admitted to the house soon after with almost oppressive decorum.

Not surprisingly, being a member of the Royal Household, Sir Bernard was a very stuffy gentleman, wearing an Old Etonian tie. Throughout tea, served by an impassive Sutton and Emily glazed with terror, he talked about the theatre, of which he knew nothing, horse racing, of which he knew a great deal, and Henley. Since he was evidently a rowing devotee, and since Charles's and Lydia's idea of boating was a river trip to Maidenhead to have lunch at Skindles, they were relieved when he refused another cup of tea, glanced at Sutton and Emily, and said, 'Now, then –' Sutton, waiting for his cue, had Emily outside in a moment, and, what's more, mindful of the occasion, didn't even leave the door ajar, but shut it quietly and firmly behind them.

'The King is a great admirer of your work, Mr Brett,' said Sir Bernard.

'That is very kind of His Majesty,' said Charles.

He knew where he was with dialogue like that. He was spouting it every night.

'His Majesty feels that so much of our theatre today reflects a regrettable lowering of moral standards.'

'Ah,' said Charles, solemnly.

Lydia's face beautifully showed the sorrow she felt at any hint of impropriety, let alone immorality.

'So often,' Sir Bernard added, 'it seems to show a lack of respect for the sanctity of married life.'

'Quite,' said Charles.

He and Lydia exchanged a tender glance of sickening connubial devotion, and then both turned their gaze earnestly towards Sir Bernard.

'Now, *your* play,' he was continuing, 'as I was able to

tell the King, celebrates honour and courage and loyalty – all the old-fashioned virtues.'

'Yes,' Charles agreed, with a touch of gloom.

'Old-fashioned' was precisely the term most of the critics had used.

'Well,' said Sir Bernard, 'perhaps I should broach the matter which I came to speak to you about.'

He lowered his voice and glanced towards the door. Lydia began to rise.

'Yes, if you will excuse me –' she began, but Sir Bernard raised his hand.

'Do please stay, Mrs Brett,' he said. 'This concerns you, too.'

Not half! thought Lydia, sinking down into her chair again. Lady Mucking Brett! I'll show Elsie where she gets off!

'I don't know if you will have heard –' said Sir Bernard, 'probably not – that the King is shortly expecting a distinguished visitor.'

Charles's face expressed polite attentiveness. What the devil is he talking about? he thought.

'I can't say who it is, except that it is the ruling monarch of a foreign country.'

'Ah.'

'And His Majesty would very much like to bring this royal visitor to see your play.'

'I should be delighted,' replied Charles, but behind his gracious smile was a sense of creeping unease. Could this possibly be *all*?

'And I did suggest to His Majesty,' added Sir Bernard, 'That perhaps Mr William Sutherland might write a special prologue, and that Miss Wheatley might deliver it.'

That brought Charles to his senses in an instant.

'I'm sure my wife would be only too happy,' he replied, hastily, 'but unfortunately she is appearing in another play –'

Lydia, however, was as quick as he was.

'But fortunately,' she cut in, smoothly, 'my play is much shorter than *The King Shall Not Die*, and our theatres are actually next door. I don't appear in the first scene, and we can certainly hold the curtain for a few moments if necessary. *Of course* I shall be only too happy to deliver the prologue!'

'Excellent!' said Sir Bernard. 'Excellent. I need hardly say that, since this is a private visit, it is essential that nothing about it should appear in the newspapers.'

Nothing could have exceeded the deep sincerity with which Charles replied.

'Oh yes, of course,' he said. 'Certainly.'

'So that is that,' remarked Lydia, when Sir Bernard had departed, and Sutton was clearing the tea things away.

'Possibly – not –' replied Charles, slowly. 'Sutton, would you call Mr Brewster, and ask him to see me tonight after the show?'

Brewster, in his usual irritating way, knocked and entered in one, without waiting to be invited in.

'Ah, Brewster,' said Charles, as he always did, 'come in.'

'Right,' said Brewster, and sat down without invitation.

'I dare say you can guess what it's about,' remarked Charles, diligently removing his make-up.

'Very poor houses,' replied Brewster, with that bluntness upon which he prided himself so much.

'About 50 per cent,' Charles agreed. 'Not enough to cover the costs.'

'So what you're saying is,' said Brewster, 'we have to close.'

He was looking at Charles in the mirror, but no one, least of all Brewster, could have guessed the warm satisfaction which Charles felt at his words.

'Ye – es,' said Charles, sadly. 'It's a pity. The King will be disappointed.'

'The King?' echoed Brewster, startled.

Charles start of dismay was splendidly convincing.

'Oh dear!' he exclaimed. 'I didn't mean to say that. The King was planning to bring a distinguished visitor to see the play. I wasn't supposed to mention it to anyone, but, of course, I would have had to tell *you*. I believe the manager of the theatre is usually presented on these occasions – and probably his wife as well.'

Brewster did not possess what is usually thought of as an expressive face, but suddenly his countenance was like a magic lantern show: The King in the royal box. Click. Brewster bowing over the King's hand. Click. Mrs Brewster, like an upholstered sofa, unexpectedly dipping into a curtsey. Brewster actually smiled.

'It's a shame we can't manage it,' concluded Charles, 'but there we are – business is business.'

Brewster seemed to come to himself.

'I'm sure you could nurse the play on for another week or so,' he said.

'Mm,' said Charles, wiping off the cold cream. 'I don't know about that. I doubt if I could manage it. The truth is, the rent was always too high. It *is* unfortunate, though, because a visit from royalty always puts up the takings.'

He turned round to confront Brewster.

'I tell you what,' he said, with an air of inspiration,

'let's say a rent of £300 and I keep the bar receipts. What do you say?'

'Er –'

Charles saw, even in Brewster's most determinedly expressionless face, the reflection of that happy vision of royal patronage.

'You're quite sure the King is coming?' inquired Brewster.

'Oh, absolutely certain!' replied Charles, heartily, turning back to the mirror. 'Distinguished foreign potentate, special prologue, everything.'

'Ah,' said Brewster. 'Well, in that case, perhaps I could agree –'

'By the way,' Charles cut in, 'the Palace insists on complete confidentiality. There must be nothing in the newspapers about the royal visit.'

With some satisfaction, he saw the look of stunned dismay on Brewster's face, as Brewster tried to decide whether he had, or had not agreed to the new terms. Charles's eyes met his in the mirror.

'Not until the next morning, anyway,' said Charles, and saw the slow smile spread over Brewster's face.

It was gratifying, though quite inexplicable, that the night of the King's visit to *The King Shall Not Die*, accompanied by the distinguished visitor, should have coincided with a remarkable increase in the size of the house. That is, it was inexplicable unless one happened to know that Lydia had scribbled a note to her sister, Lady Carstairs, saying, 'Elsie, darling, you'll never guess who's coming to see Charles's play on Thursday,' and that, just to be on the safe side, she had also telephoned her friend, Maud Protheroe, Elsie's sworn enemy, to give her the same news in strictest secrecy which, she said, she had not even divulged to her sister. The fact that a photographer was present to take a highly flattering photograph of Lydia delivering the prologue, and another one of Charles bowing over the King's hand in the royal box was even more mysterious, unless one happened to know that Charles had arrived home and remarked to Sutton, 'Nip round to Fleet Street, will you, Sutton? Tell them we've got a royal performance of the play, but nothing to appear until next morning?'

However it happened, the more than satisfactory result was that *The King Shall Not Die* suddenly became 'fashionable', and Charles, descending from the taxi next day, saw the 'House Full' board outside the Princess Theatre, and went swaggering blithely along the narrow alley towards the stage door, his camel-hair coat swinging, his hat on the back of his head. It was very pleasant, of course, to appear in an excellent play and give a superb performance and be justly praised for it. But something in his half-Irish ancestry, with generations of horse-trading behind it, made him feel even greater pleasure in having sold the public a sway-backed animal with a distinct spavin and got clean away with it.

Chapter Nine

Charles, in vest, trousers and dressing-gown, his braces hanging down, had his head in the basin and was washing his face, when he heard Lydia come in, as usual, from the Regency Theatre stage door across the alley.

'You're late tonight,' remarked Sutton.

'Yes,' Lydia replied. 'They *insisted* on another encore.'

'Oh dear!' said Sutton. 'What a pity!'

Charles emerged, scrubbing his face with a towel, and saw with amusement Sutton's solemn face, as he turned to leave with the costume from the last act. Funnily enough, Sutton was a far better comedian as a dresser and butler than he had ever been on the stage. Lydia's eyes met his, sharing his amusement.

'House full,' she remarked.

'Advance bookings are good, too,' remarked Charles, and bore down on the waiting bottle of champagne.

Lydia sat down, disposing herself elegantly, as usual.

'I'm sorry about the knighthood, darling,' she said.

For a moment, his face reflected the disappointment he felt, but he was facing the mirror, and thought she could not see him. The cork came out with a pop, and he turned towards her, pouring champagne into a glass.

'You said you'd stay until I got it,' he said. 'I suppose this means I'll never get rid of you.'

She answered lightly, following his mood as she always did. No one feels more foolish than an actor or writer who fondly believed that his talent was about to be recognized and discovered that he was mistaken.

'I wouldn't be too sure of that,' she said. 'Just one more episode like Lady Agatha –'

'Oh!' groaned Charles. 'If you only knew how glad I was to get rid of her!'

Lydia put her glass down, rose, took Charles's glass, put that down on the dressing table, and put her arms around him.

'Do you think I didn't know?' she inquired, and kissed him, as only she could.

Reluctantly drawing away, Charles wondered how he could broach the matter of her returning to their bedroom. Perhaps, he thought, that cosy little supper for two might do the trick.

'I booked a table at Rules,' he said. 'Suit you?'

'Very nicely,' Lydia replied.

They were toasting each other as there was a knock at the door.

'Damn!' said Charles, and then, in his most charming leading actor's voice, 'Come in!'

The young woman who appeared in the doorway was enough to make both their hearts sink. She was about twenty-five years old, thin and plain, timid but determined, a stage-door admirer if ever they saw one. Her clothes proclaimed her class – a shopgirl, perhaps – and were of that poor quality which let the rain in. Rich people could ignore the weather, stepping beneath an umbrella held by butler or commissionaire from house or restaurant to car and back again. But young women like this arrived wet and bedraggled, chilled to the bone, but expecting nothing else. She fixed her eyes on Lydia.

'Miss Wheatley?' she said.

Lydia glanced, surprised, at Charles, and back at her. 'Yes?'

The girl understood her faint surprise. She was no fool, then.

'I went to the Regency Theatre first,' she said. 'They told me I'd find you here.'

'Oh,' responded Lydia, and kept the surprise out of her voice and out of her face. What on earth could Tubby have been thinking of to send the girl on here? Stage-door keepers usually had more sense. The next words began to explain it.

'I don't know if you remember Betty Lacy?' said the girl.

'Of course I do!' Lydia exclaimed. 'She was my dresser. She –'

'She drank,' said Charles.

And, a second later –

'She was my mother,' said the girl.

It was one of those appalling moments when there is nothing to be done except to wish that it could be the end of the scene and that the curtain would fall. But, while Charles was trying to think what he could say to improve matters, the girl put her hand in her pocket and drew out a gold locket studded with diamonds.

'Why –' said Charles.

'That's my locket!' finished Lydia.

They both knew it well. Charles had given it to her

when Martha and Edwin were born, and she had worn it on her frilly bedjacket as she fought her way back to life.

'Yes,' said the girl. 'My mother did drink. She stole as well.'

'My dear girl,' said Charles, 'I'm so sorry.'

'It's quite all right,' said the girl, with chilling self-possession. 'She stole this locket and pawned it to buy drink. When she was dying, it weighed on her conscience.'

She looked at Lydia.

'She said you'd been very kind to her. I promised to get it back and give it to you. Here it is.'

She put the locket into Lydia's hand, and turned to leave.

'No!' cried Lydia. 'Don't go! Wait!'

Suddenly they were both eagerly drawing her back into the room.

'Have a drink!' begged Charles. 'A glass of champagne?'

'No!' she exclaimed.

Of course not, thought Charles. Her mother was a drunk. Damn!

Lydia drew her towards a chair.

'Come and sit down and tell us all about yourself,' she said. 'What's your name? I should remember, but –'

'There's no reason why you should,' said the girl, with the same chilling detachment. 'It's Jean.'

'Of course!' cried Lydia, and, for once, was almost gushing. 'Jean! Of course I remember! Do you work in the theatre?'

The girl seemed to draw within herself more than ever. The theatre, it seemed, like alcohol, was anathema to her.

'No!' she replied. 'I had a secretarial job, but I had to give it up when – when my mother became ill.'

'Secretarial!' Lydia exclaimed.

She exchanged a look with Charles.

'Do you,' inquired Charles, with great earnestness, 'by any chance have a typewriter?'

'Yes,' Jean answered. 'When my mother was ill, I used to do some typewriting at home.'

'And, if the ribbon wears out,' demanded Charles, hardly daring to wait for the reply, 'can you put in a new one?'

For the first time, a look of involuntary astonishment broke through Jean's armoured self-possession.

'Well – yes – of course,' she said.

'I really do need a secretary,' said Charles. 'Is there any chance that you might consider taking the job?'

'I'd like to,' she replied, 'but –'

There could be few people whose faces could be so totally uncommunicative.

'Naturally,' said Lydia, 'you will want time to think it over. If you could give us your address –?'

'Yes,' said Jean. 'The only thing is, after tomorrow, I shan't have an address –'

'My dear girl, why not?' Charles demanded.

'It's just that I –'

She seemed to be reluctant to continue.

'Please tell us,' urged Lydia.

She reached out and took the girl's hand. It was icy cold and quite unresponsive.

'It's just that my mother's funeral took all the money I'd saved, and – and I can't afford to stay in our flat after tonight.'

'My dear girl,' exclaimed Charles, heartily, 'you must come and stay in Nightingale Grove.' He looked at Lydia. 'She can have the little room,' he said.

Sutton had just picked up the letters when he heard the ring at the front doorbell.

'Huh!' he thought. '*She* didn't waste much time!'

He didn't answer the door at once, but paused to sort through the letters. He wondered if she'd ring again, but she didn't. He could imagine her standing outside, very quiet, very patient. He had met her the night before in the dressing room.

'Oh, Sutton!' Charles had said. 'This is Miss Lacy. She's going to be my secretary, and she'll be staying at the house.'

Sutton had kept his face expressionless, but he was aghast. He remembered Betty Lacy very well. A liar and a thief, who had betrayed Miss Lydia's trust again and again. Like mother, like daughter, and he didn't fancy having her in the house.

'Give her a chance, Alfred,' Lydia had said, when he expressed some of his misgivings.

He'd give her a chance, Sutton thought, but he'd watch her jolly carefully, too. And if she thought she was going to have a butler at her beck and call, she was much mistaken! He walked to the door with a stately tread and opened it. She was standing there in her ugly hat and coat, a battered cardboard suitcase in one hand and a typewriter in the other.

'Good morning,' she said.

Sutton stood back, and allowed her to enter. He would normally have taken a visitor's luggage, but in this case he made an exception.

'Good morning, Miss Lacy,' he said, briefly, and closed the door.

'Is Mr Brett –?' she asked, uncertainly.

'Not down yet,' Sutton replied. 'Would you care to see your room?'

'Yes. Thank you.'

There was a touch of pleasure in her voice. Sutton nodded towards the staircase.

'First floor,' he said, 'along the corridor – the little room at the end, on the right.'

She hesitated, clearly expecting him to take her case, but when she realized that he had no intention of doing any such thing, she simply nodded.

'Thank you,' she said, and slowly began to climb the stairs, carrying the case and the typewriter.

Sutton watched her go with some resentment. It had not been much trouble to get her room ready. Fortunately Miss Martha had got so fed up with the thunderous water pipes and the small window which always stuck that she had moved back into her tiny flat in Shepherd's Market, so it had simply been a matter of sending Emily up to put clean sheets on the bed and make sure that Miss Martha had left nothing behind. Sutton had checked on that himself, and taken possession of a gold bracelet and some lace-edged handkerchiefs which he had no intention of leaving around for Miss Lacy to find. But it was not only resentment that he felt as she turned the bend of the staircase and vanished from his sight. He felt a deep disquiet at the thought of Betty Lacy's daughter being admitted into that beloved house, with its easy-going, unsuspicious inhabitants, and given the run of the place.

Jean Lacy went into the little room, put down her case and the typewriter, closed the door and leant against it. She drew a deep breath of satisfaction, and smiled.

Charles had been quite right about the aphrodisiac effect of that elegant little supper at Rules – intimacy surrounded by just the right combination of admiring public throwing awed glances in their direction and friends who, having recently avoided his gaze, were now eager to catch his eye and toast his success. They mounted the staircase of Nightingale Grove with arms round each other's waists. Charles thought at first that he had miscalculated when Lydia, with an affectionate kiss, turned towards the room which had always been known as 'Martha's Room' and where she had been sleeping for the past weeks. But just as he was tying the string of his pyjama trousers and wondering if he dared to invade her bedroom, Lydia drifted in, all pink ribbons and négligé.

'You know,' she remarked, 'I really *do* miss my own bedroom.'

'Only that?' inquired Charles.

It was just as he was drifting off to sleep in a state of considerable satisfaction that Charles remarked, 'I shall buy myself a Rolls-Royce.'

'What?'

'Every successful man should have a Rolls-Royce.'

'And *you*, my darling, are a *very* successful man,' said Lydia, with that sensuous chuckle in her voice which he had always found irresistible.

In fact, it nearly set him off again – nearly, but not quite. *The King Shall Not Die* was physically an extremely tiring part.

It was, after all, a Bentley that caught Charles's attention.

'I say,' he remarked, 'wouldn't I – we – cut a dash in this?'

126

'Oh, certainly,' Lydia agreed. 'I can just see us sailing grandly down Rosslyn Hill, pursued by hordes of tradesmen waving unpaid bills.'

'They'd be hard pressed to catch us in this!' Charles observed, with satisfaction.

An unctuous voice spoke behind him.

'Mr Brett. Miss Wheatley. An honour. A great honour!'

One could not call him a salesman. In his pin-striped suit with a red carnation in the buttonhole, he looked more like the Governor of the Bank of England – and, as it emerged, not without reason.

'My name is Pyke,' he said. 'I see,' he continued, 'that you are admiring our new Six-point-six.'

'A very nice-looking motor,' Charles responded, casually puffing his cigar.

'Indeed it is,' Mr Pyke agreed. He cleared his throat. 'I wonder, though, Mr Brett, if I might ask you to desist from smoking.'

He met Charles's astonished look with a practised air of courtesy and firmness.

'We do find, sir,' he remarked, 'that it deposits an unpleasant amber film upon the surface of the motor.'

'Oh,' said Charles.

He took the cigar out of his mouth, and instantly a white-coated assistant was at his side with a large ashtray. Charles parted with the cigar with some regret. He had only just lighted it, and it was not a cheap one.

'I take it you have owned a Bentley before, sir?' inquired the Governor of the Bank of England.

'Er –'

Charles saw the look of amusement in Lydia's face, and feared the worst, but was too late to stop her.

'We had a Jowitt,' she said, 'but unfortunately Mr Brett lost an argument with an elm tree.'

'A Jowitt,' said Mr Pyke as though merely pronouncing the name gave him some pain.

'Appalling brakes,' said Charles, ingratiatingly.

'Quite,' Mr Pyke agreed. 'However, sir, Bentleys all have four-wheel brakes and forced lubrication with baffle plates.'

'Have they?' responded Charles. 'Good.'

If Mr Pyke had said 'four wheels and a nice emblem on the bonnet', he might have understood him. He and Lydia walked round the Bentley.

'Rather a dreary colour, Charles,' Lydia remarked.

The Governor of the Bank of England drew himself up.

'Black,' he said, 'is generally considered to be the most – appropriate – colour.'

'Mm,' said Lydia. 'I believe Lord Berners has a yellow Rolls-Royce with a piano built into the back.'

'Lamentably, yes.'

Charles threw Lydia a reproving look.

'Might I ask,' he said, 'what is the price of this car?'

'Of course, sir, if you would come this way –'

Charles, alarmed, realized that he was about to be ushered to the Chippendale-style desk to write a cheque.

'I think Mr Brett was asking,' said Lydia, 'what exactly this car costs?'

'Oh, I see.'

Clearly, his customers never felt the necessity to ask the price of anything.

'I thought – I assumed –'

'You assumed wrongly,' said Charles, drawing himself up. 'How much is the blessed thing?'

'The cost of the vehicle,' said Mr Pyke, distantly, 'is

three thousand, two hundred and twenty pounds. Including, of course, a full tank of petrol.'

'Good God!' exclaimed Charles, taken by surprise. 'I could mount a production in the West End for less than that!'

'How much is it *without* a full tank of petrol?' inquired Lydia.

In the end, they settled for a Vauxhall, which, in the event was quite large enough.

'That entrance looks awfully narrow,' said Lydia, grasping the window handle nervously as they approached the timber gateposts of Nightingale Grove. 'Are you sure that it will be –?'

'Yes, of course it will!' replied Charles, irritably. 'Anyone would think I'd never driven a car before.'

They had already missed a coal cart by inches, and a mongrel dog by the whiskers of its feathery tail. Entering the gateway of the house at an angle proved to be the moment of truth. There was a very nasty grinding, crunching noise and the car came to a halt.

'Damn!' said Charles, and endeavoured to put it into reverse. And then, 'Oh, damnation!'

The young man seemed to come from nowhere.

'Good day to you, Mr Brett,' he said. 'Can I be of any assistance?'

'Bloody car's stuck!' said Charles.

'If the lady and yourself would care to descend, I might be able to get it free. I have some experience with motors.'

He had fair hair and green eyes and an Irish accent, and wore ill-fitting clothes, like a soldier recently demobbed. Charles had a notion that he had seen him somewhere before.

'Hegarty,' said the young man. 'Patrick Hegarty. I dare say you don't remember me.'

'Oh – yes, of course –' said Charles, trying to remember.

'Dublin? Two years ago? Molly O'Hara's?'

'Oh yes, of course!' exclaimed Charles. 'Certainly I remember you!'

'Oh yes,' said Lydia, at her most icy. 'But I believe it was then Constable Hegarty.'

The young man came round the bonnet of the car to open the door for her.

'Detective Constable, ma'am,' he said. 'But now it is just Hegarty.'

'I am not surprised,' said Lydia, and descended from the car and swept away up the drive towards the front door.

Hegarty looked apologetically towards Charles.

'You did say that if I ever found myself in London –'

'Certainly I did,' said Charles, 'and I'm delighted to see you.'

He clambered out of the car, doing a little extra damage to the paintwork in the process.

'If you can get this blasted vehicle free,' he said, 'park it outside the garage and come and see me in my study.'

'Sutton,' said Charles, when he got inside the door, 'there's a young man out there called Hegarty. As soon as he has parked the – er – the Vauxhall, he's coming to see me.'

'Very good, sir,' said Sutton, who had carefully observed the whole incident at the gate from the useful little window beside the front door.

Lydia, heading for the garden room, turned sharply back.

'You're not letting that man inside the house?' she demanded. 'If I were you, I'd call the police.'

'He *is* the police – or was.'

'And now he has obviously come to blackmail you.'

'Of course he hasn't!' said Charles, crossly, and then added with some haste, 'There's nothing to blackmail me *about!*'

'Molly O'Hara, perhaps?'

Charles knew that they both had the same unfortunate image in their mind's eye, of himself arriving back at the Gresham Hotel in Dublin extremely drunk and rather dishevelled, with his arm round the shoulders of a plain-clothes policeman, who, if not drunk, was also distinctly dishevelled.

'I told you at the time –'

'No, you didn't.'

'Only because you wouldn't listen.'

'And I'm not listening now!' said Lydia, with sublime unreasonableness. 'It was obviously an extremely sordid episode, in which I take no interest whatever.' Before Charles could speak again, she had turned to Sutton. 'I did say I'd be out for luncheon, didn't I?'

'Yes, Miss Lydia. Rehearsing a new understudy?'

'Yes, I just hope she's better than the last one.'

Charles had an inspiration.

'Why don't you go in the car?'

'Don't be silly. You know I don't know how to drive.'

Charles glanced towards the study, where he had set Jean Lacy to work before they left, sorting letters and bills.

'I can't take you myself,' he said, 'because I really must tackle some of those letters with Miss Lacy, but –'

The beautiful wine-coloured car hummed gently past the front door.

'Why don't you let Hegarty drive you?' suggested Charles.

Lydia gazed at him with the stunned horror of a virgin goddess who has just been invited to take a leading part in Bacchanalian orgies.

'You must be mad!' she said. 'Sutton, get me a taxi in half an hour, will you?'

Sutton had just returned to the kitchen when there was a gentle tap on the back door.

'Hm,' he said. 'At least he has the decency not to come to the front door, unlike Miss Butter-Wouldn't-Melt Lacy!'

'Mr Sutton,' said Flora, reprovingly, 'I don't think your attitude to that young woman is very Christian.'

'I speak as I find,' said Sutton, ominously, and trod heavily to open the door.

'Mr Hegarty?'

'Patrick Michael Liam Hegarty.'

There was a touch of flamboyance in this which Sutton hadn't expected.

'Oh,' he said.

'Mr Brett is expecting me.'

'So I understand,' said Sutton, at his most butlerish, and stood back to allow Hegarty to enter.

'Miss Evans,' said Sutton, performing the introduction with all the austerity at his command.

'Delighted to meet you, Miss Evans,' said Hegarty, shaking her warmly by the hand.

'Oh – yes,' responded Flora, taken by surprise, as she withdrew her hands from the pastry. 'I'm afraid I'm a bit floury.'

'Like the roses in summer,' Hegarty replied.

Sutton should have looked disapproving, but his actor's *persona* could not resist an enjoyable performance. Emily turned round from the sink, where she was peeling potatoes.

'And this is Emily,' said Sutton. 'Emily Watkins.'

'Miss Watkins,' said Hegarty, with a little bow which he wisely substituted for a handshake, Emily's hands being red and wet. 'May the light in your eyes never grow dim.'

'Oo-er!' said Emily.

'Step this way, Mr Hegarty, if you please,' said Sutton.

By the time Lydia came to Charles's dressing room, as usual, after the performance, she seemed to have forgotten the morning's *contretemps*.

'How was the understudy?' inquired Charles.

'Very good,' she replied.

'Not *too* good, I hope?' said Sutton, and Lydia gave him one of her wicked smiles.

'Just right,' she answered. '*Just* good enough, but not *too* good.'

Charles turned away from tying his tie, and spoke casually.

'By the way,' he said, 'we can go home in our own car tonight.'

Lydia groaned.

'Oh, Charlie!' she exclaimed. 'I'm not sure that I'm quite up to dicing with death at the end of a long day.'

'No need,' replied Charles, even more casually. 'Hegarty will drive us.'

'*Hegarty*?'

'We need a chauffeur. I've offered him the job.'

'You've *what*?'

'O Lor'!' thought Sutton. 'Here we go again!' He seized the nearest costume and made a hasty retreat. Apart from anything else, they both tended to overplay in front of an audience.

'Do you really think,' demanded Lydia, 'that I will accept a chauffeur whose chief recommendation is that he was your confederate when you were spending the night boozing and whoring through Dublin?'

'Utter rubbish!' said Charles. 'Hegarty was a highly respectable policeman who helped me out of a – slightly awkward situation.'

'If he was so *highly respectable*,' said Lydia, 'why is he not a *highly respectable* policeman now?'

'Irish politics,' replied Charles, loftily. 'We need a chauffeur, and he is well qualified. I have offered him the job, and he is waiting outside now with the car.'

Lydia took a breath.

'And don't say that you intend to go home by taxi,' said Charles, 'because you will only make yourself look ridiculous.'

Lydia knew that he was right.

The sight of Hegarty in his Irish tweed suit and large tweed cap, looking like a bookie's clerk, did nothing to improve Lydia's mood, and the charming smile he bestowed upon her as he opened the door only exasperated her more. They drove back to Nightingale Grove in icy silence.

'Sutton,' said Lydia, ignoring the *recherché* little supper which awaited them in the dining room, 'would you ask Flora to bring me a bowl of soup up to my room?'

'Yes, Miss Lydia,' replied Sutton.

'Oh, and Charles,' added Lydia, as the kitchen door

swung shut behind Sutton, 'would you mind very much sleeping in the dressing room tonight? I have a headache.'

She set off up the stairs.

'Headache, or Hegarty?' demanded Charles.

Lydia turned.

'Both!' she said.

Oddly enough, Patrick Hegarty, for all his exotic Irishness, fitted into the Nightingale Grove household much better than the unobtrusive Miss Lacy. He ate in the kitchen, and slept in the room over the garage which, until the Bretts bought the house, had, in fact, been the coachhouse, with the coachman housed above the stables in the little room beside the hayloft. And, for all his poetic compliments and cheeky jokes, Flora and Emily felt quite safe with him. It was like exchanging badinage with the milkman at the back door – 'just a bit of fun', as Emily said.

Miss Lacy was different. She was in the house, but not of the house. She took her luncheon on a tray in the study, and in the evenings ate alone in the dining room, except at the weekend, when she ate with the family, silent and wary. It was Thomas who accidentally broke into this solitary existence, which made sense because he was living a solitary existence there himself. He burst unexpectedly into the study one evening, and stopped short, seeing Jean sitting reading. She started up.

'I'm sorry!'

'No. I'm sorry. I didn't think you'd still be working.'

'I'm not. I –' She was embarrassed. 'I should be in my room.'

'*The little room*?' said Thomas. 'It's like the engine room of a very small tramp steamer. No one can spend more than seven hours there without going mad.'

Suddenly Jean was laughing, and it was like catching a glimpse of the swan behind the ugly duckling.

'So I've found,' she said.

Laughing with her, Thomas subsided into the armchair.

'I suppose I should confess,' he said, 'that I came here to steal your typewriter.'

'Really? Why?'

'Well,' said Thomas, embarrassed in his turn, 'I – you see – I write plays.'

'Is that bad?'

'There is no one more ridiculous in the whole world than an unsuccessful playwright.'

'Surely, an unsuccessful actor –'

'No,' Thomas replied, firmly. 'At least an actor can perform somewhere, good or bad. But if you write plays, and haven't yet had one performed – people say, "What do you do?" and you say, "I write plays," and they say, "Oh yes, where have they been put on?" and you say, "Well, actually, nowhere yet." And then suddenly you're not a playwright at all. You're just some idiot who thought he could write plays.'

'And can you?' asked Jean.

There was suddenly something wonderfully straight and challenging about her question, and Thomas felt an extraordinary sense of relief as he met her eyes and answered it.

'Yes,' he said. 'I think so. I've just finished one which – I really think it's good.'

'Then you'd better let me type it.'

'Oh – no, I –'

'Can you type?'

'No, not really, but I thought I could probably manage to –'

'Please let me type it,' said Jean. 'You'd be doing me a favour.'

'Blast!' said Charles. 'Damn, hell and blast!'

He staggered into the dressing room where Lydia was enjoying a quiet chat with Sutton, awaiting the curtain.

'What on earth happened?'

'Vincent was drunk!' said Charles, sinking into the nearest chair. 'He botched the duel. If my reactions had been an instant slower, I'd've been playing Horatio Nelson.'

He clasped his arm, groaning, and saw a tiny trickle of red on the back of his hand.

'Blood!' he cried. 'I knew it! I had to play the whole of the last scene in agony, and pouring blood.'

'Let's get your jacket off and have a look,' said Lydia, with deplorable calmness.

There was, in fact, a nasty scratch from the wrist to the forearm, where the sword had slid up the jacket sleeve and ripped the shirt, and Sutton and Lydia were just bandaging it when Vincent Kendall tapped at the door and put his head round.

'Are you all right, old boy?' he inquired. 'You gave me a nasty shock.'

'*I* gave *you* a shock?'

'You know,' Vincent added, 'you *were* a trifle slow on that parry.'

'I certainly was not!' roared Charles. 'Ouch!'

Vincent opened his mouth to protest, but felt Sutton's restraining hand on his arm, saw Lydia's friendly and apologetic smile over Charles's head, and thought it best to withdraw.

Fortunately, the next day was Sunday, and, even more fortunately, there were no guests at the usual Nightingale Grove Sunday luncheon. Charles reclined on the sofa in the garden room, with his arm in a sling.

'I think I would like some more coffee,' remarked Charles, 'if there is any left.'

'There's plenty,' Lydia replied, briskly. 'Bring your cup over.'

'Never mind,' said Charles, wanly. 'Don't bother.'

Thomas grinned and came to collect his cup.

'Is it *very* painful, Pa?' inquired Martha.

Charles ignored the hint of irony in her voice.

'It does throb a little,' he said, stoically.

'Oh, come on, Charles, it's only a scratch,' said Lydia.

'A *scratch*?' Stoicism vanished in a moment. 'My shirt and jacket were ripped to pieces and covered with blood. God knows how Sutton will get them ready for the performance tomorrow!'

'Ah,' said Edwin, 'so your understudy is not about to have his moment of glory?'

'Certainly not!' said Charles, exasperated. 'My understudy is Vincent Kendall, and he is the swine who wounded me. Drunk, of course.'

'You do amaze me, Pa,' remarked Martha, sipping a Cointreau. 'When I was on tour with Vincent Kendall, he was a dedicated Methodist, and he was always trying to get me to sign the pledge.'

'I take it he failed?' inquired Thomas, giving Charles his refilled cup of coffee.

There was a brief silence. Lydia cleared her throat.

'Is it just possible, Charles,' she asked, 'that *The King Shall Not Die* is a tiny bit too taxing for you?'

'You mean, I'm too old for it!?'

'I mean,' said Lydia, with an asperity which was somehow rather comforting, 'that bounding up and down a staircase with a sword in your hand is not necessarily the sign of a distinguished leading actor.'

Charles gratefully accepted the compliment. It was not so bad to be no longer young if one was accepted as being a distinguished leading actor.

'Admit it,' said Lydia. 'You were late on that move during the duel.'

'I will admit,' said Charles with dignity, 'that I may have had a momentary lapse of concentration. The truth is that the play no longer stimulates me intellectually.'

'Or, indeed, anyone,' put in Thomas.

'Oh, come on, Thomas!' said Edwin. 'It may not be the best play in the world, but –'

'But it's still doing good business,' said Charles.

His eyes rested on Edwin, a younger version of himself, slimmer, and (possibly!) just a little better looking, and suddenly he saw the solution to the whole problem.

'Eddie,' he said, 'why don't *you* take over the part?'

'You wouldn't really, Eddie, would you?' inquired Martha, as they walked towards the tennis court.

'It's not a bad part.'

'But it's Father's part,' said Martha. 'You'd just be copying him.'

'I might be able to bring something new to the interpretation.'

'Interpretation of *what*? All you can do is to fight the duel a bit better. And if they don't change the casting, you'll look as if you're making love to your mother!'

They arrived at the rather bumpy grass court which

once a week was mowed and marked out by the jobbing gardener.

'Anyway,' Martha remarked, 'Father's only making use of you. He knows the duelling's too much for him, but he thinks there's still some money to be made out of the play.'

'I'm perfectly well aware of that,' said Edwin, irritably, taking off his blazer.

'He thinks he won't have to pay you too much, and all he has to do is to take a few tucks in his costumes.'

'I'll have my own costumes, thank you!' exclaimed Edwin, and knew in that moment that he had given himself away.

Martha stared at him, horrified.

'Eddie!' she said. 'You *are* going to do it!'

'I'm merely – thinking about it,' replied Eddie, with dignity.

He unscrewed his racket from its press and prepared to toss.

'Rough or smooth?' he said.

Thomas, meanwhile, had made his way to the nursery. He hated these family luncheons and dinners, and always, somehow, felt slightly out of place. Perhaps it was because he was not an actor, and because even successful playwrights were never quite admitted to that magic circle of those who actually stepped out before the footlights to face the audience. Even as a child, he had been the odd man out – stuck between the twins, Martha and Edwin, and the startlingly attractive but determinedly independent latecomer, Perdita. But since coming down from Cambridge and losing the cheerful comradeship of those to whom the theatre was no more important than rowing or cricket, he had felt it more than ever. A failure! Oh, God! Amongst all the famous and successful Bretts, was he to be the one failure? Was it *that* which set him apart from the others? He opened the nursery door and stopped short, surprised, seeing Jean Lacy by the window, looking down into the garden.

'Oh!' he said.

Jean turned, startled.

'I'm so sorry!' she said.

It occurred to Thomas that she was always apologizing for something, and that it was about time she stopped.

'I – finished typing your play,' she said, 'and I thought you'd want it as soon as possible.'

'You're right!' said Thomas. 'Thanks!'

He picked up the folder, with the label on the front which read: '*If The Truth Be Told*, by Thomas Brett.'

'It never looks like a real play until it's typed,' he said. He flicked through it. 'Sometimes not even then,' he added. And then – unable to resist the question which all authors ask – 'What did you think of it?'

'Well –'

'Not that I imagine you were really able to take it in,' said Thomas, hastily. 'I mean, I imagine it's a sort of mechanical operation – you probably didn't even read what you were typing.'

'I did, as a matter of fact,' said Jean. 'I liked it very much.'

'You *did*?' cried Thomas, his author's insecure vanity immediately gratified.

'Not that my opinion means anything –'

'Of course it does!' said Thomas. 'I hope you didn't think I meant –'

'I didn't,' said Jean, smiling reassuringly. 'When I was typing it, I couldn't wait to find out what happened, and when I'd finished it, I read it through again, and I admired it very much.'

'You *admired* it?'

'Yes,' said Jean. 'It's very unusual – very modern. Do you think you'll get the last scene past the Lord Chamberlain?'

'I don't know,' replied Thomas. 'I never thought about it.' He laughed. 'Father says a little scandal never yet hurt the box-office.'

'There was just one thing I didn't like about it,' said Jean.

'Oh?' said Thomas, and scowled.

Authors, like actors, always prefer praise to criticism.

'The title,' said Jean, hesitating, 'seemed rather old-fashioned. *If The Truth Be Told*. It sounds sort of – Victorian.'

'Oh,' said Thomas, 'that's rather clever of you. It did actually belong originally to quite a different play – a comedy.'

'That's what it sounds like. I think it needs something much – sharper. Something like – well – like *The Liar*.'

Thomas sank down into a chair, holding the typescript between his hands as though she had just given it to him, and he had just taken it into his possession.

'*The Liar*,' he said. 'That's it. That's what it's all about. All the lies and self-deception about the war, and how Crawford lied about it, to himself and to everyone else, and how it was that which destroyed him.' He looked up at her. 'Jean, you're a wonder!'

She blushed.

'I'm nothing of the kind,' she said. 'But I do think it's a good play.'

Then she was gone, but Thomas didn't mind. He settled down with total self-absorption to read through his play which, with its new title, suddenly seemed to have a new life of its own.

Chapter Ten

It was only a week later that Thomas received the most important letter of his life. It read:

Dear Mr Brett,

Thank you for sending me your play, *The Liar*. I think it is most unusual, and I would like to produce it at the Little Theatre, Euston Road, as soon as possible.

Yours sincerely,
Giles Peabody
P.S. Please let me know if you have any ideas about casting.

'It's very kind of you, Tom,' said Edwin, 'but Giles Peabody is rather *avant-garde*, isn't he? I hardly imagine that I am precisely his kind of actor.'

'Perhaps it's about time you were,' said Thomas. 'Crawford's your part. You know that.'

'Well – it's a very good part,' replied Edwin. 'But I've

already promised Father to take over in *The King Shall Not Die*. Sorry.'

He rose from the nursery tea which they had been sharing with Martha, and left the room.

'*He's* sorry?' Thomas repeated, indignantly. 'So he should be. Crawford is his part.'

'Oh, don't be stupid, Tom,' said Martha. 'Crawford isn't his part. It's *him*. That's why he can't play it. I can, though.'

'Play the part of Crawford?'

'No, you ass! Play the wife. Just ask Giles Peabody. He'll be thrilled.'

Somewhat to Thomas's annoyance, Giles Peabody, that pillar of socialist realism, was embarrassingly gratified at the notion of having the well-known and socially acceptable Martha Brett in the play. Sitting in the narrow, adapted church hall, Thomas knew for the first time that mixture of trembling excitement and despair which is inflicted upon every author of a new play. Once or twice Jean crept in to the darkened hall to sit beside him, and then, mysteriously, he knew that it was all going to be all right. At least – once she had gone – he hoped so.

Rehearsals were not at all what he had expected. He had thought that once the play was written and typed, the actors would simply learn it and play it. He had no idea that he would find himself fighting the producer and the actors to protect his words and intonations, and, even more difficult, trying to decide when they were right, and a change would be an improvement – only to find when he had yielded, that this change now affected another scene which they would joyfully pull to pieces in its turn. Martha was the worst of them all, picking at every line like a blackbird with a snail, until there seemed to be no life left in it at all, just a crumbling shell. He was very sorry that he had ever suggested her for the part, but he knew that it would have made no difference if he hadn't. As she told him at the time, she would only have invited Giles Peabody to her flat and *wooed him*. Thomas was never sure how far Martha went with her constantly changing court of young men or not-so-young-but-rather-rich men, but it always seemed to be enough to ensure that she got her own way.

It occurred to Thomas that, although he had occasionally sat in the stalls while Charles and Lydia were rehearsing their plays, he had always seen the rehearsals from *their* point of view, unconsciously accepting their attitude towards the author as being a tiresome man who couldn't write good scenes and kept interfering while they were trying to improve his work. As the three weeks of rehearsals wore on, leaving him ragged and exhausted, he thought, 'Even if it's a success, I shall still be an outsider.'

At Nightingale Grove, meanwhile, Charles and Lydia were still in a state of armed truce. Their sleeping arrangements were always the key to matrimonial accord. If they were sleeping together in their big bedroom, all was well. If Charles was in the dressing room with the adjoining door closed, things were bad. In the present instance, he was still sleeping in the dressing room, but tended to wander to and fro.

'Where the devil are my gold cuff-links?' he demanded, as he and Lydia were dressing to go out to a luncheon.

'Where you left them, I imagine,' Lydia replied.

If they had been on more cordial terms, she would

have come into the dressing room and helped him to look for them.

'I shall have to wear the mother-of-pearl ones.'

'Good idea,' Lydia called back, as she draped a silver-fox stole gracefully over her left shoulder.

As they descended the stairs, Jean emerged from the study.

'Excuse me, sir,' she said. 'I thought you ought to see this letter.'

'Oh. Is it urgent?'

Charles took it reluctantly, began to glance idly through it, and then started violently.

'That – that ignorant, jumped-up, presumptuous – troglodyte!'

'Which troglodyte is that?' inquired Lydia, admiring herself in the mirror which was judiciously placed by the front door.

'Brewster.'

Sutton, preparing to open the door, looked Lydia over critically, and she raised an eyebrow inquiringly.

'Very nice,' he said. 'Although I would have preferred your emerald brooch.'

'I know,' said Lydia, 'but I couldn't find it. I must have put it down somewhere. Ask Emily to look out for it when she does the room.'

'Oh yes, and my gold cuff-links, too,' said Charles. 'I swear I left them on my dressing table.' He became aware of Jean standing very still beside him. 'Would you care to hear Brewster's letter?'

'Have we time?' said Lydia.

'We'd better make time,' replied Charles, grimly. 'Listen to this.'

He adopted an uncannily accurate flat Yorkshire accent.

Dear Mr Brett,

It is with some surprise that I read in the press that you intend shortly to give up the leading role in *The King Shall Not Die* and hand over to your son, Mr Edwin Brett. May I draw your attention to the terms of our contract, which clearly indicates that the Princess Theatre is only leased to you on the understanding that you shall take the leading role in this play. Should you be replaced by a lesser actor, I am entitled to terminate the lease.

'Lesser actor!' Lydia exclaimed. 'How dare he!'

Charles glanced at her.

'Not the way I would have expressed it. Less well known, perhaps.' He reverted to his Brewster voice. '"I shall be glad to meet you in the theatre office as soon as possible. Best regards to your wife." Bloody cheek!'

He folded the letter up and gave it back to Jean, and pondered the matter.

'Don't much fancy a meeting in the theatre office. Shan't get anywhere with that, with the contract on the desk. A nice little supper party for Brewster and his "lady wife" would be much better. What do you say, Liddy?'

'Er – we–ell –'

Lydia appeared to be thinking it over.

'Is Hegarty still in your employ?'

Charles glared at her.

'He certainly is! And he will remain "in my employ" for the foreseeable future.'

Lydia advanced towards the door, and Sutton opened it for her. Outside was the shiny burgundy-coloured car, and Hegarty, in his smart new uniform, standing beside it. Lydia paused and looked back at Charles.

'Then it looks like a meeting with Brewster in the theatre office,' she said, and flung the silver fox over her shoulder.

'They never can resist those bloody exit lines,' thought Sutton. 'Never mind poor Master Eddie.'

As he closed the door and turned, he saw Jean moving towards the study.

'Well,' he said, aloud, 'I'd better tell Emily about that emerald brooch and the master's gold cuff-links. Funny the way everything seems to be going missing all of a sudden!'

Jean turned, and looked at him, and paused, and then disappeared into the study like a mouse vanishing into the wainscot.

⁓

As Charles had surmised, the theatre office was not the ideal setting for his meeting with Brewster.

'I just don't think,' said Brewster, 'that young Edwin will bring in the audiences. After all, we always knew that the play was a bit old-fashioned.'

'The King seemed to like it.'

'He may have given your audiences a leg up for a while, but I've seen the latest figures –'

'That's really none of your business. We agreed a rent, which I'm perfectly willing and able to pay –'

'Not for much longer, if you leave the cast. And it *is* my business, Mr Brett. If the weekly takings fall below a certain amount, I have the right to close the production.'

Charles glared at him. That was true, of course, but –

'I've had several approaches from other managements looking for theatres,' said Brewster, 'and, as I say, business is business.'

'Don't you have any feeling for the theatre at all?' Charles demanded.

'It pleases the wife for me to own a theatre,' replied Brewster, 'and as long as it makes a profit, I don't mind. But, it's just like a factory: if it stops making a profit, then I close it down, or I sell it.'

'Sell it?' repeated Charles, startled. 'Would you sell it to me?'

''Course I would, for the right price.'

'And what is the right price?'

'Ah well,' said Brewster, 'I'd have to talk to my accountants –'

'Come on, Brewster!' said Charles. 'I'll bet you know the price of every brick you own!'

'All right,' said Brewster. 'I'd reckon you could have the freehold of the Princess Theatre for a quarter of a million.'

'Done!' said Charles.

In the study at Nightingale Grove next afternoon, John Caldwell stared at Charles, aghast.

'*How* much?' he said. 'How on earth do you think you can raise a sum like that?'

'Well – my investments. What about those Rhodesian Zinc? Thirty-five thousand shares at fifteen shillings each. And that was in 1923. Now they must be worth – what?'

'One and three halfpence each,' replied John. 'Apparently, they've dug five hundred feet down, and they still haven't found enough zinc to line the mine shaft.'

'Then why did you tell me to buy the damned things?'

'I didn't,' replied John, drily. 'If you recall, that was

your previous stockbroker, shortly before he emigrated to Rhodesia, where I believe his brother-in-law owns a zinc mine.'

'All right, all right,' said Charles, irritably. 'What about all the rest?'

'Gilt-edged, on my advice,' replied John, adding hastily, 'which means you can't cash them in – not till next year, anyway.'

'Thank you very much,' said Charles, with profound ingratitude.

'Of course,' said John, 'if you could raise part of the money, you might be able to find investors who'd join you as – as sleeping partners.'

'Don't let Lydia hear you say that!' said Charles, and then, in a flash of inspiration, 'Harry Carstairs! He has more money than sense!'

'Unfortunately, his wife hasn't,' responded John, suppressing a smile.

'True,' said Charles, gloomily.

Ever since Lydia's sister, Elsie, had married the stage-struck baronet, Charles had been attempting to persuade Harry to invest in productions, and had never yet succeeded.

'Still,' said John, 'a theatre is a more substantial investment than a play. Bricks and mortar in the centre of London are always valuable. Lady Carstairs might well give her permission for that. I might even be interested myself.'

'Splendid!' exclaimed Charles, hope soaring again. 'How much do you think I'd have to put down myself?'

'Quite a substantial sum,' replied John. 'I should say about – fifty thousand.'

'Fifty thousand? *Cash?*'

'I'm afraid so.'

'Oh,' said Charles. 'Well, I suppose we'd better go and tell Edwin the bad news.'

Edwin had stayed the night at the house, as he often did when he was going riding next morning. The children had all been taught to ride when they stayed in the country with Harry and Elsie Carstairs, but only Edwin had shown a real aptitude for it, and the local livery stables kept an excellent horse almost entirely for his own use. He and Lydia had finished their after-luncheon coffee in the garden room while Charles talked to John Caldwell, and Lydia had now gone upstairs to prepare for a visit to her dressmaker.

Edwin was happily engaged in planning the duel in *The King Shall Not Die*. The duel between Charles and Vincent Kendall had been designed to look quite flashy while not actually involving too much danger or exertion, but Edwin was determined that *his* duel should be quite spectacular.

'Very sorry, old chap,' said Charles. 'It looks as though the king will have to die after all. John says I simply don't have the wherewithal.'

'But, even if you can't buy the theatre, can't you persuade Brewster –?'

'The swine says it's in the contract that I should play the leading part and –'

'And he won't accept me as a leading actor.'

Edwin stood up. Hurt feelings, disappointment and wounded pride provoked one of his rare fits of temper.

'Thank you, Father, very much!' he said. 'You do realize I was offered the part of Crawford and turned it down?'

'Crawford?'

'The leading part in *The Liar*.'

'Oh. Thomas's play. Surely you didn't want to –?'

'It's a very good – modern – play, and a marvellous part, and I turned it down for *The King Shall Not Die*,' said Edwin.

He did not tell his father, and perhaps by now he hardly knew himself, that he had turned it down because it struck too close to home, that he would, in effect, have been playing himself, but a self with emotions and weaknesses laid bare to the gaze of an audience, something few actors care to do.

'Now I'm out of work,' he said, and walked out of the room.

'Damn!' said Charles.

Half an hour later, Hegarty, in shirt-sleeves, was polishing the Vauxhall, which already gleamed with almost ostentatious brilliance. Sutton approached the drive outside the garage.

'Very nice,' he said. 'Where's my winnings?'

Hegarty, it appeared, knew as much about horses as he did about cars, and had already found a reliable bookie.

'Safe and sound,' he said, feeling in the pocket of his jacket on the front seat. 'And Mr Brett had a fiver on it, too.'

Hegarty gave Sutton a nice little wad of pound notes, and as Sutton, gratified, counted them, Hegarty's eyes went beyond him to the entrance gates, and the taxi driving up to the front door.

'Is that for the mistress?' he inquired.

Sutton, with difficulty, abstracted his mind from his unexpected windfall.

'That's right,' he said. 'I'd better –'

'Where's she going?'

'Her dressmaker,' replied Sutton. 'Ascot coming up. She's determined to outshine Lady Carstairs this time.'

He was turning away again, but was checked by Hegarty's voice.

'Why doesn't she take her own car?' he inquired. 'Could it be that she doesn't like the chauffeur?'

Sutton was actually embarrassed, which didn't often happen to him.

'Well, I –' He was torn between liking for Hegarty and his indissoluble loyalty to Lydia. 'Let's just say it's between her and Mr Brett, and you're the poor bugger caught in the middle.'

As Sutton turned towards the kitchen door, the first big splotch of rain fell on the shining bonnet of the car.

'Now, wouldn't you know it?' demanded Hegarty. 'And just when I've polished this car within an inch of its life.'

Sutton paused at the door and looked back at him.

'But there,' exclaimed Hegarty, gazing up at the threatening clouds, 'it never rains but it does some bugger some good!'

Lydia, emerging from the front door and getting into the taxi, was vaguely aware of Hegarty standing by the corner of the house, but ignored him, giving the name and address of her dressmaker to the cabby. Sutton waited until Lydia had climbed into the cab and the cabby had closed the door on her and gone round to the driving seat before he retired inside. Hegarty waited until Sutton had retired inside before he returned to the Vauxhall, put on his jacket and cap, got out the starting handle and cranked the car into life.

It was one of those spring storms which seems determined to empty the heavens, like a housewife spring-cleaning before summer comes. Lydia, emerging from her dressmaker, had no such poetic thoughts. She just thought she was going to get bloody wet and arrive at the theatre looking like a drowned rat. And, of course, there was never a taxi when one wanted one! It was then that she saw Hegarty.

'Excuse me, madam,' he said.

She endeavoured to look through him, but it wasn't easy when he was five foot eleven and standing right in front of her.

'I just wished to say, madam,' he continued, 'that I'll be giving in me notice today, but until it takes effect, would you care to drive to the theatre in your own car, or would you prefer to be soaked to the skin?'

Before she could think of the right answer, he had put up a large umbrella, and escorted her to the car.

'So you are giving in your notice,' said Lydia, having had time to think of something to say.

'I am, madam, on account of not wishing to make trouble between yourself and the master.'

He glanced at Lydia's face in the rear mirror, and saw it quite expressionless.

'I don't know if you've ever heard of Molly O'Hara, madam?' inquired Hegarty.

'I seem to have heard the name mentioned once,' replied Lydia, frostily.

'I'm glad to hear it, madam,' said Hegarty, heartily, 'for, sure, she was famous throughout Dublin.'

'Really?'

The frost turned glacial.

'She kept a pub just behind the Gaiety Theatre. She was sixty if she was a day, but –'

'*Sixty?*'

'I could be wrong. She might have been seventy. But she was a great lady just the same, and she ran the best pub in Dublin.'

'And, naturally,' said Lydia, but rather resignedly than indignantly, 'Mr Brett fetched up there after the performance.'

'He did so, madam. Now it was well understood that at closing time, Molly O'Hara would say, "Time, Gentlemen, please!" and the polliss would be there, and they would say, "Goodnight, Molly," and she would say, "Goodnight to yez all," and the polliss would leave, and then she would say to her customers, "Come into the back room beyant, and have a jar on the house." But on this particular night, didn't Mr Brett chance to make a few injudicious remarks on the subject of the Irish Republican Army, and wasn't there a bit of a barny, and didn't someone call the polliss?'

'And they raided the place,' said Lydia, always one for cutting through unneeded verbiage.

'They did so, madam. But luckily I was in the raiding party, and being an admirer of the theatre meself, I didn't fancy the thought of Mr Charles Brett being up before the magistrate for disorderly behaviour, not to mention drinking after hours, so –'

'How did you get him out?'

'Ah well, in Ireland, there's always a back window. The only trouble was – it was rather a small one.'

'So that's how his jacket got torn.'

They had arrived outside the Regency Theatre.

'It was, madam,' said Hegarty.

He came round to open the door for her.

'Mind,' he said, 'I'll not pretend that when I brought Mr Brett back to you at the Gresham Hotel, he was entirely sober. If not drunk, I'd say he had definitely drink taken.'

Lydia got out of the car and turned to look at him.

'I'd say he was drunk,' she said.

'You could be right, madam,' replied Hegarty. 'And I'll quite understand if you would rather not employ a chauffeur who was first encountered in such unfortunate circumstances.'

'Unfortunately,' she said, 'I seem to have very little choice.'

She swept on down the narrow passage towards the stage door of the Regency Theatre, but unexpectedly paused and turned back.

'And, Hegarty –'

'Yes, madam?'

'Take that smile off your face.'

'I will, ma'am,' said Hegarty.

But when she had disappeared into the stage door, the smile returned. Thanks be to the Blessed Virgin and all the saints that she didn't know about the lively young actress from the Abbey Theatre who had taken Mr Brett to Molly O'Hara's in the first place!

Late that night, Lydia roamed into the dressing room as Charles was unbuttoning his shirt. Not only was she wearing her best nightdress and négligé, but a waft of perfume entered with her. She sat down on the hard little bed.

'I went to my dressmaker's today, Charles,' she said.

'Oh yes?'

'And when I came out, it was pouring with rain, and Hegarty was there, so I allowed him to drive me to the theatre. Did you arrange that?'

'Certainly not!' replied Charles, indignantly. 'As a matter of fact, I had to take a taxi to the theatre myself!'

'Oh,' said Lydia, not entirely displeased. 'Well,

anyway, on the way to the theatre, Hegarty told me about Molly O'Hara's.'

'Oh. He did?'

'An after-hours drinking bar. Charles, honestly!'

She stood up and put her arms round him.

'Why didn't you tell me, you stubborn old fool?'

'Because you made me so angry, you moralizing old cow!'

'This really is a beastly little room, Charles,' said Lydia, drawing away. 'I think I shall go back to our bedroom.'

'*Our* bedroom?' inquired Charles.

Lydia paused in the doorway, and gave him an unmistakably inviting look.

'I'll just brush my teeth,' said Charles.

It was delightful to be together again in the big matrimonial bed, where confidences flowed so naturally and comfortably.

'Dammit, Liddy,' said Charles, 'it never occurred to me that I wouldn't have enough money to buy the Princess Theatre. I just thought I'd sell a few shares –'

'Oh, really, Charlie!' said Lydia. 'Don't you know anything about the value of your investments? I knew your Rhodesian zincs were sinking further than the mine shaft.'

'You did?' inquired Charles, startled. 'How?'

'I read the financial press, naturally,' replied Lydia.

'Really?' said Charles. 'I can never make head or tail of it.'

'Obviously,' said Lydia.

Charles cleared his throat.

'Why do you read them? The financial pages?'

Lydia turned her head on the pillow to look at him.

'What do you think I do with my money, Charles? Keep it under the mattress?'

He moved closer to her.

'I've never thought about it. Spend it on hats?'

'Not all of it,' replied Lydia, responding to his embrace. 'Most of it is invested. About fifty thousand pounds, actually.'

'Good God!' exclaimed Charles. 'And you'd give it to me to buy the Princess Theatre?' He drew her closer into his arms. 'You really are an incredibly beautiful woman.'

'Thank you, Charles dear,' said Lydia. 'But I'm not *giving* you the money.'

Charles froze.

'You're not?'

'No–o. Mind, I might be persuaded to invest it, as full partner in the enterprise.'

'Oh.'

'And I've talked to Harry and he's game. He'd be a sleeping partner, of course.'

'But you wouldn't?'

'Only in a manner of speaking. I really do think that one partner in any business should be able to read the financial news. Do we have a deal?'

'I suppose so,' replied Charles, rather grumpily. 'Beggars can't be choosers. I'll telephone Brewster in the morning.'

'You'll do no such thing!' said Lydia, with spirit. 'I'll deal with Brewster. A quarter of a million pounds, indeed! The Prince of Wales went for two hundred thousand. You leave Brewster to me.'

Charles was not quite sure whether he felt relieved

or insulted, but Lydia drew him closer into her arms.

'What were you saying,' she inquired, 'about my being an incredibly beautiful woman?'

The purchase of the Princess Theatre went satisfactorily ahead, all the negotiations being firmly if unobtrusively under Lydia's management. Even Brewster was pleased. Charles would have taken Harry Carstairs to an expensive lunch at the Ivy, with a good deal of vintage wine, and then endeavoured to con the money out of him, in the fond hope that he could slip it past Elsie until it was too late. Lydia, on the contrary, went straight to her sister, and, over a cup of tea, they sat down together in the old Winsome Wheatleys' style, and examined the proposition, just as they had once worked out a strategy for circumventing a grasping music-hall manager. Elsie quite agreed that buying the Princess Theatre was a good proposition, even on the most hard-headed business terms.

'That's true,' she said. 'In the form of bricks and mortar, it's worth a great deal – and if the worst came to the worst, we could always turn it into a cinema.'

Fortunately, Charles did not hear that remark, and Lydia let it pass. Elsie was not only prepared to allow Harry to invest in the Princess Theatre, but actually put some money into it herself. 'Get your bank roll together, girls!' a famous American vaudeville star of indubitable fame but dubious morality had once adjured them, and Elsie had carefully heeded the advice. Long before she met Harry Carstairs, she had somehow managed, without a hint of scandal, to amass quite a considerable, if discreet, little bank balance – and that was quite apart from the diamonds which dear boys of the aristocracy took such pleasure in bestowing upon her.

Once Lydia had landed her two big fish, she tackled Brewster, and persuaded him that his lady wife would be very sad to part with the social glitter and prestige of owning a theatre – especially since Sir Harry and Lady Carstairs would be fellow directors.

'Your good lady's done you proud, Brett,' said Brewster, as he prepared to sign the documents. 'If you ask me, she's a very clever businesswoman.'

'Oh, nonsense, Mr Brewster!' said Lydia. 'You're still getting ten thousand more than the Princess is worth, and you keep 10 per cent of the stock. If anyone is clever at business –'

Brewster threw her a shrewd look. He did not come from Yorkshire for nothing.

'Mm,' he said, and signed.

'And I very much hope,' said Charles, 'that you and Mrs Brewster will come to the first night of Edwin's debut in *The King Shall Not Die*, and join us for a little supper party at the Savoy afterwards.'

'Oh,' said Brewster, 'well – thank you very much. I'm sure Mrs Brewster and me will be happy to accept.'

His regret at the loss of that ten thousand and his uneasiness at having been done down by a woman vanished in a happy smile. *His* good lady wife had not been best pleased when he told her that he was selling the Princess Theatre. Factories may make more money, but rarely produce royal command performances, and never supply first nights at which one can wear one's best up-holstered dress and be photographed with the nobs. On the other hand, the Princess Theatre had proved to be a very shaky investment. It looked as though, this way, he gained all round.

The advance publicity for Edwin's appearance in the part of Sebastian was very satisfactory. Charles had seen to that. His determination to ensure that Edwin should not succeed him without a considerable fanfare was by no means purely altruistic – if altruistic at all – and not entirely due to a desire that the play should continue to make money. It was far more importrant to him, though he would never have admitted it, that no one should be under the misapprehension that he was leaving the play because of ill health or because he found it too much for him. And since he had no other play immediately in view for himself, it seemed best to distract everyone's attention from that fact by building up Edwin's importance.

'Famous Son of Famous Father to appear in the King's Choice,' was the headline which most took his fancy.

'That should do the trick,' he said, spreading the paper out on the desk.

'Oh, but Mr Brett,' cried Jean, 'that's the same night that Thomas's play is opening!'

'Oh, is it?' said Charles. 'Well, it can't be helped.'

'But if you're going to have a big opening-night party for *The King Shall Not Die* –'

'We've got to feature it. Don't want it to look as though my understudy is taking over. We'll go to Thomas's play on the second night. Probably be better then, anyway.'

'Oh, you can't!' cried Jean. 'He'll be heartbroken if you're not there for his first night. You know he adores you.'

Charles looked up at her, startled. Miss Lacy was such a little mouse of a thing, one didn't expect her to say things like that.

'Nonsense!' he said, always embarrassed by expressions of emotion in real life, however brilliantly he conveyed them on stage.

He paused and thought it over. How on earth could he have made such a stupid mistake? He was uneasily aware that the reason was that he had never really taken Thomas's playwrighting seriously, and that, without precisely wondering why, he had pushed the whole matter of Thomas's career into the back of his mind. However appalling the play, of course the boy would want his family to be there.

'They'll – just have to move the date,' he said.

'They can't!' said Jean. 'They just can't afford to. The Little Theatre Company haven't much money, and they've already got the posters printed.'

'You seem to know a lot about it,' said Charles.

She appeared to be taken aback.

'Oh – well – I typed the play,' she said, as if that explained it, and she added hastily, 'in my own time, of course.'

'Well,' said Charles, 'it's very unfortunate, but I don't know what I can do about it now.'

'Couldn't you change the date when Edwin takes over? Don't forget – it's Martha's first night in the play, too.'

'Oh, Lord! so it is! How on earth could I have been such an idiot? But I really don't see – I mean, if we did postpone Edwin's opening, what would we say?'

'Why not tell the truth?' suggested Jean.

'What a revolutionary idea!' responded Charles. 'I wouldn't like it to become a habit. What had you in mind?'

Jean quoted an imaginary newspaper headline.

'Younger Son of Famous Actor Has First Play Produced. Miss Martha Brett to play Leading Role.

Opening of Mr Edwin Brett at Princess Theatre Postponed to Avoid Clash of First Nights.'

'Ye–es. I suppose that might –'

'It would be good publicity for both. You could all go to Thomas's first night, and then have a grand opening of – of Mr Edwin Brett in *The King Shall Not Die*.'

'Mm, not bad,' said Charles.

'It would cause quite a stir when you all turned up at the Little Theatre.'

'What do we wear?' inquired Charles. 'Workmen's overalls?'

But the idea clearly appealed to him, until he saw the snag. *Twinkle-Toes* had finished its run, so Lydia would be able to go, but he didn't quite fancy her causing a stir without him. 'If I'm playing at the Princess Theatre for an extra night,' he said, 'I still won't be able to go to Thomas's play.'

'You could say,' Jean suggested, 'that because it is a totally new production of *The King Shall Not Die*, the Princess Theatre will be closed for one night.'

'Totally new production?' exclaimed Charles. 'Not likely! Edwin's insisted on having new costumes for himself as it is. The scenery might get a lick of paint, but that's all.'

'Ah,' said Jean, 'that's where truth stops becoming a habit.'

Charles, glancing up, saw an unexpected twinkle instead of the usual unexpressive look, and he began to laugh.

'Miss Lacy,' he said, 'you're a treasure! You ought to be manager of the theatre.'

He was glad to get a little chuckle from her in reply, before she quickly became serious again, as though afraid of giving something away.

'By the way,' Charles added suddenly, 'now we own the theatre, we shall be needing a manager. We'd better put an advertisement in *The Times*.'

'Yes, Mr Brett,' said Jean, making a note in her book.

Sutton, on his way into the dining room, had heard the sound of laughter from the study and frowned.

'She'll be putting her shoes under his bed next!' he said to himself.

Edwin wasn't too pleased to have his opening date postponed because of Thomas's play. There had always been a certain subterranean jealousy between the two of them. Thomas never failed to get in a dig or two wherever possible about Edwin's good looks and athleticism – as though he had nothing else – and Edwin knew that his brother envied him the closeness which being an actor gave him to their mother and father, not to mention Martha (but then Edwin would have been close to Martha anyway). For his part, Edwin resented the fact that Thomas had arrived into the family at a time when his parents had become successful, and were making enough money to send their son to a small public school, and to the university. Edwin looked back on a childhood spent with his parents on the stage or on tour, or else staying with Uncle Harry and Auntie Elsie, picking up an education of sorts at one school or another, wherever he happened to be. Then he was pitchforked into the war, and had emerged fit for nothing but to be an actor. He desperately needed to be as good an actor as his father, or, if possible, a better one. And now, suddenly, he had the chance to prove that he *was* better, in the very part that his father had created and in the same theatre, only to have Thomas upstage him, and with a play which he knew in his heart he should have appeared in himself.

But Edwin, like his father, was accustomed to concealing his deeper emotions, and therefore, with excellent grace, accompanied Charles and Lydia to the Little Theatre in the Euston Road. Understanding that the Little Theatre was a sort of Workers' Co-operative which despised the vulgar ostentation of a West End first night, they had all carefully dressed down for the occasion, and were slightly shaken to see all the leading dramatic critics present. Jean was in a seat behind them, and, at the last minute, Thomas slipped into the empty seat beside Edwin.

'Good luck,' said Edwin, perfunctorily, and then saw Thomas's face, dead white and desperate, and affection overcame jealousy. He put a hand on Thomas's arm, smiled at him, and saw Thomas's anguished, grateful smile in return as the curtain rose.

The Liar was one of those plays which come only once in a generation. It expressed feelings unconsciously suppressed, but which, like a volcano, once released above the surface, could not be checked, nor their existence denied. During the intervals, the audience, except for those who had walked noisily and indignantly out, retired to the back of the hall to drink cups of weak coffee. Charles, Lydia, Edwin and Thomas were hastily removed to a sort of vestry where, with Giles Peabody and the manager of the hall, they drank bad sherry in cheap glasses, and made awkward conversation.

But, as the third act continued, Charles and Lydia, sitting motionless, staring at the stage, were aware of what was happening. Thomas had written a play which had a life of its own, which turned the audience into a single, sentient being whose whole life and emotion existed on the stage.

Martha, in a dressing-gown, confronted the actor playing Crawford, the young, destroyed ex-officer.

'What more can I do?' she demanded. 'I've left my husband, my home, my life. I don't understand, unless you're saying that you're incapable of loving a woman!'

'No!' he cried. 'That is – Oh God, Diana, it was the war!'

'The war!' cried Martha, despairingly. 'That was ten years ago! That's all in the past. What about the future?'

'I don't think we have a future.'

Crawford turned towards the door.

Martha flung off her dressing-gown. There was a gasp from the audience.

'My God!' said Charles. 'She's in her knickers!'

'Camibockers, darling,' said Lydia.

Charles turned his head to look at her, and then looked back at the stage.

'I'm offering you my body!' cried Martha, falling on her knees and clasping Crawford.

He broke free and made an exit. Martha rushed to the chest of drawers and took out his service revolver as the curtain fell. A shot rang out.

After a moment's stunned silence, the audience began to applaud, doubtfully at first, and then with increasing confidence and enthusiasm. Charles looked at Lydia. Lydia looked at Charles. They hated it. But – all around them, the audience was applauding, and they had been in the business long enough to know a success when they heard it.

Very different was the occasion at the Princess Theatre next night. Elsie Carstairs, for the sake of her favourite nephew, and in honour of her new position as co-director of the theatre, had drummed up a fine selection of what Mrs Brewster approvingly assessed as 'nobs', all sporting their best jewellery and generating an air of excitement. In spite of the advance publicity, they had been obliged to paper the house (a fact which they had been careful to keep from Edwin) but Charles's and Lydia's theatrical friends had also rallied round, and all who were not working were there in the stalls, having drawn satis-factory oohs and aahs from the small crowd outside and from the gallery. The stage was set, as far as it could possibly be arranged, for what they hoped the gossip columns would describe as 'a glittering occasion'.

But it very soon became evident that something was wrong. Whenever Charles had made his entrance, he had been greeted with a spontaneous burst of applause, the audience responding not only to his fame, but also to the surge of energy which entered with him. Edwin, coming on in his smart, new, well-fitting costume, could have been any nice young man playing a supporting role, and the round of applause, initiated by his family and friends, was faltering and uncertain.

'He's very good,' everyone said earnestly in the intervals, and so he was, but he was good in the way that an understudy is good – and not, at that, an understudy who has suddenly become a star. When he took his curtain call, despite the frantic clapping of his family and friends, and a few shrill whoops from the gallery, where the shopgirls thought that Edwin was 'ever so handsome', it was fearfully difficult to keep the applause going, and to raise the curtain for the third time was to invite the inevitable experience of thin and desperate clapping in a house already heading for the exit. Even the duel, to which Edwin had devoted so much thought and practice, achieved no more than a slight gasp, as he leaped down the staircase and turned to parry a blow at the last minute. It had no more effect than the feat of an acrobat at the circus, momentarily wondered at and then immediately forgotten.

Everyone was very high-spirited and congratulatory at the elegant Savoy supper party afterwards (with the exception of Mr Brewster, who had never yet pretended that he thought a failure was a success, and had no intention of starting now). But the real moment of truth came for Edwin next night, as he sat in the star dressing room, preparing to make up and go through the whole thing again. He looked at two newspapers which lay side by side before him. One read: 'Miss Martha Brett shocked some members of the audience by appearing on stage in her underwear, but gave a brilliant performance as the wife who abandons her husband for the man she loves, only to discover that he can no longer return her love. Mr Thomas Brett in *The Liar* has daringly told the story of those walking wounded of the Great War whose tragedy has never been portrayed before.' The other read: 'Lacking his father's fine talent and huge authority, Mr Edwin Brett's athleticism could not disguise the shallow nature of this old-fashioned play.'

Chapter Eleven

In spite of being produced in the thoroughly un-fashionable Little Theatre in the Euston Road, Thomas's play achieved a thoroughly fashionable success, with queues outside the box office every day. Martha insisted that it all derived from her final appearance in her camibockers. (Harrods, superior-quality crêpe de Chine with needlerun lace and low-cut back for evening wear, thirty-nine and six.) Certainly, the photograph of her in the *Daily Sketch* which so shocked Flora had something to do with it. But journalists from such respectable papers as the *Times*, the *Telegraph* and the *Morning Post* came to interview Thomas, describing him as a remarkable young dramatist, and photographing him looking world-weary and enigmatic in the garden room, or in the summerhouse, which was usually used for storing deckchairs, but somehow seemed more appropriate than the nursery.

Meanwhile Edwin struggled on at the Princess Theatre with ever-diminishing audiences.

'I don't know why Master Eddie doesn't try his hand at the motion pictures instead,' said Flora. 'He's got the looks for it. Better than John Gilbert any day.'

Sutton shook his head, pityingly. He sometimes thought Flora was going soft in the head with those damned moving pictures of hers.

'And at least,' added Flora, 'if nobody comes to watch you in a picture, you don't know anything about it.'

Sutton looked at her, startled. Not for the first time, Flora had brought him up short. She was right there.

They heard the swing door to the kitchen banged open, as with a sharp blow from a wooden cleaning-box, and heavy footsteps approached.

'She never thinks of the paintwork,' said Sutton, irritably.

Flora glanced at him reproachfully.

'Just making your tea, Mrs Chapman,' she called.

Mrs Chapman had been the charwoman at Nightingale Grove for the past six months. As she said, if the housemaid just kept the dust down, she could give it a 'proper clean through' once a week. She arrived early in the morning, had breakfast, a cup of tea and a bit of bread and dripping at eleven, and left after dinner, which Flora always ensured should consist of a good meal of meat and potatoes. Mrs Chapman's husband had been killed in the war, and their children were now all married and had left home. Flora suspected that this midday dinner at Nightingale Grove was the only proper meal that Mrs Chapman had all week.

'Did I hear someone say a cup of tea?' inquired Hegarty, entering unexpectedly from the back door.

'Mr Hegarty!' exclaimed Flora. 'I think you smell it!'

'Well, Mr Brett wants the car at eleven, so I thought there might be just time for a quick one.'

Hegarty, sitting down, saw Mrs Chapman taking the cork out of a medicine bottle, and putting it quietly to her lips.

'Now, don't tell me, Mrs Chapman,' he said, 'that you've taken to strong liquor in the middle of the day!'

'Really, Mr Hegarty!' said Flora, reprovingly, putting his cup of tea in front of him.

'I wish it was,' Mrs Chapman replied. She took a swallow from the medicine bottle, and made a face. 'Ugh! The doctor gives it to me for wind, but, I don't know, I think it makes it worse.'

She corked the medicine bottle and put it away in her pocket, and stirred her tea.

'Where's the guv'nor off to?' inquired Sutton, who always liked to know exactly what was going on.

'Interview with the new theatre manager,' replied Hegarty. 'Mr Piers Longford-Price, related to Lord Wishbury.'

'Why should *he* need a job, if he's related to a lord?' demanded Flora.

'Ah, Miss Evans,' said Hegarty, 'there's a great many needing jobs since the war that never needed them before.'

'Longford-Price, eh?' said Sutton. 'Hm. Sounds a bit posh for a theatre manager.'

He never did like anyone being allowed inside the family circle without his knowledge.

'By the way, Mr Hegarty,' he added, 'would you have a look in the back of the car? Mr Thomas has mislaid his cigarette case.'

'I can tell you here and now it's not there,' answered Hegarty. 'The mistress asked me to make sure her emerald brooch hadn't slipped down behind, and I had a good search this morning. There's not so much as a speck of dust hidden in that car.'

'It's not that silver cigarette case Miss Martha gave him for the first night of his play, is it?' said Flora. 'Oh, don't tell me something else has gone missing!'

Mrs Chapman looked up from her tea and bread and dripping.

'Gone missing?' she said. 'Funny you should say that. I can't find my purse.'

Sutton and Flora exchanged a quick, horrified glance.

'Oh, Mrs Chapman!' exclaimed Flora. 'Wherever did you put it?'

'Well, I put it in the pocket of my pinny, same as I always do. And when I was polishing the hall floor, I took it out to get to me 'ankercher', and I'd swear I put it down on that little table outside the study. Then when I went back to look for it, it wasn't there.'

'Wherever can it be?' said Flora.

'Oh, don't worry, Miss Evans,' said Mrs Chapman, comfortably. 'It must be somewhere in the house. It'll turn up.'

Charles, briskly entering the study, saw Jean with her back to him. She turned quickly, her hands behind her back, and he received an impression that she was disconcerted.

'I'm sorry, Miss Lacy,' he said. 'Did I startle you?'

'Oh – no – I was just – Did you want me?'

'Just to say that I'm off to the Garrick,' said Charles. 'I'm having lunch there with Mr Longford-Price, settling terms and so on. He won't be starting until Monday, but I thought perhaps you might meet him at the theatre office this afternoon, show him the ropes.'

'Oh, but – Mr Brett,' Jean protested, 'I don't know anything about running a theatre.'

'No,' replied Charles, airily, 'but you've given a hand in the office now and then. You know where everything is filed and so on.'

'Er – well –'

'I'll tell him you'll meet him there about half-past two,' said Charles, and was gone.

'Oh, I found my purse, Miss Evans,' said Mrs Chapman, as Flora put her plate of dinner in front of her.

It was part of the lingering below-stairs class system that Mrs Chapman didn't eat with the rest of the staff, but had her dinner on the corner of the kitchen table, before the cloth was laid.

'What a relief!' said Flora. 'Where was it, then?'

'Well, it was on that little table outside the study. But I'd swear I looked for it there before. My eyes must be going wonky.'

'Nothing missing from it, I hope?' inquired Sutton, casually.

'I never looked,' replied Mrs Chapman, 'but I'm sure there wouldn't be, would there? I 'spect I just put it down on the floor, and someone picked it up and put it on the table, and that's where I found it.'

She took a satisfying mouthful of meat and potatoes, but Sutton's eyes met Flora's above her head.

Jean had her lunch on a tray in the study as usual, and then travelled to Shaftesbury Avenue by underground train. She walked in on Piers Longford-Price at the theatre office of the Princess Theatre much as Charles had walked in on her in the study, and found him ransacking the drawers of the desk. Unlike her, however,

Piers was quite undismayed at being taken by surprise.

'Hullo,' he said. 'You must be Miss Lacy. Thank goodness you're here! I'm just trying to find my way about.'

'Oh,' said Jean. 'I'm afraid I won't be much good –'

'I don't believe that,' said Piers. 'Mr Brett said you were one in a million.'

Jean felt herself blushing.

'I'm sure he said no such thing!'

Piers laughed and stood up. He had a thin, almost haggard face, and dark eyes, but when he smiled or laughed, his whole face seemed to glow, rather as a lighthouse sends a warm, friendly beam briefly out into the darkness.

'Well, perhaps what he said was that you were invaluable,' he said, 'and I'm sure you *are*.'

He held out his hand, and Jean took it with a hint of hesitation. She was not accustomed to human physical contact, and so almost shrank from it. But Piers's thin hand was cool and yet comforting, as though he understood her hesitation, and yet gently gave her reassurance. It was reassuring, too, that he released her hand immediately, and became businesslike.

'Now,' he said, 'if you can show me where everything is, I'd be most grateful.'

'Yes, of course,' said Jean.

She took off her hat and coat and set to work.

'You know, I'm beginning to think our Miss Lacy is a bit of a dark horse,' remarked Hegarty, that evening. 'You'd never guess where I saw her today. Going into a pawn shop.'

Sutton and Flora looked at each other, startled, and Hegarty glanced between them, amused. For all his friendly, easygoing ways, he sometimes had the air of a man who was a visitor, rather than precisely belonging to the world in which he now lived and worked.

'That's what *I* thought,' he said. 'Either she has expenses we never knew about, or else she plays the horses – and that's something I never knew about, either!'

'Well, Mr Hegarty,' remarked Flora, primly, 'that's her business, I'm sure.'

But it was very different next afternoon when Sutton and Flora were alone in the house. It was Emily's afternoon off. Martha had a matinée, and Thomas had gone to the Little Theatre to make sure she didn't play ducks and drakes with his lines. And Hegarty had driven Charles and Lydia, dressed up to the nines, to Ascot.

'I couldn't do it!' cried Flora. 'I couldn't, really!'

'You must admit', said Sutton, 'that this thieving began just when she arrived.'

'I dare say. But someone else arrived just then, too.'

'I thought you liked Hegarty.'

'So I do. But I like to see fair play.'

'Hegarty doesn't have the run of the house, and she does.'

'He goes into the hall,' said Flora, 'and the garden room. And now and then Miss Lydia or the master ask him to bring something down from upstairs.'

'It's not the same,' said Sutton, obstinately. 'She has the run of the house, night and day. And she was seen going into a pawn shop.'

'Then we won't find anything, will we?'

'Might find some pawn tickets.'

'Never!' said Flora, with that touch of practical realism

which always surprised him. 'She'd keep them in her purse!'

'We don't know what else she's nicked,' said Sutton. 'You know what this family is for leaving things about. They come home tired from the theatre. The guv'nor chucks his cuff-links down on his dressing chest. Miss Liddy takes off her jewellery and leaves it on her dressing table. They all leave money lying about.'

'And why shouldn't they?' said Flora. 'If they can't trust the people in their own house –'

'Exactly,' said Sutton.

So it was that Flora, deeply uneasy, found herself preparing to enter the little room, which was now Jean's room.

'Supposing she comes home and catches me?' she said, feeling like a criminal.

'Not she!' replied Sutton. 'I heard her telling the guv'nor that she'd brought these papers home from the theatre office to sort them out, and if he didn't need her, she'd take them back there, and "leave everything in order for Mr Longford-Price". Oh, very prim and proper she was, real little Sunday School Miss. I only hope they didn't leave no petty cash lying about!'

'Now, Mr Sutton, you don't know –'

'No, and we never shall, unless we do something about it.'

Flora crept into the little room, feeling like a thief herself. It was odd, after all these years, to have the notion that she had no business there. There was very little sign of Miss Lacy's occupancy of the room – just a cheap brush and comb on the dressing table, and a cheap alarm clock by the bed.

Well, if she *is* a thief, she doesn't spend much on herself, that's certain, thought Flora.

She would have turned back there and then, but Sutton was in the doorway, and gestured at her indignantly.

Flora opened the top drawer of the dressing table, very slowly and quietly, as though she was afraid of being caught doing it. Inside she saw a pair of cotton gloves, a couple of scarves, a string of beads, and a home-made handkerchief sachet. She lifted the handkerchief sachet. It felt heavy. Inside it was a silver cigarette case.

'Oh no!' said Flora.

She searched further amongst the handkerchiefs and found an emerald brooch, a pair of gold cuff-links and a pair of dangling ear-rings which she recognized. They were Martha's.

Just like Miss Martha, she thought, not to know she'd lost them.

She turned to show Sutton.

'Like mother, like daughter,' he said, grimly, and held out his hand.

'What shall we do now?' inquired Flora, when they were safely back in the kitchen. 'I couldn't face her, I couldn't, really.'

'I'll deal with it,' Sutton replied. 'You go off to the pictures.'

'You'll have to tell the mistress,' said Flora.

'I'll think about it,' said Sutton.

He had no intention of telling Miss Liddy if he could avoid it. She was so blooming soft-hearted, she'd given half a dozen chances to Betty Lacy, and she'd probably do the same to Jean. Sutton had no intention of giving her the opportunity, not if he could help it. He lay in wait behind the kitchen door until he heard Jean let herself in at the front door. He'd soon have that key off her, he thought, and stepped out.

'Miss Lacy,' he said, 'I wonder if I might have a word with you.'

She looked startled for a moment.

'Oh – yes, of course,' she said. 'As a matter of fact, *I* wanted to speak to *you*.'

I'll bet you did! thought Sutton. And then, aloud, 'Perhaps you'd come into the kitchen – if you wouldn't feel that that is demeaning yourself too much?'

'No, of course –'

He thought he saw a flash of anger in her eyes as she realized that his tone was ironic.

'It's just that I wanted a word with you in private,' she said, very quietly.

'There's no one here,' replied Sutton. 'Just you and me.'

He held the door open for her. It was a trick he'd often used before, and it worked this time. She walked through like a circus animal trotting through the open grille into the ring. Sutton followed her, but she spoke before he could.

'It's about these things which have been – been going missing,' she said.

'That's what I wanted to talk to you about,' said Sutton.

'That's what I thought,' she said.

Sutton took the cigarette case and other things out of his pocket and put them on the table, and then she did look angry.

'But I didn't think you'd search my room,' she said.

Sutton met her eyes calmly, and she turned away and

sat down. Now comes the sob story, he thought, but she surprised him.

'I found the pawn tickets in Mrs Chapman's purse,' she said.

'Oh, come on, Miss Lacy!' said Sutton.

'I spotted her at once.'

'Spotted her?'

'I saw her taking a swig out of that bottle when she was cleaning the stairs.'

'That was medicine.'

'It always is,' said Jean. 'She kept a bag of mints in her pocket, and sucked one afterwards to hide the smell.'

'Mrs Chapman', said Sutton, 'has been working here for six months.'

'My mother was Mrs Brett's dresser for ten years,' said Jean. 'They start by taking a bit of money here and there, and when it isn't missed, they get careless.'

'They?'

'Drunks,' said Jean, flatly. 'Don't forget, I lived with one for twenty years. I expect Mrs Chapman is a bit unsteady on her feet now and then.'

'She has dizzy spells.'

'So did my mother.'

She looked up at Sutton.

'I can give you the address of the pawn shop. They'll tell you that Mrs Chapman pawned the things. She said that her mistress had been gambling, and didn't want her husband to know. She took a bit of a chance with the emerald brooch, but she said it was just imitation, and settled for a few pounds. That's what my mother used to do.'

There was a brief silence.

'Why didn't you tell me or the mistress?' asked Sutton.

'I don't know,' she replied, and hesitated. 'I suppose I

thought I could – deal with it myself.' She hesitated again. 'What will you do?'

'Oh, I see,' said Sutton, amused. 'You thought I'd be the 'ard-'earted butler and give her the sack on the spot. No, I think if I show her the evidence of the crime, and give her a sharp warning – She'll've missed the pawn tickets by now, that'll make her think! She won't do it again.'

Once more Jean surprised him.

'Oh yes, she will,' she said, 'as soon as the bottle is empty. She'll do anything to get another one, no matter what promises she's made. She'll steal anything, pawn anything – even her wedding ring.'

Sutton looked at her, startled. How could that smooth little face, with its childishly round shape, look suddenly so hard and so old?

'Well, I –' He was at a loss, which didn't often happen to him. 'I don't know what we can do, then, except –'

'I thought perhaps', said Jean, 'that possibly – There is a vacancy for a cleaner at the theatre. The ushers go through the theatre after the performance looking for lost property, and by the time the cleaners come in the morning, everything's locked up tight. There's nothing left lying about – no temptation. I think I could probably persuade –'

Sutton, a sharp-eyed observer, saw a little colour come into her cheeks.

'I think Mr Longford-Price would give her the job. I'd have to tell him, of course.'

She stood up, and turned towards the door, but paused and looked back at him.

'By the way, I'll be giving in my notice, anyway.'

'Here, just a minute!' said Sutton, startled again. 'Don't let's be hasty.'

'Supposing something else "goes missing"?' said Jean. 'You'd never be quite sure it wasn't me, would you? "Like mother, like daughter."'

She saw the expression on Sutton's face, and smiled, but the smile was a very grim one for such a young woman.

'The Bretts will always leave valuable things lying around. I sometimes thought –' her voice hardened – 'I sometimes thought that it wasn't quite fair of Mrs Brett to leave such valuable things lying on her dressing table, and all that money in her bag, when other people –' She stopped short. 'I know you won't like my saying this.'

'Not like your saying it?' said Sutton.

Suddenly his old hard-working middle-class background claimed him for its own.

'The way this family carries on, I wonder they're not stolen blind. They deserve to be, that's certain! But they'll never change their ways. They're like royalty. They depend on being looked after by a lot of loyal servants who'll protect them from the follies of their ways.'

'Oh!' said Jean.

Sutton grinned at her.

'I don't know why everyone thinks I'm a mug, just because I play the part of the butler. When I was a young actor –'

'You were an *actor*?' repeated Jean, astonished.

'Yes – well – I don't tell everyone that.'

He saw her expression change again. For a young woman who seemed so self-contained, she had a dangerous way of allowing her emotions to show in her face when she was off her guard.

'Miss Lydia often sent me out to buy a bottle of stout –'

Jean's face hardened again.

'You must have had some difficulty in keeping it away from my mother,' she said.

'Ah come on, now,' said Sutton. 'We're none of us angels, and this was long before your mother's time. "Keep the change, Alfred," Miss Liddy used to say, and she'd give me five bob. I knew it was more than she really meant, but – it didn't mean nothing to her, and I had my rent to pay. Was that stealing?'

'Well, I –'

'Or, take my dad – he had a greengrocer's shop. If you'd seen the way he used to juggle the tomatoes so that the customer got the rotten ones from the back instead of the nice, bright shiny ones she thought she'd bought, you'd say he belonged on the halls – or in gaol!'

Jean laughed, and then suddenly was crying. She tried to stop, and struggled to apologize, but Sutton patted her shoulder.

'Now, now,' he said, comfortingly. 'You've been going through a bad time, haven't you? In fact, I doubt if you've ever had many good ones.'

That broke the floodgates. Jean sat down and put her face on her arms and sobbed aloud. Sutton knew better than to try and stop her. He could only guess at the years of lonely struggle, starting in her childhood, to save her mother, while always being dragged down herself, and at the dreadful mixture of guilt and resentment so long repressed, even at her mother's funeral, which now was being washed away at last.

'I'll put the kettle on,' said Sutton, when she had nearly cried herself out.

She started up, trying to pull herself together.

'Oh – no – I –'

'You get the cups,' said Sutton. 'And look out for the chipped ones. Emily's idea of washing up is to put everything in the bowl and stir it round with the mop.'

He had the satisfaction of seeing her smile, as she wiped her eyes and went towards the dresser.

They sat drinking their tea in companionable silence. Jean glanced round the comfortable old kitchen and then caught Sutton's eye.

'I like this house,' she said. 'Do you know, I think it's the first real home I've ever been in.'

'Is your father dead?' inquired Sutton.

'I don't know. He left when I was three. He said he was going to Australia, and he'd send for us, but he never did. I suppose that's when she took to drink.'

She finished her tea and put the cup down, as though putting everything else behind her, too.

'I suppose Mrs Brett will have to know,' she said. 'I mean, about Mrs Chapman.'

'I'll tell her,' answered Sutton, 'That is, unless *you* –?'

'Oh no!' said Jean, hastily. 'I'd much rather you did.'

'Don't worry,' said Sutton, 'I'll tell her it was you that sorted it all out. Credit where credit is due.'

Jean smiled wryly.

'I don't think I managed it very well,' she said.

'Still,' said Sutton, 'it's all worked out for the best in the end.'

She glanced at him shyly, stood up, and prepared to take the cups to the scullery.

'You leave them,' said Sutton. 'I'll wash them up. Won't leave them to Emily's tender care.'

She smiled at him again, and that little shared joke was, once more, companionable. She turned towards the door, and then paused.

'You – you're sure I shouldn't give in my notice?'

'You'd better not!' said Sutton. 'The last time the guv'nor tried to manage on his own, we had the duns at the door. This time, it'd probably be the bailiffs in the house!'

She looked back at him very gravely.

'Thank you, Mr Sutton,' she said.

He very nearly said, 'Call me "Alfred",' but not quite.

Chapter Twelve

The fact that Lydia intended to be a good deal more than a sleeping partner in the running of the Princess Theatre was soon made clear to Charles, and, suitably enough, in their bedroom. The chief disadvantage of having a partner who was also your wife was that she could always get you alone sooner or later, and usually at your most defenceless moments.

Because she had worked in revue and been a quick-change artist, Lydia dressed and undressed extremely quickly, and was always reclining on the pillows in a becoming bedjacket while Charles was still pottering about in his dressing room. He dressed and undressed very slowly and methodically, just as he did in the theatre, putting everything in its proper place. This ritual was his way of disposing of the strains and stresses of the day, just as in the theatre he laid aside the performance with his clothes and make-up. On this particular night, he had just paused to examine himself in the mirror on his dressing chest, trying to decide whether he was or was not getting a double chin. Fatal for 'the profile' that would be! It was at that moment that Lydia called, 'Charles! We shall have to do something!'

Charles started uneasily. He despised vanity in actors, and always fondly believed that he himself was not vain, so he turned hastily away from the mirror, and felt that Lydia, even if she had not seen him, already had him at a disadvantage as he came to the door of the bedroom with his tie and collar off and his braces hanging down his back.

'Do something about what?' he inquired, grumpily.

Usually, when they were out of work, they read play scripts before they went to sleep, but Lydia was not reading a play. She was studying the returns from the Princess Theatre.

'These returns are appalling,' she said. 'We simply cannot allow *The King Shall Not Die* to bleed us white.'

'Oh,' said Charles.

'Yes, "Oh",' said Lydia.

Charles had always felt guilty about persuading Edwin to take over from him. It had been a bad error of judgement, and Edwin had suffered for it. Charles felt all the worse because he knew that it was his own reputation and popularity which had ensured Edwin's failure.

'If it had been anyone but Edwin, you'd have taken it off at the end of the first week,' Lydia continued. 'I don't know how we've managed to keep it going so long.'

'No – well –'

She did not know, and Charles devoutly hoped that she never would know that he had mortgaged Nightingale Grove to get the necessary cash to keep the play going. He had told himself that he was just 'tiding it over', 'nursing the production along until it finds its audience again', 'giving the boy a chance', but he knew in his heart that he simply could not allow Edwin to suffer the humiliation of opening with such a fanfare and folding within a week because he wasn't as good as his father.

'You're not doing Edwin any favours,' said Lydia, looking at him over the top of her glasses like a particularly severe schoolteacher who just happened to be wearing a baby-blue bedjacket. 'It's soul-destroying to any actor to go on playing to an empty house. We must put the notice up immediately.'

Charles sat down and began to untie the laces of his patent-leather shoes. It meant that he had given in, though not entirely.

'That's all very well,' he said, 'but it's no good closing without having another production to come in, and we haven't found one yet.'

He looked distastefully at the pile of scripts on the floor by his side of the bed.

'I've been through all those, and there's nothing there for us. Or, indeed, anyone,' he added, gloomily. 'With all these authors who say they are panting to write for the stage, I can't imagine why one or two of them can't bestir themselves to write something decent.'

'You seem to forget', said Lydia, 'that we have an author in the family.'

'Who? Oh. Thomas.'

'Yes, Thomas. And he's just written a play which is a huge success. Martha says they're full every night, and could sell every seat four times over.'

'Just because they're prepared to traipse out to the Euston Road to see Martha in her knickers –'

'Camibocks.'

'If you ask me,' said Charles, momentarily distracted

from the main issue, 'they are a great deal more revealing than knickers and a camisole or whatever you call it.'

'A great deal more revealing,' Lydia agreed, calmly. 'That's why she chose them. I should have done the same. Anyway, it's not just a – a *succès de scandale*. It's a very good play. And it's modern. Just what we need.'

Charles had stood up and turned towards the dressing room with his shoes in his hand. He turned back in astonishment.

'You're not suggesting that we bring that – that depraved piece of Thomas's – whatever it's called –'

'It's called *The Liar*,' said Lydia. 'I got Martha to let me have a note of the takings. Here they are. They're doing better in the Euston Road than we are in Shaftesbury Avenue.'

Charles looked at the takings, and blinked.

'Yes, that's all very well,' he said, fighting what they both knew to be a rearguard action, 'but – a small cast, only two sets – it'll probably die the death in a big theatre like the Princess.'

'It's a very cheap get-in,' said Lydia, 'and if it doesn't go – though I'm pretty sure it will – it'll cost a lot less to run than *The King Shall Not Die*.'

She took her glasses off.

'Come on, Charlie, you know I'm right. You'd better get on to Giles Peabody first thing tomorrow and arrange to bring *The Liar* in as soon as possible. We won't be the only West End management after it, you know. In fact, we'll be lucky to get it.'

That was the clincher. Charles took his shoes through to the dressing room and began to put them on the shoe-trees. Lydia raised her voice.

'Who's going to tell Edwin?' she asked.

Charles turned his head towards the door, but didn't answer.

'If only it wasn't Thomas's play,' said Lydia.

She spoke more quietly, but Charles heard her.

'Why do you say that?'

'Because – it'll be so much worse for him, being ousted by his brother.'

But that wasn't what she meant, and they both knew it.

In the end, it was Charles who had to tell Edwin. He decided that it would be less hurtful if he kept it strictly formal – a management decision – and asked Piers Longford-Price if he could have a meeting alone with Edwin in the theatre office.

'Oh, certainly, sir,' replied Piers, with his usual ready smile. 'As a matter of fact, I'm meeting someone for lunch that day, so I'll just make it a little earlier than usual.'

Charles, looking down from the half-moon window of the theatre office into Shaftesbury Avenue, was slightly disconcerted to see that it was Martha who met Piers outside the Princess Theatre and went off with him, laughing, arm-in-arm.

Edwin took the bad news well. In his position, Thomas would have been a great deal less gracious.

'After all,' said Charles, 'the play had had its run, that was the trouble – and it wasn't a very good play in the first place.'

'The trouble was,' said Edwin, 'that, good or bad, you were able to carry it, and I wasn't.'

'Nonsense!' said Charles. 'A change of cast is always tricky.'

'Yes, Father, of course,' said Edwin.

Charles smiled, relieved, but at the door, Edwin paused, and spoke without looking at him.

'Do you know,' he remarked, 'I sometimes wish I had been born with ginger hair and buck teeth.'

The Liar was a huge success at the Princess Theatre. Fashionable people had realized, in their own mysterious and distinctly despicable way, that although this play was, my dear! too shocking! one absolutely *must* see it. And the genuine playgoer, recognizing beyond the camibockers something new and true and moving, passed on that even more mysterious something called 'word of mouth', which ensured that, not only the stalls and dress circle but the upper circle and gallery would be filled. The critics, having praised *The Liar* at its first production, but with reservations, now that they grasped the fact that it was a success (critics, like the fashionable people they tend to be, have their own antennae) discarded all reservations, and hailed Thomas Brett as a brilliant new playwright and congratulated themselves on having recognized his talent from the very beginning. For his part, Thomas, snatched in a moment, as it seemed, from total failure to unimaginable success, behaved like a small boy who has just discovered that it is his birthday, and that everyone has to do what *he* wants for a change. He was witty, impudent, clever, triumphant – and almost unbearable.

Edwin, fortunately, was not in London to witness the opening of *The Liar* at the Princess Theatre, and it was entirely due to Mr Brewster.

'My good lady wife,' he said, 'reckons that *The King Shall Not Die* would do very well on tour.'

'No, thank you!' Charles exclaimed. 'If I didn't want

to go on playing it in London, I certainly don't mean to exhaust myself taking it all round the provinces –'

'No, not you,' Brewster interrupted. 'Let young Edwin do it.'

'Oh,' said Charles. 'I wouldn't like to ask him. He hasn't proved a big enough draw here –'

'Maybe not,' said Brewster, 'but the provinces are different. They know it was successful in London with Mr Brett, and, after all, Edwin's played it in the West End, same as you. Just bill it as "the London production".' He added with that far-from-engaging frankness of his, 'They'll never know the difference.'

Mr Brewster, not for the first time, proved to be right. Edwin, tentatively approached, was perfectly willing to take the play on tour. The truth was, he was only too glad to get away as soon as possible from his failure and Thomas's success. And, as a matter of fact, having toured before, he had quite a following in the provincial theatres, just as any young, handsome actor can win a gratifying, if illusory fame in his local repertory theatre. So *The King Shall Not Die* played to full houses in all the best touring dates, and Edwin, warmed by such approbation, undoubtedly played the part a great deal better than in London.

Meanwhile, Brewster had another idea.

'I have an interest in the Queen Anne Theatre,' he said, 'and I wouldn't mind putting a bit of money into a production there – that is, if it suited.'

'Oh,' said Charles, gratified. 'Well, Mrs Brett and I haven't found a new play to suit us yet, but I'm sure a comedy revival –'

'Not interested in a revival,' said Brewster. 'I thought that son of yours, Thomas, might have a new play. Didn't like *The Liar* myself – nor did my wife! – but it was a big success. I reckon anything he wrote now would go.'

'Yes,' said Charles. 'I dare say it would.'

A sudden thought struck him.

'I thought you weren't interested in investing in the theatre any more.'

Brewster, astonishingly, seemed to be embarrassed.

'Well –' he said, 'it – it has to be the right production.'

Thomas, it emerged, had indeed written a new play, his first since the production of *The Liar*. He did not tell them that he had written it with fearful difficulty and with none of the old, self-confident *élan* he had enjoyed before. It was as though the success of *The Liar* had imbued him with a fear of failure. But it was done at last, and he was now sure that it was the best thing he had ever written.

'I hope it's a comedy,' said Charles. 'Your mother and I could do with a good comedy.'

'No, Father,' Thomas replied, kindly. 'It's not a comedy. It's more like Strindberg, or Ibsen.'

'Oh dear!' said Lydia. 'Ibsen never does well in the West End.'

'That's what Father said about *The Liar*,' said Thomas. 'It's called *Dark Dimensions* and I don't honestly think that it has any parts in it which would be suitable for you or Mother, though you're very welcome to read it, of course. There is a part for a younger woman which might suit Martha – but I need her in *The Liar*.'

He put his coffee cup down and rose.

'Anyway,' he said, 'I'll send a copy to Brewster, and see if he's interested. If he isn't, I'm sure plenty of other people will be.'

Lydia's eyes met Charles's as Thomas left the room.

'"Younger woman", indeed!' she said.

'"I need her in *The Liar*,"' said Charles. '*He* needs her! He's not the producer. He's only the bloody author!'

'The truth is,' said Lydia, 'that Thomas was a pain in the neck when he was unsuccessful, and now that he is successful, he is quite insufferable! I really would like to take him down a peg or two.'

If Nemesis was listening to her words, Nemesis must have been laughing her head off.

Charles, in bed with Lydia beside him, read *Dark Dimensions* through in total silence. When he had finished it, he closed the script, and sat staring straight ahead.

'Well?' inquired Lydia.

'*I* don't know,' Charles answered. '*I* don't like it – but then, I didn't like *The Liar*.'

He passed the script over. Lydia read it in total silence as well, and Charles had gone to sleep before she had finished it.

'Well,' he said next morning, 'what did you think of it?'

Lydia put on her bedjacket and plumped up her pillows, ready for her breakfast tray.

'I think it's utter rubbish,' she said. 'But then, I think most of Ibsen is utter rubbish, too.'

Brewster's reaction was very different.

'I hear that play of yours is very good,' he said. 'And that it has a nice part for a young lady in it.'

They were sitting in the small, dusty office from which Mr Brewster transacted his business when he was in London. (In Bradford, naturally, his business premises resembled rather the Acropolis in Athens, all pomp and pillars. No point in having brass, they said in Bradford, unless people know it.)

'Yes,' Thomas replied. 'I thought of it for Martha, but –'

'No, no,' said Brewster. 'Don't want to take her out of *The Liar*. Soon lose the audience if you do that.'

Thomas opened his mouth to remark that the success of the play did not depend wholly upon seeing Martha in her underwear, but Brewster was speaking again.

'I think I know a young lady,' he said, 'who might just suit the part.'

'Oh,' said Thomas, taken aback.

'Daphne Villiers.'

'I don't think I've heard of her.'

'I dare say not,' replied Brewster, flatly, 'but she's a talented girl, and I'd like to see her get her chance.'

A certain uneasiness began to creep into Thomas's gratification at the prospect of his play's production. Could it be that –? No, surely not! He found a natural means of prevarication.

'Well,' he said, conveniently forgetting all previous declarations that the author should have the last word in casting, 'naturally, the producer will have to decide –'

'Julian Williams has read the play,' remarked Brewster, casually, 'and he likes it very much.'

'Oh,' said Thomas.

'He's a bit too much of a nancy-boy for my taste,' said Brewster, 'but he seems to have quite a reputation.'

'Yes,' Thomas agreed.

It had occurred to him that he ought to offer his second play to Giles Peabody, in gratitude for giving him his first chance in the theatre. On the other hand, he and Giles had not always seen eye to eye about *The Liar*, and because it had been his first play, there had developed between them a sort of master–pupil relationship which Thomas did not wish to continue. The play had been a success, but Thomas felt an author's natural resentment at having had changes forced upon him. *He*, after all, was the creator. Perhaps the play would have been just as great a success without those changes, and would have remained much more his own. Next time –

'Julian Williams,' said Brewster, 'is quite prepared to produce the play, and he seems to think that Daphne Villiers would be just right for the leading female role.'

'Ah,' said Thomas.

Charles had taken it for granted that Thomas would want him to play the leading part in *Dark Dimensions*, and, since he was out of work, he was quite prepared to overcome his initial antipathy to the play. So, Thomas, returning from his meeting with Brewster, found Charles having tea with Lydia in the garden and carefully studying the typescript, pencil in hand.

'It's not a bad play,' he told Thomas. 'Just needs a bit more work on it, a bit more light and shade.'

'The central character has been blinded on the Somme, and you want jokes?'

'When we played to a blind ward during the war,' remarked Lydia, 'that's exactly what they *did* want. We made them laugh, and they made us cry.'

'That's not what *my* play is about!' said Thomas, in that state of irritable thin-skinnedness which every playwright suffers before the play is produced. 'It is a scorching condemnation of war and all its works –'

'So the central character is a sort of mouthpiece for your ideas?'

'Certainly not!'

Charles wasn't listening to either of them.

'Ah, the central character,' he said. 'That's the chief thing I wanted to talk to you about. As it's written, I really can't see myself playing the part, but there's no great problem. You've made him a young corporal. Now, if he's a senior officer –'

'Are we talking about the same play?' inquired Thomas.

'We will be,' said Charles, and made another pencil note in the margin. 'Now, this line: "The crown of thorns was barbed wire, the stigmata were the piercings of the bayonets . . ."'

'Well?' said Thomas, defiantly.

'Much too flowery. You wouldn't find a brigadier delivering a line like that.'

'I'm very sorry, Father,' said Thomas, exasperation beginning to be overtaken by amusement, 'but he is *not* a brigadier. He is a young corporal – a working-class lad, self-educated, with a gift for poetry. To get the full tragedy of the thing, he has to have been blinded before he had even begun to see, in the true sense of the word.'

Charles ignored everything except the one crucial fact.

'If he's as young as all that,' he said, 'the other part wouldn't be suitable for your mother. What I suggest is that – all right, make him working class, if you like – I dare say I could manage that – but make him, say, thirty-five to forty, and make the girl his wife.'

'I'm afraid that is out of the question,' said Thomas. 'The part of the girl is already cast.'

'*What?*'

Thomas endeavoured to sound businesslike, matter of fact – and not in the least defensive.

'The producer, Julian Williams, has seen her, and –'

'You're not letting that pansy produce the play?' inquired Charles.

'He's very sensitive – much more sensitive than Giles Peabody.'

'That's what I mean,' said Charles. 'Besides, you know I always direct my own plays.'

'Where did he find this girl?' inquired Lydia. 'And what is her name?'

'Daphne Villiers,' answered Thomas, and then decided that he had better tell them the truth, since they were bound to find out later. 'She's a – a protégée of Brewster's. He has great faith in her talent.'

'And he won't put the play on unless she plays the leading part?'

'It's not really the leading part,' said Thomas. 'It's just the ingenue role. She's only twenty-three and hasn't much experience, but –'

'Twenty-three!' exclaimed Charles. '*I* can't play opposite *her*! It'd look like baby-snatching.'

'Charles, darling,' said Lydia, 'Thomas doesn't *want* you in the play. He doesn't want either of us in the play. And I think he's quite right. It's not our style at all.'

'Oh well,' said Charles, greatly miffed, 'if that's the case, there's no point in my doing any more work on the piece.'

He threw the script down on the table, and wound his silver propelling pencil up and put it away in his breast pocket. Thomas finished his cold and rather stewed cup of tea.

'None at all,' he said.

He picked up the script, which now had a very nasty tea stain on the front cover, something he particularly disliked.

'But, thank you all the same, Father,' said Thomas, with exquisite courtesy.

When he had departed, Charles and Lydia looked at each other.

'I must say,' Lydia remarked, 'I never imagined Mr Brewster as having a light o' love.'

'I suppose,' said Charles, dropping into his 'oop North' accent, 'that with the lady wife up in Bradford –'

'It still doesn't seem like him,' said Lydia. 'I mean, that he should be so blatant about it. Of course, she could be his niece –'

'I'll tell you what doesn't seem right to me,' Charles broke in, 'and that is that my son should agree to have this girl in his play, when she is obviously totally unqualified and entirely unsuitable.'

'Oh, come on, Charlie!' said Lydia, smiling. 'You and I have often, in our younger days, agreed to play opposite charming young men and pretty young girls who were totally unqualified and entirely unsuitable, but just happened to be the dear friends of the manager or the producer, or the principal backer.'

'Huh!' said Charles, somewhat mollified. 'I suppose that's true, although recently I always seem to be including in the cast some doddering old fool just because he's somebody's father. Talking of which – I had a letter from Mother today.'

'Oh,' said Lydia, and endeavoured to convey in face and voice a cordial interest. 'How are they?'

'She says he's doing too much, as usual,' Charles replied. 'They were just off on a tour of Galway. Galway! I ask you! During the potato famine, the people of Galway, even though they were starving, didn't have enough sense to eat the lobsters in the sea. I can't see them being riveted by a rendering of *Romeo and Juliet*, as performed by Mother and Father.'

It was a great relief, thought Lydia, that Charles found his parents as irritating as she did. Why on earth couldn't they retire into decent obscurity and a nice seaside bungalow like her own parents?

'I just hope', she said, 'that your father doesn't try to climb the balcony.'

Chapter Thirteen

In his folly, Thomas had believed that during the rehearsals of *Dark Dimensions*, he would suffer none of the torments he had endured with *The Liar*. It was, after all, his second play, and he was now a successful author. Martha would not be in the cast to drive him mad, and Giles Peabody would not be there to treat him like an absolute beginner, an ignoramus, as though he had not been born and brought up in the theatre! He had yet to learn that every play has its own agonies, and that the author, unless he is as ferocious as W. S. Gilbert, as brilliantly and wittily destructive as Noël Coward and as disagreeable when crossed as George Bernard Shaw, is always treated as an intruder into mysteries of which he knows nothing, and that his work, unlike that of any other artist, is considered to be nothing more than a rough sketch, to be changed and improved by any hand which finds itself nearby with a pencil, preferably an indelible one.

In the present instance, Thomas found that he had an additional and quite new source of anguish – an actress who not only could not act, but seemed to be quite incapable of delivering a line correctly even when she knew it, which was not often. The Brett family slipped into speeches as lightly and elegantly as they slipped into costumes, and Charles and Lydia, easygoing as they often seemed, were fiercely selective when it came to casting, flatly refusing to work with amateurs or incompetents. Daphne Villiers was both. It would have been funny, if it had not been so painful, to see how many wrong inflexions she could find in one line. And then, the actor who was playing Ronald – he was handsome enough, and had a sort of determined dash about him, and Julian Williams said he was extremely gifted, which possibly he was, but there was something not quite convincing in his performance, and the same was true of his cockney accent.

'A bit "on again, off again", old boy, if you ask me,' Thomas could hear his grandfather saying.

Huddled in the stalls, a week before the opening night, Thomas watched his hero in dark glasses and carrying a white stick as he pronounced the moving words: 'To catch the last of the light. A distant glimmer.'

Daphne was late on her cue as usual.

'Er – for how long?' she said.

The next line should have been spoken quietly, but the actor seemed to think that he ought to prove that, like Mr Peggotty, he was rough, sir, but he was ready.

'To the ends of time, if I have to.'

'Then *there*,' said Daphne, firmly, 'will be light enough for both of us.'

Julian Williams rose up from his seat in the row in front of Thomas.

'Daphne, darling,' he said, 'I think it should be, "*Then* there will be light enough for *both* of us." Or possibly, "Then there will be *light* enough for *both* of us." '

'Oh,' said Daphne. 'Um. What did I say?'

Thomas saw Julian's shoulders droop, but he answered kindly.

'Don't worry, Daphne dear. Just – have another look at the script; the meaning gives the intonation, you know.'

'Oh,' said Daphne, blankly. 'Yes.'

Julian raised his voice.

'All right, everyone!' he called. 'Break for lunch. Back at two o'clock sharp.'

He turned back to Thomas, and, amidst the general bustle, he said softly, 'Don't worry, dear boy, I'll get a performance out of her.'

'Before the first night?' inquired Thomas.

'Perhaps you could help her out a bit more,' said Julian. 'Have a look at her speeches in the second act – see if you could trim them a bit. She does have trouble remembering lines –'

'Let alone saying them,' said Thomas. 'Her part is cut to the bone now.'

'Yes – well – just see what you can do. Oh – by the way – while we're talking about difficult lines – Ronald –'

'What about Ronald?' asked Thomas, sharply.

'Graham is still having a little trouble with that "barbed-wire, crown-of-thorns" speech.'

'I am *not* cutting that!' said Thomas.

Graham, no longer in dark glasses and having discarded his white stick, vaulted athletically down from the stage.

'Ready, Julian?' he called.

'Coming!' responded Julian, suddenly bright and cheerful. He smiled at Thomas. 'Don't worry,' he said. 'Everything's going to be fine.'

In that state of gloom which can only be produced by the producer telling you twice in two minutes not to worry, Thomas sat staring at Daphne's part in Act Two. When an actress of Martha's quality had trouble with a line, then, maddening as it was, it probably meant that there was something wrong with it. But what did you do with an actress who had trouble with every line, good or bad? He became aware of Daphne approaching, and felt a deep loathing for her, as though she was a vandal deliberately destroying his masterpiece.

'I'm awfully sorry,' she said. 'I hope I won't ruin your marvellous play.'

Thomas reluctantly stood up, script and pencil in hand.

'Of course you won't,' he said. The lie stuck in his teeth, but he knew enough to know that actors and actresses needed confidence, or they couldn't go on at all. 'You're going to be very good,' he said.

'For an amateur?' she said.

She saw his expression, and smiled.

'I heard Graham say that. "My dear, she's a perfect amateur!" He was right, of course.'

Suddenly Thomas saw her as she was – not a vandal or a cretin, but a nice, pretty girl, who had been put in an impossible position, and was intelligent enough to know it. He smiled at her.

'Let's go and have lunch at the Savoy Grill,' he said. 'I think we deserve it.'

'I'm sure *I* don't deserve it,' said Daphne.

'But you need it,' replied Thomas, 'which is often the same thing.'

⧆

The luncheon was a great success. The head waiter ushered Thomas in with a respect which all the other guests could not fail to notice, and they all nudged each other and said, very audibly, 'My dear! Thomas Brett! You know – that quite shocking play, *The Liar*. And *who* is that very pretty girl with him?'

'Goodness!' said Daphne. 'Everyone knows you!'

'They'll all know you,' replied Thomas, 'once *Dark Dimensions* has opened.'

He saw a sparkle in her eyes. She had, after all, aspirations to be an actress, and perhaps confidence was all she needed.

'If they do,' she said, 'it will be entirely because of your play. So marvellous, so – so *deep*.'

Thomas knew that, although she was not a fool, Daphne was not, on the other hand, precisely an intellectual. She really did not understand the deeper meaning of the play at all. On the other hand – he had not asked Jean to type this play, because she was so busy working at the theatre office, when she was not answering Charles's letters or paying his bills. So he had had it typed by a professional typing agency, which, anyway, seemed more appropriate to his new status. He had thought of asking Jean to read it, but decided against it. She was busy, and – there really wasn't much point. His parents had hated the play, and Brewster had said it was good simply because it had a part for Daphne. In the same way, he knew that Julian Williams had agreed to direct the play chiefly because he saw in the part of Ronald an opportunity for his friend, Graham. At least Daphne was sincere when she said she liked the play, and just now he badly needed reassurance, in spite of all his outward show of confidence. He reached across and put his hand on hers.

'It's very sweet of you to say so,' he said. 'I'm awfully glad you're playing the part. I really am.'

Martha's voice spoke above them.

'Well, well! Don't tell me you're playing truant from rehearsals.'

Trust Martha to be there at exactly that moment! thought Thomas. He stood up, firmly keeping Daphne's hand in his.

'Oh, Martha,' he said, 'I want you to meet my very charming leading lady, Daphne Villiers. My sister, Martha Brett.'

Daphne threw him a grateful glance, as she drew her hand away and stood up. That showed her inexperience, thought Thomas. Martha would have remained firmly seated, taking it for granted that, whatever the circumstances, *she* was the superior talent.

'Of course –' said Daphne, and her north-country accent crept nervously in. 'I mean – I'm a great admirer of yours, Miss Brett.'

'How very kind of you,' replied Martha – but Thomas knew that she was inwardly saying, 'Sit down, you fool! You're the leading actress of a new play, lunching with the author. Play the part!'

'Won't you join us?' said Thomas.

'No, thanks,' Martha replied. 'I'm meeting someone – Oh, there he is.'

Thomas saw Piers Longford-Price signalling to her from a table in the corner. Trust Martha, he thought, to have added the new manager of the Princess Theatre to her bag.

It happened – Nemesis, perhaps, having arranged it – that Charles and Lydia were in London that weekend. Usually, at that time of year, if they weren't playing, they went away for the weekend, but Lydia's friend, Maud Protheroe, was giving a coming-out ball for her daughter, Anthea. Lydia had agreed to be there in the cause of friendship, and Charles for the sake of matrimonial peace and quiet.

In fact, Lydia being a cockney born and bred, and Charles having a London-born father and a Dublin-born mother, they both rather enjoyed that subtle pleasure, appreciated by Keats and Charles Lamb, of an early summer weekend in London, even when, as now, the rain, beating upon the late lilac blooms and the early rosebuds, had driven them indoors. Martha put her head round the door, having discovered – Nemesis again? – that she had left her favourite pair of evening shoes at Nightingale Grove.

'You're cutting it a bit fine for getting back to the theatre, aren't you?' said Charles.

'I might be, Pa, dear,' Martha replied, 'if you hadn't kindly suggested that Hegarty should drive me there.'

'Really?' said Charles. 'I don't remember.'

'Dear Pa,' said Martha. 'You're getting old.'

'I may be getting old,' said Charles, 'but there's nothing wrong with my memory. If you want a chauffeur, why don't you hire one of your own? We're paying you enough.'

'Thank you, Pa,' said Martha, 'but I prefer Hegarty. He really is rather attractive.'

Lydia's attention was caught.

'Martha,' she said, 'you leave Hegarty alone.'

'Don't worry, Mother,' Martha replied, 'just at the

moment, I have other fish to fry. Talking of which – guess who I saw lunching at the Savoy Grill today, and holding hands, what's more?'

Charles and Lydia looked at each other blankly, and then at her.

'Thomas and his new leading lady,' said Martha. 'Miss Daphne Villiers.'

'Oh dear!' said Lydia. 'I met Sheila Paton at the dressmaker's yesterday. She's playing the mother, you know. She said the girl was embarrassingly untalented.'

'She's very pretty,' said Martha.

Charles began to laugh. Lydia eyed him suspiciously.

'What's funny about that?'

'Just that I'm sure Brewster thought that she was extremely pretty. But it looks as though Thomas is cutting him out. It serves him right!'

At about the time that Martha was rummaging for her evening shoes, Sutton was sitting with his feet up, drinking a cup of tea and reading the *Evening News*.

'I see Mr Thomas's new play has got an item in the gossip column,' he said.

'Oh, I wish they wouldn't,' responded Flora, preparing the fillets of fish for *sole véronique*. 'What do they say about him now?'

'Not about him,' replied Sutton. 'About Miss Daphne Villiers.'

'Who's she?'

'Mr Brewster's lady friend, from what I can gather,' Sutton answered.

'Mr Sutton!' said Flora, casting an anxious look towards the scullery, where Emily was peeling potatoes. 'Hear no evil, speak no evil.'

She cast another quick glance towards the scullery, lowered her voice, and inquired, 'What has that to do with Master Thomas's play?'

'Only that Miss Daphne Villiers is playing a leading part – owing to her being Mr Brewster's fancy bit.'

'Disgraceful!' said Flora, enjoyably shocked. 'You wouldn't find that sort of thing happening in the movies.'

'I'm sure you wouldn't,' said Sutton, with a note of irony which he knew Flora would not catch. He returned, grinning to himself, to the newspaper, and then suddenly sat up. 'Gordon Bennett!' he exclaimed.

'Whatever is it?' inquired Flora.

Sutton was not aware of Emily coming through from the scullery on her rubber-heeled black shoes, carrying a saucepan of potatoes.

'"Miss Daphne Villiers",' he read aloud, '"is the charming newcomer playing the ingenue role in Thomas Brett's new play, *Dark Dimensions*. Although a newcomer, Miss Villiers's family is not unknown in the West End. Her mother was Miss Edith McAveetie, the delightful actress who appeared with Mr Charles Brett in the famous comedy *Summer Lightning*."'

'Oh no!' cried Flora, fillet of sole in hand. 'Oh no! I don't believe it!'

'Don't believe what, Miss Evans?' inquired Emily.

Flora and Sutton exchanged a startled glance.

'Never you mind,' replied Flora. 'Just put those potatoes down and go and lay the table.'

'Lay the table now?' said Emily. 'It's only –'

'I don't care what time it is,' said Flora, even more unreasonably than usual. 'Just go and do as I say.'

She and Sutton waited until the door had swung to behind Emily's indignant back, and then they looked at each other.

'I suppose there's no harm,' said Flora, 'as long as she's Mr Brewster's – what you say. Not that I approve of that, of course. Still –'

'Still,' said Sutton, 'as long as it isn't Mr Thomas who's –'

'Oh, Mr Sutton!' exclaimed Flora. 'Don't! Don't even think about it. Besides, Master Thomas has never been like that – I mean, not one to carry on – not like – '

'Not like the master,' Sutton finished. 'No, I dare say, but if I know Mr Thomas, when he does fall, he'll fall like a ton of bricks.'

A sudden thought struck Flora.

'Do you think Miss Lydia knows?'

'I'm very sure she *doesn't*,' replied Sutton. 'She and the guv'nor have been dining alone together quite a lot lately, and they've talked about Mr Thomas's new play when I was serving them, and about the casting – even joked about Miss Villiers and Mr Brewster when Emily wasn't in the room. Miss Lydia would never have done that if she knew.'

'Will you tell her?'

'I don't know!' replied Sutton, and suddenly banged the table and swore. 'I don't want to upset her, but she ought to know. Why couldn't that stupid bitch have stayed where she belonged, her and all her family?'

But he qualified the 'family' with a word which made Flora gasp.

After some painful thought, Sutton decided to keep the information to himself, for the time being at least. Lydia's comfort and happiness was his sole consideration, and he knew how upset she would be. With any luck she would never need to know, and the miserable past need never be raked up again. Nemesis, however, thought otherwise.

Charles and Lydia had gone upstairs to dress for dinner, and Sutton was decanting the wine when Thomas let himself in at the front door and yelled, 'Sutton!'

'Hullo, Mr Thomas,' said Sutton, emerging. 'How did the rehearsal go today?'

'Pretty ghastly,' Thomas replied, and then added with a slight grin, as though at a secret joke, 'but better after lunch than before.'

'Well, you've got a nice dinner,' said Sutton. 'Knowing you were going to be in, Flora's making all your favourites.'

'Oh, Lor'!' said Thomas. 'I'm afraid I won't be in after all. I'm going away for the weekend.'

'Forgot, did you, sir?' inquired Sutton, coldly.

He always did his best to convey reproof to members of the family who took things for granted or overstepped the mark. The only person who was almost immune from such reproof was Lydia.

'No, didn't forget,' answered Thomas. 'It was a last-minute invitation from Miss Villiers.'

'Miss – Villiers?'

'Miss Daphne Villiers, the leading actress in my play.'

'Oh – yes, sir.'

Thomas smiled again. In Sutton's estimation, it was what one might describe as a tender smile.

'I really couldn't refuse,' he said. 'It was a very special invitation. Would you apologize to Flora for me, and ask Hegarty to drive me to Paddington station?'

He set off for the staircase.

'Er – I'm not sure that Hegarty will be back,' said Sutton. 'He was taking Miss Martha to the theatre –'

'Damn!' said Thomas. 'Well – you'd better telephone

for a taxi in half an hour if he's not back. I must catch that train. I've arranged to travel with Miss Villiers.'

He raced away up the stairs, and Sutton gazed after him in dismay.

Lydia, sitting at her dressing table in petticoat and silk dressing-gown, was surprised when Sutton knocked at the door and came in, carrying a copy of the *Evening News*.

'Excuse me, Miss Lydia,' he said, 'but I thought you ought to know that Mr Thomas is going away for the weekend.'

'Oh,' said Lydia. 'Well –'

'It seems that it was a last-minute invitation from Miss Daphne Villiers,' Sutton cut in.

Charles appeared in the doorway which led to his dressing room, and laughed.

'Well, well!' he said. 'So he *is* cutting out Brewster.'

He came towards Lydia in his shirt-sleeves. It was one of their little rituals that she always, when they were on speaking terms, fastened his cuff-links. Before she could do so, Sutton put the paper down in front of her.

'I thought you'd want to see this, Miss Lydia,' he said, and then glanced at Charles to include him as well. 'Sir,' he said.

Lydia picked up the paper, glancing at him, puzzled, and Sutton pointed out the paragraph, and then went quietly out of the room. He was on his way downstairs when he heard the door open, and looking up, saw Lydia on the landing. She seemed to have aged ten years.

'Where is he, Alfred?' she called, softly.

'Upstairs, Miss Liddy, packing. He said he wanted a taxi to go to the station in half an hour.'

She nodded, and went back into the bedroom.

Charles was sitting on the stool by the dressing table with his back to the mirror. He was still looking at the paper, and she thought he didn't want to meet her eyes.

'I suppose we'll have to tell him,' he said.

'Yes, of course we'll have to tell him!' said Lydia, crossly. 'We should have told him years ago! Not that it would have helped now. Where the hell did that name come from? Do you suppose she married again?'

'I've no idea,' said Charles.

Lydia was suddenly overwhelmed by a rage which drew its strength from an ancient wrong, an ancient hurt and fury.

'For heaven's sake, Charles!' she said. 'Don't just *sit* there! You've got to go upstairs and tell him. He's catching a train in half an hour.'

Charles stood up, and began to fasten his cuff-links.

'What am I going to tell him?'

'The truth, of course!' said Lydia. 'The whole truth. It's about time!'

'Yes,' said Charles.

She saw that his hand was shaking, and came to fasten the cuff-link, but more in exasperation than affection, until her eyes met his.

'I can't tell him, Liddy,' he said. 'It's no good. I just can't.'

Lydia finished fastening one cuff-link, and beckoned, and he gave her the other. They stood close together in silence, and she didn't look up at him. She didn't need to. She knew too well that expression on his face when he had come up against emotions which he couldn't deal with, and somehow, while all his other faults exasperated her, this inability to express his deepest feelings had always touched her, made him seem vulnerable and – oh damn! – made her want to protect him.

'I really think, Charlie,' she said, 'that you ought to tell him yourself.'

She did look up then, and saw the panic in those blue eyes.

'I can't, Liddy!' he said. 'What would I say to him? I – just can't!'

Thomas, hastily packing a suitcase in the old Night Nursery which was now his bedroom, heard Lydia's voice from the doorway.

'Thomas.'

He turned.

'Hullo, Ma,' he said, cheerfully. 'Sorry about dinner tonight.'

Lydia thought that she had never seen him looking so happy, or so much at home in the world. He turned away to the cupboard and reached up to take his dinner-jacket down from its peg.

'Daphne's going to spend the weekend down in the country, and she's asked me to go with her.'

'Yes – I know – I mean, Sutton told me, but – you can't. That is –'

'My dear Ma,' said Thomas, pausing in amazement, 'what on earth's the matter? You look all of a doo-dah.'

'Do I?' said Lydia, trying to laugh, but feeling like crying. 'Perhaps that's because I am – all of a doo-dah.'

'Poor old Ma,' said Thomas. 'Sit down and tell me all about it while I pack. Only, I'm afraid you'll have to make it snappy, because I'm catching a train from Paddington in about –'

'I can't "make it snappy",' said Lydia, beginning to be annoyed, 'and I wish you wouldn't call me "Ma"!'

Thomas always had the power to annoy her, and it was infuriating that he should make a difficult scene so much more difficult to play by doing it now. She didn't sit down, but walked across to the barred window and stood looking out into the garden, where the roses were in full bloom, and the scent of honeysuckle came up from the porch over the garden door. Looking over her shoulder, she saw Thomas's look of puzzled inquiry, and, almost without thinking, she said the first words which offered themselves.

'I'm not your mother,' she said.

She saw his face, at first incredulous and then shocked, and she was horrified at herself. She should not have been the one to tell him. There was too much resentment festering inside her from all those years ago, turning to poison like a wound which has been covered for too long. Thomas stood quite motionless, the dinner-jacket on its hanger still in his hand.

'Are you –? Are you saying I'm adopted?'

'No. That is – No. But –'

She did sit down then because her knees were trembling and she could feel her heart beating. It was like stage-fright, but it was much worse than stage-fright, because there was a confused, nightmarish quality about it. Charles had been right for once. They should not have told him. They should just have let him blunder on. Perhaps nothing would have happened – and even if it did – but then, supposing he had decided that he wanted to marry the girl? She was aware of Thomas putting the dinner-jacket down and coming to stand beside her.

'I wish you'd tell me what this is all about,' he said, with that sharp edge to his voice which none of the others had. 'I know you've never loved me as much as the others –'

'That's not true!' Lydia broke in, with a righteous indignation which wore itself out even as she looked up at him. 'I always –'

'Tried, but couldn't succeed,' Thomas finished. 'Because you're not my mother? Would you mind telling me who my father is?'

'Oh, don't be so absurd!' said Lydia. 'Your father is – is your father. Charles Brett. But –'

When she came up the nursery stairs, she had only thought how much it would hurt Thomas, but now, as she tried to tell it, she was aware of feeling the pain all over again, as though telling it made it happen once more. She spoke very coldly and calmly, as people often do who are in great pain.

'He had an affair with a young actress,' she said. 'Not altogether unusual, you will say. But this time, unfor – But this time, there was a baby. I mean, there was going to be a baby. She was married, and they'd been on tour, and the husband was in Belfast. There was no way the baby could be his. He came of a very strict Protestant family. They were – they owned a big linen business. He never would have accepted – he never would have agreed to bring up another man's child.'

'Who would?' said Thomas, ironically. 'So –?'

'So she continued with the tour, and allegedly set off on another one, arranging to go on sending postcards to the husband, but actually she had the baby in Torquay – and then returned to Belfast without it.'

'Having dumped the little bastard on you,' said Thomas.

'Nobody dumped –!' began Lydia, angrily, and stood up. 'I agreed – I wanted –'

'"Agreed" is probably nearer the mark.'

'All right!' said Lydia. '"Agreed". I agreed to take

you, because she knew her husband wouldn't, and you were Charles's son. But –'

Looking at him, she saw once more that combative little baby with the dark hair and hazel eyes, its tiny hands already clenched into fists. It had been like trying to take to her heart a changeling, and yet –

'Why didn't you tell me before?' inquired Thomas, abruptly.

'I suppose we hoped that it would never be necessary.'

'Then, why now?'

'Oh. Yes. I forgot. Your mother's name was Edith McAveetie. She apparently had another child, a daughter, called Daphne.'

Thomas looked at her, startled.

'Daphne Villiers?'

'I suppose that is her stage name. There was an item in the *Evening News* today which said she was Edith McAveetie's daughter.'

'I see,' said Thomas, and turned away.

Lydia sat trying to find the right words where no right words existed.

'You said I didn't love you as much as the others,' she said, 'but that's not true. Well – I suppose it was at first, but – later –' How could she describe her feelings for him when she really didn't know them herself? 'I loved you all differently!' she said, despairingly. 'Not more, or less, but differently!'

'I really would much rather not talk about it,' said Thomas.

Hearing him moving about, Lydia had thought that he was unpacking, but now she saw that he had finished putting things in the suitcase, and snapped it shut. He picked it up and went towards the door.

'You're not still going?' said Lydia, startled.

He paused and looked back at her.

'Yes, of course,' he replied. 'I said I would.'

Lydia, following him uncertainly down the stairs, saw Charles come to the doorway of their bedroom. He had evidently got his courage together, and was preparing to do his duty, but Thomas didn't give him the chance.

'Hullo, Father,' he said, and continued briskly towards the main stairs.

'Thomas!' said Lydia. 'You can't. She's your half-sister.'

'One of many, I imagine,' said Thomas, glancing back at Charles.

As Lydia came to stand by Charles, Thomas paused at the top of the staircase and looked at them both.

'There really was no need', he said, 'for you to tell me the news in this sudden and dramatic manner. I'm not going off for an illicit and incestuous weekend. It's a house party, and highly respectable. Mr and Mrs Brewster are going to be there, and their son, Harold. The people who own the house are great friends of Harold's and Daphne's. They're giving a party tomorrow especially to announce their engagement – Harold's and Daphne's, I mean – and she said she would particularly like me to be there. Sweet of her, wasn't it?'

He continued down the stairs, and they heard his voice in the hall.

'Hullo, Sutton, is the taxi here? Oh well, don't bother, I'll pick one up.'

They heard the front door slam.

Chapter Fourteen

There had been dreadful moments during the weekend when Lydia wondered whether Thomas would ever return to the house, but he came back on Monday morning, unpacked his suitcase, changed and set off for the theatre. He seemed to have decided to deal with the new situation by pretending that it didn't exist. He was like his father in that respect at least, thought Lydia, bitterly.

'Don't worry, I'll have a word with the boy,' Charles kept saying, but he never did.

It wasn't altogether Charles's fault. In normal circumstances, they didn't see a great deal of Thomas, and with the first night of *Dark Dimensions* approaching, they didn't see him at all. He left the house early, returned late, and never joined them for meals. He slept in Nightingale Grove, but that was about all.

'Treating the place like a hotel!' grumbled Charles, like a thousand fathers before him. 'It's no good – I'll have to have a word with the boy.'

'Wait until his play has opened,' begged Lydia.

The first night of *Dark Dimensions* was so calamitous that it made Edwin's modified failure in *The King Shall Not Die* resemble a triumph. Thomas had never been blinded, and had never lived through the Battle of the Somme. In *The Liar*, he had drawn on the character and experiences of Edwin, whom he knew well. But the truth was that, although at Cambridge Thomas had engaged in an enjoyable flirtation with Fabian Socialism, he actually knew nothing of the working classes, and his portrait of the corporal was as false as Graham's cockney accent. Oddly enough, Daphne, because she was so patently a nice girl, and sincere, was much less damaging to the play than Graham, whose performance, like the play, seemed to insult all those unpretentious, ordinary, hard-working men who, in their simple patriotism, went off to the Great War and were gassed, or blinded, or blown to pieces. The line about the crown of thorns got a huge and disconcerting laugh.

'Bound to,' thought Charles, resignedly, and clutched for Lydia's hand.

There was an empty seat beside them. Thomas had elected to watch the play from the back row of the stalls, but when the cast took their curtain call, he was there on the stage with them, and faced with them the awful barrage of boos and hisses that came from the audience – but, above all, from the upper circle and the gallery.

There was a party of sorts on the stage afterwards. Charles could only be thankful that the play had not been produced at the Princess Theatre, and that he did not have the unpleasant task of closing it down immediately.

'Poor Thomas!' said Lydia, as they went to bed that night.

'I'll have a word with him in the morning,' said Charles, and then, in response to an accusing look from Lydia, 'I really will.'

But in the morning, the telegram arrived from Ireland. Addressed to Charles, it read: 'Father dying. Come at once. Mother.'

It was amazing how completely and instantly death took precedence over everything else. The trouble with Thomas, the disaster of his first night, Charles's anxiety over the sudden decline in profitability of the Princess Theatre, and all other matters, big and small, which had previously occupied their minds vanished into insignificance because one rather tiresome old actor was dying in Galway.

Even Jean and Emily, who had never known him, found themselves involved in the general worry and distress, as Flora and Sutton talked about 'poor Mr George' and 'poor Mrs George' and Lydia and Martha exchanged fond reminiscences. Jean, in particular, found that she received a remarkably clear image of George Brett and Maeve O'Brian – he the son of a Drury Lane musician who became an actor, who at the age of about twenty-seven had set up his own company, playing all the leading parts himself in the provinces and Ireland, though never in London, and she the lovely young actress from County Kildare whom he had caught up, married, and kept with him ever since to play Juliet to his Romeo and Desdemona to his Othello, long after either of them had any business to be doing any such thing – except that it was the only thing they knew, or wanted to do, and they shared the same illusion that he was a brilliant actor and she a beautiful young girl, an illusion untarnished by failure and untouched by time. And now the old man was dying in Galway, with his wife at his bedside and a company who had not been paid for three weeks because the takings had been so low.

Except that apparently he wasn't. Charles had caught the first train to Liverpool, tossed across the Irish Sea, and hired an extremely battered taxi in which he was bumped and shaken across the wild middle of Ireland, arriving triumphantly, if sorrowfully, in time to attend his father's deathbed. The excellent local doctor was there when he arrived, and said that there was nothing he could do except to make his patient as comfortable as possible. On the second day, the doctor declared that the old man had a remarkable constitution. On the third day, the doctor said that he was holding his own, but that they mustn't hope too much. On the fourth day, George was sitting up drinking beef tea.

Thus it was that Lydia, tearing open a telegram in the expectation of reading the sad news of George's demise, learned that, although far from well, he had survived, and Charles was bringing him, with Maeve, to Nightingale Grove for convalescence. Charles also asked her to telegraph some money to the bank in Galway, so that he could pay off the company. And thus it was that Thomas, returning from a visit to some Cambridge friends, encountered Emily emerging from the nursery with an armful of his books and papers.

'What on earth's going on?' he demanded.

Lydia emerged from the night nursery, carrying most of his shirts and ties.

'Oh, Thomas,' she said, 'I'm glad you're back. Grandma and Grandad are coming to stay, and since he'll need a lot of nursing, we thought we'd better put them in the nursery. I knew you wouldn't mind.'

'I'm afraid you were mistaken,' said Thomas.

Lydia was heading for the stairs, but the tone of his voice stopped her dead.

'All right, Emily,' she said. 'Put those things back on the table in the nursery, and then take these shirts down to Mr Edwin's room.'

'Yes, madam,' said Emily, awed.

It wasn't often that Lydia spoke to her in that 'mistressy' voice, and she knew an impending row when she saw one. Lydia and Thomas watched her in silence while she went into the nursery and returned, and took the shirts, and set off down the stairs.

'Now, please, Thomas,' said Lydia, when Emily had disappeared, 'don't be difficult.'

'*Difficult*? I thought these were my rooms, but without even consulting me –'

'You weren't here!'

He wasn't listening to her. All the shock and wounded feelings which he had formerly suppressed now found expression in his indignation at this much smaller wrong.

'Of course, if it had been Martha or Edwin, it would have been different.'

'I'm putting you in Edwin's room!' said Lydia, exasperated.

'Oh, goodness!' exclaimed Thomas. 'The room belonging to the legitimate son and heir. And me just a bastard!'

Suddenly Lydia lost her temper.

'You've been treated as a member of this family all your life,' she said, 'and just because –'

'Just because this time I'm treated like a bastard –'

She could have hit him, but she didn't.

'If you think that,' she said, 'you *are* a bastard.'

'Well, I promise you one thing,' he said. 'That's the last chance you'll ever have to call me that. In fact, I hope that you and I will never, ever meet again.'

By the time that Charles arrived at Nightingale Grove with George and Maeve, Thomas was long gone, complete with all his possessions. George and Maeve, however, had brought possessions of their own. Hegarty, who had met them at the station with the car, had been obliged to hail a taxi to transport the huge skip full of props and the large wardrobe trunk.

When the splendid old progenitor had tottered inside, supported by his wife and greeted by the sympathetic Flora, Sutton eyed the mountain of luggage with deep suspicion.

'If you could give me some idea, sir,' he said to Charles, 'of what is theatrical and could be stored in the cellar, and what might be immediately required –'

'Oh – yes,' said Charles, looking frayed. 'Perhaps if we ask Mrs George –?'

'Rather unwise, sir, if I may say so. I fancy she will want it all upstairs with her and Mr George.'

'Ah. Yes. Quite right. Well – I leave it to you, Sutton.'

He tottered inside himself. Hegarty grinned at Sutton.

'I'd say, the two suitcases and the hatbox upstairs,' he said, 'and the rest in the cellar.'

About to put his hands to the skip, he paused, looking towards the front door.

'He's a grand old fellow, all the same,' he said. 'I saw him playing once at the Gaiety Theatre in Dublin. I'd not say it was the greatest performance in the world, but – once seen, never forgotten.'

'I dare say,' said Sutton, gloomily. 'But, once here, will he ever leave? That's what I want to know.'

'Darling!' said Lydia, putting her arm round Charles in the hall. 'You look exhausted.'

They turned their eyes towards the staircase which George was mounting nobly, step by step, assisted by Flora and Emily, with Maeve, trailing draperies, in attendance.

'You know, Liddy,' said Charles, 'my father makes me feel dreadfully old.'

He looked about him.

'Where's Thomas?' he inquired.

Lydia took her arm away.

'I'll tell you later,' she said. 'I'd better see them settled in.'

Charles's first engagement next day was with the manager of the Princess Theatre, a meeting he had postponed when he went rushing off to Ireland.

'I don't quite understand', he said, studying the figures once more, 'why we seem to be short of cash when *The Liar* is doing such good business.'

Piers Longford-Price sat on the corner of the desk, swinging one elegant leg.

'Overheads, sir, I'm afraid,' he said.

'Overheads?'

'A little trouble with the roof.'

He glanced at Jean, who was sitting working at a small desk at the other end of the room, and Charles, slightly puzzled, saw them exchange a smile.

'What's wrong with the roof?' inquired Charles.

'That rather high wind displaced some of the tiles, and then, unfortunately, a heavy rainstorm damaged some of the top dressing rooms.'

The public-school accent filled the room with gentle assurance.

'I have the bills here somewhere – Ah, thank you.'

As Jean brought them over to him, he gave her his charming smile, and she felt herself blushing.

'Good heavens!' Charles exclaimed, gazing at the accounts with starting eyes. 'How many tiles did you say were replaced?'

'Quite a few, sir, I'm afraid. And then the men always displace quite a number more when they're clambering about. I remember my uncle complaining about that at Wishbury Hall, with the men back and forth for weeks –'

'I hope they won't be back and forth for weeks here!' exclaimed Charles.

'Oh no,' replied Piers, reassuringly. 'It's just that it *is* an old theatre, and, just in case there are any other problems, I've decided to consult Brown Brothers. They're the roofing specialists. Used by all the big country house people.'

'What problems?' inquired Charles, with his useful habit (useful to him, that is!) of homing in on the relevant word or sentence in a deal of verbiage.

'Well – it is an ancient roof –'

'Not *that* ancient!' said Charles.

'No–o, but it could possibly be nail-sick, and then the timbers – I fancy there could be some sagging and shifting.'

'Good God!' said Charles, throwing an apprehensive glance up at the ceiling. 'Are we safe?'

'Oh yes. All old timbers tend to sag, but I do feel that we need some expert opinion, just in case.'

'You'll let me see the quotations for any work which needs doing?'

'Oh yes, sir, of *course*!' said Piers, shocked at the thought of any other course of action. 'By the way,' he added, 'I've had the ceilings replaced in the top dressing rooms, and I'm afraid they'll have to be redecorated.'

'Can we afford it?'

Jean spoke from her little desk across the room.

'It does seem sensible to have them done while we have a play with such a small cast.'

'Exactly!' said Piers, and smiled at her again. 'Miss Lacy is so practical. I don't know what I'd do without her help. The next production might be a big one, with all the dressing rooms occupied.'

'All right,' said Charles, grumpily. 'We'd better have it done.' He scowled at the weekly returns. 'But what I can't understand is why the takings are down. I thought we were playing to full houses.'

'I'm afraid they've gone down a bit. And the box-office manager was rather inefficient. Miss Lacy has had to pick up the pieces after him several times when he'd made a stupid mistake. I've got rid of him, and I'm hoping things will be better now. The same with the barman.'

'The barman?' said Charles, startled. 'I thought he was quite a good chap. Mind, I've noticed that the bar receipts were down.'

'Partly the result of reduced attendance, but partly that I'm afraid the fellow was getting slack. That's what happens when there isn't a theatre manager on the premises. However, I've replaced him, and I'm hoping you'll notice a big improvement from now on.'

Jean looked up with a little frown. Surely –? But it was

none of her business, she told herself. She must be mistaken, anyway.

Charles pushed the papers away and sat gloomily back in his chair.

'The trouble with running a theatre', he said, 'is that there always seems to be more money going out than there is coming in. Just as you think you're out of the wood –'

Piers suddenly stood up.

'I've just had an idea!' he said. 'What a fool I was not to think of it before! My cousin, Lord Wishbury, is a tremendous theatre enthusiast, and he's got pots of money –'

'You think he might consider investing some of it in the Princess Theatre?'

'It's possible,' said Piers. 'Shall I arrange a meeting?'

'Ask him to come to lunch on Sunday,' said Charles.

The Sunday luncheons at Nightingale Grove were famous. They were essentially family affairs, when all the Bretts came together from their various productions to talk and gossip and bitch and laugh, but with the addition of certain selected close friends, like Willie Sutherland, and the occasional celebrity whose work they admired and who seemed likely to prove congenial. They did not include in the Sunday luncheons people whom they did not like.

Lydia was not best pleased when Charles announced that he had invited Piers Longford-Price and Lord Wishbury, especially since Edwin was still away on tour, and Thomas was – who knew where? Worse still, Maeve had announced that George felt himself so much recovered that he proposed to Join Them for Luncheon.

'O God!' said Martha, when she heard the news. 'You don't think he'll tell the story about the herd of cows invading the church hall, and how the audience were so held by his performance of Othello that they never noticed until they rose to go out, and slipped on the cow pats?'

'Probably,' said Lydia, grimly. 'He's already told it once to your father and me, and twice to Emily.'

George near to death was an object of pity and concern; George convalescent and in her house was a pain in the neck.

George, it must be said, lived up to their worst expectations, but Lord Wishbury proved to be remarkably congenial. He was a thin, pale man, a little younger than Piers, crippled as Piers had told them, by a childhood hunting accident. Lydia, looking at him with the eye of an artist, suspected that he was in continual pain. It has to be admitted that he did not make an entirely auspicious beginning.

'I say!' he exclaimed, when he was introduced to Lydia and Charles. 'I really am quite overcome, quite overwhelmed. I've been an admirer of yours for years.'

He had absurdly innocent pale blue eyes, like a baby who is not sure what colour to decide upon, but settles for these for the time being.

'I must tell you, sir,' Lord Wishbury continued, earnestly, 'that I have been in love with your wife for years, ever since I first saw her in that play – what was it?'

'*Tell All, Tell Nothing*,' said Piers. 'We saw it together.'

'Of course!' said Lord Wishbury. 'We came up from school.'

'Really?' responded Lydia, frostily.

Wishbury turned to her, eagerly.

'I fell hopelessly in love with you!' he said.

'Oh. Really?' said Lydia, slightly mollified.

Lord Wishbury turned to Charles.

'And you, sir, you were simply splendid as the husband.'

'I dare say I would have been,' said Charles. 'But in fact I played the lover.'

'Oh dear!' said Lord Wishbury. 'I'm afraid I'm making the most complete fool of myself.'

'You certainly are!' said Lydia, and suddenly they were all laughing. They really liked each other.

'I know I'm a perfect fool,' said Lord Wishbury. 'Piers is always telling me I am, and I know he's right. But, although I'm a complete ignoramus, I really do love the theatre, and if there's any way I can be involved – I mean –'

It was at that moment that George chose to make his entrance, escorted by Maeve. There was nothing for it but to introduce him to Lord Wishbury.

'I understand', said George, when the formalities were completed, 'that you are interested in investing in the theatre. I'm sure the time is ripe for a West End production of *King Lear*. I myself have always wished to essay the part –'

Piers moved swiftly but smoothly in.

'Excuse me, sir,' he said to Charles, 'but I believe you have a splendid collection of old theatre prints. I rather think my cousin would like to see them.'

'By all means,' Charles answered with alacrity. 'They're in the study, if you'd care to –?'

'Oh, thank you very much,' said Lord Wishbury. 'Er – excuse me, sir.'

George eyed them balefully as Charles and Lydia led Piers and Lord Wishbury out of the room.

'I don't like that fellow,' he said.

'Lord Wishbury, Grandpa?' said Martha, surprised.

'No, that Longford-Price fellow. Got shifty eyes. Reminds me of a touring manager I had once. Used to fiddle the books.'

Much to Charles's delight, it was arranged that Lord Wishbury would invest a sizeable sum of money. Piers and the Wishbury Estate financial adviser both agreed that for tax purposes it was better that it should be put into something called 'The Theatre Development Fund', but Charles and Lydia could call upon it to finance the next production, in which Lord Wishbury would have a small interest, although, as he told them, he wasn't really in it to make money.

'Makes a nice change from Brewster,' said Charles, watching complacently as Piers drove Lord Wishbury away in his Lagonda.

In fact, everything in the garden was lovely, with one exception – Thomas. Jean had been able to tell them where he was living, since he had been obliged to send her his address so that he could receive his author's royalties from *The Liar*. She had even visited him more than once, though she did not tell them so. He had asked her not to, and she was so horrified by what she found that she did not want to tell them. Martha, however, had no such inhibitions.

'I went to see him,' she said, 'and, I must say, trailing all the way out to Chelsea in order to be kicked in the teeth was not precisely what I had in mind.'

'What – exactly – happened?' inquired Charles,

230

keeping his face and voice expressionless.

'He blames you and Mother, of course,' said Martha, and then, 'Though, why he should blame Mother –'

'Please, Martha, darling,' said Lydia.

'And he blames Eddie and me for knowing and not telling him. I said we only discovered by accident, but I don't think he believed me.'

'Is he writing?' asked Charles.

'No,' replied Martha. 'He's drinking, though. And if you ask me, he's on the edge of a complete breakdown.'

Charles knew that he must do something about it, but he certainly wasn't going to risk walking in on Thomas, unbidden and unwelcome. Their meeting was going to be difficult enough without that. Charles-like, he took the easy and conventional way out, and wrote a letter in his angular, elegant, slightly old-fashioned handwriting.

Dear Thomas,

I really do feel that we should meet and have a talk. I am busy on Wednesday, but otherwise please name any day that suits you and come and have lunch with me at the Garrick. Much love,

Father.

Three days later, he found the envelope on his breakfast table. On it was written in Thomas's handwriting, 'Return to Sender'. He sat looking down at it, and he could feel his heart beating. A kick in the teeth, he thought, just like Martha. And now he didn't know what else he could do. He picked the envelope up with a hand that shook a little and put it in his pocket. Later, he tore it up into tiny pieces and threw it in the waste-paper basket in his study. He never told Lydia about it.

Chapter Fifteen

It had gradually come to be accepted that Jean would spend the first hour of each day dealing with Charles's correspondence and bills, and that she would then go on to the theatre office, where she would spend the rest of her time working as Piers's secretary. In fact, with Charles and Lydia both 'resting', she would not have found enough to occupy her time at Nightingale Grove, so she was more than grateful to be busy and needed at the Princess Theatre. Otherwise, she thought, she might well have found herself out of a job. As it was, she had more than enough to do, and, if the truth were known, could well have been called assistant manager, since Piers was out of the office a great deal, frequently leaving at lunchtime and not returning until six o'clock, if then.

There was no doubt in Jean's mind about Piers's honesty, and she was able to smile at George's churlish remark. But she did think that he was too trusting, perhaps, she thought, because he was a 'gentleman', and unaccustomed to keeping a sharp eye on his subordinates for fiddling and petty thieving. No doubt, she thought, he had been right to dismiss the box-office manager and the barman, but it troubled her that he seemed to think that takings would thereafter improve, whereas, in fact, they were still declining. In fact, they were declining even more than with the old box-office manager and barman.

Piers, coming into the theatre office late one evening, stopped short at the sight of Jean sitting at his desk. She started up.

'I'm so sorry,' she said. 'I shouldn't be sitting at your desk. I thought you'd gone home. It's just that I wanted to check the box-office receipts for last week, and it's easier to spread them out –'

She was dismayed by the look of fury on his face.

'What on earth business is that of yours?' he demanded.

'I'm sorry,' she said. 'It was just that I noticed that the takings had actually gone down since Mr Hibbert came, and I wanted to make sure that he'd remembered to include –'

'Who the devil do you think you are?' said Piers, his anger increasing. 'I'm the theatre manager, and I'm perfectly capable of looking after my staff. You're not part of the management. You're simply here to do secretarial work, and otherwise kindly stop poking your nose into things that don't concern you!'

'Yes, of course,' said Jean. 'It was stupid of me. I was so afraid that you might – I was just trying to – I'm so sorry!'

The ferocity of his attack had shocked her into tears. Her one thought was to escape, but as she went towards the door, he stopped her, putting his hand on her arm.

'What a funny little thing you are!' he said. 'You were

just trying to help me, weren't you? And then I blast off at you – and you apologize. You're much too sweet, you know, much too nice.'

As she looked up at him, startled, he took her in his arms and kissed her. She had only been kissed once before, by a drunken old lecher of a stage manager. It had given her a horror of sex as he fondled and fumbled her in a dark corner backstage. She had to fight to break free, her blouse torn and her hair dishevelled. This kiss was firm but gentle. Piers didn't smell of drink, but of soap and tobacco, and when he held her closer and kissed her again, passionately this time, she could not resist, did not even want to resist. She had no thought or power of thought as he kissed and caressed her, murmuring endearments. She was in the hands of an immensely experienced lover, and she was lying on the couch with him and had lost her virginity before she even knew what was happening.

He stroked her hair back from her forehead as she lay in his arms afterwards, half tearful, half excited.

'What a dear, innocent little thing you are!' he said. 'I know I shouldn't have done that, but I couldn't resist you. Good heavens! If Mr and Mrs Brett knew, I should probably lose my job.'

'Oh no!' said Jean. 'I mean – there's no reason why they should know.'

'It'll be our own special secret,' he said, and kissed her again. 'And at least we can go on working together.' He tapped the tip of her nose fondly with his forefinger. 'But you must stop trying to protect me. I'm quite capable of looking after myself.'

Edwin's tour of *The King Shall Not Die* was drawing to a

close, and Lydia was profoundly thankful for it. She had been quite truthful when she said that she loved all her children, but loved them differently. She had not been like so many stage beauties, who either pretended that their children did not exist or else that they were a great deal younger than they were. Partly from genuine affection, and partly from native good sense, she had ensured from the earliest days that she should be photographed with her lovely young family about her (in soft focus, of course) and since she had married Charles when she was seventeen and he was twenty-four, she was able, without being too precise about their ages, still to cling on to the official age of thirty-five, an age which she had no intention of abandoning until she had to.

'I was married so young,' she would say, with perfect truth, 'and I'm afraid the first of my children arrived almost exactly nine months later!'

Thus, rather daringly, would she hint at Charles's ardour and virility, and fortunately, since Nell and John Caldwell were not in the theatre business, she was not obliged to admit that she was a grandmother. That really would be going too far! But, in anticipation of times to come, she did take the precaution of indicating, erroneously, that Nell was older than the twins.

So it was that Lydia was able to accept her grown-up sons, Edwin and Thomas, and not to compete with her daughters, Martha, Nell, and the astonishing latecomer, Perdita. In fact, Perdita, as a schoolgirl, was rather helpful, so that Lydia could be photographed with her (in soft focus) as 'The Beautiful Miss Wheatley and her Young Daughter'.

Still, it was certainly true, though never admitted, that there was a particularly close and tender relationship between Lydia and her elder son. (Indeed, as it was now admitted, her only son.) They always exchanged frequent letters when they were apart, so he knew what had been going on. Charles, of course, was a hopeless letter-writer, but even he had scribbled a note to tell Edwin about the failure of *Dark Dimensions*, and Martha, too, had sent one of her scrawls to tell him that the gaff was blown about Thomas's birth, and that he had taken it very badly indeed. But it was only when Edwin came to Nightingale Grove and sat on Lydia's bed and shared her breakfast coffee in the old childhood way that he realized how very upset she was.

'It's so ridiculous, Eddie,' she said. 'Thomas has always been the awkward one. Even when he was a baby, he cried more than the rest of you, and always poked people in the eye when they went to kiss him. That's something he's been doing ever since.'

Edwin smiled sympathetically, and dipped a lump of sugar in her coffee and ate it.

'But now he's gone,' said Lydia, 'I miss him dreadfully, and I suddenly realize how much I really do love him. I blame myself so much. If only I'd realized it sooner, I would have handled the whole thing so differently. I would have – well – just put my arms round him and told him that I loved him.'

'And risked a poke in the eye?' inquired Edwin.

She smiled, but she was nearly in tears.

'Don't worry, Mother,' said Edwin, fondly. 'It's just the failure of *Dark Dimensions* coming at the same time which has knocked him off his perch. He'll pull himself together and come round to apologize. It's too late for him to stop being a member of the family now.'

'I'm not so sure,' said Lydia. 'Oh, Eddie, I'm not sure he'll ever come back!'

Edwin, the cautious one, did not reply to this. He

stood up, and leaned over and kissed her.

'I'd better go and unpack,' he said, 'and then start looking for a job. I suppose *The Liar* is still doing good business?'

'Not quite as good as it was. Your grandfather is certain that Piers Longford-Price is fiddling the books.'

'Hardly likely.'

'I know,' said Lydia, 'but he reminds your grandfather of a tour manager they once had. He had shifty eyes.'

'*All* grandfather's tour managers had shifty eyes,' said Edwin. 'They needed them.'

Jean, descending the stairs from the theatre office that evening, was surprised to see George lurking outside the circle bar.

'Mr Brett!' she exclaimed. 'I thought you had seen *The Liar*. Have you come to see it again?'

'Not likely!' said George. 'Didn't care for it the first time. Here, come into the bar with me.'

'I don't drink,' said Jean, but he took her firmly by the arm.

'You can have an orangeade,' he said.

The first of the theatregoers were just coming in, and George and Jean sat at a small table in the corner of the bar.

'Now,' said George, 'watch this.'

The barman was taking an order for drinks. He was a man of quick actions and sharp eyes, and clearly conscientious. As he waited for payment, he wiped the bar clean with a linen cloth. The customer paid, and the barman took the money.

'Thank you very much, sir,' he said, and moved to the till.

He leaned his hand on the top of the till while he rang up the amount, and then returned to the customer with the change.

'There we are, sir,' he said. 'Hope you enjoy the play.'

'How much did he ring up?' inquired George.

'I couldn't see,' replied Jean. 'The cloth was over it.'

George turned to look at her.

'You don't mean –?' she said.

'Oldest trick in the world,' said George. 'Take in the money, ring up a smaller amount – or possibly even "No Sale" – and cover the till so no one can see it. Then you put the difference in your own pocket. Some of them do it with a cloth. Some put their hand over it. Some of them have an accomplice. Ever seen anyone standing in front of the till while he was serving drinks?'

'No!' said Jean, quickly.

But she had an instant, unwelcome image of the glimpse she had received, more than once, as she came down the stairs from the office, of Piers standing in front of the till, sometimes talking to the barman, and some-times with his back to the till, chatting with customers.

'Hm,' said George, who, for a silly, vain old ham actor, had uncomfortably sharp eyes himself. 'If you ask me, the box-office manager is on the fiddle, too.'

Jean's face showed her dismay.

'My son tells me that the takings have gone down,' said George, 'and yet we seem to be playing to full houses.'

'Not quite,' said Jean.

'Very nearly,' said George. 'And I understand there's a new box-office manager.'

'Er – yes – Mr Longford-Price said that the old box-office manager had been making too many mistakes, so he engaged Mr Hibbert.'

'And did the takings go down before Mr Hibbert arrived, or afterwards?'

Jean knew the truth too well. She could not answer.

'New barman, new box-office manager,' said George, 'and both engaged by Mr Piers Longford-Price. He's in on the fiddle.'

'No!' cried Jean. 'That's impossible. I know it is. He's a very kind, gentle, honest man. He may not be good at spotting dishonesty in other people –'

'But you're sure he's not a con man.'

'Of course not!' said Jean.

'Then I suggest,' said George, magnificently, 'that it is up to you to clear his name.'

Through the loudspeaker in the theatre office, Jean heard the rather turgid ending of the play, and the sound of applause. She sat back and looked at the theatre plan, the ticket stubs, and the account books, and at the initials, P. L.-P. at the foot of each page. The door opened, and she looked up, startled.

'Piers –?' she said. And then, 'Oh. Martha.'

'Yes,' said Martha. 'Sorry to disappoint you. An assignation, was it? He must have forgotten that he is taking me out to supper.'

'Oh – yes – that is –'

'So I'm just sending out a little warning signal.'

'Warning signal?'

'Yes, Jean, dear, I know you're much too innocent and naive to know what I'm talking about, but I feel that I should mention to you that Piers Longford-Price suits me very well, especially in bed, so if you were planning –'

'No!' cried Jean. 'No, of course not!'

'I'm so glad,' said Martha, sweetly, 'because I have no intention of letting him go.'

'He's a thief,' said Jean.

'What? What on earth are you talking about?'

'Mr George was right.'

'My grandfather is never right about anything.'

'He was right about this. Box-office takings, bar receipts, petty cash – it none of it tallies. And he – Mr Longford-Price – must have known about it.'

'What nonsense!' said Martha, but came to look over her shoulder.

Martha had left the door ajar, so the first thing they heard was Piers's voice.

'Well, well! My office full of beautiful women! What a lucky fellow I am!'

'Aren't you, though?' said Martha.

She straightened up.

'I was just telling Miss Lacy that she shouldn't be working here so late.'

'I quite agree with you,' said Piers, with a hard edge to his voice, his eyes flickering to the papers on the desk and then away again. 'Good night, Miss Lacy.'

Jean rose, and hesitated, looking from him to Martha.

'Good night, Miss Lacy,' repeated Martha, mockingly.

Jean paused a moment longer, looking from one to the other, and then picked up her handbag, fetched her hat and coat from the stand and walked out.

'Poor Miss Lacy!' said Martha, laughing. 'I really do believe she has a teeny bit of a crush on you.'

'What nonsense!' said Piers, but there was a note of complacency in his voice which was not lost on Martha.

She walked away towards the window, where the bright theatre lights of Shaftesbury Avenue were being switched out.

'Have you really been fiddling the books?' she inquired.

'Don't be childish!'

She turned.

'I never am,' she said. 'I grew up a long time ago.'

He came towards her.

'I'm glad to hear it,' he said.

He took hold of her and kissed her, and she felt the same sense of danger and excitement she had experienced on that first afternoon when they had gone back to her flat in Shepherd's Market and made love. It was not just that he was a strong and experienced lover, but that there was a touch of cruelty in him which gave an added spice, almost a sense of danger, as though he was a tiger who could at any moment turn and rend her.

'It's quite exciting being kissed by a criminal,' she said.

She broke free, and sat on the desk, swinging her leg. Piers glanced towards the papers and ticket stubs, and then back at her, and smiled.

'Oh, come on!' he said. 'What if I have turned a blind eye to a fiddle or two?'

'I wouldn't say you were the blind one,' said Martha. 'In fact, I'd say that stealing from my father was rather like taking pennies from a blind man.'

She had taken out a cigarette and was lighting it with a gold lighter on the desk.

'Well, it wasn't your money,' said Piers, easily, and then laughed. 'Although, as a matter of fact, you went out to lunch and dinner on it a few times.'

'Did I?' said Martha.

She tossed the lighter in her hand for a moment, and then slipped it into her evening bag.

'Hey!' said Piers. 'That's my lighter. You gave it to me, remember?'

'Stupid of me, wasn't it?' she said.

His face hardened for a moment, and then he began to smile again.

'Not particularly.'

He came very close, and took the cigarette out of her mouth and stubbed it out.

'You knew I could give you something you wanted. You still want it.'

He took her by the shoulders in a grip that hurt, and bent her back over the desk, leaning over to kiss her, his lips parted and his teeth showing in a tigerish smile. The smile turned to a grimace as Martha brought her knee up into his groin.

'Did you really think,' she said, as he staggered back, gasping and doubled up, 'that I would let my father be robbed and swindled by a vulgar, over-sexed con man, just because he was good in bed?'

He *had* thought so, as the look of astonished fury on his face showed. Martha straightened up, picked up her evening bag, and began to walk out of the room. But she had been right about something else, too. As she passed him, he seized her arm and swung her round and she saw the danger just before he struck her full on the cheek with his clenched fist.

The swindles of Piers Longford-Price had been more extensive than even George had suspected. When Jean got back that night, George was in bed, but next morning she told him what she had discovered, and together they went to see Charles. Before Martha's entrance, Jean had put in her handbag enough papers and notes to put

Piers's guilt beyond doubt, and they had just decided that, before calling the police, Charles should go to the theatre and confront him with the evidence, in the hope of avoiding scandal and obtaining restitution, when Martha walked in with a bruised cheek which was almost closing her left eye.

'What on earth,' demanded Charles, 'has happened to you?'

'I collided with a bedpost,' replied Martha, her eyes resting briefly on Jean's face, and added, 'I've just been in to the theatre to tell them that they'd better put my understudy on, and I really think you'd better get down there.'

'What? Why?'

The bird had flown, together with those minor predators, the box-office manager and the barman. Although Piers had cleared his desk and done his best to remove incriminating evidence, the papers which Jean had seen or extracted, together with some he had missed, were enough to reveal the extent of the fraud. The Fortune Ticket Agency was owned by a man called Philip Fortune, alias Piers Longford-Price. He had, with the connivance of the box-office manager, been sending blocks of tickets there for sale and pocketing the proceeds. The Brown Brothers, those stately home experts on ancient roofs, did not exist. A couple of tiles had been blown off the roof of the Princess Theatre in an admittedly high wind, and had been replaced by a small firm of builders for a very modest fee. When Jean went to see them, they assured her that they had found the roof in excellent shape, and had inspected also the timbers, and advised Mr Longford-Price that no further work was required for the time being. A very small amount of damage done to the top dressing rooms by the rain seeping through the missing tiles had been put right with a lick of paint, and the remaining cost of redecoration had gone into the ready pocket of Mr Piers Longford-Price.

Charles was furious with Martha for having confronted Piers with his depredations, thus giving him the opportunity to get away, but Jean could only be thankful that she would not have to face him, or, worse still, give evidence against him. It was Lydia who suddenly remembered Lord Wishbury.

'The Theatre Development Fund,' she said. 'We must make sure that –'

'Mr Longford-Price,' said Jean, 'had the account made out in his name.'

'You mean,' demanded Lydia, incredulously, looking at Charles, 'that he could sign withdrawal cheques without your signature or mine?'

Investigation of the Theatre Development Fund revealed a nil balance. Mr Piers Longford-Price had drawn out the entire sum that morning, in cash.

Lord Wishbury, summoned to Nightingale Grove, begged them not to prosecute. He promised to replace the money in the Theatre Development Fund, and also to make good the missing money, as far as the sum could be ascertained, from the box office and the bar.

'It's not just for the sake of the family name,' he said, and limped to the door, and turned. 'Poor Piers,' he said. 'It was the war, you know. I wasn't in it myself – stupid cripple – but, I do know that nobody who was in it came out undamaged. Piers was – one of the casualties.'

As Sutton saw him out, Edwin cut ruthlessly across the prevailing sentimental sympathy.

'The war?' he said. 'From what I heard, Longford-Price was rejected for active service. The general opinion was that he bribed the MO. As far as I know, he spent the war in close proximity to the quartermaster's stores – which could explain why they never quite managed to balance their books.'

Annoyingly enough, it emerged that Piers Longford-Price had presided over what should have been the final successful weeks of the run of *The Liar*. Theatregoers had always been a limited élite, and now were, as Charles remarked with justifiable annoyance, still further depleted by the absurd and undoubtedly passing enthusiasm for the moving pictures, where shopgirls who had once gathered outside the stage door to gaze upon their matinee idols now swooned over the flickering image of Rudolph Valentino or John Gilbert. Still, *The Liar* had enjoyed a remarkably good run, and Charles planned to give a party to celebrate the closing night. Thomas, of course, would be invited, but would he come?

'Of course he'll come!' said Charles, irritably. 'Why shouldn't he?'

Edwin, glancing at his father, realized that Charles was just as upset as Lydia, and decided that he had better do something about it.

His welcome at Thomas's new abode was not exactly encouraging. Thomas had rented a flat from an old Cambridge friend who had gone to continue his studies in Germany. It was on the top floor, above a chemist's shop in the King's Road, and access was gained through a narrow entrance and up three flights of linoleum-covered stairs. Edwin walked straight up, tapped at the door of the flat, and went in.

'Oh, it's you,' said Thomas, scowling.

He was sitting in a sagging armchair, drinking whisky, and the room was full of cigarette smoke.

'Just thought I'd come and see you,' said Edwin.

'You're about twenty years too late!' said Thomas, bitterly.

'Sorry,' Edwin replied. 'I've been on tour.'

He sat down and gazed at Thomas earnestly.

'That was a joke,' he said.

Thomas scowled more than ever. Edwin yawned and leaned back.

'I hear your play was a disaster,' he said.

'Thanks for mentioning it.'

'Why, hasn't anyone else?'

For the first time, Edwin caught a sharp glance which looked like the old Thomas.

'They all tiptoed round it,' replied Thomas.

'Mm,' said Edwin, 'that's what they did over my failure in *The King Shall Not Die*. God! what an idiot I made of myself over that! All it did was to prove what everyone knew, that I'm a second-rater. I've got to accept that.'

'Well, I won't!' said Thomas, furiously.

'You don't have to,' said Edwin. 'You've written one superb play, and no doubt you'll write many more. You've written one failure, and no doubt it'll do you a lot of good.'

'Thanks,' said Thomas.

'Not at all,' said Edwin. 'Are you writing anything now?'

'Do I look as if I am?' demanded Thomas, with dramatic bitterness.

'No,' Edwin replied, thoughtfully. 'You look as if you're sitting there drinking too much and feeling sorry for yourself. Come on, Tom, snap out of it!'

'*Snap out of it?*' repeated Thomas, outraged.

It did not seem quite the appropriate adjuration to someone whose life and career were in ruins.

'I can do without advice on how to behave from you,' he continued. 'You're part of the conspiracy.'

'What conspiracy?' inquired Edwin, puzzled. 'Oh – that. Martha and I found out about it by accident. Slip of the tongue by Flora. We weren't best pleased, I can tell you.'

'*You* weren't best pleased. How do you think *I* feel?'

'Sorry for yourself,' answered Edwin, pleasantly. 'Can't say I'm surprised. I always said you ought to be told. I knew you were bound to find out sooner or later. You really are making too much of it, though. You're part of the family, and you always will be.'

'Yes,' said Thomas, angrily, and rose, and walked to the window and turned. 'Kept on like a mongrel dog, a stray brought in and fed and given somewhere to sleep because everyone was sorry for it.'

'Mm,' said Edwin, critically. 'Not bad. Walk upstage, turn, deliver line with a touch of defiance mixed with pathos. You were a bit late on the turn, though.'

'This isn't a bloody play!' said Thomas.

'Dear old boy, you're turning it into one,' said Edwin. 'And as it has a juicy leading part for you, and you're obviously enjoying it enormously, I'd leave you to it, except that it is rather upsetting Mother, who for some reason that I can't fathom is devoted to you.'

'Devoted to me?' repeated Thomas, contemptuously. 'Of course she isn't. She can't stand the sight of me. She's always biting my head off.'

'Ye – es,' replied Edwin, thoughtfully. 'I've been trying to work that out ever since she told me how much she loved you.'

He said it quite casually, as though it was of no importance, and Thomas was suddenly quite still, looking at him attentively.

'I think,' remarked Edwin, 'that if she didn't give a damn for you, she'd probably be extremely polite, as if you were a guest in the house. But you know Mother – never can do things by halves. Once she took you in, she had to get fond of you, too. Silly of her really.'

'Damn you, Edwin!' said Thomas.

Edwin laughed and stood up and came to put his arms round Thomas's shoulders.

'Cheer up, old lad,' he said. 'Look on the bright side.'

Thomas didn't poke him in the eye, but he did shake himself impatiently free.

'What bright side?' he demanded. 'That I'm the result of a sordid little affair? A by-blow? That I was forced upon this family, who've all lied to me about it ever since, because my real mother didn't care enough to have me with her –'

'*That*,' said Edwin, 'is the bright side. You must admit that Thomas Brett looks far better on the playbills than Thomas McAveetie!'

And then, at last, Thomas did laugh.

They all went to the last night of *The Liar*, and sat in the royal box. It was very nearly a full house, a number of people having realized belatedly that the play was coming off and that they hadn't seen it, so the final performance, like the first, had about it the atmosphere of energy and excitement. Halfway through the first act, the door of the box briefly opened and Thomas came in and stood quietly in the shadows at the back.

During the first interval Lydia and Edwin went off to visit Martha in her dressing room and Jean ensured that George and Maeve were served drinks in the little withdrawing room at the back of the royal box.

'Come and have a drink in the bar,' Charles said, casually, to Thomas.

The new barman was doing excellent business. Charles kept his eyes on the money being rung up on the till, and listened to the excited talk of the playgoers around them, occasionally giving a nod and a gracious smile to those who recognized him. He and Thomas drank their whisky in silence for some time, and then Charles heaved a sigh. Thomas thought he was going to launch into a prepared speech on fatherhood.

'Yes,' said Charles, 'well, this is all very well, but after tonight, we're all out of work, and that thing we were planning to bring in has fallen through. You'll have to write us a play, Thomas, and you have exactly one week to do it in.'

Thomas stared at him.

'I hardly thought you'd want a play from me after *Dark Dimensions*. It's obvious that nobody else does.'

'My dear boy –' began Charles, and caught the look in Thomas's face, and stopped short, and then went firmly on. 'If everyone gave up after one failure, there'd be no theatre left.'

'How do you know that *The Liar* wasn't a flash in the pan?'

Charles sipped his drink and pondered. Thomas suddenly realized that the answer meant a great deal more to him than any speech on fatherhood.

'I'm quite sure it wasn't,' said Charles. 'There was too much genuine talent in it, genuine quality. Even that

Dark Dimensions rubbish had some excellent moments in it.'

Thomas blinked slightly, but accepted the insult, because it meant much more that Charles was speaking to him as one professional to another.

'But this time,' Charles continued, 'give it a setting and a subject that you know something about – and, for God's sake, make it a comedy!'

'If the truth be told –' Thomas began, and this time *he* stopped short.

He had been about to say that he didn't think he could write comedy, but he had just remembered that play of which he had written the first act, and then got stuck. He might just – read it through – and see if there was anything in it.

After the performance and the prolonged applause of an audience reluctant to leave and all the bitter-sweet aftermath that marks the end of a successful production, they all went back to Nightingale Grove for a small party, and it was taken for granted by everyone, including Thomas, that he would accompany them. When the rest of the cast and the other guests had left, George took up a position centre stage on the hearth rug, and announced that he and Maeve were most grateful for the hospitality, but that they would shortly be leaving.

'Went to see a touring manager I know,' said George, amidst the general exclamations of astonishment and alarm. 'Very decent chap, and more honest than most touring managers. At least he doesn't fiddle the books.'

Jean's eyes met Martha's involuntarily across the

room, and the smile they unexpectedly exchanged took them both by surprise.

'Father, I really don't think you're up to it yet,' said Charles.

'Up to it? Nonsense! It's just a little tour – a week here, a week there – and he's making all the arrangements. It'll make a nice change, quite a holiday, really. We shall enjoy it, shan't we, Maeve?'

'Oh, yes, indeed we shall,' responded Maeve, her round face as innocent as a baby's beneath its halo of unconvincingly red-gold hair. 'It was very clever of your father to fix it up,' she added, confidingly, 'because Mr Pitt didn't really want us at first – thought he needed someone younger – but your father agreed to go for half the money, and then he was as pleased as Punch.'

'Yes, yes, never mind that!' George broke in, exasperated.

'What do you say, Lydia?' inquired Charles.

'Well –' Lydia began.

Conflicting emotions strove within her breast. It really was hell having George and Maeve in the house, with George interfering in their business all the time, and Maeve always pottering down to the kitchen to make a cup of tea and gossip with Flora just when she was trying to prepare the meals. On the other hand, tiresome old devil as he was, they really didn't want George to drop dead on the road. No, she must put her foot down and stop it.

'Father, I really think –' she began.

George, slightly deaf, was always able to raise his voice above anything he didn't wish to hear.

'It's all settled now, anyway,' he said. 'We leave on Sunday. Come on, Maeve. Time for bed.'

Lydia, turning away, found herself facing Thomas.

'Saved by the bell!' he said.

They both grinned before they had time to think, and then looked at each other gravely.

'I'm sorry,' said Thomas. 'What I said to you that day was unpardonable.'

'Nothing is unpardonable,' said Lydia. 'At least, I hope not.' She hesitated. 'You heard that – that your rooms are going to be empty. Do you feel like – like moving back?'

'Well,' replied Thomas, hesitating in his turn, 'I can certainly work better here than – than in my –'

'In your garret?' supplied Edwin, helpfully.

Thomas and Lydia ignored him, and he glanced at Martha, amused.

'Thank you, Ma,' said Thomas, and then caught himself up, 'I mean –'

'Thomas,' said Lydia, 'if you stop calling me "Ma" after all these years, I will kill you with my bare hands!'

She put her arms round him and held him close, just as she had held that ugly, combative little baby twenty-three years earlier. And Thomas now, like the baby, didn't respond to her embrace, but he didn't reject it, either.

Chapter Sixteen

Like most former nannies, Flora was a light sleeper.
It was a fine early morning in the September of that
same year, 1927, when she awoke, certain that she had
heard the creak of footsteps on the stairs. She slept in the
same little room where she had always slept, along the
passage from the night nursery, and at first she wondered
if it might be Thomas going down to the lavatory on the
landing. But somehow she thought that she would have
slept through Thomas in his slippered feet, and that the
sound she had heard was heavier. If it wasn't Thomas,
then – No one in that family got up early. It must be
burglars. With beating heart she got quietly out of bed
and put on her dressing-gown. If the last trump had been
announcing the end of the world, Flora would always
have put on her dressing-gown before answering the
summons.

She tiptoed to the door and opened it very cautiously,
and crept to the top of the stairs, relieved not, so far, to

have come face to face with a desperate criminal. But in that moment she heard, quite unmistakably, the creak of the staircase below her. Terrified but determined, she crept down the stairs, and peered down into the hall. She was just in time to see Edwin, nattily dressed in tweed jacket and Oxford bags, slipping quietly through the front door.

Two hours later, Sutton was preparing Lydia's breakfast tray and Flora was having a cup of tea.

'Do you know what time Master Eddie left the house this morning?' she inquired. And then, triumphantly, 'Five o'clock!'

'Bit early for riding,' remarked Sutton.

'He wasn't wearing his riding clothes,' said Flora.

Sutton, intent upon bringing Lydia's breakfast tray to its usual elegant perfection, answered idly enough.

'Then, if he's not going riding, why did he stay here last night?'

'That's what I'd like to know,' said Flora, darkly.

Emily emerged from the scullery with her wooden cleaning-box, just as Sutton put an autumn rosebud in the little silver vase.

'You'll have to start buying flowers soon,' said Flora.

'She likes them better from the garden,' responded Sutton.

Flora caught sight of Emily gawping at them.

'Stir your stumps, girl, for goodness' sake!' she exclaimed. 'Haven't you done those grates yet?'

'What about my cup of tea?' demanded Emily.

'Never mind your cup of tea!' said Flora. 'You get to work!'

Emily set off for the door, but she had been working herself up to say something, and this was just the impetus she needed.

'Miss Evans,' she said, 'when I went home yesterday, my mum spoke to me.'

'Doesn't she usually, then?' inquired Flora.

Emily, having once begun, doggedly continued.

'She reckoned I was being put upon.'

'Oh yes?' said Flora. 'So what did she think you should do about it?'

Sutton gazed at Flora, astonished. He knew a cue when he heard it.

'She said I ought to give in my notice,' said Emily, and gazed defiantly at Flora for a moment, and then turned and trudged out.

'Take it easy with her, Flora,' said Sutton. 'She's just beginning to settle down. We don't want to lose another one.'

He glanced at Flora, and saw her sipping her tea, her face expressionless.

'Flora,' he said, suspiciously, 'you're not trying to get rid of that girl, are you?'

'No,' Flora replied quickly. 'Certainly not! But –'

She met Sutton's accusing eye, and put her cup down. She took out of the pocket of her apron a crumpled letter written on cheap, lined paper.

'It's just that I had a letter from my sister yesterday, and she said, she wondered if there might be a place here for one of my nieces.'

'I see,' said Sutton, grimly.

It was an odd thing that, after all these years of working together, he and Flora had never really become close friends. They got on perfectly well together, but in a way it was like working with a foreigner, and it was at moments like this that he felt it most strongly. She had left Wales thirty years before, and yet her accent was as strong as ever, and even now, there was no doubt where her loyalties lay. The Bretts came first, perhaps, but after that –

'You know how it is, Mr Sutton,' she said, defensively, but stubbornly. 'My brother-in-law's out of work, and the pit closed down – the whole valley's out of work. There's no money coming into the house, and no jobs to be had. Mr Sutton, they're starving!'

'I know it's very hard,' said Sutton, 'but, after all, Flora, fair's fair.'

'Of course,' said Flora, glancing towards the kitchen door through which Emily had vanished, 'and I wouldn't be unfair to the girl, of course I wouldn't. Still, if she *did* want to leave – well – no harm done. Ah, there's Mr Hegarty!'

And avoiding Sutton's accusing eye, she hastily stuffed the letter away in her pocket and got up as Hegarty came in by the back door, fresh and trim in his chauffeur's uniform, his boots gleaming.

'I'll get your breakfast on now,' she said.

'Miss Evans, you're the queen of me heart,' said Hegarty, with that extra bit of Irish which he always put into his voice when he was teasing Flora.

'That's enough of that,' she said, going to fetch the bacon, and, despite her severe tone, by no means displeased, 'I'll have you remember, I was brought up Chapel.'

'Ah,' said Hegarty, 'isn't that just your fatal attraction for me?'

He grinned at Sutton, took the cosy off the teapot and sat down, pouring himself a cup of tea. He had shown a remarkable capacity to make himself at home and fit into the household, and he had brought into the kitchen a welcome touch of liveliness. He was friendly without being familiar, and his compliments were audacious without being impudent. And yet, if any of them had stopped to think, they knew almost nothing about him, except that he had been a policeman in Dublin. They took it for granted that he was not married, since he never mentioned a wife, and the only letters he received came from one of his sisters, who, he said, was a nun. But whether he had any friends in London, or how he spent his off time, when he was not at the races, not even Sutton knew.

'You're early,' Sutton now remarked.

'Mr Brett wants the car prompt at nine,' Hegarty replied. 'Isn't himself and the mistress off to the first rehearsal of Mr Thomas's new play? We're picking Miss Martha up at her flat on the way.'

Sutton groaned.

'I see trouble ahead,' he said.

Thomas had delighted, and, it must be said, astonished Charles and Lydia by actually writing the comedy in the week that Charles had stipulated. And a charming comedy it was, with excellent parts for Charles and Lydia, and a small but showy role for Martha in the last act. In fact, it was that part which had given him the key to the play. When he went back to read the first act he had written all those months ago, he found that it was witty and well constructed. Hardly a word needed to be changed, and, in some mysterious way, the experiences of the intervening time, both personal and professional, had taught him how to finish it, keeping it light and funny, and yet giving a little depth of feeling to the humorous façade. And, almost without knowing it, he used the stage *personae* of his parents and Martha to bring that extra individual gleam of life to his characters. There was also a part that Edwin might have played, but, rather to their surprise, he turned it down.

'I think one Brett writing the play and three Bretts acting in it is about enough,' he remarked.

Thomas's pleasure at his father's enthusiasm for the play soon received a slight dampener.

'It needs a few changes here and there,' said Charles.

'*Changes?*' repeated Thomas. 'What changes?'

He had not worked with his mother and father before, and had yet to learn that players of their stature and popularity tended to mould plays to their own shape, rather than adapt their style to the play. And then, of course, there was Martha. He had experienced Martha in *The Liar*, but he had yet to experience Martha, his mother and his father all together. Sutton was not in the least surprised when voices enjoyably upraised in argument heralded their return from the first rehearsal, as they continued the discussion begun in the car.

'I tell you, Martha,' roared Charles, 'there's not the slightest need for you to upstage me there. Mother's downstage.'

'Mother's in the light,' Martha countered.

'Mother's always in the light,' replied Charles. 'She bribes the electricians.'

Only the slightest twitch of Sutton's lips betrayed his amusement, as he took Lydia's tapestry bag from her.

'I don't have to bribe the electricians,' said Lydia, with dignity. 'I simply have a quiet word with them.'

Her eyes met Sutton's and she winked at him.

'By the way,' she added, walking on into the garden room, 'they say we're going to have to rewire sooner or later.'

'Never mind that now,' said Charles. 'Martha, we'll walk through that scene again.'

'There's a telegram for you, sir,' said Sutton.

'Not now!' said Charles, irritably.

They were all in that state of heightened excitement and twitchy nerves which came from the first rehearsal, when that part which had seemed on paper to offer such rich and easy opportunities was suddenly hampered by difficult moves, lines that didn't work, props at present invisible but soon to present endless possibilities for disaster, and, worst of all, fellow actors, who upstaged, topped good lines, suggested damaging changes, and generally contributed to the painful process of pulling the play to pieces with no real assurance that it would ever be satisfactorily put together again.

Charles had expected Martha to follow him into the garden room, but, as Hegarty came in, carrying her overnight case, she threw a furtive glance after her father and then turned back.

'You will do it, Patrick, won't you?' she begged.

'Ah, now, Miss Martha,' Hegarty protested, 'it's more than my job's worth!'

Sutton, who was waiting to follow Martha into the garden room, paused, unobtrusively by the staircase. He liked to know what was going on – and obviously something was.

'Come on, Patrick,' said Martha, a seductive note creeping into her voice, 'no one will ever know – and it really doesn't matter if they do. I'll say it's all my fault.'

'Well – I don't know, Miss Martha –'

Charles's voice preceded him as he came to the doorway.

'Martha, where are you?'

'That's settled, then!' whispered Martha, hastily. 'See you tomorrow evening!'

Hegarty shook his head and grinned slightly as he

watched her innocently and obediently obeying Charles's summons. Sutton spoke at his elbow.

'What's going on?'

'Oh, just a little favour she wants me to do her.'

'What kind of favour?' inquired Sutton, more suspicious than ever.

Hegarty only grinned at him.

'I should watch yourself with Miss Martha,' Sutton advised, with dignity. '*She* may be able to get away with anything, but that's not to say *you* can.'

He had meant it to be a stately admonition from the senior member of the staff, but Hegarty took it as a friendly warning.

'Mr Sutton,' he remarked, 'I may come from Ireland, but no one ever said I was green.'

He put Martha's case down by the stairs, and went outside to put the car away. As Sutton was looking after him, frowning, he heard Lydia's voice.

'Sutton, have you got that telegram?'

One of the great advantages of Nightingale Grove was that it had a room large enough for fairly lavish entertaining, but also suitable for use as a rehearsal room. Moreover, the garden end of the room was on a slightly higher level, so that it formed a little natural stage, with a piano on it. Sutton, having given the telegram to Lydia, watched with an experienced eye as Charles and Martha, script in hand, walked through their moves and declaimed their lines.

'Father – dearest Father!' cried Martha. 'Didn't it occur to you –?'

'Didn't – what – occur to me?' responded Charles, in a voice shaken with emotion.

He turned the page.

'That Mother understood you so much better than I did,' said Martha, movingly, 'and loved you so much more?'

'Dearest girl –'

Charles, glancing up, was shaken by a very different emotion.

'Dammit!' he exclaimed. 'You're upstaging me again!'

'Bound to, on that line,' remarked Sutton, drawing on his years of experience of watching in the wings. 'When she says that, the audience should be looking at her, not at you.'

'Thanks, Alfred,' said Martha, gratified.

Charles suddenly lost his temper. Just as Thomas always had the power to irritate Lydia because of the circumstances of his birth, so Charles tended to be particularly testy with Sutton, chiefly because he knew that Sutton's loyalty was given to Lydia far more than to him. It was noticeable that never in all their relationship had he ever addressed him as 'Alfred'.

'Sutton!' he roared, 'why don't you mind your own business? I pay you to be a butler, not a critic! You were no bloody good as an actor, so I don't know why you think *your* opinion should be worth anything!'

If Charles had planned it for years (which he certainly hadn't!) he could not have said anything more deeply wounding. Lydia was only listening with half an ear because she was reading the telegram. She had sat down, but now suddenly stood up again.

'Oh no!' she cried. 'Your blooming parents! "Gap in tour. Arriving Tuesday. Maeve and George." That's tomorrow!'

Charles was suddenly overtaken by one of his irreverent fits of laughter.

'Let's face it, me darlings,' he said, 'they're guaranteed to upstage us all! Sutton –'

Having recovered his temper, he was about to make some mildly conciliatory remark, but he was in time to see Sutton going quietly out of the room.

'Damn!' said Charles.

Time was when Flora would never have dreamed of going out on a day when visitors were arriving, even if the visitors were members of the family. But nothing short of the direst emergency would keep Flora away from the picture house and the arrival of George and Maeve, though considered to be dire by Charles and Lydia – and by Martha who was obliged to give up her room this time – was definitely not an emergency. Flora did, of course, go to some trouble to ensure that everything should go smoothly.

'Have you got it clear, now, Emily?' she demanded. 'Mr and Mrs George Brett will be arriving at about six o'clock, and dinner will be at eight.'

'Yes, Miss Evans,' said Emily, nervously.

Flora was wearing her best coat, and the hat with the cherries on it which she had bought for Miss Nell's wedding. It was rather a large hat, and those cherries, nodding about the images on the screen, had more than once received unfavourable comment from other patrons of the cinema who chanced to be sitting behind her, but it was Flora's best hat, and she always wore it in the summer. In the winter, she had another one with an equally irritating little tuft of feathers but she wore the cherries as long as possible because they seemed more festive. Flora always wore her best clothes to go to the picture house, rather as though she was dressing with particular care to meet her lover – which, of course, she was.

'I'll be back well before then,' she said, 'but I want you to get the dinner started.'

'I'll do my best,' said Emily, more alarmed than ever, 'but I don't know nothing about cooking.'

'So I've noticed,' replied Flora, crushingly, 'the way you keep burning the porridge! Now, all you have to do is to prepare the vegetables – I told you what I wanted – and then there are the two dishes in the larder, all ready. The baked fish takes an hour, and the veal takes an hour and a half, so you can just light the gas in the oven, and I can pop them in when I get back. Is that clear?'

'Yes, Miss Evans,' said Emily, who had lost track soon after the word 'vegetables'.

Flora looked at the clock on the mantelpiece and set off for the back door, a happy glow of anticipation in her plump cheeks.

'I'm off, then,' she said. 'And, mind, I want everything perfect tonight. Mr and Mrs George will have been living on boiled eggs and 'addock for the past two weeks.'

Sutton was sitting in his shirt-sleeves with his feet up, reading a copy of the *Stage*.

'What is it today, then, Flora?' he inquired as she passed him.

Flora paused, happy to share her enjoyable anticipation.

'John Gilbert and Greta Garbo,' she said, reverently, 'in *Flesh and the Devil*.'

'I say!' Sutton exclaimed. 'That sounds a bit risky. Are you sure your father would have approved?'

'Of course he would,' replied Flora, indignantly. 'It's a quotation from the Bible, that is.'

She had a slight qualm as she said it, because she

couldn't quite remember where it came in the Bible – if, indeed, it was there at all – but she soon suppressed it. As she proceeded towards the door, she was already moving into her dream world.

'I always like John Gilbert,' she said. 'He puts me in mind of Master Eddie.'

The return of George and Maeve to Nightingale Grove was not attended by quite the same sympathetic drama as last time, and when dinnertime came, the rallying-round element was notably absent, together with several members of the family. Thomas was already committed to dining out and going to the theatre. Martha also pleaded a previous engagement, though she did not say what it was. Edwin said that he would be busy all day, but that he would try to arrive in time for dinner. By eight o'clock, he had not appeared, and it was in the depleted and reluctant company of Charles and Lydia, supported by a faithful Jean, that George stood on the hearth rug and held forth upon the triumphs of their tour. Maeve sat and sipped sweet sherry, gazing at him admiringly.

'I must say,' George remarked, 'our season at Shoreham was a great success. And then we moved on to East Preston –'

'East Preston?' repeated Charles. 'I didn't know there was a theatre at East Preston.'

'Oh, darling, really!' exclaimed Lydia, impatiently. 'Theatre – village hall – what does it matter?'

'"Village Hall"?' said George, deeply offended. 'Certainly not. Jubilee Hall. Very decent little place.'

'So it was,' Maeve agreed. 'It was just that the roof leaked a trifle.'

George decided not to have heard.

'Very well attended,' he continued, 'and a very appreciative audience. When we did *Othello*, and I said, "Put out the light", a woman in the front row said, "Look out, Missus!"'

'He did so,' Maeve agreed, proudly. 'And a gentleman in the back called out – excuse the language, dear – "Don't you trust that black bugger!"'

'Well, there you are,' said George, complacently. 'That's what the theatre is all about – bringing the first experience of the drama to those who have never known it before.'

'That's what they say about the Moving Pictures,' remarked Jean.

'My dear Jean!' exclaimed Charles, who had been becoming increasingly restive. 'I never heard such rubbish! Moving Pictures, indeed! A ridiculous pantomime, with actors opening and shutting their mouths and no words coming out. Actors! They're not actors. They're like a lot of performing dogs.' A sudden thought struck him. 'Do you know who was voted the most popular film-star this year?'

'John Gilbert?' suggested Lydia. 'Lillian Gish?'

'Ronald Colman?' offered Jean.

Charles shook his head. Lydia pondered.

'Rudolph Valentino!' she said, triumphantly. And then, 'Oh, no, he's dead. Who, then?'

'Rin Tin Tin,' said Charles, triumphantly.

He saw George and Maeve looking blank.

'He's a dog, dammit!' he said.

Jean and Lydia laughed, but George and Maeve still looked blank.

'Are we ever going to get any dinner?' Charles demanded.

Jean, emerging from the garden room in answer to a despairing glance from Lydia, encountered Sutton lurking in the hall.

'What's happened to dinner?' she whispered.

'It's Flora,' replied Sutton. 'She's not back yet. I've had to put the understudy on.'

'"Understudy"?' repeated Jean, puzzled, and then, 'You don't mean Emily!'

As she gazed at him, aghast, Lydia made a gracious exit from the garden room. She closed the door firmly behind her before turning, fuming, on Sutton.

'Alfred,' she said, 'if I have to listen to one more word about taking culture to the natives beneath corrugated iron roofs, I shall strike that aged Thespian dead where he stands. What in hell's name has happened to the dinner?'

She sniffed. They all sniffed. Sutton turned towards the door which led to the kitchen.

'Emily!' he called. 'Have you burned the dinner?'

'*Emily?*' Lydia repeated, and threw an astonished glance at Jean. 'Where's Flora?'

Lydia, following Sutton into the kitchen, was in time to see Emily removing from the oven the charred remnants of both fish and veal.

'Oh, madam!' exclaimed Emily, dismayed. 'I'm very sorry, madam. Miss Evans said as how I was to light the oven, but she never said how hot I should make it.'

Maeve, hearing of the disaster which had befallen the dinner, sprang immediately into delighted action.

'Now, Lydia,' she cried, 'don't you be worrying about a thing. I'll make some scrambled eggs on toast for us all.'

'Now, Maeve,' said George, 'don't interfere.'

'Nonsense,' replied Maeve, looking fondly at her son. 'If there's one thing Charlie likes, it's my scrambled eggs.'

'Er – yes, Mother dear,' replied Charles. 'Delicious. But – er –'

266

He looked towards Lydia for inspiration.

'Why don't we all go out,' said Lydia, 'and celebrate – er – celebrate the success of your tour!'

'Good idea!' said George, readily leaping up.

He, too, liked Maeve's scrambled eggs, but felt that he had had quite enough during the past fortnight.

'Sutton,' said Charles, resignedly, 'ask Hegarty to bring the car round.'

'Very sorry, sir,' replied Sutton, standing to attention, butler-wise. 'Hegarty's not here.'

'What?' exclaimed Charles, indignantly, and then, 'Oh yes. He did ask me if we'd need him again tonight, and I said we wouldn't.'

'I'll make my scrambled eggs!' cried Maeve.

A second later – 'I'll drive the car myself,' said Charles.

'Car's not here, either, sir,' said Sutton, boot-faced.

'What?' exclaimed Charles, indignantly, 'Are you telling me that Hegarty's gone joy-riding in my motor car?'

'Not exactly, sir,' replied Sutton, clearly driven into a corner. 'Er – I believe Miss Martha asked him to drive her out into the country.'

'Where in the country?' inquired Lydia.

Sutton's expressionless voice was the butler's voice, but his eyes met hers with absolute honesty. He never lied to Lydia.

'I don't know, madam.'

At that precise moment, Emily, trying to scrape some edible remnants of the veal off the dish, saw Flora coming in at the back door, hat askew and eyes wild.

'I'm ever so sorry, Miss Evans,' said Emily, 'but – I'm afraid I burned the dinner.'

'Never mind that,' said Flora, astonishingly.

She surged on towards the kitchen door, calling, 'Mr Sutton!' Emily, like any decent Londoner, scenting drama, followed her as she would have followed a fire engine.

Sutton met Flora, emerging from the garden room with the others behind him.

'Are you all right?' he inquired.

'Flora!' exclaimed Lydia. 'Have you had an accident?'

'Knocked down by an omnibus, I shouldn't wonder,' said Maeve, sympathetically. 'Nasty great red things. Come inside, now, and sit down, and I'll make you a nice cup of tea.'

They supported her inside, and Sutton and Maeve assisted her to sit down. Lydia, Charles and George gathered round, with Emily, all agog, in the doorway.

'Oh, sir!' said Flora. 'Oh, madam!'

'Emily,' said Jean, 'would you make a cup of tea?'

'Yes, Miss Lacy,' said Emily, and backed away, but then came to a halt, reluctant to leave the drama.

'Flora,' said Lydia, in a tone of sympathy, with exasperation lurking just below the surface, 'what exactly has happened? Are you hurt?'

'Oh, no, madam!' cried Flora. 'It's not me. It's – it's –'

'Martha!' exclaimed Charles, alarmed. 'Hegarty crashed the car, and Martha –'

'Oh, no, sir,' gasped Flora. 'It's Master Eddie!'

Lydia turned away, shocked, and Charles, equally shocked, put his arms round her.

They all looked at each other in dismay.

'Flora,' said Sutton, determined to get the news out of her, for good or ill, 'has Master Eddie had an accident?'

Flora looked up at him with tears streaming down her face.

'He – he –'

As they all stood round her, frozen in grief and horror, the front door slammed, and Edwin appeared in the doorway.

'Hullo?' he said. 'What's going on?'

'Oh, Master Eddie!' cried Flora. 'Why didn't you tell me?'

'Oh,' said Edwin, seeming to be rather taken aback.

'Tell her what?' asked Charles.

Lydia, drawing out of Charles's loosened embrace, went to fling her arms round Edwin.

'Eddie, darling!' she cried. 'Are you all right?'

Flora was single-mindedly answering Charles's question.

'There he was, sir,' she said, 'up on the screen as large as life.'

Lydia suddenly took her arms away from round Edwin's neck.

'The screen?' she said, sharply.

She looked at Edwin. He guiltily returned her gaze.

'I just looked up, madam,' Flora pursued, 'and there he was.'

'Where?' inquired Maeve, confused. 'Where was he?'

'Not under a bus, that's one thing sure,' said George, and went to pour himself another drink.

Sutton decided that it was time to assert himself and clarify the matter, for everyone's sake.

'I think she's talking about the Moving Pictures,' he said. 'It was John Gilbert, Flora,' he added, kindly. 'You said that he put you in mind of Master Eddie.'

'Oh, him!' said Flora, with a contempt which bordered upon blasphemy. 'He's not a patch on Master Eddie! I had to sit through the big picture twice, Master Eddie, just so I could see your film three times.'

She turned to Lydia.

'He was wearing that tie, madam,' she said, 'the one you gave him for Christmas, and he played the part of the nice young policeman, the one that was in love with the young lady, but she went off with the other one – and a good thing, too! She wasn't nearly good enough for him. And Master Eddie got him off, but if you ask me, he did it all the time.'

'Flora,' said Charles, feebly grasping at reality, 'are you saying that Mr Edwin is appearing in a film?'

'It was only a quota quickie, Father,' said Edwin, apologetically.

'And what, might I ask, is that?'

'Oh, come on, Charles,' said Lydia, 'you know quite well what quota quickies are.'

'Well, I certainly don't,' said George.

'I'm sure there's no harm in them,' Maeve interposed, smiling fondly at Edwin.

'There was an Act passed in Parliament,' said Lydia, 'called the Cinematograph Films Act, or something like that, which said there had to be a certain proportion of British films shown in cinemas in this country. That's right, Eddie, isn't it?'

'Quite right, Mother. Lots of film companies sprang up to take advantage of the Act and make British films to be shown here. They're cheap and not very good, and –'

'And you're appearing in one of them,' said Charles.

'Yes,' Edwin answered, with more than a touch of defiance. 'It brought in a bit of money – and no one else was offering me any work.'

As he glanced round at them all, his eyes fell on Flora, gazing at him, with tears still on her cheeks, and he went to go down on his knees beside her and take her hand.

'Flora,' he said, 'I'm sorry I didn't tell you, but I knew you'd only be disappointed. I'm no good in films.'

'Oh, Master Eddie!' cried Flora. 'You were beautiful!'

Edwin laughed and kissed her cheek, and then stood up and looked defiantly at Charles and Lydia.

'Well,' he said, 'they pay quite well, anyway. As a matter of fact, I'm making another one now, with a Hungarian director, Laszlo Sandor.'

There seemed to be absolutely nothing to say in reply to this. Lydia decided to try to return to some sort of normality.

'Flora,' she said, 'about dinner –'

But Flora was still in a happy daze.

'It's very kind of you, Miss Lydia,' she said, 'but I couldn't eat a bite.'

Chapter Seventeen

Sutton's foreboding of trouble at the prospect of Charles, Lydia, Martha and Thomas all working together in the same production was more than justified. Charles was accustomed to having his own way in everything, and so, in her more subtle way, was Lydia. Thomas was a perfectionist by nature, and his terror that the failure of *Dark Dimensions* might be repeated caused his perfectionism to verge upon paranoia.

As for Martha, she had never manifested the same single-minded dedication to the theatre as the rest of them. She had always delighted in doing outrageous things, ever since, at the age of three, she stood up in the drawing room of the Carstairs' country house and sang one of Marie Lloyd's fruitier songs with all-too-appropriate gestures to a stunned audience of distinguished guests. ('Where did she hear it?' her Auntie Elsie and Uncle Harry had asked each other, aghast.) Since her husband's death in the war, she had had a series of love affairs which she had conducted with such a total lack of discretion that somehow they had caused no real scandal. Perhaps it was because, like Talullah Bankhead, she had come to be accepted as a 'character', part of the post-war society scene. The danger was that, playing this part with such gusto and success, the time might come when she could play no other, and that, loving so easily and carelessly, she might in the end be incapable of ever really loving deeply again. Irresponsibility, though not one of the seven deadly sins, is certainly one of the most destructive. All the family were irritated by Martha's irresponsibility, but it was, perhaps, only Edwin, her twin, who was aware of its danger.

It was unfortunate that in *If The Truth Be Told*, Martha appeared only in the last act. Her rehearsals, therefore, were not as frequent or as regular as the others', and her attendance became increasingly belated and, somehow, dilatory. The part itself, too, as she never failed to mention, was a great deal smaller than she had thought at first.

In addition to everything else, it was the first time that Thomas had worked with his father not only acting in the play, but also acting as manager and producer, thus holding the purse strings – and uncommonly penny-pinching he turned out to be.

When Piers had departed, it had been taken for granted, in typical Brett fashion, that Jean would continue to work in the theatre office, so she had, in effect, been acting theatre manager, without the slightest increase in salary, or any acknowledgement of her changed situation except that they all unerringly turned to her to solve their problems or to complain when anything went wrong.

Shortly after the revelation of Edwin's dubious

activities in the film world, Thomas banged open the door of the theatre office in a blazing temper whose expression was only slightly hampered by the effort of climbing five flights of stairs. (It had often occurred to Jean what an advantage those stairs were, and she hoped that Charles would never get around to installing a lift in the Princess Theatre.)

'Jean!' gasped Thomas. 'That blasted scenery hasn't arrived!'

Jean, working at the large desk by the window, glanced up and answered vaguely.

'Oh, hasn't it?'

Thomas took several deep breaths, and was off again.

'Father promised faithfully that by now we would be rehearsing in the set,' he said. 'He and Mother are wandering about all over the place – and as for Sophie, she spends half her time straddling the french windows.'

Jean's attention had already returned to the papers, which were giving her some trouble, and needed all her concentration.

'If Sophie gets too set in her ways,' she said, 'we can always leave the french windows open on the first night.'

'*Jean*,' said Thomas, ominously.

Jean, giving him her full attention for the first time, recognized the all-too-familiar crisis of artistic integrity. She pushed aside the account book with its non-matching vouchers.

'I'm sorry, Thomas,' she said. 'I know they did promise to deliver it yesterday, but –'.

'It's not as if they've got to build it,' said Thomas, resentfully. 'We're renting most of it.'

This was another of Charles's little economies – saving money on newly-designed scenery.

'They've got to build the summerhouse for the last act,' said Jean.

'Well, why can't they send the rest?'

'It's cheaper', Jean replied, 'to send it all together.'

'Oh, I see!' exclaimed Thomas, preparing to work himself up into a rage all over again. 'This is one of Father's cheese-paring notions!'

'No,' replied Jean, 'I'm afraid it's mine.'

'Oh,' said Thomas, taken aback. 'That's what's known as "cutting the ground away from under someone's feet". I'm not sure exactly how it's done, but the effect is the same.'

Jean laughed, and he perched on the little desk and they smiled at each other. They had always been friends since he first surprised her in Charles's study six months earlier, and if he had not been so much engrossed in his own affairs during the Piers *débâcle*, she might have confided in him and saved herself a lot of anguish.

'I tell you what,' said Jean. 'I'll go round in my lunch hour, and see what's holding the scenery up. They *did* promise it.'

'You haven't had a lunch hour since Piers left,' said Thomas, and then, seeing her flinch, 'Sorry. Shouldn't I have mentioned him?'

Jean stood up and answered briskly.

'Don't be silly,' she said. 'Since I'm still trying to clear up the mess he left behind, his name comes up every day.'

There was a file on the desk, and, in order to hide her face from Thomas's observant eyes, she picked it up and went to put it away in the filing cabinet.

'And that's the worst of it,' said Thomas.

She replied without looking round.

'No,' she said. 'The worst of it is having been such an idiot.'

'We're all idiots,' said Thomas. 'The worst of it is being found out.'

That made Jean laugh, and she shut the drawer of the filing cabinet and turned.

'Oh, Thomas, yes!' she cried. 'That's the worst of it. Everyone knows. They know that Piers got away with barefaced robbery for so long because I fell in love with him. And they must all know, as I do, that he never gave a fig for me. He just made me think that he did, so that –'

She stopped laughing, and her face had that grimness of youth betrayed which had dismayed Sutton, and which she had thought was behind her.

'Never again,' she said. 'I will never trust anyone again, as long as I live.'

'I know how you feel,' said Thomas. 'But it's rather a lonely feeling, isn't it?'

Jean found a tear running down her cheek, the first since she had learned of Piers's betrayal. Thomas came to put his arm round her.

'Bastards are alone, too,' he said. 'They have to find their own place in the world.'

She leaned against him for a moment, and then broke free.

'How absurd you are!' she said. 'You've found yours. You're a talented and successful playwright.'

She returned behind the desk, as though taking refuge.

'Talented, I grant you,' said Thomas, who, like most writers, knew his own worth, even if others didn't. 'But, successful? That remains to be seen. But *you* –'

'Oh yes?' replied Jean, scornfully. 'What am I supposed to be? I'm not trained for anything except secretarial work, which I hate, and I've no special talents –'

'Except for being you,' said Thomas. 'That's quite special.'

He had come to take her hand, and was pressing it tenderly when Charles surged into the room.

'Jean?' he said, as he made his entrance. 'Oh, there you are, Thomas.'

Jean hastily withdrew her hand, but Charles's mind was on other things.

'Jean,' he said, 'did you send Hegarty to pick something up?'

'No, sir,' Jean replied. 'I haven't seen him this morning.'

'What's the matter?' inquired Thomas, calmly enough.

'That blasted sister of yours', replied Charles, 'hasn't turned up for rehearsals.'

Thomas's calmness disappeared in an instant.

'*What*? She is the bloody limit!'

Jean picked up the rehearsal schedule.

'She wasn't called until twelve o'clock,' she said.

'Exactly,' replied Charles. 'I arranged for Hegarty to go and pick her up at her flat, and he hasn't come back, and neither has she.'

It was at about that time that Martha walked into her tiny flat in Shepherd's Market. It had formerly belonged to a prostitute, which could explain its slightly disproportionate design, with a huge bed, a tiny kitchen, a small bathroom and one armchair. It suited Martha perfectly, not least because it could never be more than a *pied-à-terre* – one foot on the ground, and otherwise no commitments. Perhaps that was why she clung so fiercely to 'Martha's room' at Nightingale Grove. After her marriage to Basil, she had still lived in her parents' house, and it was there that she heard of his death. To set up a proper home elsewhere might be to take responsibility for her own life, and that she was not yet – if ever – ready to do.

Martha was wearing a cloche hat and a fur coat which she slid out of like a snake shedding its skin, leaving it behind her on the floor as she advanced, looking over her shoulder at Hegarty, as he came in, his cap under his arm, carrying her small but expensive suitcase. He put it down just inside the door, where he prudently remained.

'Thanks, Patrick,' said Martha.

He really was awfully attractive, she thought, with his fair hair and green eyes and face with a hint of the leprechaun about it.

'I thought I made quite a good choice of outfits,' she remarked. 'Which did you like best?'

'I'm really not a great judge,' replied Hegarty, primly.

'The négligé?' Martha suggested.

'That was very becoming,' Hegarty answered, 'but I think I preferred the evening dress.'

'There!' cried Martha, triumphantly. 'I knew you were taking an interest!'

Hegarty's face gave nothing away.

'Never having been in such a place before,' he said, 'I naturally took an interest in all that was going on.'

'Naturally,' said Martha, and then, 'Including me?'

Hegarty stooped and picked up the fur coat, and held it out for her to put on.

'Will I be driving you to the theatre now, Miss Martha, for the rehearsal?'

Martha took the coat from him and threw it down on the bed.

'Oh, it's much too late,' she said. 'By now, Father will have lost his temper and stormed off to have lunch at the Ivy.'

She wandered into the kitchen and found a bottle of champagne and two glasses. Hegarty was standing in the same place, quietly attentive, like a good chauffeur – or a good policeman.

'Can you open a bottle of champagne?' inquired Martha, putting bottle and glasses down on a small table.

'I haven't much experience in such things,' replied Hegarty, in the manner of an Irish country boy.

Martha subsided on to the bed, her short dress revealing a long length of silk-stockinged leg.

'It really isn't difficult,' she said. 'It just needs – strength.'

Hegarty came and picked up the bottle of champagne, and Martha prepared to direct the proceedings.

'You just unscrew that wire –' she began.

But Hegarty had put his cap down, twisted the wire, taken off the foil, and had the cork eased off and the first of the champagne into the glasses while Martha's mouth was still open. Glancing up, he saw the expression on her face.

'Me old granny taught me,' he said, apologetically, and filled one of the glasses and brought it to her.

'Patrick,' she said, 'you're a fraud.'

He went to fill the other glass.

'Excuse me, Miss Martha,' he said, 'but it is customary to call the chauffeur by his second name. Mine's Hegarty.'

'I prefer Patrick,' said Martha, leaning back seductively.

'You're the boss's daughter,' said Hegarty. 'You can call me what you like.'

Martha inwardly acknowledged that this was a palpable hit, but she certainly wasn't going to let him know that it had landed.

'Oh, don't be so stuffy!' she said. 'Have a nice glass of warm champagne, and you'll feel better. After all, it's only policemen who don't drink on duty.'

She eyed him thoughtfully.

'Did you like being a policeman better than being a chauffeur?' she inquired.

For a second, Hegarty's face showed a flicker of resentment at this invasion of his private feelings, but the next moment he was smiling, and Martha realized that his smile was a form of defence.

'The hours are about the same, and so is the pay,' he said, 'but you meet a better class of person.'

'Here, or in the police?'

'Sure, I wouldn't like to say.'

He raised his glass to her, a twinkle in his eye.

'Here's good fortune to you, Miss Martha,' he said, 'in all your ventures.'

'All of them?' inquired Martha. 'Oh, thank you, Hegarty!'

He put the glass down and picked up his cap.

'Will I wait in the car?' he asked. 'Or have you decided where you want to have lunch?'

'I don't think I care about lunch,' said Martha.

She got up from the bed. She knew she was doing something appalling, but she couldn't stop herself. It was like that moment when a man who drinks too much finally slips into alcoholism. If Hegarty had made any kind of approach to her when he came in, she would probably have repulsed him, but as it was, she felt that he was a challenge, and she couldn't resist trying him out. She came close to him and took his cap and put it down again.

'I find you awfully attractive,' she said, 'and I think

you find me attractive, too, though one never likes to take these things for granted.'

'Oh, I think you can take that for granted,' replied Hegarty, mildly.

'Oh, good!' said Martha.

She was about to put her arms round his neck, but before she could do so, Hegarty spoke again.

'It's just the matter of the luncheons and the dinners and the suppers,' he said, earnestly.

She looked at him, frowning.

'When I take a young lady out,' Hegarty explained, 'I like to pay, but you're accustomed to the Savoy or the Ritz or the Ivy, and on a chauffeur's pay –'

'I told you,' said Martha. 'I don't care about lunch!'

'I don't know about that,' responded Hegarty, even more earnestly. 'As time went by, you'd get very hungry.'

Martha eyed him for a moment in silence, and he looked back, sober as a judge.

'Patrick,' she said, accusingly, 'you're not only a fraud, you're a – a –'

'Yes, Miss Martha?'

'An escape artist!' she said.

'Yes, Miss Martha,' he said, and now the twinkle was back in his eye.

It was while they were still standing close together and smiling at each other that Lydia walked in. She stopped dead, and then spoke in a voice of cool detachment.

'Oh, Hegarty,' she said. 'Mr Brett was wondering where you were. Perhaps you'd be good enough to wait in the car.'

'Yes, madam,' said Hegarty, and picked up his cap and walked quietly out.

Lydia waited until Hegarty had gone before turning on Martha.

'Really, Martha!' she said. 'How *could* you?'

'Sorry I missed the rehearsal,' said Martha.

'Never mind that,' said Lydia. 'You don't give a damn about the theatre.'

'That's not true!' said Martha, indignantly.

'No? Perhaps one day you'll prove it. Meanwhile –'

She walked forward into the room. There was no play-acting now. She really was distressed and shocked.

'However outrageously you've behaved in the past,' she said, 'you've always got away with it, because on the whole it was funny without being vulgar. But – but to have an affair with a chauffeur – and the family chauffeur at that –! How could you? Martha, how *could* you?'

Martha shrugged. The fact that she felt uneasy, guilty and, in a strange way, puzzled by her own behaviour made her all the less inclined to admit as much to her mother.

'I suppose you realize', said Lydia, 'that he'll lose his job.'

'Not if you don't tell Father,' said Martha. 'Nothing happened, anyway. He wasn't interested.'

'Which means that you did make a play for him,' said Lydia. 'Martha, *really*!'

'Oh, come on, Mother!' said Martha, beginning to recover her equilibrium. 'Haven't you ever thrown out a lure just for the hell of it?'

'Certainly not!' replied Lydia, swiftly, and received, equally swiftly, the unwelcome image of Gerard Lee, his dark eyes glowing in his young, thin face. 'Certainly not with a chauffeur,' she added, regaining safer ground. 'All right, I won't say anything to your father, as long as you promise me that in future you'll turn up to rehearsals on time, and that there'll be no more of this taking Hegarty off into the country.'

'Mm,' said Martha, thinking it over. 'I'd like to promise that, Mother, but the trouble is, I may need Hegarty again to take me to Richmond.'

'Richmond? Why on earth should you want to go to Richmond?'

'At least it's not Winchmore Hill,' said Martha.

'Winchmore Hill?' Lydia repeated, beginning to look slightly dazed. 'Where's Winchmore Hill?'

'There's a film studio there,' said Martha.

Lydia stared at her, aghast.

'Don't tell me you're making quota quickies, too!'

'Certainly not,' replied Martha, with dignity. 'Eddie introduced me to Laszlo Sandor, and he's given me a very nice part in quite a big film.'

If she hoped to pacify Lydia with this information, she was disappointed.

'You're not telling me that you've been missing rehearsals of a play – and Thomas's play at that – just so that you could appear in a film! I don't believe it. It's so – so unprofessional. And you know what your father thinks of films.'

'Only because no one has ever offered him one.'

'Rubbish!' said Lydia.

'Laszlo wants to offer him a part.'

'In a quota quickie?' inquired Lydia, with supreme contempt. 'He wouldn't even consider it.'

'No – o,' replied Martha. 'Not a quota quickie. Quite an important film, actually.'

Lydia eyed her sceptically.

'*The King Shall Not Die*?' suggested Martha.

Lydia looked back at her, stunned and speechless.

An imposing notice which read BRITISH EMPIRE FILMS marked the entrance to Laszlo's film studio. It was decorated with a rather dubious coat of arms, consisting of two lions rampant who were either supporting or wrangling over an imperial crown, beneath the legend, set in a curly scroll: 'Per artis ad astra'. The fact that this large board was hung on a gate which was slightly off its hinges did not escape the attention of Charles and Lydia as they approached it in the car, with Hegarty driving and Sutton sitting beside him in the front, clutching a wig stand and the wig Charles wore for *The King Shall Not Die*.

Hegarty brought the car to a halt and looked hopefully round for someone to open the gate.

'When I brought Miss Martha here,' he said, 'there was a commissionaire – but he did tell me that sometimes he did a bit of acting as well.'

'Good heavens!' exclaimed Charles, glancing nervously at Lydia.

He had thought that a film studio would simply be like a theatre, but with camera instead of an audience. It seemed that he was mistaken.

Hegarty resignedly got out and opened the gate and drove inside, braking slightly to avoid a horse which was approaching up the drive. The horse itself seemed moderately normal, but its rider appeared to believe that he was Napoleon, and was practising horse management with one hand tucked inside his military jacket and a cocked hat on his head which tended to slip from side to side with the motion of the horse. A sudden outbreak of barking from a huge dog chained up nearby upset his perilous equilibrium, and horse and Napoleon disappeared at a gallop through the gate and down the road, leaving the cocked hat behind. Charles craned round to look through the back window, and then turned back to see that they were approaching a large and somewhat eccentric-looking house, with a huge, castellated portico.

Hegarty opened the door for Lydia, and Sutton, still clasping wig stand and wig, opened the door for Charles, who, as he descended, observed that something very odd seemed to be going on near the big cedar tree in the grounds. A number of Arabs were gathered round a Bedouin tent, from which a scantily clad young lady emerged, and started back, hand on bosom. One of the Arabs stepped forward and, in a dramatic gesture, tore the veil from her face. Sutton cleared his throat.

'Er – yes,' said Charles, withdrawing his attention from this scene with difficulty, and walking round the car to join Lydia. She took his arm.

'Hollywood, here we come!' she said.

As they went inside, they could not help noticing that both the portico and the corridor into which it led were somewhat down at heel, and that the stag's head, which was the dominant feature of the entrance, was indubitably moth-eaten.

'Orange groves, palm trees and Charlie Chaplin?' suggested Charles, glancing round.

'And fame and fortune,' said Lydia.

He paused.

'I thought we had that already,' he said.

'Of course,' answered Lydia. 'But one can't have too much of a good thing.'

She grasped his arm more firmly and they advanced together along the corridor.

On a large oak staircase at the end of the corridor,

Edwin, in the uniform of 'Sir Hugo', the dastardly villain, was practising the duel, counting the stairs and working out the camera shots in a highly professional manner. A props man descended the stairs carrying a candelabra and Edwin nearly decapitated him.

'Oh, sorry Herbert,' he said, cheerfully, and then spotted Charles and Lydia approaching.

He leaped athletically off the staircase and came to meet them. He seemed very much at home in these extraordinary and disconcerting surroundings.

'Hullo, Father,' he said, hastily sheathing his sword. 'Mother, dear, you look lovely.'

As Edwin kissed her, Charles reflected that Lydia did, indeed, look stunning. She was dressed up to the nines, and he felt proud of her, as he always did. On the other hand – it was *his* screen test, and not hers.

'Well,' he said, 'where's this Hungarian of yours?'

'Yes, of course,' replied Edwin. 'You must come and meet Laszlo.'

'He's in the studio, I presume,' said Charles.

'Er – Father,' replied Edwin, 'this *is* the studio. All of it.'

He led the way into a big room, once the elegant drawing room of a country house, but now, with peeling paint and flaking plaster, housing two or three different sets. It was rather like a disorganized dolls' house where the various rooms were scattered about at random, here a boudoir, next to it a garret. In addition to the hammering of carpenters, various men were wandering about with ladders, lights and bits of furniture, apparently at random.

'I hope I'm not expected to act in this – this shemozzle,' said Charles, nervously.

'Oh – no, Father,' replied Edwin, but threw an anxious glance at Lydia.

'Harry!' yelled one of the scene-shifters from the hall, 'you seen that *chez* long?'

'The what?'

'The sofa!'

'It's in the boudwar.'

'Right!'

'This way,' said Edwin, leading the way towards the glass doors which gave on to the garden.

'Sofa?' said Charles, puzzled. 'I didn't think we were doing the bedroom scene. I thought we were –'

'No, no, that's not our set, Father,' replied Edwin. 'It's Martha's.'

'I might have known,' said Charles, resignedly, and followed Edwin and Lydia outside.

Sutton, having done some exploring of his own, and disposed of the wig stand and wig, came into the drawing room and paused, glancing disgustedly about him. He peered round the wall of the boudoir and found three men playing pontoon in the garret. He withdrew, shaking his head disapprovingly, and trod in a stately manner towards the door to the garden.

'Good heavens!' exclaimed Lydia.

Beyond the rose garden was – it could not be – but surely it was? – Versailles.

'Ah, there he is!' cried Edwin, and vanished.

'Where's he gone?' asked Charles, and added, feebly, 'Have they really built Versailles in – in –?'

'Who knows?' answered Lydia.

Edwin reappeared round the corner of Versailles, which turned out to be a pane of glass hung between two posts. He was accompanied by Laszlo Sandor, who was in his late thirties, prematurely grey, with a thin, quirkish face. He wore a Savile Row suit, with silk shirt and tie, and, quite incongruously, a beret. As he hastened towards Charles and Lydia, he was followed by Violet, the continuity girl, who wore an unbecoming dress and her hair curled round her ears in 'earphones'. Wherever Laszlo went, Violet followed, anxiously taking notes. One felt that if Laszlo went to bed with a girl, Violet would be there to ensure that the sheets next morning would be rumpled to exactly the right degree.

'An honour!' exclaimed Laszlo, shaking hands with Charles. 'A true honour to meet one of our greatest actors.'

'Thank you,' responded Charles, graciously. He extended an expansive hand towards Lydia. 'My wife, Miss Wheatley.'

Laszlo bent, with Continental elegance, to kiss Lydia's hand.

'Everyone', he said, 'knows the beautiful Miss Wheatley.'

He kept her hand in his, and smiled into her eyes. Charles, however, felt that it was time to get down to business.

'Are we – er – are we filming in the garden?' he inquired.

'But, no, Mr Brett,' replied Laszlo, readily. 'Did you not see your staircase?'

'My –?'

Laszlo laughed engagingly.

'Other film producers', he said, 'rent warehouses, build sheds – I buy this house. It contains everything I need – but, above all, it has a staircase! Never do I have to build a staircase. That is the secret of my success!'

He laughed again, it was hard to tell whether in triumph or self-mockery.

'I see,' said Charles, quite out of his depth.

'Ah, there's Martha,' said Edwin.

His tone of relief showed that he felt that he needed some support.

Martha emerged from the drawing room, wearing an extremely low-cut dress in the Empire style. Charles now vaguely recollected that she had said that she was playing Josephine.

'Hullo, Father,' said Martha, kissing him, and then to Lydia, 'Mother, you look marvellous.'

'Thank you, Martha, dear,' said Lydia, sedately. 'I'm just here to support your father.'

'What do you think of this dress, Laszlo?' asked Martha.

Laszlo surveyed Lydia thoughtfully before turning to look at Martha.

'Perfect, my darlink,' he said. 'Perfect. After the screen test, we shoot your next scene.'

'We shoot back to back, Father,' explained Martha, helpfully.

'Not literally, I hope,' said Charles, in what he hoped was a jovial manner.

'No, no,' Laszlo explained, seriously. 'We shoot one scene in one set while we prepare the other set. So we save money.'

'Yes,' said Charles, 'but surely, the noise, and the hammering –'

He caught the expression in Laszlo's face, and laughed cheerily.

'Of course,' he said. 'No sound.'

Laszlo spread out his hands, beaming in acquiescence.

'So,' he said, 'we get to work. Edwin has agreed to do the screen test with you. Very kind. Very generous. And so much better so. Then you don't have to play the scene with a stranger.'

Charles, as the leading actor, was not altogether happy

at the suggestion that playing the scene with Edwin was a privilege.

'Well – yes – Edwin knows the moves,' he said.

'Ah,' replied Laszlo. 'The moves. Yes. I tell you those as we go.'

'My dear fellow,' exclaimed Charles, 'I know the moves! I did them for six months.'

'On the stage,' said Laszlo.

Charles was about to reply, 'Of course, on the stage!' but something stopped him.

'In the theatre,' said Laszlo, 'you rely on the eyes of the audience. Here you depend upon the eye of the camera, which can follow you – but not so fast!'

He saw Charles's mistrustful look, and smiled his impish smile.

'It is all a trick, Mr Brett,' he said. 'We are conjurors. It is all a trick. Violet, my darlink, give Mr Brett the script.'

'I have my own copy of the play,' replied Charles, and saw with relief Sutton standing waiting just outside the glass door. 'Sutton –'

'No, no, I should have said, scenario,' Laszlo corrected himself. 'In film, Mr Brett, what you see is everything. The words is the servant, not the masters.'

Violet offered a very thin typescript and Charles took it.

'Yes,' he said, heroically. 'Yes. I understand that. Quite different from the stage, of course.'

As Charles began to study the scenario, Lydia was on the move, gazing around her with enthusiasm.

'It's all too fascinating for words!' she exclaimed. 'Versailles. Fancy.'

In that moment, the glass shot was dismantled, and Versailles disappeared.

'Fancy!' said Lydia, again, and moved towards the

house, and Sutton.

'Alfred,' she murmured, 'this is awful!'

'He'll be all right once he's on,' said Sutton, reassuringly.

'I hope so,' said Lydia, far from reassured. 'Can't you do something?'

She turned away, and found Laszlo closer than she thought.

'Tell me, Miss Wheatley,' he said, 'have you appeared in many films?'

'None at all, Mr Sandor, I'm afraid,' she replied. 'You see, most of my work is in musical comedy, and I'd look very silly opening and shutting my mouth with no sound coming out.'

Oops! She was aware of Charles carefully *not* looking up from his perusal of the 'scenario', and she added with some haste, 'I mean – you can't do a silent musical comedy, but, of course, if a good dramatic role should be offered to me, I should be delighted.'

Charles was becoming increasingly restive. No one could enjoy idleness more than he did when he was on holiday, but in his professional life, he was accustomed to be in charge, and to keep things moving at a brisk pace. All this hanging about exchanging courtesies when he had to go to work, and when he was feeling unsure of his ability to undertake a new kind of work, was beginning to get on his nerves.

'Mr Sandor,' he said, briskly, 'if you would kindly ask someone to show me to my dressing room –?'

Laszlo seemed to start slightly, but then his charming smile returned.

'Ah, yes,' he said. 'Shall we go inside?'

But the moment they were back in the drawing room, his attention appeared to be distracted elsewhere.

'Ah!' he cried, 'they are lighting the staircase now. I must go. Everything must be perfect for such an important screen test. Edvin, you look after your father. So kind.'

And he seemed to vanish in a puff of charm and good will, with only the faithful Violet hastening along to show where he had been. Charles looked resentfully after him.

'If you ask me,' he said, 'that fellow has a damned cheek, asking me to give an audition!'

He saw Edwin and Martha exchange a troubled glance.

'It's not an audition, Father,' said Edwin. 'It's a screen test, to see how you look in front of a camera – I mean – what make-up you need –'

'Dammit,' said Charles, 'I've been making myself up for forty years. I should think I know by now what make-up I need!'

He intercepted another anxious look between Edwin and Martha.

'Oh well, all right,' he said, impatiently, 'where's the dressing room?' And then, when Edwin didn't answer at once, he added, 'I take it you don't expect me to fight a duel in plus-fours?'

'Er – no,' said Edwin, 'but – Laszlo should have told you –'

'Told me what?'

Sutton was suddenly at his elbow.

'Excuse me, sir,' he said. 'It would appear that, this being a new studio, the dressing rooms are not yet ready. But I think you will find the caretaker's room quite convenient, and I have laid your costume out there.'

Charles was immensely relieved to find himself once more in a situation of normality. Sutton had not only found the small caretaker's room, with a table and chair, but had got hold of a cloth to cover the table, put the wig stand on it, and already hung the costume on a hook on the door. It was not the first time that Charles had found himself in a makeshift dressing room, and he set to work to change into his costume with renewed confidence.

'Not much of a light for making up,' he remarked, casually.

Sutton stood ready to help him into his jacket, his face expressionless.

'It appears, sir,' he said, 'that in the cinema, all artists are made up in the same room, there being a special kind of make-up required.'

'I see,' said Charles, his confidence slightly shaken.

When he saw in the mirror the result of the make-up, it vanished altogether.

Lydia and Martha had found chairs in front of the staircase, which was now lit by overhead lights, with Laszlo, full of energy and excitement, shouting directions and exhortations to the extraordinarily large number of men who seemed to be busying themselves in an extraordinarily small space.

'What on earth is going on?' demanded Lydia. 'Why didn't they get all this ready beforehand? We shall be sitting here all morning.'

'Mother, it's always like this with filming,' Martha replied. 'You spend three minutes acting, and the rest of the time sitting around, waiting.'

'Really?' said Lydia. 'That will never suit your father. I'm not sure that it would suit me,' she added, thoughtfully. 'Good heavens! Who is that?'

A tiny, waif-like girl had emerged from the drawing room. She looked about fourteen years old and had dark hair, huge eyes, a little rosebud mouth, and wore a very simple long dress with a cloak over it.

'Ah, my Eva!' exclaimed Laszlo, and hastened towards her.

'Eva Dronka,' said Martha. 'She's a Hungarian actress – one of Laszlo's protégées. He's testing her for the part of Celestine.'

'She's a bit young, isn't she?' said Lydia, startled.

Celestine was the girl that Sebastian fell in love with, and with Charles playing Sebastian –

'She's older than she looks,' remarked Martha, drily.

Laszlo had taken Eva's hand in his and drawn her just inside the drawing room. He was talking to her earnestly, no doubt about the screen test, but Eva, while listening with devout attention, had a little trick of looking coyly and admiringly up through her eyelashes –

'I see what you mean,' said Lydia. 'All the same, I still think she will look like Charles's granddaughter.'

Turning her eyes anxiously towards the corridor, she saw Charles approaching, and her mouth came open.

'Streuth!' she said.

Charles's face was a singularly unbecoming shade of yellow, his eyes seemed to have turned black and his lips were blue.

'Well, Liddy,' he said, grimly, 'what do you think?'

Edwin and Sutton followed apprehensively behind.

Lydia by now had her countenance under control. She stood up, deciding that only honesty would serve.

'Darling,' she said, 'it's not very attractive off stage – but then, neither is stage make-up.'

'I dare say,' said Charles, resentfully, 'but I don't have to be painted yellow to go on stage.'

Martha decided to take a hand, and stood up in her turn.

'The point is, Father,' she said, helpfully, 'the camera can't manage red. It just comes out as black. And if your face turns red –'

'Why should it?' demanded Charles.

'Film lighting is very hot, Father, much more so than stage lighting.'

'Without make-up, you'll just look as though you're playing Othello,' said Martha.

'With it, I look like Mr Wu!' said Charles.

Laszlo hastened towards them, all enthusiasm.

'Ah, Mr Brett!' he cried, throwing a quick glance over Charles's costume, wig and make-up. 'Perfect! Perfect!'

He threw out a triumphant hand.

'What do you say to our staircase? Lights! Murder the lights in the studio!'

With dramatic suddenness, the corridor lights were switched off, and the powerful overhead lights came on. Charles was surprised to find that the staircase really did look rather impressive.

'Come, come,' said Laszlo, 'we get to work.'

Lydia and Martha sat down, and Sutton lurked in the corridor. Hegarty came unobtrusively to join him.

'But first,' continued Laszlo, 'you must meet Miss Eva Dronka. Since we do the scene with Sir Hugo and Celestine, I give her a test at the same time.'

'Oh,' said Charles, not best pleased.

But as the charming, delicate little girl advanced, he responded to her shy smile with his usual gallantry.

'I hope you're not as nervous as I am, Miss Dronka,' he said.

'Oh, she speaks no English,' said Laszlo, blithely, 'but a very talented actress.'

'Yes, I – I'm sure,' said Charles, stunned, 'but if she doesn't speak any English, how can she –?'

'I talk her through it,' replied Laszlo, casually, and turned away to check that the man operating the directional spotlight was correctly placed.

Charles turned a despairing gaze towards Edwin.

'She'll follow the scenario, Father,' explained Edwin, in an undertone, 'and act the part – and then, of course, when the film is shown, the words are written on the screen.'

'She – as it were – mimes it?' said Charles, and then, with another heroic attempt to appear at home in this alien territory, 'Yes. Yes, of course. Naturally. I understand.'

Laszlo, having checked the spotlight and the camera, turned back. It might have occurred to a suspicious observer that he tended to absent himself, in one way or another, whenever some little snag or difficulty presented itself to his actors, returning to sweep them along with his unbounded enthusiasm as soon as the problem appeared to be solved.

'So,' he cried, 'we get to work. Eva –'

He addressed his little protégée in Hungarian, and then turned to Edwin.

'Edvin, you stand beside her, with your foot on the bench. Mr Brett, here is where you will enter.'

He waved a vague hand towards the long, dark corridor behind the camera.

'Yes,' said Charles. 'Er – where, exactly –?'

'We pick you up on camera as you enter, on the words, "Ah, Sir Hugo –"'

'Right,' responded Charles, highly professional and businesslike.

But he threw a nervous glance at the camera, as he saw the operator peering into it, hand at the ready. Edwin and Eva took their places.

'Ready, Mr Brett?' he said. 'Camera! Action!'

Charles had played the part of Sebastian in *The King Shall Not Die* more than two hundred times, including once before the King. As he prepared for his entrance, he took a deep breath, and told himself that it was quite absurd to be nervous just because he was playing the part before a camera instead of an audience. He had never been exactly reluctant to present his well-known countenance to the camera; in fact, he had always photographed extremely well. At Laszlo's cry of 'Action!' Charles strode confidently forward into the lights.

'Ah, Sir Hugo!' he began. 'I thought –'

'Not quite so far, if you please,' said Laszlo.

Charles stopped short.

'I beg your pardon?'

'You are masking our little Eva.'

'Surely not.'

'Er – from the camera, Father,' interposed Edwin, softly.

'Oh.'

Charles looked, dismayed, up at that blank glass eye, losing in a moment all his fifty years of experience of how to move on the stage, making an entrance, taking up a position centre stage, upstaging, perhaps, but never masking, because that was bad stagecraft. Instinct told him when he was stepping between a fellow actor and the audience, but how on earth did he know when he was between a fellow actor and the camera, unless he kept his eye, all the time he was performing, on that terrible, sightless but all-seeing globe? Trying to conceal his alarm, he turned to Eva.

'I'm so sorry, Miss Dronka,' he said. 'I do beg your pardon.'

Then he remembered that she spoke no English.

She raised her hand in a charming gesture, smiling adorably past his left shoulder.

'Cut!' said Laszlo. 'Shall we try another take?'

'Er –'

Presumably, thought Charles, that meant that he should go off and prepare to come on again. He did so.

'Ready when you are, Mr Brett,' called Laszlo. 'Camera. Action!'

Charles strode on, threw a cautious glance towards the camera, and took a step backwards before speaking.

'Ah, Sir Hugo,' he said, 'I thought I should find you here.'

He turned to Eva with his usual gesture of out-thrown hand.

'And your daughter, too. No doubt, Celestine, you knew what your father intended to do?'

Eva stood up, clasping her hands. It occurred to Charles that her strong point appeared to be clasping her hands in various poses of innocence, alarm, love and despair, or sometimes, as in the present instance, all together, with those huge eyes reinforcing the emotion. Charles looked at Edwin expectantly, waited for a moment, and then said, 'It's your line.'

'It's been cut, Father.'

'What?'

'That line. It's been cut.'

'Shall we continue?' said Laszlo.

'Yes,' said Charles. 'Of course.'

In the kitchen of Nightingale Grove that night, Sutton was giving a caricatured impression of Laszlo at work, with a folded duster on his head to suggest the beret, and an egg whisk to represent the camera, which, apparently, Laszlo was operating himself.

'No, no, no!' he cried, in a wild exaggeration of a

Hungarian accent. 'Ven I say battlements, I vant battlements vot you can battle from. Not just a hop, skip and how's your mother?'

Emily giggled delightedly, but Flora, though amused, felt a little uneasy at this frivolous treatment of her beloved motion pictures. Hegarty, drinking a glass of beer, was an appreciative audience.

'Oh, Mr Sutton!' exclaimed Flora. 'He was never like that, was he?'

'Near enough,' replied Sutton, well satisfied with the success of his impersonation. 'A bit of a poe-seur, Mr Laszlo, if you ask me.'

He took off the duster, put down the egg whisk and sat down to continue his own glass of beer. The family was dressing for dinner, and Flora and Emily were in the last stages of preparing the main course.

'Did you see anyone else at the studio, Mr Sutton?' inquired Emily. 'Like – Ivor Novello?'

'What do you know about Ivor Novello?' demanded Flora, annoyed at this further invasion of her private world.

'He was in *The Rat*,' replied Emily. 'I saw it at the Rialto with me mum.'

'Oh, *did* you?' said Flora, and sniffed.

She had never met Emily's mother, but in some mysterious way, carried on a vendetta against her, at one remove.

'And how did the master get on with this Hungarian gentleman?' she inquired.

Sutton exchanged a cautious glance with Hegarty.

'Oh, you know the guv'nor,' he replied. 'Always the perfect gent.'

'When will they be showing the master's film?' asked Emily, eagerly.

'Here, steady on!' answered Sutton. 'They've got to look at the screen test first!'

With sinking heart, Charles realized that his mother and father proposed to come to the studio and view his screen test.

'Isn't this grand?' said Maeve, as they trooped out to the car. 'I love a magic-lantern show.'

'It's not a magic-lantern show, Maeve,' said George, irritably. 'It's a film.'

'Sure, I know that,' replied Maeve, 'but it's the same sort of thing. Won't it be great to see Charlie up on the screen?'

'I wish everyone would stop treating this like a Sunday School Outing!' said Charles, exasperated. 'We're not going there for fun. The whole point of the screen test is to see whether my make-up is right and – and the lighting and so on.'

'I'm sure you'll look lovely, me darling,' said Maeve, patting his cheek fondly. 'You always do.'

As she turned to get into the car, Charles grasped Lydia's arm.

'Why did you say they could come?' he demanded in a fierce undertone.

'I didn't,' replied Lydia between clenched teeth. 'They just took it for granted.'

When they arrived, Maeve trotted ahead of the others with the happy air of a child at a circus. She and George were both dressed in their best. She wore a coat with a slightly moth-eaten fur collar and a Queen Mary toque. George had dignified the occasion with spats.

'So this is a fillum studio,' Maeve remarked. 'Would you believe that, now, George?'

'Looks more like an old ruined house to me,' replied George.

'Ah, come on, now, don't be a spoilsport,' cried Maeve. 'Here's Eddie. Hullo Eddie! Isn't this a great gas?'

'Er – yes, Grandma,' replied Edwin, correctly assessing his father's expression of gloomy indignation. 'If you'd like to come this way –' He added, 'Laszlo will be here in a minute, Father. He's just shooting the last scene of Martha's film.'

'The last scene?' said Lydia. 'Thank goodness for that! Perhaps now she'll be in time for rehearsals.'

'But if the screen test goes well,' said Edwin, softly, 'Father will be late.'

Lydia groaned.

In Laszlo's office at the top of the house, a screen and projector had been set up, with two rows of folding chairs. Sutton, who had somehow managed to get himself quietly included in the expedition, was just placing the chairs more conveniently when Martha breezed in, still in her 'Josephine' costume, her face a becoming shade of yellow.

'Holy Mary!' cried Maeve. 'Is it jaundice she has?'

'No, Mother, of course not,' said Charles. 'It's just make-up for the films.'

'I hope they didn't make you look like that,' said Maeve.

'Gran, Grandpa,' said Martha, 'don't you both look spiffing? Laszlo's just coming, Father.'

'So I should hope,' said George. 'You want to put that fellow in his place, Charles, keeping you waiting. I remember a theatre manager in Budapest –'

'Mr Sandor is here, sir,' interposed Sutton, smoothly, from the doorway.

Laszlo came in, all bustle and charm, with Eva Dronka following shyly in his wake. Introduced to Maeve and George, he was more charming than ever, but then paused to throw an appraising glance over them before turning away with an expansive gesture.

'Now we will view the screen test,' he said. 'Leonard, are you ready?'

An extremely dour man had been threading film into the projector. He nodded. It seemed to be a characteristic of the technicians that they viewed actors and directors with supreme contempt, as though they were idle persons who interfered with the serious business of the cinema.

Charles and Lydia sat in the front row, with George and Maeve on his other side. Laszlo sat behind, between Martha and Eva, but Lydia observed that he seemed to be paying rather more attention to Martha. Little Miss Dronka, Lydia thought, had better bestir herself if she did not want to be ousted as Laszlo's 'protégée'. Edwin had placed himself at the end of the second row, where he could watch the screen without himself being observed. Laszlo, glancing round, saw Sutton standing unobtrusively by the door.

'I wonder,' said Laszlo, 'if you would pull down the blinds? So kind.'

Sutton, glad to make himself useful and justify his presence, moved to lower the blinds over the windows. The light sprang up on the screen.

'Oh, look!' cried Maeve. 'There he is! There's Charlie! And Eddie. Eddie's there, too.'

Charles looked with dismay as his image on the screen strode on, stopped short, turned jerkily, mouthed something, listened to Edwin mouthing something, and then

302

turned to Eva, who raised a coyly sweet, deprecating hand.

'Ah, look!' cried Maeve, 'there's that dear little girl, now. Is she playing your daughter, Charlie?'

'No, Mother,' replied Charles, exasperated. 'She –'

He fell silent, seeing himself stride on once more, his movements and gestures far too large, as he rolled his eyes and mouthed inaudible lines. The make-up seemed to make his face look heavy and coarse, whereas Edwin, turning into camera, was stunningly handsome and full of vitality.

'Doesn't Eddie look grand?' exclaimed Maeve.

'Huh!' grumped George. 'It's hard to tell what's happening without the words.'

'It's the same as in the play, Grandad,' put in Martha. 'Sebastian knows that Sir Hugo has arranged to have the King killed, and he's going to try to stop him.'

'You mean, Eddie's playing Sir Hugo?' exclaimed Maeve. 'I thought he was supposed to be older.'

'That make-up doesn't do you any favours, Charles,' remarked George.

'Indeed it does not,' Maeve agreed. 'I should get that changed.'

In the darkness, beneath the flickering images on the screen, Charles's hand felt for Lydia's, and her hand found his and held it tight.

The projector ground inexorably on. Charles, with exaggerated gestures, accused Edwin, who bravely but falsely declared his innocence. Charles, turning the back of his head to the camera, waved his arms about, evidently accusing Eva of complicity, and she clasped her hands in innocence. Charles drew his sword, and so did Edwin, and they fought a duel on the staircase, in which Charles looked heavy and clumsy, and Edwin was slim, precise and full of energy.

'Bit late on that one, Charles,' remarked George, helpfully, as Edwin made a thrust which really should have struck Charles dead, except that Edwin, as the camera showed, allowed him a belated parry.

Charles, signalling his intention to the gallery with a flourish of his sword, struck Edwin to the heart, and the camera stayed with Edwin as he fell, moving in on his face which, in close-up, was suddenly breathtakingly beautiful.

'Ah, there now, he's dead!' exclaimed Maeve. 'What a shame!'

Eva clasped her hands in dismay, and Charles made an all-too-declamatory speech, ending with the words mouthed with a wild gesture of the hand: 'The King shall not die!' He then ran heavily up the staircase. The screen went blank.

'Oh, God!' thought Charles. 'Oh, God!'

At least if you made a fool of yourself on the stage, it was just for that one time and that one audience. No one recorded it so that long afterwards other people could gawp at it and you yourself crawl with embarrassment.

'Shall I raise the blind, sir?' said Sutton.

'If you would be so good,' replied Laszlo.

Charles and Lydia were still sitting side by side, their eyes fixed on the screen, but as the daylight was admitted to the room, Charles disengaged his hand and rose.

'Well,' he remarked, with great good cheer, 'that was immensely interesting, most amusing.'

He was aware of an inaudible sigh of relief, as though they were all together on stage and had been afraid that, most embarrassingly, he did not know his lines, but now found to their delight that he did.

'But, you know,' he added, 'there's more to this film acting than meets the eye.'

'Edwin seems to have got hold of it,' remarked George, with his unfailing gift for coming out with unwelcome truths.

'Oh yes,' echoed Maeve, more innocent, but equally fatal, 'Eddie's got it down to a "t".'

Edwin and Laszlo stood up, and Edwin exchanged a quick glance with Martha.

'I've had a bit of practice, Grandad,' said Edwin. 'It's just a matter of learning the tricks of the trade.'

'No,' said Charles. 'No, it's more than that. It's a different technique altogether, and I wish I had the time to learn it. I always enjoy a challenge. But, with Thomas's new play coming on – you young people may be able to act in films all day and in the theatre all night, but I'm getting a bit long in the tooth for that kind of thing.'

He turned to Laszlo.

'Very kind of you, Mr Sandor, to offer me the part, but now that I see what it entails, I'm afraid I really can't spare the time.'

He met Laszlo's eyes, expecting to see there sympathy or embarrassment, but instead seeing only respect and admiration.

'I am sorry,' said Laszlo. 'It would have been such an honour. I am a great admirer of yours.'

He shook Charles's hand, and bowed his head from the neck, as though to royalty.

'A great admirer,' he said.

Lydia came to join Charles, slipping her hand into his arm. They turned towards the door, but Charles paused, glancing back at Laszlo.

'If you'll take my advice,' he said, 'you'll offer the part to Edwin.'

Laszlo, in a lavish gesture, had insisted on taking them all out to luncheon, so it was late in the afternoon when Maeve came surging into the hall at Nightingale Grove, with George behind her, and Lydia, Charles and Sutton resignedly following.

'Flora!' cried Maeve. 'Flora!'

She had never lost the Irish country-house habit of her youth, whereby you always shouted for the servants, because the bells never worked. It was true that Charles often did the same, chiefly because he was too impatient to wait for the answer to a bell, but it never failed to annoy him when his mother did it.

Flora emerged through the swing door.

'You'll never guess what's happened!' exclaimed Maeve.

'Mrs George,' said Flora, 'whatever is it?'

'The best news you ever heard,' said Maeve. 'Mr George and me are going to be in the fillum. That nice Mr Sandor offered us the parts of the Grand Duke and the Grand Duchess, and he's paying us twenty pounds a week – each!'

'It would have been thirty,' remarked George, 'if you hadn't shown him how keen you were.'

'For heaven's sake, Father!' said Charles. 'You got him up from fifteen as it was. Damned embarrassing.'

'It certainly was,' agreed Lydia, her eyes meeting Sutton's.

'Nonsense!' said George, giving his coat and hat to Sutton. 'These managers expect you to bargain with them, especially if they're foreigners.'

'So,' said Flora, gratified, 'you'll be acting with the master.'

'No, no,' replied Maeve, cheerfully. 'He decided that he didn't care for acting in the fillums – and, anyway, it didn't suit him at all, so Master Edwin's taking his part.'

Instinct, more powerful than knowledge, told Flora that all was not well, but Sutton, having taken George's hat and coat, had now moved to take Charles's.

'Now, come in to the kitchen,' said Maeve, 'and I'll tell you all about it.'

'Mother,' protested Lydia, 'we shall all be having tea very soon, anyway –'

But Maeve's Queen Mary toque with its curling feather had already vanished through the swing doors and George's spats were not far behind. Flora threw an apologetic look at Charles and Lydia before following.

'Well,' said Charles, left alone with Lydia and Sutton, 'we'd better get back to the theatre, where we belong.'

He spoke with forced joviality, and, as Sutton returned from hanging up his coat and hat in the hall cupboard, he added, 'We've got a first night to prepare for, eh, Sutton?'

'Er – yes, sir,' said Sutton. He hesitated. 'Excuse me, sir, but I wonder if I might have tomorrow off?'

'What, the whole day?' answered Charles, surprised.

Lydia, drifting towards the garden room, paused and turned.

'No, sir,' replied Sutton, 'just the morning. Er – Mr Sandor asked me to come and see him at the studio.'

'Do you know why?' inquired Lydia.

'He – er –' Sutton was embarrassed but determined. 'He said he wanted to offer me a job. So, sir, if you wouldn't mind –?'

Suddenly it all became too much for Charles to bear. He had suffered the humiliating *débâcle* of the screen test, increased four fold by the involvement of Maeve and George. He had been made to realize that he was growing old, and that his son, young, romantic and virile, could reflect on the screen those qualities which once had been his own. He had behaved quite superbly throughout the entire ghastly event, and throughout an extremely testing luncheon. Now, suddenly, he had had enough.

'Oh, by all means!' he shouted. 'Take the car. Take Hegarty. Go to the studio. Stay there as long as you like. Apparently that's where everyone else will be!'

He stormed off to his study and slammed the door behind him. Lydia bit her lip and looked at Sutton, and he looked guiltily back at her.

Chapter Eighteen

Next morning, Flora, checking the gas under a pair of kippers in a pan of boiling water, heard the sound of a cup rattling in a saucer, and glanced over her shoulder at Sutton. The cup was rattling as he put it down because his hand was shaking. Before she could say anything, Hegarty came whistling in by the back door. Sutton started up.

'Is it time to go?' he said.

'Ah no, we'll have a bite of breakfast first,' replied Hegarty cheerfully.

He poured himself a cup of tea and sat down with it. Sutton sank back. He was in his best 'walking out' suit, and was wearing a slightly flashy tie.

'What time are we picking up Miss Martha?' he inquired.

'Eight o'clock,' answered Hegarty, 'but she'll not be ready. She never is.'

Sutton took another sip of tea, holding the cup in

both hands. It was strange to be experiencing again stagefright, that unique blend of terror and excitement and total self-engrossment which he thought he had left behind him for ever.

'Would you like a nice pair of kippers, Mr Hegarty?' asked Flora.

'Ah, that'd be grand.'

'I was really cooking these for Mr Sutton,' said Flora, 'but he says he can't seem to fancy them this morning.'

'I never could eat before going on stage,' Sutton explained.

'I didn't know you were an actor,' said Hegarty, surprised.

'Well, it was a long time ago, but they say you never forget the knack of it.'

'Easy as falling off a bicycle, eh?' said Hegarty, with all the heartless cheerfulness of a good sailor in the presence of sea-sickness.

Flora gave him a reproachful look as she put the plate of kippers in front of him. Hegarty grinned and helped himself to one of Flora's good bread and butter doorsteps and set to work dissecting a kipper with gusto.

'You pass me your cup, Mr Sutton,' said Flora. 'Nothing like a nice cup of tea to soothe the nerves.'

She refilled his cup, and sat down herself.

'I wonder what part they want you to play,' she said.

'You'd think Mr Sandor would have told you that yesterday,' remarked Hegarty, 'when he said he wanted you to come and see him.'

'I suppose he wouldn't like to,' replied Sutton, 'not with the guv'nor there and – and after all that had happened. It might have looked as though I was being offered a job and he wasn't – and me in his employ.'

'I can't get over you being in the theatre business,' said

310

Hegarty, extracting a tricky kipper bone. 'How did you get into it?'

'Just for a lark, really,' answered Sutton. 'Funny to think about it really.'

He stirred his tea and gazed into the past.

'I saw an advertisement in the paper for walk-ons, and I thought, Oh, I might as well go along; it'll be a bit of a lark. And then I got on the stage, and I saw Miss Lydia and the guv'nor, and they were – well, I'd never seen anything like it! And I thought, This is what I want to do. My poor old dad! I'll never forget his face when I said, "I want to be an actor." "You must be mad," he said. And he was right, you know, because I wasn't good enough. The guv'nor knew it. So did Miss Lydia, but she was too much of a lady to say so.'

Hegarty's look of amusement had vanished. He glanced at Flora, and she glanced back at him, both touched by the ancient disappointment, the old hurt.

'It's a long time ago, Mr Sutton,' said Flora, gently.

'Ah, yes,' said Sutton, and was suddenly eager and excited, as they had never seen him before, 'but now I've got a second chance!'

He looked from Hegarty to Flora, and back again to Hegarty, because he had been to the studio, and would have a better idea of what he was talking about.

'You see,' said Sutton, 'I saw the guv'nor do that screen test, and I saw what he did wrong. And I saw what Mr Eddie did right. You don't stand in the wings all those years, and not learn something. I've learned a lot. I've often thought I'd like to have another go at it, and now –'

He gazed into the distance again, but this time his eyes were bright.

'I've got a second chance,' he said.

Charles and Lydia were not best pleased to realize that, having given Sutton and Martha permission to go to the studio in their car, they themselves were obliged to go to the theatre in a taxi. On the other hand, it was very pleasant to be back in the world where they belonged. They repaired to the theatre office, where Jean was both efficient and encouraging as she reported on the progress of *If The Truth Be Told.*

'The advance bookings are excellent,' she said.

'That's a relief,' remarked Lydia.

'I don't know why you say that,' responded Charles, with some indignation. 'You and I are usually quite a draw.'

'Yes,' said Lydia, 'but with Thomas's last play being such a flop –'

'Pooh!' said Charles, outrageously. 'They don't come to see the play. They come to see us.'

'Yes, darling,' said Lydia, and exchanged an amused glance with Jean.

Jean had vacated the big desk for Charles, but sat between them, papers and accounts readily to hand as never before since they had bought the Princess Theatre.

'This is more or less the final budget for the production,' she said.

'I must say, Jean,' Lydia remarked, 'you've kept the costs down wonderfully. This will probably be the first time one of our productions will have kept within the original estimate.'

Jean smiled.

'Don't forget,' she said, 'that I used to have to keep two people on twenty-six shillings a week. That teaches you to count the pennies.'

'Jean, you're a treasure,' said Lydia, and stood up. 'We'd better get down to the stage,' she said. 'With any luck, Martha will have arrived, and she and Thomas will have had a glorious stand-up row about that speech she wants changed, and then we can all get on with the rehearsal.'

Seeing that Charles was also on the move, Jean spoke hastily.

'Before you go –' she said, 'you said that you were going to find a new business manager –'

'My dear girl,' replied Charles, 'that's easier said than done. I can't exactly put an advertisement in *The Times*: "Wanted, Theatre Manager, sober, honest and guaranteed not to make my daughter fall in love with him."'

Lydia looked at him in exasperation, but Jean, rather to her surprise, found herself able to smile a little. Perhaps she really was getting over Piers. If so, the turning point, like the moment in a sickness when the fever breaks, dated from the moment when Thomas put his hand in hers and told her that she was something special. Perhaps it was because it was not only her infatuation for Piers but also a long-lived contempt for herself which Thomas had begun to cure.

'I really do think,' she said, 'that with a new production coming into the theatre, you ought to find a temporary manager.'

'Darling Jean,' said Lydia, sweetly, 'that's you. You're our temporary manager.'

'Yes, I know,' said Jean. 'But –'

Thomas slammed into the room.

'Where the hell is Martha?' he demanded.

'Oh, not again!' said Lydia. 'Hasn't she arrived yet?'

'Hegarty was supposed to drive her straight back from the studio,' said Charles.

Thomas swore.

'I thought that bloody film was supposed to be finished!' he said.

Thomas considered that drama consisted of the author's words which actors delivered precisely, audibly, and, if possible, with the right inflexion. The idea that any dramatic art could lie in the photography of players miming emotions while truncated captions appeared at the foot of the screen was, to him, like suggesting that one could perform a concerto on a piano from which the strings had been removed while scrawling a few notes of music on the wall above it.

'Martha said that there were just a couple of retakes,' said Lydia, pacifically, 'but she swore they'd only take an hour.'

'Perhaps she waited until Sutton had had his meeting with Mr Sandor,' suggested Jean, rashly.

As soon as she had said it, she felt it could have been a mistake, and so it proved.

'Oh, how marvellous!' cried Thomas. 'Martha particularly asks me to be here because she's not happy about her last speech. I turn up, dead on time, and where is she? Hanging about at the film studio waiting for the butler, who has suddenly developed an overwhelming ambition to make his name in motion pictures!'

'Thomas,' Lydia intervened, hopefully, 'we don't *know* that she waited for –'

Thomas, somewhere between rage and hysteria, was certainly beyond reason.

'Oh, don't we?' he said. 'Well, one thing I *do* know. Throughout this entire production, everything else has come first, and my play absolutely nowhere. I wonder you bothered to put it on at all!'

He stormed out of the room, slamming the door satisfyingly behind him. Jean, Charles and Lydia looked at each other.

'I'm sorry,' said Jean. 'That was stupid of me.'

Lydia surprised her with a chuckle. One of the charms of living and working with the Bretts was that all of them were capable of surprising her.

'Don't worry,' said Lydia. 'It gave him a chance to blow off steam. He's been feeling a bit out of things lately.'

'I suppose I keep forgetting,' said Jean, 'that writers have temperaments as well.'

Lydia looked at her, startled.

'You're right,' she said. 'I never thought of that. None of us do, I suppose.'

Charles's attention had ceased with the slamming of the door.

'What's the matter with that boy?' he inquired.

'Charles, I keep telling you,' said Lydia, 'his last play was a total disaster, and so naturally he's terribly nervous about this one.'

'Really?' said Charles, whose chief experience of authors in the past had been such sterling old practitioners as Willie Sutherland. 'Well, let's go and run through the first act – cheer him up.'

'Good idea,' said Lydia. 'The first act's the best, anyway.'

'For Gawd's sake,' said Charles, 'don't tell him that – or Martha! Don't forget, she only appears in the last act.'

Jean realized with alarm that they were once more on the move.

'Before you go,' said Jean. 'About the theatre manager –'

Too late. They had gone.

Sutton had shown something less than his usual astuteness in travelling to Richmond with Martha. As Hegarty had predicted, she was late, and by the time they arrived at the British Empire Films studio, Laszlo was busily engaged, with Edwin, in setting up the first scene of *The King Shall Not Die* in the portico.

'Martha, my treasure,' he cried, 'what a wicked girl you are to keep me waiting!' He kissed her fondly. 'Dress, make-up – ' and a burst of Hungarian which could have been endearments, scolding, or simply an adjuration to hurry. Laszlo used his native tongue, as he used everything else, skilfully and ingeniously for his own purposes.

For a moment, Sutton thought that he had been forgotten, and was wondering if he would have to put himself forward and risk rebuff, but Laszlo's eye rested on him blankly for a moment, and then with recognition.

'Ah, Mr Sutton. Yes. Yes. I want to see you, but not now. Soon. Soon. Would you be so good as to wait in my office, and I will come very soon.'

Two hours later, Sutton was still waiting, his confidence and optimism at a very low ebb. He still clutched in his hands a brown envelope in which he had carefully placed the photographs and press cuttings from his theatrical career. They were not exactly profuse: butlers did not often feature prominently in production photographs. But he had paid for a studio portrait in the first flush of enthusiasm at being taken into the company, and there was also a rather flattering picture of him in the evening paper when he first returned to his native city. Fortunately, in that production he had been playing not a butler but a footman, so he wore a becoming livery and a wig, and the caption underneath read: 'Local Boy Makes Good in Theatre'. He glanced at his watch. Supposing Mr Laszlo had forgotten him again? Supposing he was left sitting there all day, and they all went home?

There were quick footsteps on the stairs, and Sutton turned eagerly in his chair and rose to his feet, but it was Edwin who came in, wearing his Sebastian costume.

'Hullo, Sutton,' he said, encouragingly, 'it won't be long now. I thought I'd just come and see how you were getting on.'

'That was – very kind of you, Mr Edwin. I was beginning to wonder –'

'Mr Sandor always seems to be doing ten things at once, but he always seems to remember everything, just the same, sooner or later.'

Sutton drew a breath of relief. At least he wasn't being made a fool of, and that, when you got right down to it, was what he had been most afraid of.

'You're starting *The King Shall Not Die* straight away then?' inquired Sutton, with a comfortable feeling of being part of the enterprise.

'Yes, filming the first scene today,' replied Edwin.

He sat on the corner of Laszlo's desk, and laughed.

'Time's money, as Laszlo keeps saying. It's a mad business, this. Talking of money, do you know how much they're paying me? A hundred and fifty pounds a week!'

'Blimey!' said Sutton, and Edwin laughed again.

Golden possibilities gleamed in Sutton's vision. Of course, he wouldn't get as much as the 'star', but even so – Edwin was speaking again.

'Mind you,' he said, 'I've heard that in America quite

ordinary actors get as much as two thousand dollars. Lord knows what that is in pounds!'

The golden gleam in Sutton's eyes became brighter still, and they both heard footsteps on the stairs, and Edwin stood up.

'Here he comes,' he said. 'Good luck, Alfred.'

'Thanks, Mr Eddie,' said Sutton, very gratefully indeed.

Edwin was the one, he thought, who had inherited Miss Lydia's loving kindness and consideration for the feelings of others. It was with renewed confidence that he turned to face Laszlo, who paused to speak to Edwin outside the door, and then came swiftly in, shook him by the hand, and went to sit behind his desk all in one movement, speaking as he did so.

'Mr Sutton, pray forgive me. I keep you waiting so long, and with nothing to do. I think you are a man who likes to be kept busy.'

'Oh –' said Sutton, taken by surprise, '– well, I – I never thought about it, sir – Mr Sandor – but I suppose I do.'

Laszlo made a gracious gesture, and Sutton sat down again on the edge of the chair. Laszlo leaned back and eyed him thoughtfully.

'And you notice everything,' he said. 'That is what a good director does.'

'Oh,' said Sutton, gratified. 'Is it?'

Laszlo suddenly abandoned his reflective tone, sat up and spoke briskly. It was these changes of mood and attitude which kept other people continually off balance.

'Well, Mr Sutton,' he said, 'are you going to come and work for me?'

This was what Sutton had been waiting for, but now he was taken by surprise, and felt himself at a disadvantage for that reason.

'Oh – yes – sir, Mr Sandor –' (it was hard to shake off the butler's habit of addressing everyone as 'sir'). 'I – I brought some photographs with me.'

His hands were suddenly clumsy, and he juggled with the envelope, photographs and cuttings, and one photograph fell to the floor. He hastily picked it up, and put them all in front of Laszlo on the desk.

'I thought – to show you how I look on camera. Mind, these were taken a long time ago, but – well, they give an idea.'

Laszlo glanced at the photographs without picking them up. The silence was unnerving, and to fill it, Sutton said, nervously, 'I've often thought I'd like to be an actor again.' He was shattered when Laszlo threw himself back in his chair and laughed aloud.

'An *actor*?' he said. 'Actors are nothing. Flim-flam. Circus animals who perform for me.'

He stopped laughing, and looked Sutton gravely in the eye.

'Mr Sutton, you do not want to be an actor.'

'I – I –' Sutton stammered. 'Well, then, what –?'

Laszlo leaned forward.

'I have been watching you. I know what you do for Mr Brett – for all that family. That takes a special gift – a gift for organization.'

'Oh,' said Sutton.

So that was it, he thought. All this build-up, and all he wanted was a servant. Well, if that was it, he'd got another think coming. But, beneath his anger, disappointment was like a blow to the heart. He had looked away, trying to cover his feelings, but when he looked back, he saw Laszlo smiling understandingly.

'No, no,' he said, 'do not be mistaken. It is a rare gift you have, and it should not be wasted on a butler.'

He leaned back again, and spoke confidentially.

'Films are art,' he said, 'but also they are money. Films need time, a lot of time, but time is money and should not be wasted.'

He pointed a finger at Sutton, like pointing a gun and saying, 'Do you understand me?' and Sutton nodded, bemusedly.

'When actors are unhappy,' he continued, 'they cost time, a lot of time, a lot of money. You understand actors. But, also, you have an eye for detail and for organization.'

'Ah,' said Sutton, his self-esteem beginning to unfold under this praise.

He had been a failed actor and a *faute-de-mieux* butler and dresser for so long that it had never occurred to him that he could actually have talents.

'I am an artist,' Laszlo continued, 'but I need at my shoulder someone who will allow me to practise my art, someone who will save me time and money, and keep my actors happy. That man is you.'

He looked Sutton straight in the eye. Sutton felt like one of the fishermen being summoned from their boats and nets and led away in a different path, whether they would or no. It was as though, to Laszlo, it was already settled.

'Er – yes, sir,' he said, dazedly. 'Er – what position would I hold?'

'You would be my assistant,' said Laszlo, magnificently.

Sutton gave an involuntary frown. What did that mean?

'In the theatre,' said Laszlo, 'everything is old, everything has been done before. What can you do in the theatre which has *not* been done before? Write a new play. What can you do with it? Act it on the stage to an

320

audience, beneath the same lights. Electricity, perhaps, instead of gas, but – apart from that, there is nothing new. But with films, everything is new, everything is possible.'

That's true, thought Sutton. In the theatre, there's all this business of theatrical tradition – old superstitions, old habits, make-up always set out in exactly the same way, bad luck to change anything – and, once a dresser, always a dresser. Laszlo seemed to know his thoughts, and nodded.

'In the cinema,' he said, 'everyone is learning. It is a new art, and we have yet to learn what can be done with it. Exciting things are going to happen, very soon. One should not be in at the death of an old art, but in at the birth of a new art.'

He's right, thought Sutton. It's like electricity or the wireless, or – remembering his roots – the Spinning Jenny. It's the future, not the past.

'So,' said Laszlo, 'I offer you a post as my assistant at twenty pounds a week.'

Sutton's butler's experience stood him in good stead. He kept his face expressionless, but – Ee, ba gum! he thought. Twenty pounds a week is better than three pounds a week, all found.

'Who knows?' continued Laszlo. 'You start as my assistant, but perhaps in time you become a director yourself. What do you say?'

Sutton very nearly said yes on the spot, but his native hard-headed north-country caution asserted itself. It was true that he had once, long ago, made an impulsive decision to go into the theatre, and had never – quite – regretted it. But he was older now, and, besides, Laszlo was not Lydia. Old loyalties rose up to draw him back.

'It's very good of you, sir,' he said. 'But, I have a good position with Mr and Mrs Brett, and, well, I think it's true that they have come to rely on me. I have to think of them as well as myself.'

'I understand that,' said Laszlo.

'If I might think it over,' said Sutton, firmly.

'Of course,' said Laszlo, understandingly. And then he was suddenly on his feet, looking fiercely down at Sutton. 'Take all the time you need, for, if you come to me, I shall demand your undivided loyalty.'

'Yes – sir – Mr Sandor,' replied Sutton, getting to his feet.

Laszlo's eyes turned towards the door, where Martha appeared, elegantly dressed. He went towards her.

'Martha, my darlink,' he said, 'we go to lunch.'

He put his arm round her and turned to Sutton.

'Mr Sutton,' he said, 'you think it over, and let me know.'

''Bye, Sutton!' called Martha.

Left alone, Sutton began to put the photographs and cuttings back in the brown envelope, and even as the new path opened before his feet, still he felt again the old pain, the old disappointment. If anything, in that moment, it was sharper than ever, for it was as though now he put away for ever the old dream.

Sutton travelled back to Hampstead by bus. He could have taken the train, but he wanted to have time to think. It certainly was a remarkable opportunity, one which would never come again. And yet, brilliant and fascinating as Laszlo Sandor undoubtedly was, he did not strike Sutton as being what one might call a solid sort of chap. With the Bretts, Sutton knew he had a job for life, and, with unemployment being what it was, it was rather alarming to think that, if British Empire Films went bust (remember the gate off its hinges!) he would find himself set adrift. On the other hand, after a few months of that salary, he'd have a few quid in his pocket, enough to allow him time to look around. And, since the war, butlers had been hard to come by. He wouldn't have any trouble finding himself a post. One thing was certain, if the job with Laszlo Sandor didn't work out, he wouldn't go back to the Bretts, for the guv'nor to give him one of his nasty set-downs.

Suddenly Sutton realized that this was the reason that he was seriously considering throwing his lot in with Sandor. Far more than the money, or the exciting possibilities of the film world, what mattered to him was that he should be treated with respect. He remembered Charles's words: 'I pay you to be a butler, not a bloody critic. You weren't even any good as an actor.' They seemed to come together with all those other remarks, insulting or slighting, irritably spoken or accidentally overheard.

'That fellow's no good,' he had said to Lydia, right at the beginning, when she insisted on keeping him in the company. 'Why don't you get rid of him?'

Perhaps this was his chance, thought Sutton, not just to be kept on sufferance, like an old dog that smells a bit but isn't quite old enough to be put down. He was only forty-five. He could make a new life for himself not in the theatre, where he had failed, but in the cinema, where anything was possible. And then he thought of Lydia, and his heart sank at the thought of telling her, and he knew that the final moment of decision had yet to come.

Back at Nightingale Grove, Sutton simply told Flora that Mr Sandor had made a proposition to him, but that he wanted to tell the guv'nor and Miss Lydia first. Since Emily was there, eyes wide and mouth agape, Flora simply nodded and spoke of other things.

Sutton changed into his butler's garb, and waited in desperate anxiety for the family's return from the theatre. Martha unexpectedly let herself in with her latch key at about half-past five.

'Sutton!' she called, as he emerged from the kitchen, 'could you get me a Martini? I think I'm going to need it.'

He thought that when he brought it, she would ask him about his meeting with Laszlo, but her mind was obviously on other things. She reclined on the sofa with her eyes half shut and asked him to leave the shaker. It occurred to Sutton that during her luncheon with Laszlo, she had probably drunk quite a lot of champagne.

Sutton lurked anxiously in the hall until he heard the car in the drive. He got himself together, and opened the door. Charles charged in, followed by a furious Thomas.

'Don't blame me,' said Charles. 'Blame your sister.'

'Half-sister,' corrected Thomas.

Lydia, following them inside, was not best pleased by this.

Charles and Thomas were hastily divesting themselves of coats and hats which they dumped on Sutton. Lydia turned to Sutton. Now she would ask him. 'How did it go, Alfred?' she would say. But, instead –

'Miss Martha isn't here, is she?'

'Er – yes, madam, she's in the garden room.'

'Oh dear,' said Lydia, and followed Charles and Thomas.

Sutton, burdened with coats and hats, stood and gazed after them as the door closed behind them. He knew that the Bretts, like members of royalty, had bursts of im-

324

mense kindness and generosity towards servants, flower-girls, stage-hands and dressers but that, unfortunately, in between, engrossed in the all-consuming business of the theatre, they forgot them completely. Sutton realized that they had all completely forgotten his meeting with Laszlo Sandor.

In the garden room, Martha, reclining on the sofa, looked up, glass in hand.

'Hullo,' she said. 'I thought you'd all be back here by now, so I didn't bother to go to the theatre.'

'You didn't *bother*?' repeated Charles. 'There was a rehearsal call, but you didn't bother to go to the theatre?'

'Oh, don't make a fuss, Father,' said Martha, languidly.

Thomas advanced belligerently.

'He may not want to make a fuss,' he said, 'but *I* certainly do! You said you particularly wanted to work on that speech –'

'I don't particularly want to do anything,' interrupted Martha, 'except slightly improve my part – which, goodness knows, could do with some improvement.'

'Martha, it's a marvellous part,' Lydia intervened.

'What?' exclaimed Martha. 'Only coming on in the last act? If you want to know, I only took it as a favour to Tom.'

'Oh, don't do *me* any favours!' exclaimed Thomas. 'There are plenty of actresses who'd be only too glad to have the part, and who would play it a damned sight better.'

Lydia knew fighting words when she heard them. She groaned.

'I should get one of them, then,' said Martha.

Charles decided to assert himself.

'That's enough!' he said. 'Thomas, you're the author, not the manager. If there's any hiring or firing to be done, I'll do it.'

He turned to Martha.

'Martha,' he said, 'we shall be rehearsing Act Three at nine o'clock sharp tomorrow morning, and if you're not there on time, your part will be recast.'

Martha put her glass down, uncoiled herself gracefully from the sofa and picked up her coat.

'In that case, Father dear,' she said, 'you'd better start looking for a replacement. Nine o'clock is rather early for me, especially since I'm dining out.'

Sutton, lurking behind the kitchen door, emerged as Martha headed for the front door.

'Miss Martha,' he said, 'did you want me to get Hegarty to –?'

'No, thanks, I'll pick up a taxi.'

'Martha!'

Lydia came out of the garden room in time to hear the front door slam.

'Oh death, where is thy sting?' she moaned.

'Miss Lydia –' Sutton began.

She turned towards the stairs.

'Alfred,' she said, 'I'm going to have a nice little nap before dinner. Will you make sure that nothing and nobody disturbs me?'

'Yes, madam,' said Sutton.

As she slowly mounted the stairs, Sutton watched until she disappeared round the bend, and then turned away with bitterness in his heart. So, after all these years, that was all he meant to her. He was useful to her, that was all. He had deceived himself even about Miss Lydia.

Charles, still in a rage, came out of the garden room, shouting a final angry remark at Thomas. Sutton was coldly determined to intercept him.

'If I might have a word with you, sir –'

'Not now, Sutton,' said Charles, heading for the study.

'About my meeting, sir, with Mr Sandor.'

Charles paused.

'Ah. Yes. Of course,' he said, and turned. 'What part did he offer you?'

'Not an acting part, sir,' replied Sutton. 'Mr Sandor asked me to be his assistant.'

'Oh, did he?' said Charles, and obviously didn't think much of *that*.

'He offered me a salary of twenty pounds a week.'

'Good God!' Charles exclaimed.

That caught his attention, thought Sutton, with some satisfaction.

'I told him I would let him know,' said Sutton, and waited.

He wasn't quite sure what he was waiting for. Perhaps it was for Charles to say, 'My dear Sutton, you can't possibly accept. What on earth would we do without you?' Instead, he simply nodded.

'Of course,' said Sutton, stiffly, 'I would stay to see you through the first night of Mr Thomas's play.'

'Thanks, Sutton,' replied Charles, casually. 'I hate having strangers in my dressing room before the performance.'

He continued towards the study.

'Bring me a whisky and soda, will you?' he added, over his shoulder.

Martha dined out with friends that evening, Laszlo being one of the party. They were then going on to a night-club, and it should all have been immensely cheerful and enjoyable, but somehow Martha didn't enjoy herself. She had a sinking feeling that she was behaving extremely badly over Thomas's play, but she was damned if she was going to admit it. Still, it was enough to spoil her evening. She said that she did not feel like a night-club after all, and Laszlo, who was always quick to feel her moods, brought her home, kissed her, and left her at the grubby door in Shepherd's Market. She hadn't yet been to bed with him, and wasn't quite sure whether or not she would. He was married to a very dowdy Hungarian wife, and had three children, and Martha was sure that he would never leave them. She could, of course, become his mistress, but she wasn't sure that she wanted that. Still, she had a notion that once she went to bed with him, the decision would be made, and it would be very difficult to go back on it. In any event, tonight was not the night, when half her mind, however reluctantly, was on that stupid quarrel with her parents and with Thomas.

As she opened the door to her flat and went in, a dark figure rose up in front of her, and she started back with a scream.

'Thought you were never coming,' said a familiar voice.

'Eddie!' she said. 'You frightened me out of my wits.' She put the light on.

'Why are you sitting in the dark?'

'Taking a nap while I waited for you.'

'What the hell are you doing here?'

'Trying to find out,' said Edwin, 'what the hell you think you're doing.'

'I'm not doing anything,' replied Martha, dropping her evening coat on the floor. 'I've had a moderately enjoyable evening, and I'm just going to bed.'

'Come on, Mart,' said Edwin, 'don't waste my time. I've got to be at the studio at six o'clock tomorrow morning. We're filming in Richmond Park.'

'So?' said Martha, with a touch of defiance.

Edwin gazed back at her and shook his head.

'I always know', he said, 'when you're doing something stupid. Remember the time you fell out of that tree, and I limped for a week?'

'Well, you don't have to limp now,' said Martha. 'I'm perfectly all right.'

I'm not really, she thought. Perhaps I never will be all right again. But she gazed back at him defiantly.

'*You* may be,' said Edwin. 'How about Thomas's play?'

'Oh,' said Martha. 'So that's what it's all about. How did you know?'

'I telephoned home,' answered Edwin, 'to find out how Sutton got on with Laszlo. Needless to say, Mother and Father had completely forgotten to ask him, but –'

'Quite frankly, Ned,' Martha interrupted, 'if it's a choice between turning up at rehearsals and having lunch with a charming man like Laszlo Sandor –'

'And you don't give a damn about Thomas or the family.'

'Of course I do,' said Martha, 'but –'

They had always finished each other's sentences and followed each other's thoughts.

'But you forget that the theatre is the family business. You're damn lucky to be so good at it. I wish I was. Anyone can be good in films.'

'Father can't!' said Martha, swiftly, and knew at once that she had made a mistake.

'Then, for God's sake,' said Edwin, 'don't let him down in the theatre.'

'Oh, Eddie!' said Martha. 'Don't be such a bore!'

Edwin smiled at her.

'He's taking a hell of a chance with this play,' he said. 'Everyone knows what a disaster *Dark Dimensions* was.'

'*The Liar* was a great success.'

'Yes, but audiences and critics remember failures much more than successes. He and Mother are hoping they can carry it, no matter what. But they need you, too.'

Martha groaned and turned her back on him so that he could unhook her dress.

'Do you know what Father's done?' she said. 'Called a rehearsal for nine a.m. tomorrow, and says I'll be sacked if I don't turn up on time. I won't be bullied and blackmailed. I just won't.'

'I don't blame you,' said Edwin, undoing the last hook. 'You know what I'd do?'

Martha looked at him inquiringly over her shoulder.

'I'd ring Thomas,' said Edwin, 'and tell him to meet you at the theatre at half-past eight. Then, when Father turns up, he'll be quite knocked off his perch to find you there already. Besides – you know how he hates to think he might have missed something!'

Martha burst out laughing, and turned and flung her arms round his neck and hugged him. Trust Edwin to find a face-saver which was also a good joke – and to know that she needed it!

'You know,' she said, 'it might almost be worth it.'

Sutton had bolted the front door, and was just going to

bed when the telephone rang. He took the message, and was just turning towards the stairs, knowing that Thomas wouldn't have gone to bed yet, when he saw a glimmering white figure on the dimly lit staircase. It was Lydia, in nightdress and silk gown.

'Alfred!' she called, softly, and came quickly down.

He didn't answer. He couldn't bring himself to say, as usual, 'Yes, Miss Liddy, did you want something?' He still felt angry and resentful.

'I'm so dreadfully sorry,' she said. 'Charles has told me – you've been offered a marvellous job, and we never even asked how you got on!'

In spite of himself, Sutton began to soften slightly.

'That's all right, Miss Lydia,' he said. 'You were upset about Miss Martha. I understand.'

'Oh, Alfred!' cried Lydia. 'You always *do* understand! That's why we depend on you so. I know we're selfish swine, but – you wouldn't really leave us, would you?'

When he didn't answer, she looked aghast. This wasn't one of her acting jobs, Sutton knew, like what she'd done on that chap Burroughs when he came to the house to dun them, or like what she was always doing to the electricians or the stage-door keeper at the theatre. She really was upset, and he knew it.

'But you're one of the family!' she said.

Only when it suits them, thought Sutton, and he hardened his heart. When he got off the bus, he thought that he was still undecided, but in the few hours since they came home, he found that he had made his mind up, and once he had made his mind up, he didn't often change it.

'I think perhaps the time has come,' he said.

'It's not – it's not just because of what Charles said the other day?'

'No. Not only that. It's been coming on a long time.'

He saw tears in her eyes, and it was hard to go on speaking firmly, but he summoned all his Manchester obstinacy, and did.

'You can get a proper butler now,' he said, 'not just a failed actor playing the part. And there are plenty of good dressers who'd feel it an honour to serve Mr Brett.'

'I dare say they would,' said Lydia, shakily, 'but – Alfred, I know I'm being selfish again, but I should miss you so horribly!'

'I know *you* would, Miss Liddy,' said Sutton, slowly, 'but I sometimes think the guv'nor would be glad to see the back of me.'

She couldn't find an answer to that. While she was still struggling to think of something to say which was not an absolute denial, but left room for doubt, Sutton spoke again, more firmly than ever.

'I'll see him through the first night,' he said, 'and then I'll write to Mr Sandor. I said I'd think it over, and I haven't given him my answer yet, but I'm pretty sure I know what it will be.'

He moved towards the stairs.

'Excuse me, Miss Lydia,' he said. 'I have a message to give to Mr Thomas before he goes to bed.'

And he went upstairs, leaving Lydia alone in the hall. He heard a little sob and sniffle, as though she was trying to suppress the sound of a burst of crying, but he didn't look back. He just walked firmly on up the stairs, knowing that it was his only chance.

After all the early agitations, the last week's rehearsals of *If The Truth Be Told* sailed triumphantly through. It was, after all, a very clever, witty, funny play, and Charles and Lydia, for all their little vanities and naughtiness, were highly professional and immensely talented comedians. As for Martha, having once decided to give the play her loyalty, she was now turning in a performance of stunning virtuosity. So the first night found them all, despite the normal and healthy nervousness, remarkably calm and confident. There was only one cloud over the proceedings, and that was the boot-faced and stultifying correctness of Sutton, as he fulfilled his duties both as butler and as dresser.

Charles, sitting in his dressing room in vest, trousers and dressing-gown, opened a telegram.

'Mm!' he said, seeing that it came from an actor whom he particularly disliked, and whom he had no intention of ever employing again.

He crumpled it up and threw it in the waste-paper basket. His eyes rested on Sutton, pottering about in the background.

'Did you remember the carnation?' he inquired.

'Yes, sir,' replied Sutton. 'I left it outside in the cool, but I'd better fetch it in now – make sure of it.'

Charles smiled a little. Of course Sutton would have remembered the carnation. He always did. Then, as the door closed behind Sutton, he saw Lydia push open the communicating door between their dressing rooms.

'Charles,' she said.

He concentrated on his make-up.

'Mm?'

'Have you asked Sutton to stay yet?'

'No,' said Charles. 'Not yet.'

'Well, you *must*!' said Lydia. 'If you don't, I'll never speak to you again.'

He didn't reply.

'*Charles?*' Lydia demanded.

He turned to look at her, but before he could speak, Martha tapped at the door and came in.

'You'd better get dressed,' said Charles to Lydia.

She glared at him.

'I mean it,' she said. 'If you don't, I'll never forgive you. Never!'

As Lydia banged the communicating door shut, Martha advanced.

'Did I interrupt something?'

'Fortunately, yes,' said Charles.

'I just came to wish you luck,' said Martha, with a little awkwardness.

Characteristically, they had not, in fact, spoken alone together since that very nasty little spat over the rehearsal, which they had both, ever since, been trying to pretend had never happened.

'Luck', replied Charles, with dignity, 'has nothing to do with it. It's hard work and talent.'

He surveyed his face in the mirror critically, and then turned round in his chair to look at her.

'Come here,' he said. 'You do know I'm very proud of you, don't you?'

'No,' replied Martha, startled. 'I don't think I do.'

'Then you're a bigger fool than I thought you were,' he said, and took her hand in his. 'Edwin's a good actor, but when he's on the stage, I can't help feeling that he's just doing what I do, only not quite so well. And Thomas is a writer. That's different. He's very good at it, but it's not quite in my line.'

'Poor Tom!' said Martha.

'Oh, he's all right,' said Charles, carelessly. 'He'll always have a hard row to hoe, but that's the way it is. Nothing to be done about it. But you –'

He looked up at her, and smiled.

'You've got your own talent. It may be inherited from your mother and me, but you've made it your own, and I admire it. The only thing is, it comes too easily to you, just as it did to me.'

Martha drew her hand away.

'Oh Pa, not another sermon!'

Charles turned back to the mirror.

'Certainly not,' he said. His eyes met hers. 'There's no need. You and I can do more when we're half trying than most other actors can manage when they're sweating their guts out.'

Martha suddenly put her arms round his neck and hugged him.

'Darling Pa!' she said.

'I suppose that Hungarian fellow is out front,' remarked Charles.

Martha withdrew her arms.

'Certainly,' she replied, defiantly. 'I'm going out to supper with him afterwards.'

'Good,' said Charles. 'We'll show him what acting is really like!'

Martha laughed and went out as Sutton came in, carrying the red carnation in a small vase.

It had been a strange week for Sutton. He had told Flora and Hegarty about Sandor's offer, and they both agreed that he would be mad to refuse it.

'It's not so easy for people in our walk of life to get ahead like that,' said Flora.

'That's true enough,' Hegarty agreed. 'Once a servant, always a servant. I should know. I took the step down meself and this is the step up for you. It's much harder to find than the other one – and if you don't take it, you won't find it again.'

Sutton knew that they were right. Lydia hadn't mentioned the matter again since that night. Perhaps, thought Sutton, she had her pride, or perhaps she knew that there was nothing more to be said. As for Charles, he had never talked about it at all.

'I was right,' thought Sutton. 'He'll be glad to see the back of me.'

And yet, as he moved about the dressing room, his heart misgave him at the thought that it might be one of the last times that he would be there. Almost without thinking, he followed the old rituals, the familiar customs, everything in its place, ready to hand, everything done in the same order, very precisely, just as he liked it – and just as Charles liked it too. He glanced towards the dressing table, and saw that Charles was just finishing tying his tie, eyeing himself in the mirror with satisfaction. He would be ready for his jacket in a moment. Sutton took it down and began to brush it.

'Sutton,' said Charles, without turning round, 'about this job – I think you should take it.'

Sutton stood quite still for a moment, and then went on brushing the jacket. Charles turned round in his chair and looked at him.

'You know,' he said, 'theatre people are like royalty – there are so few people they can trust, that when they find someone, they wear them out. Laszlo Sandor is right. You deserve something better than that.'

Sutton stopped brushing, and looked up at him.

'That's funny, sir,' he said. 'You remembered his name. You've always called him "that Hungarian fellow" before.'

Charles grinned.

'First rule of survival in the theatre,' he said. 'Always despise those who can't recognize your talent. This chap –whatsisname – has recognized yours – and it's not just for fetching bottles of stout for Lydia and covering up my shortcomings.'

He saw Sutton's startled look.

'Do you think I didn't know?' he said. 'I'm very grateful, but I don't think you should spend the rest of your life doing it.'

It was as though Sutton had been waiting for thirty years to hear him say that – and yet now it didn't really seem to matter. It was as though, now he heard him say it, Sutton had known how Charles felt all along.

'Oh, I don't know, sir,' he said. 'It keeps me busy. I like that. And, as you said, you and me, we belong in the theatre.'

He gave the jacket a final touch, put the brush down, and heard the voice of the call boy coming along the corridor.

'Overture and beginners, please! Overture and beginners!'

Sutton brought the jacket to Charles and held it out for him, and Charles rose and slipped into it.

'Thanks, Alfred,' he said, casually.

Chapter Nineteen

A few months later, Lydia walked into her dressing room feeling that God was in his heaven, and that everything was as good as it could ever be in this imperfect world. *If The Truth Be Told* had been extremely well received, and, among the excellent notices, the two headlines which had pleased Charles and Lydia most had been, in *The Times*: 'The Brilliant Bretts', and, in the *Morning Post*: 'Mr and Mrs Charles Brett, the Brightest Stars in the British Theatre'. The party they gave after the show was one of the most successful they had ever given, not least because of Edwin's generosity. He knew, as they all did, what terrors Thomas had suffered in putting his work before the public after the abuse he had received after *Dark Dimensions*, and he called for silence, and raised his glass.

'Let's drink to the success of the play,' he said, 'and of that very successful playwright, Thomas Brett. Congratulations, Tom!'

'Thanks,' said Thomas, and suddenly was himself again, a member of the family, always a little bit outside, but a member of the family, nevertheless. 'Personally,' he remarked, 'I think we should drink to the new theatre manager, Miss Jean Lacy.'

Charles looked at him, startled, and then at Lydia, and then at Jean.

'You're right!' he exclaimed. 'Jean, we all know that you've been doing the job –'

'Yes,' said Lydia, 'and it's time we started paying her the bloody wages for the job, too!'

And then they were all laughing, and all wonderfully part of the same family – except for Laszlo, who stood on the edge, smiling a little, as if to say, 'You are all children living in a grown-up world.' He reached down and, entirely for his own amusement, turned over one of the newspapers so carefully folded at an excellent notice for the play. Lydia, catching sight of the gesture, looked down and saw the headline: 'Success of "The Jazz Singer" in New York. Talkies Are Here!' She looked, startled, at Laszlo, and he raised an apologetic and deprecating hand and turned the paper back again.

Still, thought Lydia, even Laszlo Sandor had his uses if he had shown Edwin where his future lay. And, meanwhile, the rest of them were happily settled in a long-running and not-too-testing success, which they might even, after its London run, take to Broadway. She hung up her coat and hat and turned towards the dressing table. Broadway, she thought. Wouldn't it be delightful to go to Broadway again? She thought of the last time, and began to smile, and in that moment she saw, beside her make-up, a cable from New York.

Lydia was so delighted that, without even thinking,

she flung open the communicating door to Charles's dressing room, the open cable in her hand.

'Guess who this cable's from?' she said. 'Gerard Lee! He's coming to London!'

She saw Charles's face freeze for an instant before he turned away, and knew what a stupid mistake she had made. She should have waited until after the performance and then remarked casually, 'Oh, by the way, I hear that Gerard Lee is coming to London. I suppose he's working on a musical here.' She didn't know how much Charles knew or guessed, but she suspected that he knew enough to be jealous. Still, it was too late now. She decided on a double bluff – to show her pleasure so plainly that it was plain she had nothing to hide.

'I've been longing for you to meet him,' she said. 'He's such a charming young man, and so talented.'

'We'd better have him to a Sunday Luncheon,' said Charles.

'Oh yes!' cried Lydia. 'What a good idea!' and knew that, double bluff or not, she had overdone the enthusiasm, and that Charles would know it.

Back in her own dressing room, Lydia read the cable again. It said: 'DEAREST LYDIA COMING TO LONDON ON 15TH. STAYING AT SAVOY. CANT WAIT TO SEE YOU. LETS DO A SHOW TOGETHER AGAIN. FONDEST LOVE. GERARD.' Lydia looked at her face in the mirror, as her dresser came in with the costume for Act One which she had just pressed.

'Marge,' said Lydia, 'would you say that I'm getting old?'

'Aren't we all?' replied Marge.

Beastly woman! thought Lydia. She had always detested her. As a matter of fact, she had never had a dresser she really liked since Betty Lacy, Jean's mother.

When she was sober, she was a very nice, sympathetic woman. All that was wrong with her was that she was a drunk. Lydia felt a sudden shiver of terror. Was that all it took to destroy a life? One fault, one weakness? I'm afraid of growing old, she thought. Is that my fatal weakness? In the mirror, she saw Marge glance, infuriatingly, at her watch.

'Yes, Marge, I know!' she said. 'It's time for me to make up and dress up and go on stage and pretend I'm still young and charming!'

Lydia prepared that particular Sunday Luncheon at Nightingale Grove with special care. Gerard Lee was not just some New York Jewish boy from a tenement in Brooklyn who had been lucky enough to write a few hit tunes. He came of a rich, cultivated Jewish family, who would have been a great deal happier if their son had become a classical pianist. Instead, he used his training as a musician to create rich, tuneful, eternal American songs and musicals. He knew everyone in New York, lunched at the Algonquin, dined at the Four Hundred, was welcome at every Long Island house party. Perhaps Lydia could not quite match Alexander Wolcott, Dorothy Parker, Paul Whiteman, and all the other brilliant talents of New York, but she certainly hoped to produce for Gerard some of the theatrical *beau monde* of London.

The family and guests were assembled in the garden room when Gerard arrived, except for Martha, who, characteristically, was late. Lydia, having taken considerable care with her dress and make-up, waited until she heard him arrive, and then set off down the stairs.

'Good morning, sir,' she heard Sutton say. 'A great privilege to meet you, if I may say so.'

'Thanks, Sutton,' replied Gerard, in his cheerful New York way. 'I've heard a great deal about you.'

'You have, sir?' replied Sutton, gratified.

Gerard's eyes went past him to where Lydia was making her entrance down the staircase.

'Hi, Legs!' he said.

'Oh, Gerard!' cried Lydia. 'Don't be so absurd!'

'What's absurd about it? They still look like pretty good legs to me.'

'They do?'

She laughed again, and came down the stairs, and took his outstretched hands, and they kissed.

There was no doubt about Gerard Lee's success at the Nightingale Grove Sunday Luncheon. He congratulated Charles and Thomas on the triumph of *If The Truth Be Told*, and commiserated with Thomas on the failure of *Dark Dimensions*, but linked it cheerfully with failures of his own, which, he indicated, were part of the business they were both in. He knew all about *The Liar*, and, while suggesting that it might be too 'British' for Broadway, remarked that it might well be bought for Hollywood, especially if Edwin would consider playing the leading part.

'I hear', said Edwin, 'that since *The Jazz Singer*, everyone suddenly wants talking pictures.'

'Right,' said Gerard. 'That's where all you British actors come in, with your beautiful voices – and British writers who can actually write dialogue, and not just captions.'

'I often wondered who wrote those,' remarked Charles.

'Oh, that's easy,' replied Gerard. 'The janitor.'

They were all laughing when Martha came in, with Laszlo.

'When did you get here?' inquired Martha, when the introductions were over.

'On Thursday,' replied Gerard. 'I sailed to Naples and hired a plane.'

'Good heavens!' said Charles. 'A plane? Trains are so much more comfortable.'

'Life's too short for trains,' said Gerard.

'But you did not fly the Atlantic, like Lindbergh?' inquired Laszlo.

Gerard laughed.

'No,' he replied, 'I guess that would be going a little too far. But, you know something? I think the time will come when taking a ship across the Atlantic will be as old-fashioned as taking a train across Europe.'

'Oh, Gerard, what nonsense!' exclaimed Lydia, affectionately.

'You said you hired a plane,' said Martha. 'You didn't fly it yourself?'

'Sure,' answered Gerard 'You ever flown a plane?'

'Well – no,' Martha answered. 'But I really would love to try it.'

'Luncheon is ready, madam,' said Sutton, in the doorway.

'Thank you, Sutton,' said Lydia, and repossessed Gerard. 'Shall we go in?' she said.

That night, as Lydia sat brushing her hair, Charles came through from his dressing room in pyjamas and dressing-gown.

'I thought it all went rather well today,' remarked Lydia.

'Ye–es,' Charles answered. 'Quite pleasant. You seemed to spend a lot of time walking in the garden with Gerard Lee.'

'We were talking over old times.'

'You seemed to have a lot to talk about.'

She turned away from the dressing table and gave him her fond, wifely smile.

'Darling,' she said, 'you're not jealous, are you?'

'Should I be?' inquired Charles.

'Of course not!' said Lydia.

Those New York days flashed across her mind like a remembered scene from a play. She saw the attractive, brilliant young man at the piano, playing the songs which he had written especially for her, and which only she could sing as he intended them to be sung. She saw the lunches at the Algonquin, with witty literary celebrities all around them, and the suppers at Sardi's, where they were treated with that peculiarly flattering delicacy of attention which Americans reserve for success and the English reserve for royalty. Indeed, members of the American theatrical royalty like the Lunts and the Barrymores always stopped to speak to them, and even while they enjoyed their intimate table for two, they were both aware all the time of being envied, he for being in the company of a beautiful woman at the height of her profession, and she for being in the company of a rich and delightful young man in the first glow of a rare talent. And every day she knew that he was falling in love with her and that she was allowing if not encouraging him to do so.

It was not sheer irresponsibility that had made Lydia behave as she did. Before she left England, she and Charles had been going through what she described to Elsie as 'one of their bad patches'. Charles's eye had been roving even more than usual, and always seemed to alight upon younger and younger women. Having always taken some pleasure in the fact that she was younger than Charles, she now began to wonder for the first time whether a man might not age more gracefully than a woman. Until now, she had been satisfied with the mildest of flirtations, but now she felt she needed something more – an absolute assurance that she was still attractive and even still dangerous.

If in the end she did not go to bed with Gerard, it was not out of loyalty to Charles, but from inbred and native caution. She and Gerard lived and worked so much in the public gaze and in the bright glare of high society that she knew that they could never keep it a secret, and she valued the respect she had earned in her profession and the dignity of her position as Mrs Charles Brett. And then, if she ever overstepped that delicate line between love and passion, could she ever step back again? Gerard was not just a witty, charming young man with a talent for sentimental tunes and memorable lyrics. He had a deliciously unexpected sense of humour, and that peculiarly Jewish gift for seeming older than he was, and wiser than most young men of his age. He adored her now. If he became her lover, would they not both be caught in a honeyed trap from which there was no escape?

Having ventured so much farther than she should have into this dangerous territory, Lydia used all her skill and experience to withdraw, and to do so without wounding Gerard too deeply. She even, to save his young and vulnerable feelings, told him the truth.

'Darling Gerard,' she said, 'I dare not. I love my children dearly, and I suppose I do love Charles, however infuriating he is. And you are so dreadfully attractive. Forgive me, darling Gerard, I dare not.'

He kissed her hand, and when she boarded the ship to return to England, her cabin was filled with cream-coloured roses. Attached to them was a card which read: 'In my heart always your lover, Gerard.'

'Anyway,' said Lydia now, taking off her gown and turning towards the bed, 'he's over here to set up a musical. He'll be much too busy to have time for *me*.'

She saw Charles's look of satisfaction before she turned, and smiled to herself. She had no intention of telling him that Gerard had spent most of the time during their *tête-à-tête* in the garden trying to persuade her to go back to America with him and star in his new show on Broadway.

Martha was still in bed next morning when she heard a gentle but firm rat-tat-tat at her door. She groaned and dragged herself out of an untidy bed and went yawning to the door in her nightdress, wondering irritably who on earth it could be. Certainly no one who knew her would expect her to be up and around at ten-thirty in the morning. She opened the door a crack and saw Gerard.

'Hi,' he said. 'Remember me?'

Martha could think of only one thing to do and did it. She slammed the door in his face.

'OK,' he called. 'I get the message.'

'No!' said Martha, and opened the door a crack again. 'Don't go away,' she said. 'Just – er – just give me a minute.'

She threw a glance over her shoulder.

'I don't suppose you could make that a couple of days?'

'One minute,' he said, firmly.

'All right.'

She closed the door, and stumbled frantically round the room, tossing the bedcover over a distinctly lumpy-looking bed, throwing clothes into the cupboard and forcing the door shut on them, pulling back the curtains, and then, alarmed at what they revealed, drawing them to again and switching on a lamp. The kitchen – there was nothing to be done about the kitchen!

'Are you still there?' she called.

'Only just,' he called back.

She grinned to herself. Somewhere she had a very glamorous négligé that Laszlo had given her – Damn! it was in the cupboard. She dragged it out, stuffed the clothes back again with tell-tale edges of white showing round the edge of the door, and struggled into the négligé, trying to brush her hair at the same time.

'Coming!' she called.

'Good!'

Her mother, she knew, would have appeared, all elegant allure, no matter what the time of day or night, and for the first time in her life, she wished that she was more like her mother.

'Come in,' she said, endeavouring to assume an air of cool sophistication, but slightly out of breath.

'Thanks.'

He glanced round him, and blinked slightly.

'This is very – er –'

'Careful!'

He paused for thought.

'Bohemian,' he suggested. 'Will that do?'

'Just,' she replied, and they both laughed, and suddenly the state of the room didn't matter in the least.

'I came to ask you out to lunch,' he said.

'When?'

'Today.'

'*Today?*' repeated Martha, indignantly. 'Haven't you ever heard of such a thing as issuing proper invitations – using the telephone –'

'I don't like telephones,' replied Gerard. 'It's too easy to say no on the telephone.'

'Well, I'm afraid I'm going to have to say no,' said Martha, 'because I already have another engagement for luncheon.'

'Break it. You'd enjoy this more.'

'I do love a man who's modest,' said Martha, 'but I'm going to have to say no, anyway. I don't break an engagement just because I've had –'

'The offer of a better one?' suggested Gerard. 'You did say you'd like to go flying.'

'Flying? In a plane?'

'I just can't seem to fancy trying it any other way,' said Gerard. 'Lunch at Croydon, and then – up, up and away, into the wide blue yonder.'

Martha was astonished to find herself tempted, and even more surprised to find herself resisting temptation.

'No,' she said. 'I'd love to come flying with you, but – another day. Today I have an engagement for luncheon.'

Martha kept her luncheon date, which was with Laszlo. She waited until they were drinking coffee, and then said, 'Laszlo, I don't think we should go on seeing each other so much.'

'Oh?'

She tried to think of a convincing reason.

'It's not fair to your wife – your children – and I've never really fancied myself as a mistress –'

'You've met someone else,' said Laszlo.

Martha hesitated, but met his eyes, and smiled. Laszlo,

accustomed to delineating the finest shades of emotion through the eye of the camera, was impossible to deceive.

'Met him,' she said. 'Not gone out with him yet.'

Laszlo smiled, too, and reached across the table and put his hand on hers.

'My dear little Martha,' he said.

'Little?' she repeated.

She was just the same height as Laszlo, and at least four inches taller than Gerard. Laszlo shook his head, still smiling.

'I knew that one day you would fall in love for the first time.'

'Oh, Laszlo, really! Have you forgotten that I was married?'

'Oh, yes,' he said. 'You married your Basil out of sentiment, and patriotism, and perhaps pity? And you were very fond of him.'

'Yes!' cried Martha.

She sought in her memory for that foolish young marriage, that mutually virginal night of sex, and seemed to see it far away, like a dream she could not quite remember.

Laszlo's hand closed round hers.

'My dear little Martha,' he said again, 'you have so much love to give, and you should not squander it as you have been squandering it. Were you unfaithful to your Basil while he was at the war?'

She tried to draw her hand away, but he kept firm hold of it. He was surprisingly strong.

'So you felt guilty, and you said, "I will punish myself. I will love everyone, and pretend that it means nothing." Am I right?'

'I –'

'I am right,' said Laszlo, 'but it doesn't matter. It is all over now.'

And suddenly it was. Because it had been spoken and the guilt acknowledged, it was over.

'Laszlo,' she said, 'you're a magician!'

'Oh, yes,' he replied, drily. 'I am a magician – that is, I am a film-maker who has one gift, to see and understand the human heart in the human race – and, I must say, the woman's heart above all.'

He laughed, and lifted her hand to his lips and kissed it.

'I hope you will be happy,' he said. 'Very happy.'

Martha and Gerard were struck by love like a *coup de foudre*. They were neither of them inexperienced, heaven knew. They had both moved in sophisticated and rather promiscuous societies. And yet they came together with absurd innocence and freshness, mind to mind, heart to heart, humour to humour, passion to passion. They did, indeed, have lunch together at Croydon, and he took her up in an aeroplane. The mixture of terror and ecstasy, of being borne up by some invisible and yet undeniably existing force was to Martha like being born again, and she stepped down shakily on to the grass and clung to him, gasping and laughing, all her languid pose of worldly wisdom quite forgotten.

'Again!' she said. 'Let's go up again very soon!'

He laughed, and held her close. They both knew that the secret and exciting world which they had just shared up in the sky was a foretaste of the even more secluded world of passion which they were soon to share in bed.

Somehow, it was part of the new-found childish simplicity of their love that they instinctively kept it secret, as though to share the knowledge of it would be to rob it of some of its magic. The moment the final curtain came down at the Princess Theatre, Martha would slip away and meet him in a little Italian restaurant in Covent Garden or a Chinese eating house in Lime-house. Or perhaps he would wait for her at the end of the alleyway opposite the theatre, and they would stroll together along the Embankment, and buy hot sausages and steaming mugs of tea at a coffee stall, and sit on a bench by the river, looking up at the frosty stars and hearing the tugs hooting along the Thames.

The family was in the habit of wandering up to Martha's flat without warning and, anyway, Gerard had taken an unaccountable dislike to the place. ('How very odd! I wonder why?' said Martha, teasing him for his neat and elegant style of living.) But Gerard was now a very rich young man, not only because of the success of his work, but also because his father's death meant that he had inherited considerable wealth from the family business. So, even though he intended to be in London for only a short time, his dislike of hotels had led him to buy a house, and in this small, white, wistaria-covered cottage in Belgravia they felt safe and secluded from the outside world.

Perhaps it was because, like many lovers before them, they had left reality behind, that they were quite un-prepared for the morning when Lydia knocked at the door and, when Gerard answered, kissed him and breezed cheerfully inside.

'Hello, darling,' she said, 'what a charming little house! I had the greatest difficulty in finding it. Hegarty kept driving round and round –'

She saw Martha sitting drinking a cup of coffee in her dressing-gown, and finished, 'I'm sorry I'm so early.'

'Hullo, Mother,' said Martha, coolly.

She stood up and looked at Gerard.

'I didn't know you had an appointment, or I wouldn't have hung around for so long.'

'We haven't an appointment,' said Lydia, and, in her turn, looked at Gerard. 'But you should have told me.'

'We tumbled head over heels,' he said, 'and we haven't picked ourselves up yet.'

Martha was suddenly and clearly in a blazing temper.

'Still,' she said, 'you should have told her. I knew you two were good friends, but I didn't realize quite *how* good!'

She went towards the little, curving staircase.

'I'd better get dressed,' she said, 'and clear out of here.'

Lydia realized that Martha was jealous, *Martha*, whereas *she*, who had every right –! She struggled to get her feelings under control.

'Oh, Martha, don't be absurd,' she said. 'I simply came here, admittedly rather early, on business. Gerard, show her the score.'

'You mean, tell her the score.'

'I mean both,' said Lydia.

Gerard went towards the piano, glancing back at Martha.

'I want your mother to open in my new revue on Broadway,' he said.

'You haven't said anything about it,' said Martha, eyeing Lydia, suspiciously.

'Well, you know your mother,' began Gerard.

'I thought I did,' replied Martha, 'but I'm beginning to doubt it.'

'I haven't made up my mind,' said Lydia, 'and I don't want everyone to start arguing and bullying me – especially your father. It might mean leaving the play before the end of the run –'

'He won't like that!' said Martha.

'Exactly. So, until I've made up my mind –'

'You haven't even heard the songs yet!' said Gerard, with a note of irritation which she had never heard from him before.

'I came to hear the songs this morning,' replied Lydia, 'but, for once, it seems my timing wasn't too good.'

She went towards the door, and turned, making one of the instinctive Brett exits.

'I'll telephone,' she said, 'and make an appointment.'

Gerard started after her.

'Lydia!' he called, but the door had closed behind her.

Gerard turned to look at Martha, and smiled, but his smile was uneasy, and already the first little cloud raced across the sunny landscape of their love.

'I have a notion,' said Hegarty, 'that the mistress wasn't too happy with her visit to Mr Gerard Lee. It took us half an hour to find the house, she was in there five minutes, and came out with a face like thunder.'

'There's something going on,' said Sutton. 'I wish I knew what it was.'

'Why, Mr Sutton,' said Flora, 'I thought you always knew what was going on.'

'So did I,' said Sutton, not best pleased.

Charles, too, had a feeling that something was going on. One of the troubles with owning a theatre was that you always had to look ahead in order to have the next production ready to move in when the current one came to an end. Lydia knew this as well as he did, and yet it seemed to be impossible to persuade her to take an interest in reading scripts and making plans for the future. Annoyingly enough, Jean, too, seemed to have lost her grip lately. She, who had always been so trim and efficient, had become lazy and slovenly, arriving late in the office and disappearing at odd times without notice. Even more irritating, her deterioration seemed to date from the time when she was officially made theatre manager. Perhaps, thought Charles, she was one of those people who can't take responsibility – and if that was the case, it was a great pity she hadn't made it clear to them sooner. Her temper wasn't what it was, either.

'My dear Jean,' said Charles one day, 'we really must find a new production to come in after *If The Truth Be Told*. It's no good waiting until the returns are so bad that we have no choice, and have to bring anything in, whether it's suitable or not. How about all those scripts? Isn't there anything in them at all?'

'I – I haven't really had time –'

'I seem to remember you volunteered to read them, and sift out anything that was any good.'

'Yes, I will!' replied Jean, with an angry note in her voice which Charles had never heard before. 'But I can't do everything at once!'

'It seems to me,' replied Charles, annoyed in his turn, 'that you're not doing a great deal. The show is running perfectly well, we haven't anything on tour –'

'I'm sorry if I'm not giving satisfaction!' said Jean, and walked out of the room, leaving Charles openmouthed.

Charles was not only astonished, however. He felt rather guilty, too. It wasn't like Jean to behave like that. He knew that something was wrong, and that it was his duty as an employer, as well as a friend, to find out what it was. But Jean had always maintained her reserve, and though she had relaxed her guard a little for a while, now she seemed once more to have retired behind the barriers which only Thomas had really been able to break down.

It was true, though, that Charles would not have spoken as he had if it had not been for the fact that he had had a very irritating and upsetting start to the day. Just as he was preparing to set off for the theatre, Sutton had told him that Hegarty had taken Lydia to keep an appointment and was not back yet.

'Appointment?' said Charles. 'What appointment? She didn't say anything to me about it.'

'I couldn't say, sir,' said Sutton.

Hegarty was more forthcoming.

'Sorry to keep you waiting, sir,' he said. 'I was taking the mistress to Mr Gerard Lee's house.'

'House? Doesn't he stay in a hotel?'

'Ah no, he has a nice little house behind Belgrave Square. Make a proper little love nest if the gentleman was that way inclined. The first time I drove the mistress there, we had the divil of a job to find it.'

Hegarty was smiling cheerfully as he held the door open.

'What time are you picking Mrs Brett up?' inquired Charles, casually.

'Oh, not till about three o'clock, sir,' replied Hegarty. 'She said she'd be having lunch with Mr Lee.'

'Right,' said Charles.

But it wasn't right at all. Lydia had said nothing to him about visiting Gerard Lee, and yet she had gone there, not once, but twice – and even more times for all he knew. Of course she had had an affair with the fellow when she was in New York. If she thought he didn't know, she must think he was a perfect idiot. Guilty about his own philandering, he had always pushed the knowledge out of his mind, afraid even to think of it. That Lydia should really have a love affair with another man was something he could not accept, so it was best to pretend that he didn't know it. But for that man now to come to London, and for Lydia to visit him secretly in his blasted 'love nest' –! No wonder Charles arrived at the theatre office and bit Jean's head off!

Lydia, having duly made her appointment with Gerard, ran through the songs with him, and found them quite delicious, quite delightful, and entirely in her style. An added attraction was that the show was to be a revue and not a musical comedy. She did not have to carry the whole thing herself, or learn a lot of lines, as for a play. She simply had to do what she did best – float on, looking lovely, deliver a charming and witty song, get great applause, and go swanning off again, and then, after a couple of amusing sketches during which she had plenty of time to change, do the whole thing again with a different but equally delightful song. She didn't even have to commit herself for too long. Everyone wanted to be in a Gerard Lee revue. Gertie Lawrence might take over from her, or Talullah – though Talullah was much younger, more Martha's age.

'What do you think?' said Gerard.

'I think, if anything, they're even better than anything you've ever done before,' answered Lydia.

'So –?'

'There's no doubt about the songs. They're marvellous. I just have to think about – appearing on Broadway again.'

'Again?' Gerard repeated. 'That's the whole point of

it. They love you there! It's not like starting from scratch. They're waiting for you with open arms.'

'Yes,' said Lydia. 'I'll let you know.'

'I need to know soon.'

'Yes, of course,' said Lydia, pettishly. 'Don't bully me.'

She didn't tell Charles where she had been, and was relieved when he didn't ask her.

The pristine freshness of the relationship between Martha and Gerard was never quite regained. The fact that Lydia knew about it had already brought that fatal invasion of reality, and they both knew in their hearts that the moment must come when Gerard would say, 'There's something we must talk about.'

'I don't like the sound of that,' said Martha. 'Whatever it is, don't let's talk about it now.'

'You know we must. I'll be going back to the States very soon. I want you to come with me.'

'Come with you? You may not have noticed, but I'm appearing in a play.'

'It'll be coming off soon.'

'There'll be another play. My work is here. You love London. Why can't you stay here?'

'Because my work is in America. Come on, honey. I put the questions in the wrong order, maybe, but what I'm trying to say is, will you marry me and come to New York?'

They were lying in each other's arms on the sofa, waiting until it was time for Martha to go to the theatre, but now she drew away and stood up.

'No,' she said.

'No, to which?'

'No to both. It's too soon. Why can't we just go on as we are?'

'I've just told you, I have to go back. I have business in New York, and then I'm going on to Hollywood. I'd like you to come with me.'

'What on earth would I do? Be a sort of – appurtenance?'

'Be my wife and my lover.'

'I'm an actress.'

'Of course. You'd get work over there. I'm hoping your mother will be in my show on Broadway –'

'Thanks,' said Martha. 'I don't know that I *particularly* fancy going to New York in order to be in competition with Mother – in any capacity.'

Gerard stood up, too, at that.

'Don't you think that remark is a little unworthy of you?'

'I've no idea. I don't know what is expected of me.'

'Damn it all, Martha, I'm asking you to marry me!'

'Yes, but on what terms?'

'On the terms that we love each other!'

He came behind her to put his arms round her, but she stood very still and did not respond.

'That would have been enough once, but now it isn't.'

'Why not?'

She broke away.

'I must go to the theatre,' she said.

'No,' said Gerard. 'Not yet. I think we should settle this here and now. Are you coming with me?'

'I'll tell you when I've made up my mind.'

Martha was getting into her fur coat. Gerard stood quite still and didn't move to help her.

'Yes or no?'

She turned on him furiously.

'I don't know!'

'If you don't know by now,' said Gerard, 'that means the answer is probably no.'

It was the kind of absurd, wounding quarrel which only lovers can have, with a hundred nuances of feeling hidden behind each simple word.

'All right!' Martha shouted at him. 'That's what it means!'

And she was through the door and had slammed it behind her, like someone who, in a temper, seizes a valuable object and flings it on the floor, dashing it into a dozen pieces before she has even thought about it.

Neither Flora nor Sutton heard Jean leave. It was Emily – it would be, of course! – who came down to the kitchen, all agog, to say that Miss Lacy had made her bed, but had left a note on the pillow addressed to the master and mistress. Sutton took the note up to Lydia while she was still in bed, and she told him to stay, and read it aloud to him and Charles. In it, Jean thanked Mr and Mrs Brett for their kindness, but regretted that she had to leave. She was sorry it hadn't been possible to give notice, but she hoped that everything would be found to be in order in the theatre office.

Charles finished dressing, ate a hasty breakfast, and was driven straight to the theatre. He wasn't particularly proud of his first instinct, which was to check the box-office returns, the advance bookings, the bar receipts and the petty cash, but it had to be done. Everything was in perfect order.

'She's even read all these scripts,' he said to Lydia, when she arrived some time later. 'She's written rejection letters for the ones that are no good, marked some as possibles, and put this one aside for production.'

'But, why?' said Lydia. 'Why should she do it?'

They had a matinée and an evening performance, so it wasn't until their late-night supper back at Nightingale Grove that they were all together, with Edwin, who was staying the night before filming the opening scenes of his new picture on Hampstead Heath. They all agreed that Jean had not been herself lately, that she seemed to have withdrawn herself from the family, that she had reverted to her old, silent ways, as well as her old, dowdy style of dressing.

'And we were all too much engrossed in our own lives,' said Lydia, 'to ask her what was happening in hers. Was it another love affair, do you think? Or was the job too much for her?'

'I'm sure it wasn't,' said Thomas.

'And even if it was,' said Martha, 'why keep quiet about it? Why should she suddenly – walk out?'

'Well,' said Charles, guiltily, 'I admit that I did have a little unpleasantness with her over –'

There were all on to him like a pack of wolves who see a sacrificial passenger ejected into the snow from the sleigh.

'Charles, really!' said Lydia. 'You are the limit!'

'Father, you never appreciated Jean.'

'I suppose your "little unpleasantnesss" was a blazing row, which made her feel –'

'Father, I don't think you understand how inadequate you make people feel, when you –'

It was Sutton, plonking flat-footed round the table, collecting the pudding plates, whose voice rose above the rest.

'Excuse me, sir, madam,' he said, 'but it is Flora's opinion that Miss Lacy was expecting.'

And with that he continued on his way out of the room.

'I take it he means expecting a baby,' remarked Edwin. 'I wonder who the father was.'

'That son-of-a-bitch, Piers Longford-Price!' exclaimed Martha. 'I might have known it!'

'But why didn't she tell us?' cried Lydia. 'Surely she must have known that we would understand? She was like one of the family.'

'I can understand her not telling the rest of you,' said Thomas. 'She was ashamed and embarrassed, especially with Longford-Price being what he was. But I would have thought she might have trusted me. Oh, God!'

His face changed. They all looked at him.

'Of course,' he said, 'I was the last person she could confide in. She could hardly say that she was going to have a little bastard, and that she was thoroughly ashamed of the fact.'

He stood up and walked out, leaving the others all glancing at each other, disconcerted.

'Eddie,' said Charles, 'for God's sake, pour us all some wine. I'm getting too old for these emotional scenes at the end of a long day.'

'Right, Father,' said Edwin, and went to the sideboard, but threw a cautious glance at Martha as he did so.

'By the way,' he said, 'I saw Gerard Lee at the Studio today.'

'Really?' said Lydia. 'What on earth was he doing there?'

'Laszlo was trying to talk him into letting him have the rights of *Head Over Heels* for a musical picture.'

'You can't make a film out of a Broadway revue.'

'Laszlo thought he could cobble some kind of story together round it. He's seen a girl in the chorus, Anna Neagle, who, he thinks, would be marvellous in it.'

'I hope she's not Hungarian,' said Charles.

Edwin smiled.

'No, I've seen her. She really is rather a beauty. But Gerard wasn't too keen. He thinks if he's going to sell out to moving pictures, he'd rather do it for more money in Hollywood.'

Edwin brought the wine and began to pour it.

'I had lunch with Gerard,' he said. 'What a nice fellow he is. By the way, he told me he'd asked Martha to marry him.'

'Oh, thank you, Eddie!' cried Martha, indignantly. 'I should sell tickets and tell the whole world!'

'What did you say?' demanded Charles.

'I said no,' replied Martha.

'Good,' said Charles.

Lydia said absolutely nothing, but drank her wine. Edwin moved on to fill Martha's glass.

'He also told me that he wanted Mother to appear in his new revue.'

'*What?*' said Charles.

'But she turned him down, too, so he's going back to New York to eat worms. He's flying from Croydon at nine o'clock tomorrow morning.'

Martha put her wine down, untasted.

'I'm going to bed,' she said, and walked out.

Lydia sat and finished her wine in silence, looked at Charles, and rose.

'I think I'll do the same,' she said.

Left alone, Charles and Edwin looked at each other.

'Not like you, Eddie,' said Charles, 'to put the cat among the pigeons. More like Thomas.'

Edwin smiled.

'I suppose it is,' he said. 'But I just had this feeling, Father, that this was something you and Mother needed to talk about.'

'Oh, damn!' said Charles. 'I suppose you're right. Let's have another glass of wine first.'

Lydia was in bed by the time Charles had come upstairs and undressed and got his courage together. He came into the bedroom, and sat on the bed beside her.

'Why didn't you tell me? Is the show any good?'

'Yes. It's delightful. Three or four charming songs, and a couple of good sketches –'

'Then, why have you turned it down?'

'Because I'm bloody terrified!' said Lydia, and buried her face in the pillows.

'You had a big success on Broadway last time,' said Charles, feeling his way.

'Yes! Last time! That was five years ago!'

Suddenly Charles saw it all. Last time, he thought, Gerard Lee was in love with you, and now he's in love with Martha.

'They'll still remember you,' he said.

'That's what I'm afraid of!' replied Lydia, looking up at him. 'How long can I go on pretending that I'm – I'm –'

Charles took her in his arms.

'A very beautiful woman, with a marvellous talent,' he said, 'and they'd be bloody lucky to get you – and I shall be bloody miserable while you're away!'

It was early in the morning when Charles became aware of Lydia getting quietly out of bed. In fact, since it was still dark, he thought it was the middle of the night.

'What time is it?' he groaned. 'Where are you going?!

'Six o'clock. Croydon. Go back to sleep.'

Martha proved a great deal more difficult to rouse,

and even after Lydia had dragged her forcibly out of bed, she showed a tendency to crawl back into it again. However, at last she had got herself into some sort of clothing, with a fur coat on top, and Sutton had roused Hegarty and made them all a cup of tea, and they were in the car, heading for Croydon. It was a frosty morning, with a little fog about, and it was still dark, so there was no question of speeding.

'We will be in time, will we?' asked Lydia.

'We're cutting it a bit fine, madam,' replied Hegarty, 'but we should just make it.'

It was then that the car ground to a halt with a puncture.

Martha, who had been huddled in the corner of the car with her eyes shut, was suddenly desperately anxious.

'Oh, hurry, Hegarty! Do please hurry!' she said, as she and Lydia stood on the side of the road and Hegarty jacked the car up.

'Darling, don't fuss. He's being as quick as he can. Come on, let's walk up and down. It'll be warmer.'

'I must see him,' said Martha. 'I simply must! I was so beastly to him. I must have been mad.'

'We're all mad when we're in love,' said Lydia.

'Yes, but – he asked me to marry him, and I turned him down so ungraciously, and it was up to me to get in touch with him, but I didn't. And he came to the flat when I was out, and put a note through the door, but I never answered it. I don't know why. And now he's going to New York, and on to Hollywood, and I'll never see him again.'

'You can always write him a letter,' remarked Lydia, drily.

'Ready, madam!' called Hegarty.

He tossed the spare wheel and the jack in the boot,

struggled into his jacket without buttoning it up, and they were off again.

Near Croydon and the country, the fog thickened, and there were times when Hegarty had to slow to a walking pace. The sun, if it was there at all, was hidden behind swirls of mist.

'Oh, damn!' said Martha. 'Oh, damn!'

The fog lifted as they reached the airfield, and they saw a small plane, and a man climbing into it.

'There he is!' cried Lydia and Martha simultaneously.

Martha reached for the door handle.

'Stay where you are, Miss Martha,' said Hegarty, and drove straight towards the aeroplane.

Gerard Lee climbed out and took Martha in his arms and kissed her.

'You're a crazy kid,' he said. 'You know that?'

'I know.'

'Maybe that's why I love you.'

'I hope so,' said Martha.

Gerard glanced towards the aeroplane, where the man in the co-pilot's seat was pointing to his watch.

'I have to go,' he said, 'or I'll miss the ship at Le Havre. It would all have been so much simpler if you would have married me and come with me.'

'You haven't asked me lately.'

'You mean, you'd come with me?'

He threw an anxious look at the plane, and at the man who was waiting to pull the chocks away.

'Wrong question,' said Martha. 'Will I come with you? No. I'm in a play.'

'Will you marry me?'

'Yes. Oh, yes!'

Gerard's face, beneath its flying helmet, was a splendid mixture of delight and exasperation.

'This is a fine time to tell me,' he said. 'I can't even buy you a ring!'

He pulled off one of his leather gloves, and took a signet ring off his little finger, and put it on the third finger of her left hand.

'Now we're engaged,' he said, 'and don't you forget it!'

'I won't,' said Martha, and they kissed again.

'Mr Lee!' called the co-pilot. 'We should be leaving. The fog's coming down again.'

Gerard, turning towards the aeroplane, saw Lydia, and paused. Elegant in tweed, Lydia came towards him, smiling.

'Strictly business,' she said. 'Gerard, darling, that little note I sent you, would you mind eating it?'

'And you'll eat your words?'

'Every one of them,' said Lydia. 'I would love to be in your show – that is, if you still think I'm good enough.'

'Lady,' said Gerard, 'in my book, you will always be the tops.'

Then he was in the plane, and the goggles pulled down over his eyes. The engine was started up, the chocks pulled away, one last wave, and with a chatter and a roar the plane was taxiing away.

'Off into the wide blue yonder,' said Martha, as the plane vanished, its wings rising and dipping in turn from side to side like a tightrope-walker, into the low cloud, and she felt the heavy gold signet ring which had joined the wedding ring on her finger.

Chapter Twenty

Martha had fully intended to visit New York as soon as possible. Unfortunately, it just happened that the play that Jean had put aside for production was an American comedy called *Scram!* which, with a little rewriting by Thomas, was an admirable vehicle for Charles and Martha, and since she knew that Gerard would be in Hollywood, Martha thought that she might as well do it. Emerging from that, with a nice little revival billed as a stopgap, Martha was quite prepared to book her passage – except that, unfortunately, on the last night of *Scram!* she stepped carelessly off the stage at the end of the final call and broke her leg.

Flowers and daily letters from Gerard cheered her convalescence, but Lydia was back from New York before Martha managed to get there. The revue had been a great success, but, ironically enough, Lydia had hardly seen anything of Gerard. Once the show was set, he was off to Hollywood again, where some mogul or other had offered him more money than was decent to turn one of his bright, witty little Broadway revues into a big, crass backstage musical comedy, with very dubious synchronized sound. Deliciously amusing letters told Martha about Charlie Chaplin, Mary Pickford and Douglas Fairbanks, and the heroic efforts of Hollywood simultaneously to ride two horses which were travelling in entirely different directions, one silent and the other talking. Only Al Jolson had unerringly followed *The Jazz Singer* with another singing, talking picture called *The Singing Fool*, which, rightly abused by the critics, had triumphantly grossed a million dollars more than *The Jazz Singer*.

Waiting for Gerard to return to New York and still limping, Martha filled the time by writing a play with Thomas. It was based on a first venture into drama by a highly respectable clergyman, but Martha, once involved in the enterprise, brought into it some much more rakish experiences of her own, when she was stranded in a railway carriage in a siding with a lecherous touring manager called Bobby Bishop. Unfortunately, in the original play, the character placed in a compromising position was a bishop. Unfortunately, also, Billy Bishop had since become an official in the Actors' Association, an organization deeply hostile to all theatre managements, and particularly inimical to Charles Brett.

The play was produced at the Princess Theatre under the title of *Taken at the Flood*. Charles was hilarious as the bishop – outraged pomposity personified – and Lydia, still glowing with confidence from her Broadway success, was quite delicious as his frivolous temptress. The play opened to roars of laughter and ecstatic reviews – and Billy Bishop promptly sued.

'We'll fight!' said Charles.

'You'll have to take the play off meanwhile,' said John Caldwell, whose original training had been in the Law. 'Otherwise, if Bishop wins, the damages will be enormous.'

Charles and Lydia looked at each other, dismayed. They had nothing else ready to come in, and it was a very expensive production, with machinery especially built to move a rowing boat across the stage. (The railway carriage in the siding had been conceived by the clergyman author as a caravan in a flooded field.) To take such a successful play off, and have the theatre dark, would represent a very considerable loss. On the other hand, if the damages were as large as John indicated, they could be ruined. Because the clergyman wished to remain anonymous, especially when he saw how racy his play had become in the hands of Martha and Thomas, only their names appeared as co-authors, and he was not cited.

'But he might give evidence,' said Nell.

'No!' said Martha, decidedly. 'Dear old Dr Woodward, it wouldn't be fair. We promised him faithfully that his name would never appear. He said his bishop would never forgive him, and that he'd probably be unfrocked.'

'I agree with Martha,' said Thomas. 'He's a jolly old chap, and he loves the play, but we made a solemn promise to him and we have to keep it.'

'Well,' said Charles, 'without his evidence, I don't see that we stand a chance. We'd better take the play off.'

'Oh, come on, Pa!' said Martha. 'It's not like you to cave in, especially to a poisonous pimple like Billy Bishop. Anyway, I think John's wrong. He's suing for defamation of character. By the time I've given my evidence about what *really* happened, he won't have a shred of character left.'

'Nor will you,' said Edwin.

Because he was now spending all his time making films, he tended to be something of an outsider in the daily life and business of the family, locked as it was into theatrical work and events, but, like John and Nell, he tended to be summoned to family councils in moments of crisis.

'Oh, darling, are you sure you ought to give evidence?' cried Lydia.

'She won't have much choice,' said Thomas. 'None of us will.'

'Still,' said Nell, always mindful of appearances, 'she could be a little discreet.'

The others roared with laughter. Martha discreet!

'That's all very well,' said Nell, 'but everyone knows that she is engaged to a distinguished American songwriter. Martha, I really do think that you should consider Gerard.'

'So do I,' Martha replied. 'We'll invite him to come over for the trial. He'll love it.'

But Gerard did not come over for the trial. He said he was too busy working on a new show. Martha went into the witness box, and, as she had predicted, her blithe account of the night spent stranded with Billy Bishop and of his unsuccessful attempts upon her virtue brought much more ridicule upon him than the play could have achieved in a year's run. The real drama of the event, however, was achieved by Dr Woodward. That elderly and highly respectable clergyman travelled up from his rectory in Norfolk and, bravely throwing aside his anonymity, gave evidence as to the origins of the play, and the fact that it was he who had made fun of the leading character, a bishop. Well, yes, he admitted, under cross-examination, the character, lamentably enough, did display certain characteristics of his own highly respected bishop.

'There goes his hopes of promotion,' remarked Hegarty, sitting with the rest of the staff in the public gallery.

'Considering the money he's made out of this play,' replied Sutton, 'I doubt if he cares.'

Dr Woodward *did* care, however, and had made a considerable sacrifice. He was not to know that the English taste for eccentric clergymen and his bishop's fear of seeming to be small-minded would lead to a small but gratifying degree of fame as an author, and the edifying position of rural dean.

Meanwhile, the family waited nervously for the verdict.

'What do you think?' said Nell.

John Caldwell shook his head.

'It's all very well,' he said, 'but whatever the first draft may have been, Martha's evidence showed that she *did* pillory Billy Bishop in the play as it appeared on the stage.'

John was right. The jury brought in a verdict of 'guilty' and the judge quite agreed with them. But the damages awarded to Billy Bishop were not as substantial as John had feared. They consisted, in fact, of the sum of exactly one farthing.

It was one week later, when they were still in a state of euphoria, especially with HOUSE FULL boards up outside the Princess Theatre every night, that the letter arrived for Martha from Gerard Lee, breaking off the engagement. He didn't give any real reason. He just said that Fate seemed to be keeping them apart, and maybe Fate knew what it was doing. Martha had been right, he said. She belonged in London, and he belonged in New York. 'Nothing is for ever,' the letter concluded. 'We had a wonderful time together, and we both have that to remember. Let's keep it that way.'

'Damn!' said Charles. 'Damn! I knew she shouldn't have given evidence. The whole blasted case made front-page news in America as well as here. Edwin was right. It may have wrecked Billy Bishop's character, but it made Martha look damned rackety, too.'

'But Gerard wouldn't worry about that, not if he loved her,' said Lydia. 'He isn't like that. There's something wrong.'

'In that case,' replied Charles, 'he's probably met another woman, and is using this as an excuse.'

Lydia looked at him despairingly. It was all too likely, after such a long absence, and with all the talented and beautiful women who surrounded him in New York and Hollywood.

'Oh, Charlie!' she said. 'It'll destroy her!'

Martha, however, once the first shock was over, surprised them all. Having at last found a man whom she considered worth fighting for, she was not giving up so easily. She sent a cable: 'SAILING TO NEW YORK NEXT WEEK. YOU'LL HAVE TO TAKE THAT RING OFF MY FINGER YOURSELF. I LOVE YOU ALWAYS. MARTHA.' Before she could pack, a cable arrived, saying: 'SAILING FROM NEW YORK ON NORMANDY. GERARD.'

It was Sutton who picked up the newspaper from the mat and read the headline. He took it straight up to Lydia, who read it, stricken. 'GERARD LEE MISSING FROM

ATLANTIC LINER. FAMOUS SONGWRITER VANISHES OVERBOARD DURING NIGHT. WAS IT SUICIDE?'

Charles, emerging from his dressing room, saw her face and came to take the paper and read the headline. He put his arms round her, but she put him aside.

'No, don't, Charlie,' she said. 'I must get dressed at once. Martha's at her flat. I must tell her before anyone else does.'

'He killed himself,' said Martha. 'He killed himself, rather than marry me.'

Lydia brought her back to Nightingale Grove, and they all tried to surround her with love and warmth, but she was frozen, and they were helpless. What words of consolation could there be for suicide, the ultimate and most destructive rejection?

Gerard must have known that she would be with the family at Nightingale Grove, because it was there that his second letter was delivered.

Dearest Martha,

Forgive me for being such a coward. I went to the doctor a few months ago. I knew that something was wrong. I've had all sorts of tests, but there's nothing to be done. I'm going to die, anyway, and I got him to tell me what it would mean. I couldn't bear to think of you remembering me as blind and half crazy, and, apparently, that's what it means when you have a tumour on the brain. Honey, I know you would have been strong enough to take it, but I'm not, so I'm making my exit in the way I love best. I know you'll understand. Believe me always,

your husband and your lover,

Gerard.

P.S. Please wear the ring for me.

P.P.S. I wish I could have been there for that trial. Oh boy! that would have been something to remember!

Lydia put her arms round Martha and held her close.

'Mother,' said Martha, voicing at last the jealous fear she had felt for so long, 'did you and Gerard –? Did you ever –?'

'No, my darling!' cried Lydia, thanking God that she could tell the truth. 'He did love me, but it was only while he was waiting for you.'

They cried together then, but they were healing tears.

Chapter Twenty-one

The beginning of December 1928 saw the Brett Family in surprisingly good shape. *Taken at the Flood* was still a roaring success, assisted by the scandalous publicity of the lawsuit. Edwin's film, *The Claws of the Eagle*, had firmly established him as the Douglas Fairbanks of the British Cinema, and had been shamelessly followed by an even more athletically romantic sequel called *The Eagle Flies Again*. Much to Charles's disgust, Edwin was pursued by adoring female fans to the very gates of Nightingale Grove. Sutton wasn't best pleased, either, since the most daring of them would penetrate the grounds and knock at the door to beg for autographs, while Hegarty didn't relish having to get out of the car to open and shut the gates, which were now kept closed whenever Edwin was at the house in a vain attempt to discourage intrusion. Only Emily was delighted, since she gained a great deal of reflected glory from working so close to this new Idol of the Silver Screen.

'Oh yes, I often makes his bed of a morning,' she would say, airily, to her family and friends, gratified by the swooning envy this provoked.

'Wasn't it a good thing, Miss Evans,' she remarked one day, when Edwin had been voted Biggest Box Office Draw of the British Cinema, 'that I never left, like what my mum wanted me to?'

And Flora, thinking of her hungry nieces in the Welsh valley, scowled. Who would have thought that Master Eddie and her beloved Moving Pictures would have landed her with Emily as a permanent and exasperating fixture in her kitchen for the foreseeable future?

They had heard nothing of Jean since she left. There was something eerie in the way she had walked into their lives and affections and then silently vanished. For a while, they tried to find her. Lydia, in particular, made discreet inquiries of all her friends in the theatre, and even asked the stage-door keeper to see if he could hear anything. For even longer, as she was driven to and from the theatre or to her dressmaker, and as she walked along Shaftesbury Avenue or through the alleyways to the Ivy, she glanced about, hoping to see that neat, slender figure moving unobtrusively through the crowds. But after a while, she forgot to look, and only a sudden resemblance would make her quickly turn her head, and then sink back, disappointed.

'She doesn't mean to be found, Miss Liddy,' said Sutton, who shared her sense of loss more than anyone except Thomas.

Jean had been an invaluable ally in a household that thrived on alarms and excursions.

Perhaps because of a secret hope that she would return, they had never replaced Jean with a new theatre manager. Instead, they had a series of middle-aged and rather tiresome female secretaries, and, in moments of emergency, summoned a bitterly protesting Nell to fill the gap.

Thomas missed Jean more than anyone, and still blamed himself for having been too self-engrossed to observe that she was in trouble. It was Jean who had nursed him through the discovery of his bastardy and the failure of *Dark Dimensions* and Jean who had helped him more than anyone to face his return to the theatre with *If The Truth Be Told*. If it came to that, it had been Jean who had given him help and encouragement with his first play, and even suggested the title of *The Liar*. And yet, when she needed him, he wasn't there, and now that she was gone, he began to think that he had cared for her a great deal more than he had ever realized.

When the *Taken at the Flood* trial was safely over, Thomas was glad to accept an invitation from a friend to go to Germany for a while. There he had a love affair with a Russian countess fifteen years older than himself, which taught him a great deal, and did him no harm whatever. There he also moved in the curious world of political passion and sexual perversion that characterized the literary Berlin of the time. He saw a play by Bertolt Brecht and met a young man called Christopher Isherwood, and returned full of enthusiasm for Communism and eager to expound his revolutionary fervour in dramatic form. If he hoped to convert his family to his new-found Marxist principles, however, he was to be disappointed.

'Oh, Tom, don't be such a bore!' Martha would say.

And Charles, urging him to write a new play for the Princess Theatre, remarked blandly that he didn't mind what the characters' politics were, as long as there were two good parts for Lydia and himself.

Into this comparatively restful household came, unexpectedly, the joker in the pack, Perdita. It had been

Perdita's habit to do unexpected things ever since her conception, which took place in Australia. Lydia had thought that she never would be able to forgive Charles for the careless liaison which had led to the birth of Thomas, and for quite a long time, she didn't. But there was something about that tour of Australia, playing under corrugated-iron roofs, travelling acrosss seemingly interminable desert wastes in hot and dusty trains, and being at once churlishly flattered and inadvertently insulted by the kindest people in the world that would have reconciled Cain and Abel, and Perdita was the result.

It was Sutton who received the news of Perdita's latest premature incursion into the family circle. He put the telephone down and went into the kitchen where Hegarty, not for the first time, was having a quiet cup of tea.

'Miss Perdita,' he said, 'calling from Victoria Station. Nip along and pick her up. She'll be waiting under the clock.'

'It's a bit early for the Christmas holidays, isn't it?' inquired Hegarty.

'Ye–es,' replied Sutton, with a tiny note of doubt. 'But she says there's measles at the school, so they've all been sent home.'

Hegarty finished his cup of tea, stood up and picked up his cap.

'I hope *she* hasn't got measles,' he said, 'for I never had it meself.'

'Oh, don't worry, Mr Hegarty,' said Flora. 'Miss Perdita had measles when she was five. In fact, I don't know why they bothered to send her home, for you don't get measles more than once. Everyone knows that.'

378

Charles and Lydia, Martha, Edwin and Thomas were all taking part in a charity show that afternoon to raise money for the Stage Widows and Orphans Fund, and Charles and Lydia, of course, were then going on to the Princess Theatre for the evening performance. Perdita, arriving in her singularly unbecoming school uniform, and being fed tea and scrambled egg by a sympathetic Flora, showed a remarkable readiness to go to bed before they returned. Next morning, however, retribution struck. The headmistress, not lovable and no fool, had not entrusted the letter to Perdita, but had put it in the post.

'Expelled?' roared Charles. 'You've been expelled?'

'What about the measles?' demanded Lydia.

Perdita shrugged.

'No measles,' said Lydia.

Charles was rereading the letter.

'For persistent misconduct. Plain misconduct wasn't good enough for you. It had to be persistent misconduct.'

'What exactly did you do?' inquired Lydia.

'Nothing, really. I just used to sneak out after lights-out to the flicks with some of the other girls. Miss Charleston said I put them up to it.'

'A ringleader,' said Charles. 'A ringleader, a liar and a – a misconductress. No school will ever accept her again.'

Perdita's expressive little face changed in an instant from gloom and guilt to a happy smile.

'Oh, good!' she exclaimed. 'Because I've no intention of going back to school, anyway. I'm going on the stage.'

'You certainly are not!' said Lydia. 'Auntie Elsie

knows of a very good school in Switzerland, and that's where you're going, directly after Christmas.'

'Oh, Mummy –!'

'And if we had ever considered the possibility of your going on the stage, we certainly wouldn't now. It's a profession which calls for effort, study, self-discipline, and – and –'

'And honesty,' put in Charles. 'Measles, indeed!'

'What *are* we going to do with Perdita?' said Lydia, that night.

'Send her to that school in Switzerland,' replied Charles.

'Ye–es. But if she's determined to make them get rid of her – You know what worries me, Charles? We're all good at getting our own way, but Perdita has a – a sort of single-minded determination which is quite frightening.'

'Be invaluable to her if she goes on the stage,' remarked Charles, closing his book and putting out the lamp on his side of the bed.

'She's not going on the stage!' said Lydia, doing the same.

They were both sound asleep when Sutton came in, his thinning hair tousled, his dressing-gown untied.

'Sir! Miss Liddy!'

Lydia had taken a sleeping pill, so was harder to rouse.

'What?' said Charles, getting up on one cross elbow. 'What the devil is it?'

'It's the police, sir. They've just telephoned to say that the Princess Theatre is on fire.'

There is no more desolate sight than a damaged

theatre. Next morning Charles stood and looked round the charred auditorium with tears in his eyes.

'She was so beautiful,' he said. 'It's like seeing the woman you love disfigured.'

Lydia was examining the blackened ruins of the scenery of *Taken at the Flood*.

'If you'd been born in Clapham,' she said, briskly, 'you'd be saying, "Thank Gawd the bleedin' 'ouse is still here!"'

She came and slipped her arm into his.

'She's not dead yet,' she said, 'and neither are we.'

Sutton emerged from the prompt corner, stepping over miscellaneous debris.

'How're the costumes, Alfred?' asked Lydia.

'Not too good, Miss Liddy,' he answered, 'especially those that were in the dressing rooms. Once those firemen get a hose in their hands, there's no stopping them.'

'Any news of how the fire started?' inquired Charles.

'They're not sure yet, sir, but they think it was in the wiring.'

'I told you!' said Lydia, irritably. 'I told you the theatre needed rewiring.'

'Yes, well, never mind that now,' said Charles. 'The question is, what are we going to do?'

It was characteristic of them that, with disaster staring them in the face, they went to lunch at the Ivy before summoning a family council. It was also inevitable that George and Maeve, who were due to come and pay a visit for Christmas, arrived instead the day after the fire.

'Thought we'd rally round, old chap,' said George. 'All hands to the pump.'

'Thank you, Father,' said Charles, 'but I believe the firemen have done all the pumping that's necessary for the moment.'

'And if any of your costumes are damaged,' said Maeve, happily, 'you can always fall back on ours.'

'Thank you, Mother,' said Lydia.

Her eye met Sutton's, and they both gazed at the huge and battered skip whose presence in the hall had always been the all-too-visible outward sign of the presence in the house of George and Maeve.

The whole family gathered in the garden room that afternoon, except for Edwin, who was unaccountably late. Charles set out the position, which certainly was not encouraging. The Princess Theatre, miraculously, had not been burned to the ground, as it well might have been, or even fatally damaged in its structure. It would, however, be out of action for at least three weeks –

'And with rewiring and redecoration,' put in Lydia, 'that's pushing it.'

'Right,' said Charles. 'If we hope to keep the theatre –'

There was a general outcry.

'Of course we must keep the theatre!'

'Oh, Pa! how can you even think of – ?'

'Can't part with the theatre, old chap.'

'Ah, now, Charlie –'

'Oh, Daddy, you can't!' cried Perdita. 'The Princess Theatre is *yours*!'

Charles smiled at her affectionately, and his mother's touch of Irish crept into his voice, as it often did when he was amused or emotional.

'Theatres aren't just ornaments, me darling,' he said.

'A theatre is like a cargo ship. Every day it's afloat costs you money. Don't forget, we're still paying the staff, and we're still liable for running costs and ground rent –'

'And we have to refund money to people who bought tickets in advance for *Taken at the Flood*.'

'That's right,' Charles agreed. 'We're still paying the box-office staff, and they're still working, but unfortunately they'll be paying money out, not taking it in.'

'I never thought of that,' said Perdita.

'Huh!' said George. '*I* did.'

'I don't understand what he means,' said Maeve, 'about cargo ships.'

Charles and Lydia exchanged an exasperated glance. Maeve, never the most brilliant intelligence in the western hemisphere, really seemed to become vaguer by the month.

'He means, Grandma,' said Thomas, 'that productions are what keep the theatre going.'

There was a sort of sigh of relief among the family. The answer was simple, and Martha voiced it.

'Then we must get a play in as soon as possible,' she said.

'Why not rebuild the sets of *Taken at the Flood*?' inquired Thomas. 'It was still playing to full houses.'

'Ye–es,' said Charles. 'But that play is probably the raciest thing your mother and I have ever appeared in –'

'And with children coming home for the Christmas holidays,' Nell put in, 'it's not exactly –'

'Quite,' said Charles.

'Not exactly what?' inquired Perdita.

'When are you putting the notice up, Charlie?' asked George, putting his finger on the painful spot as usual.

'Tomorrow,' replied Charles.

They all glanced at each other, and Perdita looked at them all in turn.

'That means the actors will be out of work over Christmas.'

'It's happened to all of us, darling,' said Lydia. 'That's the business we're in.'

'So what *are* we going to do?' asked Thomas.

'Well, your mother and I have been discussing it, and –'

Charles stopped short and glared round, angrily.

'Where the devil is Edwin?' he demanded. 'He should be here.'

'He said he had a meeting,' said Lydia, 'but he'd come as soon as possible.'

'So I should bloody well hope!' said Charles. 'This affects him as much as the rest of us.'

'Not quite,' said Martha. 'He makes his living out of the cinema, not the theatre.'

As Charles took an angry breath, John Caldwell decided to intervene on a practical note.

'So you need to get the theatre repaired, and a production in as soon as possible,' he said. 'I take it the insurance will pay for the repairs –'

'Oh yes,' replied Charles, briskly, 'that's something *you* can sort out, John.'

'Really, Father,' Nell broke in, exasperated, 'John isn't a member of your staff!'

'No, darling,' said Lydia, sweetly, 'but he is a member of the family.'

John smiled at Nell with a touch of ruefulness which said, I am a member of the family when it suits them! And then he turned back to Charles.

'All right, sir,' he said. 'I'll see the insurance people first thing tomorrow morning, and make sure that everything is in order. But that will only take care of the repairs to the theatre, and that still leaves the problem of financing a new production. Presumably you have some money in the bank?'

'Ah – yes,' answered Charles, with a touch of uneasiness. 'But we have rather tended to live up to our income.'

'Servants' wages,' put in Lydia, 'food, wine bills –'

Sutton, having been admitted to the council of war as an interested party, saw fit to put his oar in.

'Quite right, Miss Liddy,' he said. 'This household doesn't run itself on nothing.'

'Yes, well, "this household",' said Charles, 'is going to have to draw in its horns and tighten its belt like the rest of us!'

'*Taken at the Flood* must have made quite a lot of money,' said Thomas.

'Huh! in author's royalties, I dare say,' replied Charles. 'But it's an expensive production, and when you include the costs of defending that damned lawsuit, it's only just gone into profit.'

There was a moment of gloom. Edwin, letting himself in at the front door with his latch key, saw Emily wide-eyed with alarm.

'Oh, Mr Edwin, sir,' she said, taking his hat and coat, 'are we all going to be out of 'ouse and 'ome?'

'I don't think so, Emily,' replied Edwin, amused. 'I'm sure we'll manage something.'

The door to the garden room was ajar. Turning towards it, he heard John say, 'It might be possible to raise some money at the bank against Nightingale Grove – that is, unless it is already mortgaged?'

Edwin, in the doorway, saw his father's face, blank and unresponsive, before he entered.

'Sorry I'm late,' he said.

'Eddie, darling!' cried Lydia. 'Come in. We're trying to work out what's best to do.'

'There's not a lot of choice,' said Charles. 'Either we get the theatre repaired and a production in as soon as possible, or else we put the Princess Theatre up for sale.'

Edwin spoke with the usual decision of someone arriving late at a meeting and seeing simple solutions.

'That's out of the question,' he said. 'You can't possibly sell the theatre. Obviously, you must get it repaired and put in a new production.'

'Yes, darling,' said Lydia, 'but unfortunately we don't seem to have any money.'

Edwin looked more cheerful than ever.

'I should have quite a lot coming in before long,' he said, 'and meanwhile – I admit I've been a bit extravagant – but I have at least five thousand pounds. It's yours.'

'I spent rather a lot in Berlin,' said Thomas, 'but I think I have about two thousand.'

'I have ninety pounds in my Post Office Savings,' said Perdita.

'Goodness!' said Martha. 'I wish I could be sure *I* had. But I'm sure I've something –'

'Maeve,' said George, loftily, 'how much do we have in our bank account?'

'Ah, would you come on now, George,' responded Maeve. 'We don't even have a bank account, let alone anything in it!'

This silenced even George, and enabled Lydia to break in, as she had been trying to do for the past few minutes.

'Darlings, please!' she said. 'We didn't ask you here to – to –'

'– to put the bite on you,' Charles finished.

He and Lydia looked at each other, touched.

'The theatre's an uncertain business,' said Lydia, 'goodness knows, and we can all be out of work at any moment. And when that time comes, what we all need is a bit of money in the bank. Believe me, I know. If I hadn't made a mess of my American income tax, your father would have more than he has now, but he's too much of a gentleman to say so.'

Charles was horrified by this breach of the rules of their no-holds-barred guerrilla warfare.

'My dear Liddy!' he exclaimed. 'Damn it all!'

'Sorry, darling,' said Lydia, amused.

'So, if you won't take our money –' said Edwin.

'Such as it is,' added Martha.

'You and Mother have obviously got something worked out,' said Thomas.

'Yes,' said Charles. 'The truth is, if we're lucky, the theatre can be open for business just before Christmas, and what we thought was –'

'Obviously, a pantomime,' said George.

'Thank you, Father!' said Charles, exasperated. 'Yes. A pantomime.'

He looked round at them all.

'It would be a damned expensive production, and we can't afford to hire a lot of actors at excessive salaries. But we thought if we rented the scenery and costumes, hired the walk-ons and the chorus, and played the principal parts ourselves – What do you say?'

'Wonderful!' cried Perdita.

'We're with you, Pa,' said Martha, and looked at Edwin, and paused, puzzled.

'Mother, Father,' said Edwin. 'I'm awfully sorry. I won't be here.'

'Eddie!' cried Lydia. 'What do you mean?'

'I told you I had an appointment. It was with my

solicitor – my lawyer – the chap who deals with my film contracts. David Green. He's my agent, really –'

'Good God!' said Charles.

Agents were fat little Jewish men with offices in Soho who arranged bookings for Monsewer Italiano and his Performing Seals.

'He's had a cable from Hollywood, offering me a leading part in a film opposite Lillian Gish. They want me out there by Christmas.'

Amidst the chorus of interest, puzzlement and congratulation, Charles and Lydia looked at each other across the room, their faces full of dismay.

'They'd like a cup of tea,' said Sutton, bustling into the kitchen.

'I thought they would,' said Flora. 'I've got the kettle on. Emily, warm the pot.'

'How's it going?' inquired Hegarty.

'Touch and go,' Sutton replied.

'*Go?*' repeated Emily, alarmed. 'Does that mean we're out?'

'Ah, come on now, Emily,' said Hegarty, 'while there's life there's hope, eh, Mr Sutton?'

'Mm,' said Sutton. 'What would you say to betting on a race when the favourite has just been scratched?'

'I'd say, it's a gamble – but then, if you only bet on a sure thing, that's not gambling.'

Sutton smiled.

'That's true,' he said, 'and the theatre's a gamble, just as much as a horse race is. Come on, Emily, Mr Edwin wants his tea. He's a big film star!'

'Ooh, yes, Mr Sutton!' said Emily, eagerly, but Flora looked at Sutton, puzzled and frowning.

The arrival of tea and some of Flora's aptly named rock cakes had broken up the solemn and businesslike nature of the gathering in the garden room. It's true that Charles was going through facts and figures with John and Nell, with Lydia taking an interest in between pouring tea, but the rest of them were noisily engaged in an absorbing discussion of the respective merits of all the pantomimes they could remember.

'*Aladdin*'s good,' remarked George. 'Mind, it depends on your Widow Twankey. Always thought I might essay that part myself.'

'Or *Mother Goose*,' said Lydia, hastily. 'Do you remember Gertie Stubbs? She was always billed as –'

'The Best Goose in the Business!' the others all recited in chorus.

'Oh, don't do *Mother Goose*,' Thomas broke in. 'There's no real story in that – just a mish-mash.'

'If I'm playing Principal Boy,' said Martha, 'I think we should do *Dick Whittington*.'

'Yes,' said Edwin, getting drawn in, 'but *Dick Whittington*'s nothing without a good Cat.'

'My Uncle Leo was a marvellous Cat,' said Lydia. 'Remember him, Charlie? He used to come on in one tremendous leap, look at the audience, twiddle his whiskers, and then when they laughed, he did a back somersault.'

'So, it's *Dick Whittington*, is it?' said Martha, stretching out her long legs complacently.

Charles put his pen down.

'Certainly not,' he said. 'I thought I had made myself clear. We are playing all the principal parts ourselves, and we certainly can't afford speciality skin parts such as geese and cats.'

'They'd all be booked now, anyway,' remarked Sutton, impartially.

'Thank you, Sutton,' said Charles, with no gratitude whatever.

'So what *are* we doing?' demanded Martha, feeling that she was playing the most important part, and had most to win, or lose.

Charles looked at the depressing figures of liabilities and assets in front of him, written down in John Caldwell's neat handwriting.

'I don't know about the rest of you,' he said, gloomily, 'but it looks as though *I* shall be playing Baron Stoneybroke!'

The response took him by surprise.

'Well done, Charlie!' cried Lydia. 'How very apt! *Cinderella*, of course!'

'Ah, sure, isn't that the best of them all?' agreed Maeve.

'Yes,' protested Charles, 'but I didn't actually mean –'

'Well, if Charlie's playing Baron Stoneybroke,' said George, raising his voice above the rest, 'I don't mind playing the Broker's Man. What do you say, Charlie?'

Before Charles knew what he had done, he took up the challenge.

'I'll give you a run for your money, Father,' he said. 'But –'

'And your mother,' George continued, instinctively casting the piece, as if he was the actor manager and not Charles, 'will play Fairy Godmother.'

'So it's Prince Charming for me,' said Martha, disappointed. 'it's not nearly such a good part as Dick Whittington.'

'Look on it as a challenge,' suggested Thomas.

A moment later, he realized that he had been rash to open his mouth.

'Ah, Thomas!' said Charles, 'we shall need you to write the script.'

To the astonishment of the others, Thomas readily agreed.

'Dear me!' said Edwin. 'What would Bertolt Brecht say?'

'It's the people's theatre,' replied Thomas. 'He'd strongly approve. And I've always wanted to write a decent book for a pantomime. Most of them are –'

'No time for that!' Charles interrupted, impatiently. 'Just nip along to Samuel French and pick out the best *Cinderella* they have, and see what you can do with it.'

'Put in plenty of topical jokes,' recommended George. 'They always go down well.'

'Yes, Grandad,' said Thomas, resignedly.

Any little notion he might have been cherishing of writing a revolutionary allegory in which Red Riding Hood was the innocent but courageous proletariat and the Wolf represented big business vanished beneath the all-powerful and immutable traditions of pantomime.

Sutton was moving quietly about the room with slices of soggy sponge to follow the rock cakes, and now paused beside Lydia.

'No decent part for you in *Cinderella*, Miss Liddy,' he remarked.

He spoke quietly, but Charles heard him.

'Dammit, Sutton, you're right!' he said. 'Liddy, I'm awfully sorry. I hadn't really thought – I suppose you could make something out of the Stepmother, or – No, no, that wouldn't do. Listen, everyone –'

'Don't worry about me, Charles,' Lydia said, calmly. 'I've had a little idea.'

Charles's concern for her welfare instantly changed to suspicion.

'What are you plotting?' he demanded.

She smiled amiably.

'I'll tell you later,' she said. 'But if what I'm thinking of comes off, it might be worth a bob or two at the box office.'

'We can certainly do with that!' said Charles. 'Oh, by the way, Nell, I shall need you in the theatre office tomorrow morning.'

'Father,' Nell protested, 'of course I'm only too happy to do anything I can, but – but you seem to forget that I have a house to run, and the children coming home from school –'

'Oh yes, glad you reminded me,' said Charles. 'We shall need Billy to play Buttons.'

'He's a bit young, isn't he?' said Edwin. 'Buttons is usually played by –'

'Well, *you* won't be playing him,' said Charles, with a distinct note of bitterness. 'And we shall have to hire a Dandini, too.'

Edwin looked disconcerted, and Lydia hastily intervened.

'Nell, I thought perhaps Giselle might do a little speciality number. Little Fairy Snowflake dance, something like that.'

'Giselle!' gasped Nell. 'Mother, really –'

She looked at John. He laughed.

'I should give up, darling,' he said. 'Just be glad they're not asking you to play Cinderella!'

'Talking of which,' said Thomas, 'who *is* playing Cinderella?'

Perdita had been sitting absolutely motionless ever since the pantomime had been decided. She had a quality of stillness which was rare in a girl of her age, and yet it was not exactly repose. It was too full of energy, like a runner on the blocks, motionless, but with every muscle, every nerve alive. Her stillness, if anything, now increased, and so did the inner energy.

'We'll have to hold auditions,' replied Lydia, carefully keeping her eyes away from Perdita. 'But it shouldn't be a problem. There are plenty of good little actresses who could play the part.'

Perdita was on her feet like an exploding grenade.

'What about me?' she demanded. 'Mummy, it's not fair! You said that all the parts would be played by the family. Well, Daddy did, anyway.'

Lydia turned her blue eyes towards Charles, and there was a look in them that would have made Napoleon press on to Moscow or Wellington give up the whole idea of Waterloo. A braver man than Charles would have obeyed it.

'Well – Perdita, my dear,' he said, 'Cinderella is a very big leading part, and you don't have the professional experience to – to – especially in the West End – so, I agree with your mother. I think we should hold auditions.'

Perdita looked at him in silence for a long moment.

'That's not fair,' she said, very quietly, and walked out.

'Mother, I really don't know why you bother,' said Martha. 'You never made a better exit yourself. What do you say, Father?'

'Do you think I'm mad?' replied Charles. 'Absolutely nothing.'

Edwin and Thomas spoke together.

'I really do think, Mother –'

'I agree with Perdita, Ma, it's not fair.'

Lydia rose and froze them all with a circular look.

'I am not going to discuss it,' she said, and walked out.

'That makes two good exits,' remarked Martha.

Lydia caught up with Perdita on the staircase. She knew that she was right, and was determined to be very calm and reasonable.

'Darling,' she said, 'your Auntie Elsie and I went on the stage before we could walk, let alone think, and so did your father. We had no choice. And with Martha and Edwin, it just – happened. But I want you to have time to think about it. Acting is such an uncertain business, so full of disappointments.'

'I don't care about that!' cried Perdita, with all the confidence of youth.

'You will,' replied Lydia, with all the experience of age. 'Don't forget, no matter how successful you are – and Daddy and I have been successful – you can still end up –' (it hurt, but she said it, anyway) '– nearly fifty, and terrified that one day you'll go out there on the stage, and the audience won't come.'

'If that's the price,' said Perdita, 'I'm prepared to pay it. But why won't you at least let me play Cinderella?'

Lydia accidentally lost her temper.

'Because I know,' she said, exasperated, 'that once you set foot on the stage –!'

She stopped short, but it was too late. Perdita completed the sentence.

'I'd know beyond a doubt that it was what I was born to do! That's true, isn't it? It's true!'

Chapter Twenty-two

'We must have been mad!' said Charles. 'Stark, raving mad. It just shows what happens when actors get involved in owning theatres and putting on productions instead of staying where they belong, on the stage.'

He was sitting at his desk in the theatre office, surrounded by plans of sets, letters, bills, estimates, lists of costumes and props, and all the horrifying mass of material needed for a hastily assembled production. Edwin, sitting at Jean's desk, was looking through the new production called *Spotlight* which gave photographs of actors and actressess all together in one compact book. He was searching for someone they might have forgotten about to play the Stepmother. Feeling distinctly guilty, he was anxious to do anything he could to help, though admittedly it didn't seem to be much, except make encouraging noises.

'Come on, Father,' he said, 'everything seems to be going ahead.'

'Yes, like a runaway horse!' said Charles. 'Here I am, ordering scenery and engaging dancers – and if we don't get that insurance money pretty quickly, we shan't even have a theatre!'

He was overcome by rising panic, and got up and walked about.

'Even if we get the damned thing on,' he said, 'do you think we'll get the audience? There's barely time to publicize it, even if we'd got the money to do it. I suppose we could hire Nellie Wallace and an elephant and go round distributing posters like a circus.'

'Oh, Father,' Edwin protested, 'you never have any trouble getting the customers in.'

'Huh!' said Charles. 'Never done anything like this before. They're not coming just to see me play Baron Stoneybroke – and I'm far from sure how they'll take to your mother's little notion. Theatre audiences don't like to be taken by surprise, you know. And Martha will make a very good Principal Boy, but she's never really attracted a big, popular following.'

He stopped and looked at Edwin.

'Not like you,' he said, 'with all your damned film fans!'

Edwin turned a page without seeing anything, in order to avoid looking at him. He knew what was coming next.

'How set is this Hollywood thing?'

'It's very "set",' said Edwin, and closed the book. 'I have to do a screen test with Lillian Gish – but since she was the one who asked for me in the first place, that shouldn't be too bad, and then, if all goes well, I shall be offered a three-picture contract.'

'Good God!' exclaimed Charles. 'If you do that, we shall never see you on the stage again. Hollywood's like a lion's den – all the footprints leading in, and none coming out!'

'The cinema is where I belong,' said Edwin. 'That's where I've made my reputation.'

He saw the expression on Charles's face.

'Father, I feel terrible about this,' he said. 'I wish I *could* stay. But my whole career is at stake!'

'Yes, yes,' said Charles, hastily. 'I understand. I didn't mean –'

They were both relieved when they heard footsteps on the uncarpeted stairs outside.

'There's John with that insurance man,' said Charles.

Edwin had meant to leave as soon as the man from the insurance company arrived, but Mr Perkins, having greeted Charles with a perfunctory handshake, showed such enthusiasm when he was introduced to Edwin that it seemed churlish to leave immediately, and once the encounter between Charles and Mr Perkins had begun, it became impossible.

Mr Perkins was a thin-faced man who wore pince-nez and a pin-striped suit and carried a small attaché case which he opened as soon as he sat down, thus missing Charles's famous charming smile.

'Now,' said Charles, briskly, 'how soon can we expect settlement of our claim?'

John cleared his throat.

'Er – it seems that there is a slight problem.'

Oh, Lor'! thought Edwin, and sat down again at Jean's desk.

'What?' demanded Charles, sharply. 'What problem?'

Mr Perkins clearly had no intention of being hurried. He had taken a folder out of his attaché case, and was taking a sheet of paper out of the folder and studying it.

'It has been established', he said, in a thin, chilly voice, 'that the fire in this theatre was caused by defective wiring.'

'My dear man,' said Charles, trying to jolly him along, 'all fires have to be caused by *something*! Nobody insures against things which can never happen!'

Mr Perkins, however, was not a jolly man.

'That's true, Mr Brett,' he said, coldly, 'but, as I understand it, the defect in the electric wiring was not unexpected, and since my company was not notified of the fact –'

Charles suddenly sat up.

'Are you saying we have no claim?' he demanded.

'No!' exclaimed John, hastily.

Mr Perkins was less definite.

'Not exactly,' he said, glancing up at Charles. 'It is not up to me.'

'Then who is it "up to"?' said Charles.

Oh God! thought Edwin. He's lost his temper.

Edwin was right. Charles was beginning to feel alarmed, and his way of dealing with alarm was always to hit out. He had his mother's trigger-happy Irish temper as well as her Irish charm.

'I take it, Mr Perkins,' he said, 'that your company insures quite a number of West End theatres?'

It was a guess, but quite correct as Mr Perkins's face showed. Ah, thought Charles. Got him!

'Perhaps you would care to notify your company that if you refuse to pay this claim, I shall fight you through the courts every inch of the way – and I'm sure that all the other theatre owners will be interested to learn that we are paying these extremely heavy premiums for nothing.'

'Threats won't do you any good, Mr Brett,' said Mr Perkins.

Charles caught sight of the dismayed glance John exchanged with Edwin.

'Threats?' he said. 'Of course not. I'm simply warning Mr Perkins that I shall exercise my rights –'

'And my company', said Mr Perkins, 'has the right to investigate every claim before paying it.'

He put the paper back in the folder and the folder back in the attaché case. Charles latched on to the words 'paying it'. He had inherited his mother's optimism as well.

'Naturally, naturally,' he said, reverting to a cheery tone. 'But you *will* pay it. Splendid!'

He had rejoiced too soon. Mr Perkins closed his attaché case, as he had already closed his mind.

'I will put in my report when it is ready,' he said, 'and it will go through the proper channels.'

He rose, preparing to depart. Charles stood up, too, alarm giving way to panic.

'Yes,' he said, 'but *how soon*?'

'In due course, Mr Brett,' replied Mr Perkins.

When he had been escorted out by John, Charles sank down into his chair. Edwin, looking at him, thought that the colour had actually gone from his face. Perhaps it was just a trick of the light, or perhaps he really had turned grey.

'That's it, then,' he said. 'Even if he does pay up, it won't be in time.'

'What will you do?' asked Edwin.

'What can I do? The repairs of the theatre are in hand, and we've begun to set up the production. If I cancel it, and the theatre's dark, we're done for anyway. If we're going down, we may as well go down with colours flying.'

He smiled at Edwin.

'We'll just have to hope that the advance bookings will be enough to keep the wolf from the door for a while.'

It was that brave smile that did it. That, and a few other things.

'I'll ring David Green,' said Edwin.

'David Green?'

'My lawyer,' said Edwin. 'He can send a cable to Hollywood and cancel the screen test.'

'Yes, but –'

Charles had a brief, visible struggle with himself, and as visibly lost. Edwin picked up the telephone.

'What will he tell them?'

Suddenly Edwin laughed, just as Charles himself would have laughed in the face of disaster, and Charles, looking at him, understood for the first time why his film fans adored him. He had not inherited the talent, but he had inherited the panache.

'He'll tell them I'm playing Dandini in a pantomime,' he said. 'They're sure to understand!'

The huge skip that had always been such a howling bore whenever Maeve and George had come to stay had at last come into its own. Open in the garden room, its contents strewn over the floor, it was being happily ransacked by Maeve, with Flora and Emily on their knees beside her. She produced a distinctly tatty white Fairy Godmother costume.

'There, now!' she exclaimed, triumphantly. 'I knew it was there somewhere!'

She passed it to Flora, who eyed it dubiously, while Maeve rummaged on.

'It needs a stitch or two, Mrs George,' said Flora.

'If you ask me,' said Emily, 'it could do with a wash as well.'

'Och, I'd be careful how you wash that, Emily,' said Maeve. 'It's none too strong – and it'll look fine under the lights. There's me wand, now!'

Emily's mouth came open at the sight of a badly bent fairy wand, with a ragged tinsel star at the end of it.

On the higher level by the piano, Charles, Martha, Edwin, George and Thomas were arguing over the script.

'If you think, Father,' said Charles, irritably, 'that I'm going to allow you to get all the laughs while I act as your feed –'

'You won't get any laughs with *that* joke, anyway,' said Thomas, preparing to cut it out.

'Which joke?' demanded George, quickly. 'Oh, that one. That's quite good.'

He tried it out.

'Why didn't the worms go into the ark in pairs?'

'Because they went in apples,' replied Martha, with a groan.

'Cut it out, Tom, for heaven's sake!' said Edwin. 'And while we're about it I absolutely refuse to come on and say, "Hullo, boys and girls, don't let me interrupt your village merriment!"'

Sutton had come unobtrusively into the room, stepping over the Demon King's costume and various unexpected props.

'Excuse me, Mr Edwin,' he said, 'there is a Mr David Green to see you.'

'Oh,' said Edwin. And then, after a moment, 'Thank you. I'll see him in the study.'

He had not been looking forward to this interview, and had to brace himself before going into the study.

David Green turned to face him. He was impeccably dressed in the dark suit and discreet tie of a London solicitor, and he had dark, curly hair and regular features, but when he was angry, as he was now, his face hardened, and a rough note came into his voice. He plunged straight in, ignoring the social niceties.

'Are you mad?' he said. 'What the hell do you think you're playing at?'

'I'm sorry, David –'

'Don't "David" me! I'm not one of your gentlemanly barristers from the Garrick Club. They wouldn't even let me in there, would they?'

'Why on earth not?' asked Edwin, puzzled.

David looked angrier than ever.

'Never mind that,' he said. 'Let's talk about you. Just because you've had it easy all your life, you seem to think –'

'*Easy?*'

Suddenly Edwin was angry, too.

'Do you really think it's been easy, always playing second best to my father?'

'Now's your chance to prove you're not!' said David. 'So why the hell don't you take it?'

Edwin's flash of anger died out. Why the hell didn't he? And how the hell could he explain to a man he had known for only a few months, and that professionally, how the Brett family, with its three or four generations dedicated to a single purpose, a single loyalty, could close around its members in a fierce and inextricable embrace? How could he explain the mixture of love and jealousy, of admiration and pity he felt for his father? How could he explain all the delicately conflicting emotions that intertwined his relationships with his mother and Martha, with Thomas, even with his grandparents? He looked at David, and saw him still taut with anger, his mouth grim, his eyes narrowed.

'I'll try to explain,' he said.

'You'd better!'

It was impossible, of course, thought Edwin, but he tried to search in his own mind for the reason why the final decision to stay had been made.

'This won't make any sense to you,' he said, 'but – When Father suggested that I should replace him in *The King Shall Not Die*, the owner of the theatre thought I wasn't good enough. Second best, you know. So Mother and Father put in all their savings and bought the Princess Theatre, and did it anyway. It turned out that the owner was right. I wasn't good enough, and I wasn't a draw. So Father mortgaged Nightingale Grove, and he kept the play going long enough to save my face. I owe it to him, and to all the family who backed him, and covered up for me –'

David suddenly interrupted him.

'Family!' he said, and gave a short laugh. 'I might have known! All right. Now I understand.'

Edwin looked at him, puzzled.

'You don't have to tell me anything about family!' said David.

He was shaking his head, still laughing to himself, when Charles came quickly in, and stopped short with an excellent interpretation of apologetic surprise.

'Oh! I hope I'm not interrupting –?'

'I imagine you hope you are,' said David.

Charles did not particularly relish this piece of impudence, especially since this rather common young man – for Charles was not taken in by the expensive suit and the unaccented voice – was, of course, quite right. Edwin hastened to make the introductions, and David assured

Charles that he was delighted to meet him. Charles made no reply. He was not in the least delighted to meet David Green, who clearly was going to do his best to detach Edwin from the family and transport him to the vulgar and meretricious world of Hollywood.

'I gather you are putting on a pantomime, Mr Brett,' remarked David.

'Always goes well over Christmas,' replied Charles, with a touch of belligerence.

'Mm,' said David. 'Any speciality acts? Any big draws? Nellie Wallace? George Robey?'

Charles glared at him.

'Oh no,' David continued. 'Of course, by now they'd all be engaged elsewhere.'

Damn the fellow, he was right again! thought Charles.

'We have the entire Brett family,' he said, loftily, 'including Edwin.'

He threw an anxious brief glance at his elder son. He *hoped* they still had Edwin, if this Green fellow hadn't queered the pitch again.

'I don't think that's enough,' said David.

'David!' exclaimed Edwin, horrified.

His father was uneasy enough as it was. David didn't look at him, but kept his eyes on Charles.

'What do you suggest?' demanded Charles, annoyed.

'You need something to bring 'em in. Something the other Christmas shows haven't got.' He pondered. 'How about a charity matinée?'

'Charity!' exclaimed Charles. 'I'm the one that needs the charity!'

David smiled, and for the first time, Charles saw the charm, which was not deliberately used, as an actor uses it, but which was as much a part of him as the tough determination to succeed in all he did, like a boxer who, however friendly out of it, once in the ring, is entirely ruthless.

'A sprat to catch a mackerel,' he said. 'I seem to remember that the Bretts have enjoyed a certain amount of royal patronage in the past.'

'Of course!' said Charles. 'A royal charity matinée!'

Everyone told them that there was not a chance of persuading the King to make an engagement before Christmas, especially with his naval preference for strict discipline and careful and precise planning. But Charles and Lydia did have an instant entrée to Court circles by means of Sir Bernard Whitgift, who certainly owed them a favour or two, and was, at least, prepared to put the proposal delicately before His Majesty. And since the King had greatly enjoyed *The King Shall Not Die* – just his sort of simple, straightforward play – and since he knew that the Bretts had done a great deal of work for charity in the past, he was prepared to consider the matter, instead of dismissing it out of hand. And in the end, what decided it was his tremendous fondness for his little granddaughter, Elizabeth.

'Lilibet would enjoy it,' he said. 'She has never seen a pantomime. We can take Lilibet.'

So, suddenly, the Princess Theatre had something to bring 'em in which none of the other Christmas shows enjoyed – a Royal Charity Matinée in the Presence of His Majesty, King George the Fifth, Queen Mary, and the Princess Elizabeth.

'That should keep the creditors at bay,' said Charles. 'Now, all we have to do is to get the theatre ready, the show rehearsed – and cast a Cinderella!'

Since the Princess Theatre was almost totally dismantled, with electricians and workmen everywhere, Nightingale Grove had been turned into a rehearsal room, a costumier's and a props room. In the kitchen, Hegarty was rubbing up swords with the polish he used for his beloved motor, and Flora was busy at the sewing machine. Perdita, bitterly unhappy and resentful, was sorting and darning the more fragile costumes.

'I hope everyone realizes,' she said, 'that at school I got nought out of ten for sewing. I got ten out of ten for singing.'

'Ah well, Miss Perdita,' said Hegarty, 'you can give us a song while you sew.'

Emily emerged from the scullery and looked about her, dismayed.

'Miss Evans,' she said, 'ain't we going to have no dinner?'

'If the family hasn't time for luncheon, we haven't time for dinner,' replied Flora, turning the wheel of the sewing machine faster than ever. 'We'll have some sandwiches later, if we're lucky – and I don't want to know what your mum thinks!'

Before Emily could answer, which she fully intended to do, there was an imperious ring at the front door.

'That'll be her ladyship,' said Flora.

Lydia was waiting for her sister in the study, which seemed to be the only room comparatively untouched by the prevailing chaos. Sutton opened the door.

'Lady Carstairs, madam,' he said, every inch the butler.

Elsie Carstairs was a very beautiful woman, although, unlike Lydia, she had been obliged to allow her hair to assume almost its normal colour, and to cut down on the make-up. She had no intention of allowing anyone to say that Harry Carstairs had married an actress, and that she still looked as though she ought to be on the stage. Instead, she played the part of Lady Carstairs with tremendous flair but considerable restraint. It was, in fact, a performance to be proud of, and she thoroughly enjoyed being her ladyship, and all the perks that marriage to a baronet had brought her way. It would be idle to pretend, however, that there were not times when she envied Lydia. She missed the stage and the old camaraderies and the adulation at the stage door, and, annoyingly enough, Lydia and Charles, rising to the head of their profession, had almost attained the social status which she enjoyed – almost, but not quite, she would think defiantly, when such thoughts occurred to her.

However, despite the ancient sisterly rivalry, she and Lydia had always been very close, and the bond had, perhaps, become closer because of the one great tragedy of Elsie's life. She and Harry were childless. In his eyes, she was perfect, but in her own estimation she had failed dismally. There was no heir to the baronetcy, which, instead, would go to a weedy and mean-minded cousin. It was, perhaps, significant that, in spite of her grief and sense of failure (a failure almost certainly due, not to her, but to the weak-chinned in-breeding of the Carstairs family!) Elsie had always given generous love and support to the children of Charles and Lydia, and, during their impoverished touring days, had never failed to provide a home for them, and an invaluable sense of security.

Whenever they visited each other, Elsie and Lydia always dressed with great care, and so now Elsie glided into the room, wreathed in furs, and wearing her most becoming hat. Ten minutes later, she was staring at Lydia, open-mouthed and outraged.

'A *pantomime*? *Me?*'

'A very special pantomime,' insinuated Lydia, 'to put the Princess Theatre back into business. You and Harry have an interest in it, after all.'

'Hm,' said Elsie, who held the purse strings in that household. 'We haven't made much money out of it.'

'But, this is something special,' said Lydia, and, like a gambler playing a trump card, passed her the letter from Buckingham Palace.

'Oh,' said Elsie, reading it carefully.

She kept her face impassive, but Lydia knew her too well.

'It'll be an entirely family affair,' she said, casually, 'and I thought it might appeal to you to be part of it.'

'Ye–es,' said Elsie, returning the letter, and disposing her furs to better advantage. 'It would be a sort of – Command Performance?'

'Exactly!' cried Lydia, gratified. 'A dazzling, limited-season return to the stage.'

Elsie was clearly tempted.

'Oh – well, darling – if it'll help you and Charlie – I did promise Harry that I would never – But this would be quite different.'

Suddenly she came down to business.

'What part were you thinking of? Fairy Godmother?'

'Er – no,' replied Lydia. 'Maeve's playing that.'

'I might have known,' said Elsie, resignedly. And then, suddenly, 'I am *not* playing Cinderella's Stepmother!'

'Certainly not,' responded Lydia, with dignity. 'I wouldn't dream of asking you.'

Elsie eyed her suspiciously.

'What part are *you* playing?' she inquired.

Lydia answered as though it was the most natural thing in the world.

'The same as you, darling – one of the Ugly Sisters.'

Elsie stared at her in silence for a moment, and when she spoke again, it was in the accents of their native Clapham.

'You bitch!' she said.

'What can you mean?' asked Lydia, who knew very well.

'You know bloody well!' said Elsie. 'I retire as a Famous Beauty – and you've been on the stage ever since, still the Beautiful Miss Wheatley – and – and I know you were three years younger than me, but – but to suggest that I should make my return to the stage as – as –'

'Be a bit of a laugh, though, wouldn't it?' suggested Lydia.

'I don't think so at all.'

'Oh, come on, Else! Here have I been battling away all these years with the lines and the chin and the bags under the eyes –'

Elsie responded to that, looking at her carefully.

'You haven't got –'

'It's only a matter of time,' said Lydia, grimly. 'Anyway, what I thought was – everyone remembers us as the Winsome Wheatleys –'

'Oh, God!' said Elsie. 'Those sunbonnets!'

'Exactly. Everyone will be expecting us to try to turn the clock back, but – Charlie isn't playing Prince Charming. He's playing Baron Stoneybroke. So I thought that if you and I – you and I –'

She met Elsie's stony gaze, and faltered.

'All right,' she said. 'P'raps it wasn't such a good idea after all.'

'I'll tell you one thing,' said Lady Carstairs. 'If we do

it, I'll be a bloody sight uglier than you, you old cow, and a bloody sight funnier, too!'

'I dare you!' said Lydia, and came to put her arms round her sister's neck.

'Champagne, madam?' inquired Sutton, entering on cue.

It was while Sutton was pouring the champagne that Elsie asked casually, 'Who's playing Cinderella?'

'We shall have to audition,' replied Lydia, distantly. 'It shouldn't be difficult to find someone with a pleasant little personality and a good voice. If there's one thing I hate, it's a Principal Girl who squeaks like a mouse.'

'Perdita's got a good voice,' said Elsie.

'I dare say,' replied Lydia, even more distantly.

Elsie's eyes met Sutton's. No go, evidently.

'All right, then,' she said, 'why don't you give Maud's girl a chance?'

Lydia was overjoyed.

'Anthea! Elsie, darling, you're a genius! Such a pretty girl. Maud will be delighted – and we won't have to pay her.'

The Honourable Anthea Protheroe was a small, thin girl, with curly hair and blue eyes. She would have been pretty, except that she had a nervous manner, as though she constantly expected something or someone, possibly her mother, to jump out at her from behind the bushes. She came prinking up the drive of Nightingale Grove in her high-heeled shoes, silk stockings and prescribed débutante clothes, and was about to ring the doorbell, when the door opened.

'Oh,' said said, startled.

Perdita, who had been watching for her from the hall, smiled and drew her inside.

'Hullo, Anthea, come in,' she said. 'Gosh, you're brave!'

'Brave?'

The hall was full of chorus girls, rehearsing tap-dancing. A man in chauffeur's uniform went past her with an armful of swords, smiled at her in a friendly manner, and took them upstairs. From somewhere came the sound of a piano, and a boy's voice singing, 'I can't give you anything but love, baby.'

'Well,' said Perdita, confidingly, 'it's just that my father – what with the fire at the theatre, and all his money troubles – and of course he's always been the most frightful perfectionist.'

'Oh,' said Anthea.

'But don't worry,' said Perdita, immensely kind and reassuring. 'Honestly. You'll be just right for the part. I know you will. Just – just don't let my father frighten you.'

'Oh,' said Anthea. 'No.'

The piano and music had stopped, and Charles emerged from the garden room, shouting at the top of his voice, which was rather like being directly beneath a thunderclap.

'Sutton!' he roared.

His eyes fell on the shrinking Anthea.

'Daddy, you know Anthea,' said Perdita, helpfully. 'She's come to audition for the part of Cinderella.'

'Oh. Yes,' said Charles.

He eyed Anthea thoughtfully. Clearly, she was even less dynamic than he remembered. He smiled at her gamely, and took her by the elbow.

'Come in, my dear,' he said. 'Nothing to be afraid of.'

Anthea was just beginning to be slightly reassured when Sutton emerged from the kitchen door, and Charles vented upon him the irritation he felt at being landed with 'Maud's girl'.

'Sutton, where the devil have you been,' he demanded, his voice ringing terrifyingly in Anthea's ear. 'Tell Hegarty we shall want him to drive us to Angell's this afternoon!'

When Charles had escorted Anthea into the garden room, Perdita looked at Sutton. He looked back at her.

'I think I'll go and stand at the back,' she said. 'It might give her confidence.'

'It might,' responded Sutton, with heavy irony.

He listened outside the door, as Anthea quavered and wavered and stumbled through her 'audition'. Listening to that high, reedy voice, with its entire lack of personality, he shook his head and turned away. Miss Liddy had made up her mind, and that was it, but he couldn't help feeling that it was a pity.

Despite all the difficulties, and fears over the readiness of the theatre, and the obvious and dire inadequacy of Anthea for the role of Cinderella, the production had now acquired its own momentum, and rolled forward like a shaky but unstoppable juggernaut. The moment came when Charles and Lydia actually felt that the worst was over. They were sitting alone together in the garden room, enjoying a quiet drink and studying their lines, with Jack Payne and the BBC Dance Orchestra playing quietly in the background. The wireless suddenly went dead. They looked at each other, puzzled. The announcer's voice came out very solemn and clear.

'We interrupt this programme by Jack Payne and the BBC Dance Orchestra to bring you an item of news of national importance.'

'Don't say we're at war,' said Charles, only half joking.

'It has been announced from Buckingham Palace,' the announcer continued, 'that His Majesty, the King, is gravely ill with blood-poisoning. We shall be broadcasting further bulletins on His Majesty's health as they are issued.'

'Well,' said Lydia, 'there goes our royal charity matinée!'

The dance music did not continue. Instead, they heard 'The Dead March' from *Saul*.

'Charlie!' said Lydia, suddenly, 'if the King dies –'

'All the theatres will be closed,' said Charles, and, being Charles, he smiled at her. 'And we shall be ruined.'

Chapter Twenty-three

It was strange how instantly and completely the country discovered its affection and loyalty towards King George V, that small, quiet, shy, bearded man, who had dutifully taken over from his dead brother the task of ruling the kingdom, as well as the marriage to his dead brother's fiancée, Princess May of Teck. Churches were kept open day and night, and men, women and children prayed and grieved, as though for their own father. On 11 December, it was reported that the King was barely conscious. Flora conducted prayers in the kitchen, with Emily, a perfect little heathen, much impressed, and Hegarty crossing himself at unexpected moments, and Sutton, keeping his agnosticism to himself, saying a courteous 'Amen' at the right moments.

It was announced that the King was to have an operation the next day, and Charles despatched Hegarty to

Buckingham Palace to await the latest bulletin. Meanwhile, on the well-worn but still prevailing principle that the show must go on, they were conducting a slightly desultory rehearsal of the ballroom scene, with everyone wearing such eccentric costumes and props as might help them.

'Come along, everyone!' called Charles. 'Whatever happens, we have a charity matinée in five days' time!'

That is, he inwardly added, unless the King dies – and then he saw Hegarty in the doorway. They were all absurdly frozen in silent attention.

'Hegarty!' said Charles. 'Any news?'

'The King has survived the operation, sir.'

'Thank God!' said Lydia, and in that moment was thinking only of the King.

'He's not out of danger, madam,' said Hegarty, 'but it sounds as though he's through the worst. They're issuing another bulletin later.'

Lydia and Charles moved together, self-interest taking over.

'He still won't be able to come to the performance,' said Lydia.

'At least we can open,' said Charles.

He raised his voice ruthlessly above the sentimental murmur.

'Come along, everyone! Back to work! The ballroom scene! Lydia, Elsie, Martha, Edwin. Anthea, dear, outside the door, ready for your entrance. Perdita, get on the book.'

'Yes, Daddy,' said Perdita.

She really was suffering such agonies as only a frustrated artist knows, and Lydia was aware of it, but tried to harden her heart. They rehearsed the opening of the ballroom scene, with the Ugly Sisters shoving Baron Stoneybroke aside and tripping each other up to get at the Prince. Martha struck her Principal Boy pose and turned to the graceful and attentive Dandini.

'Dandini,' she cried, 'who is that lady who has just come in?'

They all looked towards the door.

'Come on, Anthea, dear,' said Charles, irritably, 'this is your big moment. Cinderella has come to the ball. Anthea?'

Anthea walked on, paused, and burst into tears.

'I'm sorry,' she sobbed. 'I – I can't!'

'My dear girl,' said Charles, endeavouring to subdue irritation by sympathy, 'what on earth is the matter?'

'I did something so *awful*!' cried Anthea. 'I prayed last night that the King would die! I'm sorry, but I did. I would have done anything, just as long as I didn't have to play Cinderella.'

'My dear girl,' said Charles, 'we thought that you *wanted* to play Cinderella. You went to the Royal Academy of Dr–ramatic Art – '

He gave it its full title, with a note of irony. Anthea gave a hiccup.

'Yes, but only because Mother said I must,' she said.

Charles started at her, stunned.

'Débutantes, Pa,' put in Martha, 'all go to Rada. It's "the thing to do".'

'I'm sorry!' cried Anthea. 'I never thought I'd actually have to go on the stage!'

She rushed out.

'If you ask me,' remarked George, 'that's the best performance she's given yet.'

'We seem to have lost our Cinderella,' said Charles, dispassionately.

They all looked at Lydia.

'I know when I'm beaten,' she said.

A week later, Charles and Lydia were standing on the stage of the Princess Theatre, where the kitchen scene was being set up, with a great deal of hammering and of coming and going with props. Workmen seemed to be wandering about all over the place carrying pots of paint and paintbrushes.

'I told them not to bother about the royal box,' said Lydia, 'but just put a coat of paint over the soot.'

'Quite right,' said Charles. 'Well, we'd better get dressed. Dress rehearsal in half an hour.'

As they turned to leave the stage, Sutton hurried on.

'Sir!' he called. 'Miss Liddy! Mr Thomas has just telephoned the stage door. There's a message from Buckingham Palace.'

'The King's dead,' said Charles. 'I knew it. Damn!'

'No, sir,' said Sutton. 'He's still very ill, and the Queen can't leave him, but it seems she said that she knew he wouldn't want to disappoint his granddaughter, so the Duke and Duchess of York are coming instead, with Princess Elizabeth.'

'Alfred!' said Lydia, urgently, 'tell the painters to leave everything else and get to work on the royal box!'

Large cars drew up outside the Princess Theatre, and chauffeurs assisted the alighting of ladies and gentlemen, little boys in velvet suits and little girls in cloaks of pink velvet and swansdown, with bronze slippers on their little feet. The small crowd gazed and shuffled, waiting for royalty.

In the dressing rooms, there was a feeling of old-fashioned comradeship, as in the old touring days, since, with the first-floor dressing rooms burned and not yet repaired, they were all doubling up. Elsie and Lydia, grotesque in their Ugly Sisters make-up, sat side by side, staring into the mirror.

'What do you think?' inquired Elsie.

'A touch more red on the nose?'

'You brute!'

Elsie obliged, however.

'Tell me,' she said, 'whose idea was our make-up and costume for the walk-down?'

'Charlie's,' replied Lydia.

Elsie smiled at her in the mirror.

'He must still love you,' she said.

Lydia smiled back, and rose.

'It's all yours, Mother,' she said.

Maeve, who was taking one of her catnaps, woke up and smiled.

'Thank you, my dear.'

'Let's go and count the house,' said Elsie.

Martha finished straightening the tights on her long legs.

'I think I'll come with you,' she said. 'I must say, I never thought I'd get stagefright at this stage of the game.'

Preparing to follow Elsie and Lydia out of the room, she saw Perdita finishing lacing her Cinderella costume behind the screen, and paused.

'Are you all right, Perdita?' she inquired. 'Need any help?'

'No. I'm fine.'

'Don't be silly, darling,' said Martha. 'We're none of us fine. We just get through as best we can. And that's what you'll do.'

Perdita took a deep breath and smiled at her.

'Yes. All right.'

'Good girl,' said Martha, and went out, leaving Perdita and Maeve alone.

'You're looking rather pale, me darling,' said Maeve. 'I should put a wee bit more colour on your cheeks. You're not nervous, are you?'

'Nervous?' cried Perdita. 'Oh, Grandma, I'm terrified!'

'Come on, now,' said Maeve, 'there's no cause for that. With all your family to help you through? Hasn't that been my good fortune all my life, to have your Grandad's hand in mine for the last curtain?'

Perdita knelt down beside her and took her hand.

'And you'll be there to help me.'

'So I will,' said Maeve, fondly. 'If I was really your Fairy Godmother, what would I wish for you? That you should find joy in doing what you love, in the company of those you love, and have the courage to go on doing it, and never lose that joy.'

'Oh, Grandma!' cried Perdita. 'Thank you!'

'Now, you finish getting yourself dressed,' said Maeve. 'I'll do my make-up, and then you can hear my lines, for I've a little trouble lately holding them in my head.'

In Charles's dressing room, Edwin was finishing his make-up while Nell gave the finishing touches to Billy's pageboy costume. George, fully dressed and made up, was taking forty winks on the couch.

'Now, Billy,' said Charles, 'play the part just as you did at the last dress rehearsal – cheeky, but not too cheeky.'

'Yes, Grandad,' replied Billy, with perfect confidence.

'And not so much of the Grandad,' said Charles.

'When we're in the theatre, you call me "Mr Brett" or 'sir".'

'Yes, sir,' said Billy, no whit dismayed.

There was a tap at the door, and Sutton went to answer it, and turned, disapproving.

'Mr Edwin,' he said, 'Mr Green is here. Says he wants to see you.'

'Oh yes, of course,' said Edwin. 'Come in, David.'

Sutton stood aside, frowning. He didn't approve of strangers in the dressing rooms before the performance. He caught sight of Lydia approaching along the corridor, and jerked his head, and she came to the doorway, as Edwin turned round in his chair.

'There's a cable for you from California,' said David.

'Oh well, nice of them to wish me luck.'

'I opened it,' said David, giving it to him.

Edwin looked at him, sharply, and then read the cable and gasped.

'What?' cried Lydia. 'Eddie, what is it?'

'They've delayed the screen test until February, and they're offering me double the salary.'

'They thought you were playing hard to get,' said David, and he and Edwin grinned at each other triumphantly.

'That's wonderful!' cried Lydia. 'Charles, isn't that good news?'

'Yes, excellent,' said Charles. 'Come on, Eddie, I need the dressing table. My dear boy, if you put any more mascara on, you'll look like a geisha girl!'

Edwin smiled, confident in his film-star image, which gazed confidently back at him from the mirror, as in the eye of a camera.

In the adjoining dressing room, Perdita put her feet into her slippers, pulled up her torn and grubby stockings and shook out her ragged skirt. She turned towards the dressing table.

'I'm all ready, Grandma,' she said.

Maeve, beautifully made up, sat at the dressing table in her pretty, faded pink silk dressing-gown.

'Grandma,' said Perdita, 'did you want me to hear your lines?'

She smiled affectionately. Maeve had fallen asleep again.

'Grandma?' she said, gently, coming to sit beside her. And then, trembling, 'Grandma!'

For Maeve was not asleep. She had died, beautifully and gracefully, sitting at the dressing table in her faded pink wrapper and her Fairy Godmother make-up.

Sutton, making his way between assorted village lads and maidens, with a smattering of walk-ons, tapped at the dressing-room door and came quickly in.

'Miss Liddy,' he said, 'the royal car's outside!'

He stopped short, seeing Maeve lying on the couch, and George kneeling beside her, holding her hand. Lydia drew out of Charles's arms, and looked at him inquiringly. He nodded. She knew what that nod meant. It was saying, 'Do what has to be done. I can't quite manage it yet.' Lydia went towards the costumes hanging on pegs on the wall.

'Nell,' she said, 'you'll have to play Fairy Godmother.'

Nell was trying to comfort Perdita, who sat, frozen, at the dressing table. She turned, and saw with a kind of superstitious dread, the tinsel and gauze costume.

'Mother, I can't!' she cried. 'I haven't been on the stage for – for fifteen years!'

'You know every line of it,' said Lydia, 'and you know she never had an understudy.'

Nell still hesitated. Charles spoke without moving.

'Please, Nell,' he said.

As Nell took the costume from Lydia, Charles seemed to come to himself. He touched George on the shoulder.

'Father,' he said, 'shall we put your understudy on?'

'No,' replied George. 'Oh no. She wouldn't like that. Especially in front of royalty.'

It was not until the call boy called 'Overture and beginners, please!' and Perdita turned and saw Nell in the Fairy Godmother costume that she knew that she could not go on.

'No!' she cried. 'No, I can't! I can't!'

Elsie and Nell were instantly all sympathy.

'Perdita, darling, we know how you feel,' said Elsie.

'Perdita, we know how much you loved Grandma, but –'

'I can't go on!' cried Perdita. 'I can't!'

Lydia's voice penetrated her rising hysteria.

'Perdita!' she said. 'Stop that at once! You're ruining your make-up. If you want to cry, cry when you get home tonight.'

'Mother, don't you think –?' Nell began.

'Shut up!' said Lydia, ferociously.

She took hold of Perdita and felt her shaking and gasping with grief.

'Perdita,' she said, 'your grandmother hacked round the provinces and all over Ireland, and never missed a single performance, and now *you* – How dare you be so unprofessional?'

'I'm sorry,' sobbed Perdita, trying desperately to pull herself together, 'but I can't remember anything. I should just go on and – and –'

'You'll go on and do your job,' said Lydia, fiercely. 'You've been telling us for the past ten years that you're an actress, well, now's the time to prove it.'

Perdita couldn't speak, but she had fought down her tears. Lydia spoke more gently.

'Come on, darling,' she said. 'Let's see to your make-up.'

'Master Billy Caldwell!' shouted the call boy from the corridor. 'Miss Perdita Brett!'

'There's your call,' said Lydia.

There are moments in the theatre of such pure magic that those who are in the audience will never forget them, but who would have thought that such a moment would occur in a rather cheap hired set of the kitchen scene of *Cinderella*?

'Oh, Buttons,' cried Perdita, and for all the ragged dress and the absurd straw broom, she shone on the stage like a golden flame, 'I don't know why you stay at Castle Stoneybroke when my stepsisters are so horrid to you. You told me that your parents were in the iron and steel business.'

'That's right,' said young Billy, as bright and sharp as the best Buttons that ever trod the stage. 'My mother irons and my father steals.'

The warm and satisfying laugh that came from the audience derived from Perdita's delightful laugh giving them the cue, something which a thousand actresses might have practised for fifty years and never caught the trick of.

'Oh, Buttons, dear Buttons!' she cried. 'You do make me laugh. Don't ever leave me.'

Billy sprang down from the kitchen table, and he and Perdita were suddenly moving into a song and dance so neatly and elegantly that the whole audience felt a sense of triumphant achievement.

'I can't give you anything but love,' they sang, and, though they played enchantingly to each other, their love affair was with the audience.

Charles waited in the wings, ready to go on and do his comic song. Lydia came and slipped her hand in his.

'When she was young,' he said, 'she was so beautiful.'

'I know,' said Lydia.

She looked at him, and saw that he had reached that moment when, like Perdita, he was prepared to say, 'No! No, I can't!' She clasped his hand tighter.

'Just go on, darling,' she said, 'and make them laugh!'

Laughter came flooding up from the audience and washed out into the wings as Charles sang the song first sung by Grimaldi in 1819.

'Guv'nor's song's going well,' said Sutton.

'Yes,' replied Lydia, her eyes on that absurd, shabby figure, playing the audience with all the loving skill of a virtuoso.

In all the years of seeing him in heroic and romantic roles, she thought that she had never loved or admired him more.

The pantomime took its cheerful and familiar course, and the love story came to its happy ending, always anticipated, always new. The Ugly Sisters were hilariously routed, Dandini proffered the glass slipper on a cushion and Cinderella slipped her foot into it, and then rose gracefully, taking the hand of her Prince Charming.

As the curtain fell and the audience applauded, they had no idea of the frantic activity backstage as the scenery swung into place for the transformation scene, and as the entire cast struggled with poppers, hooks and buttons to achieve an instant change into glittering costumes and silver wigs. George, wandering like a sleepwalker in his baggy silver broker's costume, paused beside Charles.

'Pity Maeve had to miss the walk-down,' he said. 'She always enjoyed that.'

The curtain rose again to display a glittering staircase which had apparently appeared, not by sweat and strain, discipline and expense, but by effortless magic. The walk-ons and supporting cast descended, and then, to increasing applause, Nell, Billy and Giselle, followed by Perdita, Edwin and Martha. There was a roar of delight as Charles and George descended together. The audience never knew that, while Charles cheerfully waved to them with one hand, he kept the other firmly round his father's waist, supporting those stumbling, sleep-walking steps.

'Will Grandad make it?' said Thomas, waiting with Sutton in the wings.

The smile was still on George's face, but it had become set and his eyes were glazed.

'Just about, I'd reckon,' said Sutton.

Charles and George took their bows to tremendous applause, and then Nell came to take George's arm and draw him to her side, while Charles turned with a fine gesture to the top of the staircase, where Lydia and Elsie appeared, no longer the Ugly Sisters, but those two famous beauties, The Winsome Wheatleys, in silver dresses and silver wigs, gracefully descending. Charles took Lydia's hand, and the whole cast bowed towards the royal box.

They saw, as in a snapshot, the Duke of York, slight and timid, but applauding with engaging enthusiasm and simplicity, and his pretty, smiling, dark-haired Duchess, and, between them, the tiny Princess with her mop of fair, curly hair, the King's beloved granddaughter, Lilibet. And Charles and Lydia, bowing and curtseying, hand in hand, saw with that wicked flash of amusement which comes even in moments of the greatest grief and drama, a smudge of white paint on the Ducal sleeve where it had rested on the newly painted royal box.

So the Bretts stood together on that stage which was at once their home and their business. When the curtain rose for the last time, where the Fairy Godmother had stood was a single empty spotlight. And yet it seemed to them that it was not empty after all, but that Maeve was there, that faded Irish beauty with the small talent and warm heart, reaching out her absurd tinselled wand towards Perdita as she claimed her undoubted right to enter the profession which her grandmother had graced with such innocence and love.

FOR THE BEST IN PAPERBACKS, LOOK FOR THE

In every corner of the world, on every subject under the sun, Penguin represents quality and variety – the very best in publishing today.

For complete information about books available from Penguin – including Pelicans, Puffins, Peregrines and Penguin Classics – and how to order them, write to us at the appropriate address below. Please note that for copyright reasons the selection of books varies from country to country.

In the United Kingdom: For a complete list of books available from Penguin in the U.K., please write to *Dept E.P., Penguin Books Ltd, Harmondsworth, Middlesex, UB7 0DA*

In the United States: For a complete list of books available from Penguin in the U.S., please write to *Dept BA, Penguin, 299 Murray Hill Parkway, East Rutherford, New Jersey 07073*

In Canada: For a complete list of books available from Penguin in Canada, please write to *Penguin Books Canada Ltd, 2801 John Street, Markham, Ontario L3R 1B4*

In Australia: For a complete list of books available from Penguin in Australia, please write to the *Marketing Department, Penguin Books Australia Ltd, P.O. Box 257, Ringwood, Victoria 3134*

In New Zealand: For a complete list of books available from Penguin in New Zealand, please write to the *Marketing Department, Penguin Books (NZ) Ltd, Private Bag, Takapuna, Auckland 9*

In India: For a complete list of books available from Penguin, please write to *Penguin Overseas Ltd, 706 Eros Apartments, 56 Nehru Place, New Delhi, 110019*

In Holland: For a complete list of books available from Penguin in Holland, please write to *Penguin Books Nederland B.V., Postbus 195, NL–1380AD Weesp, Netherlands*

In Germany: For a complete list of books available from Penguin, please write to *Penguin Books Ltd, Friedrichstrasse 10 – 12, D–6000 Frankfurt Main 1, Federal Republic of Germany*

In Spain: For a complete list of books available from Penguin in Spain, please write to *Longman Penguin España, Calle San Nicolas 15, E–28013 Madrid, Spain*

Dreams of Other Days   Elaine Crowley

'A magnificent and unforgettable story of love, rebellion and death. 'You will never forget Katy and the people of her place . . . a haunting story' – Maeve Binchy, author of *Light a Penny Candle*

Trade Wind   M. M. Kaye

The year is 1859 and Hero Hollis, beautiful and headstrong niece of the American consul, arrives in Zanzibar. It is an earthly paradise fragrant with spices and frangipani; it is also the last and greatest outpost of the Slave Trade . . .

The Far Pavilions   M. M. Kaye

The famous story of love and war in nineteenth-century India – now a sumptuous screen production. 'A *Gone With the Wind* of the North-West Frontier' – *The Times*. 'A grand, romantic adventure story' – Paul Scott

The Mission   Robert Bolt

History, adventure and romance combine in the most exciting way imaginable in this compulsive new novel – now a major motion picture.

Riches and Honour   Tom Hyman

The explosive saga of a dynasty founded on a terrible secret. A thriller of the first order, *Riches and Honour* captures the imagination with its brutally chilling and tantalizing plot.

The World, the Flesh and the Devil   Reay Tannahill

'A bewitching blend of history and passion. A MUST' – *Daily Mail*. A superb novel in a great tradition. 'Excellent' – *The Times*

FOR THE BEST IN PAPERBACKS, LOOK FOR THE

PENGUIN BESTSELLERS

To Have and To Hold   Deborah Moggach

Viv was giving her sister, Ann, the best present she could think of – a baby. How Viv, Ann and their husbands cope with this extraordinary situation is the subject of this tender, triumphant and utterly absorbing story. Now a powerful TV drama.

Castaway   Lucy Irvine

'A savagely self-searching tale . . . she is a born writer as well as a ruthlessly talented survivor' – *Observer*. 'Fascinating' – *Daily Mail*. 'Remarkable . . . such dreams as stuff is made of' – *Financial Times*

Runaway   Lucy Irvine

Not a sequel, but the story of Lucy Irvine's life *before* she became a castaway. Witty, courageous and sensational, it is a story you won't forget.

A Dark and Distant Shore   Reay Tannahill

'An absorbing saga spanning a century of love affairs, hatred and high-points of Victorian history' – *Daily Express*. 'Enthralling . . . a marvellous blend of *Gone with the Wind* and *The Thorn Birds*. You will enjoy every page' – *Daily Mirror*

A Daughter of the Nobility   Natasha Borovsky

A magnificent and spellbinding blend of fiction and history, set in the Russia of Nicholas and Alexandra. 'An enchanting tale that richly recaptures the glorious days of Imperial Russia' – *Booklist*

Love, Honour and Betray   Elizabeth Kary

Destined to love, doomed to part, Seth and Charl become part of a seething drama of treachery, tragedy, pain and desire. History and romance entwine spectacularly in this climactic story, as highly charged and memorable as any story told before now.

FOR THE BEST IN PAPERBACKS, LOOK FOR THE 🐧

PENGUIN OMNIBUSES

Author's Choice: Four Novels by Graham Greene

Four magnificent novels by an author whose haunting and distinctive 'entertainments' and fiction have captured the moral and spiritual dilemmas of our time: *The Power and the Glory*, *The Quiet American*, *Travels with My Aunt* and *The Honorary Consul*.

The Collected Stories of Colette
Edited with and Introduction by Robert Phelps

'Poetry and passion' – *Daily Telegraph*. A sensuous feast of one hundred short stories, shot through with the colours and flavours of the Parisian world and fertile French countryside, they reverberate with the wit and acuity that made Colette unique.

The Penguin Complete Novels of George Orwell

The six novels of one of England's most original and significant writers. Collected in this volume are the novels which brought George Orwell world fame: *Animal Farm*, *Burmese Days*, *A Clergyman's Daughter*, *Coming Up for Air*, *Keep the Aspidistra Flying* and *Nineteen Eighty-Four*.

The Great Novels of D. H. Lawrence

The collection of the masterworks of one of the greatest writers in the English language of any time – *Women in Love*, *Sons and Lovers* and *The Rainbow*.

Frank Tuohy: The Collected Stories

'The time has come for him to be honoured for what he is: a great short-story writer, an absolute master of the form' – Paul Bailey in the *Standard*. From Poland to Brazil, from England to Japan, Tuohy maps the intricate contours of personal and racial misunderstanding, shock and embarrassment. 'Exhilarating fiction' – *Sunday Times*

The Nancy Mitford Omnibus

Nancy Mitford's immortal, unforgettable world in one scintillating volume: *The Pursuit of Love*, *Love in a Cold Climate*, *The Blessing* and *Don't Tell Alfred*.

Life with Jeeves   P. G. Wodehouse

Containing *Right Ho, Jeeves*, *The Inimitable Jeeves* and *Very Good, Jeeves!*, this is a delicious collection of vintage Wodehouse in which the old master lures us, once again, into the evergreen world of Bertie Wooster, his terrifying Aunt Agatha, and, of course, the inimitable Jeeves.

Perfick! Perfick!   H. E. Bates

The adventures of the irrepressible Larkin family, in four novels: *The Darling Buds of May*, *A Breath of French Air*, *When the Green Woods Laugh* and *Oh! To Be in England*.

The Best of Modern Humour   Edited by Mordecai Richler

Packed between the covers of this book is the teeming genius of modern humour's foremost exponents from both sides of the Atlantic – and for every conceivable taste. Here is everyone from Tom Wolfe, S. J. Perelman, John Mortimer, Alan Coren, Woody Allen, John Berger and Fran Lebowitz to P. G. Wodehouse, James Thurber and Evelyn Waugh.

Enderby   Anthony Burgess

'These three novels are the richest and most verbally dazzling comedies Burgess has written' – *Listener*. Containing the three volumes *Inside Enderby*, *Enderby Outside* and *The Clockwork Treatment*.

Vintage Thurber: Vol. One   James Thurber

A selection of his best writings and drawings, this *grand-cru* volume includes *Let Your Mind Alone*, *My World and Welcome to It*, *Fables for Our Time*, *Famous Poems Illustrated*, *Men, Women and Dogs*, *The Beast in Me* and *Thurber Country* – as well as much, much more.

Vintage Thurber: Vol. Two   James Thurber

'Without question America's foremost humorist' – *The Times Literary Supplement*. In this volume, where vintage piles upon vintage, are *The Middle-aged Man on the Flying Trapeze*, *The Last Flower*, *My Life and Hard Times*, *The Owl in the Attic*, *The Seal in the Bedroom* and *The Thurber Carnival*.